"A writer of ... ... and sensitivity."

Mary Jo Putney

She had no recourse but to accept the position...

Impoverished and untitled, with no marital prospects or so much as a single suitor, Beatrice Sinclair is forced to accept employment as governess to a frightened, lonely child from a noble family—ignoring rumors of dark intrigues to do so. Surely, no future could be as dark as the past she wishes to leave behind. And she admits a fascination with the young duke's adult cousin, Devlen Gordon, a seductive rogue who excites her from the first charged moment they meet. But she dares not trust him—even after he spirits them to isolation and safety when the life of her young charge is threatened.

... and no choice but to fall in love.

Devlen is charming, mysterious, powerful—and Beatrice cannot refuse him. He is opening new worlds for her, filling her life with passion ... and peril. But what are Devlen's secrets? Is he her lover or her enemy? Will following her heart be foolishness or a path to lasting happiness?

By Karen Ranney

If You've Enjoyed This Book,
Be Sure to Read These Other
AVON ROMANTIC TREASURES

Coming Soon

ATTENTION: ORGANIZATIONS AND CORPORATIONS
Most Avon Books paperbacks are available at special quantity discounts for bulk purchases for sales promotions, premiums, or fund-raising. For information, please call or write:

Special Markets Department, HarperCollins Publishers, Inc., 10 East 53rd Street, New York, N.Y. 10022–5299.
Telephone: (212) 207–7528.   Fax: (212) 207–7222.

KAREN RANNEY

An Unlikely Governess

An Avon Romantic Treasure

AVON BOOKS
An Imprint of HarperCollinsPublishers

This is a work of fiction. Names, characters, places, and incidents are products of the author's imagination or are used fictitiously and are not to be construed as real. Any resemblance to actual events, locales, organizations, or persons, living or dead, is entirely coincidental.

AVON BOOKS
An Imprint of HarperCollins*Publishers*
10 East 53rd Street
New York, New York 10022-5299

Copyright © 2006 by Karen Ranney
ISBN-13: 978-0-06-075743-4
ISBN-10: 0-06-075743-4
www.avonromance.com

All rights reserved. No part of this book may be used or reproduced in any manner whatsoever without written permission, except in the case of brief quotations embodied in critical articles and reviews. For information address Avon Books, an Imprint of HarperCollins Publishers.

First Avon Books paperback printing: January 2006

Avon Trademark Reg. U.S. Pat. Off. and in Other Countries, Marca Registrada, Hecho en U.S.A.
HarperCollins® is a registered trademark of HarperCollins Publishers Inc.

Printed in the U.S.A.

10 9 8 7 6 5 4 3 2 1

If you purchased this book without a cover, you should be aware that this book is stolen property. It was reported as "unsold and destroyed" to the publisher, and neither the author nor the publisher has received any payment for this "stripped book."

Chapter 1

Kilbridden Village, Scotland
November 1832

"**I**'ll work very hard, I promise."

"Gimme your hands."

Beatrice Sinclair stretched out her hands. Because she was trembling, she placed them palm up on the bar.

"You've got calluses all right. But you look like you'd fall over after a few hours of good work. I need a healthy lass, one who can be on her feet twelve hours."

"I'll be your best worker. I'll even work for free the first week to prove it."

"Can you wipe a table down in the wink of an eye? Or give a little saucy wiggle to the patrons?"

She nodded.

"Laugh at my customers' jokes, even if they be sorry ones?"

"I can."

1

"You don't look the type my customers like. You're too pale, and you've got an air about you." He frowned. "Are you sick?"

"I'm very healthy."

"Then why are you shaking?"

"I'm just cold."

He didn't look as if he believed her.

"Who told you I was looking for another tavern wench?"

"The owner of the Sword and Dragon."

"Went there, did you? Bet he wanted someone younger."

"He said he didn't have need for another helper."

"That's not true. His business has been near as good as mine. For the last half year, at least. Before that, no one came to drink or talk." He began to wipe down the bar with a spotted rag, looking as if he were thinking about the matter. "Did you have the sickness?"

She shook her head again, afraid to tell him the truth. But all the assurances in the world wouldn't matter. The minute the tavern maid entered the room Beatrice knew she'd lost the post. She couldn't wear a blouse that revealed all her assets or a skirt that bared her ankles. Nor was she given to simpering smiles or coy looks. While she didn't object to dispensing spirits, she wasn't about to sell herself along with them.

The innkeeper grinned. Several teeth were missing, and the effect was more of a leer.

"Go up to Castle Crannoch. They'll have a job for you."

She'd heard of Castle Crannoch ever since coming to Kilbridden Village, but she'd never considered it a source of employment.

"Castle Crannoch?"

He jerked his chin toward the ceiling.

"Aye, where the duke lives. Go ask the duke for a job. He'll give you one, but I won't."

Beatrice tightened her hands on her reticule and thanked the tavern owner with as much grace as she could muster. She'd come all this way for nothing.

She left the inn and stood outside. The cold rain seeped through her thin dress, a reminder that she'd traded her cloak for a sack of flour and a few eggs a week ago. Beatrice tightened her shawl around her hair, held it closed with one hand at her neck, and looked up at the mountain in front of her.

Castle Crannoch stood at the very top, overlooking the village. The fortress dominated the countryside, visible to anyone approaching, a sentinel of the past that looked capable of protecting its inhabitants well into the future.

Occasionally, word would seep down from the top of the mountain as to the lives of the occupants of Castle Crannoch. There had been tragedy there not long ago, she recalled. But her own life had been so difficult that she'd paid the gossip little attention.

The castle was oddly shaped, constructed as if it were a large box with a smaller box pulled from inside it. The two square buildings sat adjacent to each other atop the mountain, the smaller structure in stages of disrepair, the larger box topped by four turrets. The only way to the place was up a long and winding road. Not only did her legs ache but the climb looked to be a frightening one.

A voice, sounding too much like her father's, spoke against the fierce wind. *Do not go, Beatrice. No single*

woman of good character would seek employment there.
There were rumors about Castle Crannoch.

She no longer had a choice.

Slowly, she began to walk up the winding road, praying for endurance. She wouldn't allow herself to look up at the castle again. Doing so would only make the task seem interminable. She concentrated, instead, on putting one foot in front of the other, leaning into the rain.

Her shawl was sodden, but she tightened it around her head, holding it close at the neck. How long had she been walking? Hours? Surely not that long.

She heard the sound of the carriage and eased closer to the parapet. In the darkness she couldn't see the drop, but her imagination furnished the distance in her mind, adding jagged peaks and huge boulders at the bottom of the ravine.

The approaching carriage was a blur of motion, a dark shadow against the wall. Four horses pulled the ebony shape, the lead pair adorned with gleaming silver appointments. Twin lanterns, also silver, sat on either side of the door, but they were unlit, leaving her to wonder if the occupant of such a magnificent carriage wanted privacy. Or secrecy.

The coach took up the full width of the road, forcing her to the edge. Beatrice gripped the wall with her frayed gloves and felt them tear further. Was God punishing her for her daring, for her journey, for the thought of working in such a place as the duke's lair?

Only the curving half wall stood between her and the abyss. She held her breath as the carriage passed, the stallions from hell blending back into the shadows, their silver appointments winking out of sight.

Was it Black Donald, the devil himself? If so, it appeared he was not quite ready to abandon her. The carriage halted on the next curve. She gripped her reticule with both hands in front of her as if the small bag could offer some protection. She debated waiting until the carriage moved forward, but the rain was getting heavier. She had to make it to Castle Crannoch tonight.

Just as she would have walked by, the door abruptly opened. She stopped, halted not only by curiosity, but by fear. She was cold, wet, and exhausted, but cautious all the same.

"The road is dangerous." A human voice, low and deeply pitched. "You could easily have been run down by my horses."

The coachman didn't turn but remained huddled beneath his greatcoat.

Beatrice took one step forward. "Your horses were taking up the center of the road, sir."

"They are skittish of heights, and since they are so valuable, they are allowed to travel down the middle of the road if they wish."

"As opposed to people, sir, who must travel at the edge of it?"

"It's raining. The least I could do is offer you safe passage to Castle Crannoch."

She almost asked if he worked there before the ridiculousness of that question struck her. He was riding in a luxurious carriage, pulled by magnificent horses. He was probably the duke himself.

She would be foolish to accept a ride in a strange carriage. Almost as foolish as declining such an offer. The heavens growled overhead as if to convince her. The door opened wider, and she entered the carriage, stepping over the stranger's long legs to sit opposite him.

Two small pierced silver lanterns illuminated the interior. As the flames flickered, dots of light danced across the blue cushions and silk of the ceiling.

"Why are you going to the castle?"

Clearly, he wasn't the least reticent about prying into her concerns.

Beatrice debated whether or not to answer him, then realized his curiosity might well be the payment she owed for the ride up the mountain. She looked down at her clasped hands.

"I had hoped to obtain a position."

"Had you? They are notoriously parsimonious at Castle Crannoch. Did you know that?"

She shook her head.

Her rescuer was a man she would have noticed in any setting. His face was absolutely faultless, the nose, chin, and forehead perfectly crafted like the sculpture of an archangel she'd once seen. His hair was brown with touches of gold, and his eyes were so dark a brown as to appear black, and so arresting she felt as if he could pin her to the seat with his gaze.

One corner of his mouth curved up slightly, in amusement or a wry acknowledgment of her examination. Surprisingly, a dimple appeared in his cheek, and it was that particular feature she studied with great care.

Surely a man with a dimple could not be evil?

"Have you seen enough?" he asked finally.

"I have noted your appearance, sir. But appearance does not matter in this world."

"No doubt a homily told to you by an ugly woman. Ugly women are the only ones who think appearance does not matter."

"Have you ever heard of the story of the Ant and the Chrysalis?"

He looked intently at her for a moment, as if attempting to ascertain whether or not she'd lost her wits.

Without waiting for a response, she began to speak. "Once upon a time there was an ant and a chrysalis. It was very nearly at its time of change, and the only thing visible in the shell was a long tail that attracted the attention of an ant. He saw that this strange being was alive, and walked up to it and addressed the shell.

"'I'm very sorry for your fate. I'm an ant, you see, and able to walk and run and play if I wish. Poor you, for being trapped in such an ugly shell.'

"The chrysalis didn't bother to respond. All of its energy was spent in its transformation.

"A few days later, however, the ant was climbing a small hill, allowing himself to fall, then running up the hill again, laughing at his own silliness.

"He felt a breeze upon the back of his head and turned to find a large blue-and-purple butterfly hovering in the air. 'Dear ant,' the butterfly said. 'Do not pity me. I can fly whereas you can only walk.'

"The moral of this story is that appearances are deceptive."

"And you thought me a butterfly?"

"No. I thought you were Black Donald."

"I beg your pardon?"

"Satan might be a tempting master, but he demands eternal servitude."

He laughed, the carriage filling with the sound.

When she didn't respond to his amusement, a corner of his lip curved up in an almost smile.

"Does your virtue shelter you, then? Is that why you don't appear afraid? If I were Black Donald, I would think you'd be trembling in terror."

"Do you often do this? Insist upon demonstrating an act of kindness only to ridicule the person foolish enough to accept it?"

"Do you often chastise your hosts?"

"Stop the carriage and let me out. I shall trouble you no more."

"Don't be foolish. It's night and not safe for a lone female. Besides, we're there."

In the next moment, the carriage slowed, then stopped.

Beatrice slid her finger alongside the leather shade, peering into the darkness. A face leered at her, one so startling that she dropped the shade.

"Has something frightened you?"

"No," she said, not altogether certain the face she'd seen was real. Perhaps it was something she'd only seen in her mind.

The man opposite her reached over and opened the carriage door.

She hesitated, unwilling to face the monster outside the carriage. Her rescuer took her delay for the fear it was, but it was obvious he didn't fully understand it.

"I have not gnawed on a pretty virgin for many years. You're safe enough with me."

She doubted any virgin was safe with him, but she didn't stay to argue the point.

Instead, she pointed one toe out the door. The cold night air caressed her ankle, reminding her that time was passing too quickly. It was already dark, and she had yet to meet with the duke. She still had to make it down the mountain again, but she doubted she had the strength to walk the five miles back to her cottage. She'd probably have to find shelter on the side of the road in the rain. The thunder overhead punctuated that thought with a dull, ominous roar.

As she emerged from the carriage, the wind tugged at her dress, revealing her petticoat. A hand flew to her shawl to keep it anchored, while the other pressed against her skirt.

The creature materialized as she navigated the last step. He was tall and chunky, with thick bands of muscle where his shoulders would be. The uniform he wore was ill fitting, his wrists hanging beyond the cuffs. His face was misshapen, as if the bones of his face had been broken once and never properly healed. His eyes, however, were alert and kind, his gaze now fixed on her face.

"*Bienvenu à Château Crannoch,*" he said, in soft but perfect French.

Surprised, she only nodded back at him.

He translated his words, bowing slowly to her from his impressive height. "Welcome to Castle Crannoch."

"*Merci,*" she said. "*Il est mon plaisir.*" How much of a pleasure was doubtful, especially since the giant had made no effort to open the tall, arched, oak doors. Beatrice doubted if she could manage one of the iron-studded pair by herself.

"How may I assist you, mademoiselle?"

Must she get through this giant to reach the duke himself? Her stomach rumbled, vying in sound with the storm itself.

"I have come to speak with the duke about a position."

The giant looked at her curiously but said nothing. Instead, his attention was drawn to something behind her. Without turning, Beatrice knew the stranger had emerged from the carriage.

Her stomach clenched as he moved to stand too close behind her. She straightened her shoulders, avoiding the temptation to turn and ask him to move aside. He would be waiting for her to do something just that foolish. Or perhaps he was goading her to do so.

"The duke is not available, mademoiselle."

"It's all right, Gaston, I'll see to the lady."

"If you're sure, Mr. Devlen."

She turned to face him. He smiled down at her, nearly as tall as the giant, Gaston.

"Devlen?" His name was too close to devil. She *had* been transported here by Black Donald himself.

"Devlen Gordon. And you are?" He inclined his head, waiting.

"Beatrice Sinclair."

"I'll take Miss Sinclair to see my father, Gaston."

"Your father is the duke?"

"No, but be certain to address him as such, it would please him immeasurably."

He offered her his arm, leaving Beatrice with the choice of refusing his chivalry or touching him. After a moment, he dropped his arm, ending her indecision and her options. She had no alternative but to follow him as he strode up the steps.

Chapter 2

~~~~~◦◦~~~~~

Castle Crannoch looked to be a vast place from the village, or even on the road leading up the mountain. Up close, however, it looked smaller, square and ugly, with turrets on all four corners and no windows to speak of facing civilization. On the other side of the castle there was the loch, and perhaps the defenders had allowed for some sunshine from that quarter. But they certainly hadn't planned for comfort when they constructed the castle of the Dukes of Brechin.

Beatrice followed Devlen into the shrouded darkness of the entranceway.

"Do you not have candles or lamps at Castle Crannoch?"

"My father is notoriously thrifty with a coin."

Beatrice had been without any source of funds for nearly a year, and in the past three months had been in dire straits indeed. She could stretch a meal to last three days, hoard provisions to last a month; but even she had lit a candle upon occasion, to keep her company during the long nights.

The only illumination was the pinpoint of light from a three-sided lantern set into an alcove far down the hall. Devlen headed toward it unerringly, as if he often traveled in the darkness and needed no marker or light.

The Devil could see in the dark.

Pray God to keep me safe and free from harm. See my sins, oh Lord, and forgive them with the alacrity I attempt to banish them from my soul. Keep me safe in this wicked place and with this wicked man.

She stumbled on the stone floor and made a sound, causing Devlen to turn. His expression was a mystery to her. She could no more see his face than she could the floor or her feet.

"Are you all right?"

No. She was tired and hungry, and more frightened than she'd been since the morning after she buried her parents.

She only nodded. He turned left and descended a set of stone steps carved into the earth. The musty, sour smell of the ground made her think this was a very old part of the castle.

There was nothing to fear with this man as her protector. He was so tall and broadly built, any ghost, goblin, or earthly presence would surely flee at the sight of him. There was nothing to fear unless it was the man himself.

Devlen abruptly stepped to the side of the corridor, as if he had some inkling of what would happen next. A keening sound echoed through the space, an unearthly noise that made her skin crawl. A small figure flew toward her, arms outstretched, a black void where his face should be. Beatrice pressed her back against the wall next to Devlen, praying the specter would pass. Instead, it halted only feet from her.

"Who are you?" he asked, pushing back the hood.

She expected to hear the voice of Hell itself, stentorian tones warning her this was no place for a gently reared woman. But the voice that emerged from the cloak was that of a young boy, high-pitched and curious.

Beatrice blinked at him.

The shadows were expansive, the single light from the end of the corridor barely enough to illuminate his narrow, pinched face. His nose was long for his face and his chin too prominent. His cheekbones were high, the skin stretched tight as if he'd lost weight recently or had always been a sickly child.

He was not an attractive boy, made even less so with his frown. His mouth was pinched and his eyes slitted into a narrow-eyed glare.

"Who are you?" he repeated.

At her silence, he glanced at Devlen.

"Cousin?"

Devlen turned to her, bowed slightly. "Miss Sinclair, may I present Robert Gordon, the twelfth Duke of Brechin."

She glanced at the boy, every faint and futile wish or hope for her future dissipating as they exchanged a long look.

"Your Grace," she said. The child acknowledged her light curtsy with a nod.

How was she possibly to obtain employment from this child?

She glanced at Devlen, wanting to slap the faint smile from his face. He'd known. All this time he'd known.

"Why did you not say something?" she asked.

"You insisted upon seeing the duke. I have provided you with a meeting."

There was nothing to do but straighten her shoulders and walk away from Castle Crannoch.

"Why did you want to see me?"

She was not used to obeying the summons of children, even one from an aristocratic child. But it was all too evident neither of them would move to allow her to pass until she gave him some sort of answer.

"I need employment. The innkeeper at the Hare and Hound said you might have need of me."

"In what capacity?" Devlen asked.

"Are you named for the Devil?" she asked, pushed to rudeness by the events of the past five minutes.

"The first duke, actually. He might well have been named for the Devil. I understand he deflowered his share of maidens."

Heat surged to her face at his words. Had he no sense of propriety?

She pushed away from the wall, clutching her reticule tightly. Hunger was making her dizzy, and the disorientation of the darkness made the situation worse. She stretched out one hand and gripped the edge of a protruding brick, hoping she would not shame herself as she retraced her steps.

Please, God, let me get through this. Endurance. One of the great assets of life. Patience, another. She doubted she had any more of the good emotions left. The last weeks had drained her.

"Let me pass," she said, reaching out and placing the fingers of her right hand on the wall.

She had to leave, to get out of here. There was nothing else to be done.

"I'll hire you," the diminutive Duke of Brechin said. "We're always needing wenches in the scullery."

Beatrice doubted she could manage the work in the scullery. In fact, she doubted she could continue to walk down this corridor without assistance. The walls were bending at the top to meet in the strangest sort of arch, and the floor was buckling beneath her feet.

She pushed past him, past Devlen, who didn't put up a hand to stop her, and down the corridor, following the beacon of that single light.

"I have not given you permission to leave me."

"I do not need it, Your Grace."

"You are at Castle Crannoch, and I am the Duke of Brechin."

"More like the Duke of Incivility," she murmured, but he heard her.

"I will set my guard on you. Or Devlen. Devlen, fetch her to me. Stop her!"

"Cousin, you have insulted Miss Sinclair," Devlen responded in a surprisingly somber voice. "I doubt the young lady would be suitable as a scullery wench."

"Then where shall I put her?"

"Perhaps somewhere where her education could be of benefit."

"How do you know she's educated?"

Beatrice slowed her steps, curious as to what they were saying about her. A part of her was loath to leave Castle Crannoch. There was nothing waiting for her outside its walls.

Her stomach no longer rumbled with hunger. There

was only pain, and a fierce sort of nausea that occasionally caught her off guard. It struck with a vengeance now, causing her to lean against the blackened brick. She climbed the steps with great deliberation.

They were still talking about her; she could hear them. Their words, however, were not as important as simply remaining upright. Dizziness threatened to level her, and it was with the greatest of wills she fought it back.

I will not faint. Not here, not in front of them.

"Are you all right, Miss Sinclair?"

"Yes, thank you."

But she wasn't. The world was tilting.

Devlen unexpectedly appeared beside her, putting his hand on her arm. She jerked away and lost her balance.

The stone floor seemed so very far away. She felt herself falling toward it, and reached out her hands to break her fall. The dizziness followed her down, became a voice etched with worry. A male voice called for assistance. How strange. How very odd.

She surrendered to the nothingness with a feeling of relief.

Devlen Gordon stared down at the figure of the young woman he'd escorted to Castle Crannoch.

"Damn." He sighed, then bent to rouse her, a feat more difficult than he'd expected. He gently tapped her cheeks with his fingertips. No sign of consciousness. She was breathing lightly, a fact he noted with some relief. The last thing he wanted was one more complication in his life.

"Do something, Devlen!"

"You would do better to cease commanding me,

cousin. In fact, I think it's about time someone advised you on your manners."

Robert didn't comment, a wise decision since Devlen was about ready to upend his young cousin and apply a few judicious paddles to his bottom.

He bent and scooped Miss Sinclair up in his arms, thinking she weighed less than he'd expected. In fact, she'd surprised him from the first moment she'd entered the carriage. She was a mouthy little thing, puffed up with prudery. But her mouth was made for kisses, and she had the blackest hair he'd ever seen. For a moment, when he'd caught sight of her in the carriage, he'd wanted to demand she remain still for as long as he wished so he might study the color of her eyes, such a light blue it looked as if she'd trapped a portion of a fair sky behind them. Where had she gotten that small mole beside one eye? It looked almost as if it were an affectation, one used often by the women of Paris.

Despite her threadbare dress, or perhaps because of it, he was most conscious of her long torso, the waist sloping gently from an overfull bodice down to long, beautifully shaped legs. She really should wear a heavier petticoat if she wanted to hide her figure.

But perhaps she didn't want to hide anything at all, and this story of applying for a position was just a ploy to wiggle her shapely little derriere past his father.

Still, she should weigh more. She wasn't a short woman. The top of her head came to his throat, and he was tall for a Gordon.

He was insatiably curious, a character trait that might be considered a flaw since he tended to use it to excess. Was she sick? The fever? Had he unwittingly brought disease to Castle Crannoch? He realized as he walked into the newer section of the castle the young woman in his arms prompted more questions than answers.

"Devlen!"

He didn't turn, didn't answer Robert.

The oldest part of the castle was comprised of a series of long, corridors sparsely lit by a candle here and there. No one could claim his father's stewardship of Robert's inheritance was rife with profligacy.

The walls widened as he climbed up the gently sloping corridor. There were no stairs in this section of the castle. When visitors came to Castle Crannoch, they did so through the north entrance, gaining a view of the sea and the surrounding undulating hills. He'd taken the family entrance, and had to pay for it now, carrying Miss Sinclair through the fortifications like a beast who'd captured a maiden and was taking her to his lair.

Chapter 3

Beatrice awoke to find herself in a strange bed.

Her fingers trailed over the coverlet tucked beneath her neck. Silk. Ivory silk. Just like the heavily ruched canopy above her head. The four posters of the bed were intricately carved with trailing vines and leaves. The mattress felt as if it was stuffed with feathers. Was there lavender in the pillows?

She had never before slept in such a magnificent bed. Naked.

Not quite naked. One hand crept across her chest and lower to measure the extent of her coverage. This garment was not her shift. The yoke was heavily embroidered, and there was lace at the edge of her cuffs.

She flattened both hands against the smooth linen of the sheet and closed her eyes, trying to recall the events that led to her being in a strange bed in a strange place.

The last thing she could remember was walking up the long and winding road to Castle Crannoch and being stopped by the carriage. A black carriage with a daunting occupant.

Devlen.

Had he undressed her, then? Was this his chamber?

Her eyes slitted open to take in the rest of the room. A tall bureau with a pediment and many drawers, a washstand, an armoire, the bedside table, a man sitting in a chair.

A man?

Her eyes widened as she stared.

Her visitor was quite a handsome man, one with a decided resemblance to Devlen. For all his name, however, Devlen's face was that of an angel, and this man's face was marked by suffering. His mouth was thin, set inside deep grooves, parentheses in his flesh. A tracery of lines radiated from his brown eyes, and she had the impression humor hadn't caused them. His hair was brown, threaded with gray, and clubbed at the back with a blue ribbon matching the fabric of his jacket.

Emerald, lavender, and sky-blue embroidery depicting thistle and heather blossoms enlivened his waistcoat, granting a touch of abandon to his otherwise somber dark blue attire.

His mouth was faintly smiling, his expression one of self-directed mockery. Beatrice wished she had a clearer memory of the night before.

"Who are you?"

"Your host, Miss Sinclair."

Beatrice tried to sit up and promptly fell back against the pillow when the room whirled around her. She pulled the sheet up even tighter, rose cautiously on one elbow, and after ascertaining she was well and truly properly covered—as properly as one might be while lying in an unknown bed being addressed by an unknown personage—addressed him again.

"It would be less confusing, sir, if I knew your name. You are not the Duke of Brechin. I've met him."

"You do not sound impressed."

She was reasonably certain she was still at Castle Crannoch. It was hardly polite to criticize the Duke of Brechin, especially since she was partaking of his hospitality, however accidentally.

"My nephew has a great deal to learn, unfortunately," the man said at her silence. "One of those lessons is how to treat guests. I offer my apologies for his behavior."

"Nephew?"

The man floated toward her. The movement was so disorienting it took her a moment to realize her visitor was in a movable chair. Large wheels in the front and smaller ones in the back allowed him to glide across the floor while seated.

"You will have to forgive me if I don't get up, Miss Sinclair. My permanent posture is the result of a carriage accident."

"I am very sorry, sir."

"Pity is a common enough emotion, but it's not the reason I've sought you out, Miss Sinclair."

He reached the side of the bed. Slowly, he bowed from the waist, the same mocking smile still in place.

"Allow me to present myself," he said. "Cameron Gordon. I am the Duke of Brechin's guardian."

"And Devlen's father," she said, recalling snatches of last night's conversation.

"Have you known each other long?"

She could feel the warmth travel from her chest to

her face at his amusement. How improper of her to call him by his first name.

"I met him only yesterday. Dear God, it was just yesterday, was it not?"

He nodded.

"How did I get here?"

"I understand from Gaston that you fainted. There are several reasons a woman faints, Miss Sinclair. Are you sickening? With child?"

She didn't comment on his rudeness, because just then the faint scent of cooking wafted through the air. For a moment, she was dizzy, then hunger like she'd never known stripped any other thought from her.

"How long has it been since you've eaten?"

"Two days," she answered absently, wondering where the smell originated.

A knock on the door preceded the arrival of a maid, who entered struggling under the weight of a heavily laden tray.

Beatrice sat up, uncaring that the sheet dropped to her waist, or that she was trembling. Nothing mattered but the sight of all that food heaped upon plates and coming toward her.

She almost wept.

The maid approached the opposite side of the bed and laid the tray on top of the silk coverlet beside her.

Her fingers touched the lace of the tray cloth, felt the pattern of it. If it was real, then surely the toast was real as well?

"Is there anything else you would like, miss?"

"It looks like George IV's breakfast."

Cameron looked startled at her statement. "What would you know of the English king's eating habits?"

She glanced at him. "My father had a vast correspondence with men in England. They said his favorite breakfast was two roast pigeons, three beefsteaks, and a variety of spirits. Did you know he was purported to be England's fattest king?"

"If not its most inebriated."

His comment surprised her, but not as much as the sudden smile transforming his face. Humor lit his eyes and curved his lips, transforming him into a handsome man.

She turned back to the tray, telling herself she had not eaten in so long that she'd be sick if she consumed very much food at one sitting. But, oh, the choices. Oatmeal with cream, a rasher of bacon, nearly a loaf of toasted bread crusty brown and warm. A pot of butter, and a pitcher of chocolate. Her fingers trembled in the air, lit on one object after another as she tried to decide what to eat first.

"You say it's been two days since you've eaten, Miss Sinclair? And not steadily, I think, before that."

Beatrice nodded, picking up a piece of the thickly sliced toast and holding it in the palm of her hand. She was trembling, and wished, suddenly, he was gone, that no one could see the almost religious reverence she felt for this bread.

She bit into it, closed her eyes, and chewed slowly. Her stomach, as she expected, lurched in spasm, a final bit of pain in response to days of hunger. She swallowed, then bent her head, ashamed for not having thought to say Grace. But surely the Almighty understood her desperate eagerness.

Her prayer quickly done, she took another bite, and while she was chewing slathered a dark red jam on the remainder of the bread. If she took one piece of toast, and a few slices of bacon, surely she wouldn't become ill. One cup of chocolate, that was all she'd drink.

Her plans made, she dismissed her visitor with the single-mindedness of the starving. For long moments he seemed content to watch her eat, neither saying anything or moving so her entire concentration was on what she consumed.

Never had a meal tasted as good. Nor had she ever been as grateful for anything in her life.

"My son says you came to Castle Crannoch looking for employment."

She glanced at him.

"Yes."

"In what capacity, if I may ask?"

"Anything. I'm a hard worker. What I don't know, I can learn. I'm diligent, and focused."

He held up his hand as if to halt her recitation of virtues.

"You've met my nephew, have you not?"

"I have."

"From your expression, I can only imagine you found him ill-mannered and rude."

She remained silent.

"He is a singularly unlikable child, and it is my duty to rear him after the death of his parents." He glanced down at his covered legs. "The same accident, you see, managed to alter the lives of more than one person."

"I think he would benefit from a tutor," she said. There, a tactful way of stating the obvious. Perhaps if the tutor also had a small whip, that would even further benefit the Duke of Brechin.

"I have employed three tutors so far. None of them have stayed more than a month. He has tormented them in some fashion, left a frog in one's bed, told tales on another, and threatened the third with a bow and arrow, I believe, a present from my son. I can't decide if the world is becoming a softer place, or if I simply had the misfortune to employ three very frightened young men."

She stared at him, wondering why he was telling her this.

"I am in need of someone to instill some discipline into the brat. A governess, if you will. You, Miss Sinclair, are obviously in need of a livelihood."

"What makes you think I could do a better job than three tutors?"

He ignored her question. "In return, I will offer you a very handsome salary, to be paid in advance per quarter, a generous allowance for new books and the like for our young duke, and as much food as you choose to consume. I do warn you, however, there are numerous stairs at Castle Crannoch. If you begin to waddle, it will be difficult for you to master them."

Was he jesting? He must be, because he was smiling at her. But as far as becoming the Duke of Brechin's governess, that was a ludicrous idea. She stared down at the tray. Perhaps even more unbelievable was the idea of returning to the cottage with no money, no food, and no prospects, and expecting to survive the winter.

She sat back against the pillow. "You have not asked my qualifications, sir."

"Your speech indicates you have been educated, Miss Sinclair. You have the manners of a gentlewoman, even as hungry as you are. You know about the king, and speak of your father's correspondence. You have come down late in the world, I suspect."

She nodded, biting back the temptation to tell him of the past three months. Burdens shared do not necessarily become burdens lightened.

"You also speak French."

She looked at him, surprised.

"Gaston relayed as much to me. Robert has a penchant for speaking in nothing but French from time to time, as if to incessantly remind me his mother was French. Neither my wife nor I speak it. Gaston does, but it is problematic to have a servant attend dinner for the sole purpose of translation."

"Doesn't your son speak French?"

"My son does not live here."

Why was she disappointed? She'd been in Devlen Gordon's company for less than an hour, not enough time to acquire any feelings about the man at all.

"Well, Miss Sinclair?"

She looked at the tray, at the piece of toast remaining in her hand, and thought of the long trek down the winding road, then five miles more to her cottage.

"I have none of my belongings with me."

"Gaston will drive you where you need to go."

She took the last bite of toast and savored it as completely as she had the first.

"Yes, sir, I'll take the position."

Governess to a hellion. Still, it was a better life than the one she'd lived all these many months. That's what she told herself as Cameron Gordon smiled, then wheeled himself out the door.

Chapter 4

❧

The family dining room faced east, and the view was of the sea in the distance now radiantly gold as the sun rose in the sky. As usual, his father sat at the head of the table, facing the view as if he commanded the land and all within it. As Robert's guardian, he did.

As always when he came to Castle Crannoch, Devlen marveled that generations of his family had coveted the place. This part of Scotland was a wild, open land harkening back to a time when they'd all painted themselves blue and fought the Romans. For some reason, there had always been strife among the Gordons for control of this castle, this acreage. Only during the last century had they become civilized, saving warfare for conflicts outside the family. Yet in the last generation, envy had risen again, to divide brother from brother.

As stark and arresting as Castle Crannoch was, Devlen preferred the civilization of Edinburgh, Paris, or London. He had homes and business interests in all three and could immerse himself in the activities of his businesses, or find some way of amusing himself. Not like his visits to the castle.

Devlen had rarely been to Castle Crannoch before his uncle's death. As a child he'd visited once when he was ten and due to be shipped off to school. His uncle hadn't married yet, and had given the impression of being a confirmed bachelor, a fact that had no doubt pleased his father. Little did Cameron know that ten years later, his brother would surprise everyone by marrying a young French countess who obviously adored her much older husband.

"There have always been men of adventure in the Gordon clan," his uncle had said on that day nearly twenty years ago. "What will you do with your life, Devlen?"

"I will be a wealthy man. I will own ships and buildings and shops. I'll be able to buy anything I want and never have to go away to school again if I don't wish."

His uncle had laughed. "I hope you do, my boy, I hope you do. The Gordon family could always use rich men."

Devlen had gone back to school, but he'd also acquired both wealth and power.

"Well, have you offered your proposition to Miss Sinclair?" he asked now. "More importantly, has she accepted?"

"I have done so, yes, my son. I'm pleased to say Miss Sinclair has accepted our little offer."

"Do not include me in your plan, Father. The less I have to do with your machinations, the happier I am." He moved toward the sideboard and selected his breakfast.

He returned to the table and sat at the opposite end of it, facing his father.

The Gordons weren't prolific breeders. He was an only child, while his father was one of two children. His uncle, in turn, had only one son. If they'd had more off-spring, no doubt there would have been less rancor in the family.

"Does she know of the attempts on Robert's life?"

His father made a gesture in the air with his hand as if he brushed away the question. "The ramblings of an hysterical child. You know Robert is prone to imagining things. He has constant nightmares."

"I would have nightmares as well if I thought my uncle was trying to kill me."

All pretense of eating was forgotten. The two men stared at each other, Devlen's eyes the exact shade of his father's, his hair the same. His appearance was similar, but his nature was drastically different. While he couldn't give a flying farthing about being duke, his father lusted after the title.

Would he harm Robert in order to acquire it, however? That was a possibility, and one he'd not been able to discount. It was the reason he was here, after all, when it would have been more advantageous to be at the launch of his new ship. Or even accompanying Felicia to Paris. Anything but staring down the man he called sire, but who felt, even now, like a stranger.

"How can you think such a thing of me, son?"

"You only use that word when you're trying to charm me. Or confound others, Father."

Cameron's smile was part mockery, part amusement. "While you do the same. I've often thought we should just call each other by our given names and dispense with labels."

"Shall I tell you what I'd call you?"

Cameron laughed. "Do I look the fool? I can assure you, son," he said, accentuating the word, "that if I'd wanted the boy to come to harm, he wouldn't be alive now. And there would be no one to tell the tale."

"No witnesses? Just a frightened little boy who insists on sending me messages?"

"How did he ever manage to do that? Is that why you're here so soon after your last visit?"

"Does it matter? I'm here. How do you account for his most recent accident, Father?"

"Do not take such a tone with me, Devlen. You may command your businesses. You don't command me."

"Someone should. Why don't you spend your time in grateful appreciation for the life you have, Father, rather than in bitter contemplation of that which you cannot change?"

"My brother's death?"

"Your nephew's survival."

If his father could have stood, he would have. If he could have stormed from the room, he would have done that as well. Forced as he was to remain seated and in place, he fisted his hands on the edge of the table and stared at Devlen.

"I find it difficult to believe you would listen to the ramblings of an hysterical child," he said finally.

"Do you?"

Devlen studied his plate. In matters of food, his father never scrimped. None of the economies that showed throughout the rest of the estate were visible in the kitchen. But he had lost his appetite. His breakfast forgotten, Devlen sampled his coffee.

"I didn't harm the child."

Devlen didn't comment.

"Would it please you if I gave you my word?"

"It wouldn't matter one way or the other."

"You've grown into a cynic, Devlen."

He sat back and surveyed his father. Something was wrong at Castle Crannoch. It was unnatural for a child to be so afraid, an emotion Robert ably tucked beneath his less-than-pleasant behavior. Miss Sinclair would have her hands full.

"Is it cynical to know one's adversaries? You have a habit of twisting the truth to serve your purposes. You always have."

"Am I an adversary? Interesting."

"What else would you call our relationship?" From the moment he was old enough to understand, Devlen knew his father didn't care for him. He was an encumbrance, a nuisance, an irritant. All Cameron's interests were directed toward the shipbuilding empire his brother had given him to manage, and the ever-present need to demonstrate to his older brother that he was capable of doing so. Cameron was caught in a paradox—needing his brother's approval and despising the necessity for it at the same time.

"I'm surprised you offered the position to Miss Sinclair. She seems an unlikely choice."

"Why would you say that? I think Providence delivered her to our doorstep. The woman needs an occupation, and I have a position."

Devlen didn't answer, didn't comment what he truly

thought. Beatrice Sinclair looked too fragile for Castle Crannoch. In addition, there was sadness just beneath her bravado, something essentially courageous that made him feel oddly protective.

Now wasn't that an unusual thought for him to have?

Breakfast forsaken, Devlen stood and left the room, uncaring that his father wore a small and secretive smile. There were some things he didn't want to know.

Beatrice had been so afraid and so hungry in the last few weeks that the sudden absence of both sensations was almost heady. As she ate, she hummed a tune, an oddity witnessed by one curious bird settling on the edge of her window.

"Hello, little bird. Have you come to beg some scraps?"

He trilled a short song at her and flew away, no doubt annoyed because she wasn't sharing.

The knock on the door startled her. Beatrice stood, walked to the door, and opened it cautiously, holding the borrowed dressing gown closed tight at her throat.

"Mademoiselle? It is I, Gaston," the man said in the French of Paris.

She peeked through the opening to find the giant standing in front of the door, one beefy hand clutching her dress. "The maid, she ironed it for you."

Beatrice extended her hand and retrieved her dress. The maid had evidently mended the garment as well. The tear on the lace at the neck had been repaired, and a button had been replaced.

"Thank you, Gaston."

"Of a certainty, mademoiselle. Whenever you're ready to go fetch your belongings, I await you."

"Thank you."

"All you need to do is pull on the bell rope beside the bed, mademoiselle. Or, if you prefer, I can wait for you."

"I'm not quite finished with breakfast."

"Then I await your summons."

She closed the door, feeling a little bemused. No one had ever waited on her before.

After she finished eating, she dressed, smoothing her hands over the threadbare material of her dress. The maid had ironed it beautifully. The wool felt almost new, the smell emerging from the fabric something reminiscent of lavender. A simple thing really, but it brought tears to her eyes.

After she dressed, Beatrice found a brush sitting on a silver tray and used it to smooth her shortened hair. She, herself, had been ill with the same cholera that had taken her parents, and she'd been subjected to same treatments as the other survivors—their hair had been cut and they'd been purged, twin indignities she'd been too ill to protest.

The square mirror in front of her was trimmed in gold. The reflection revealed a woman too old for her years, perhaps. There was a look in her eyes that hadn't been there before, a bone-deep sadness, an enormous sorrow that didn't fade even when she practiced smiling.

The epidemic that had swept through Kilbridden Village had taken a member of every family. Some, like hers, had been doubly struck. Both her mother and father had died, three days after the first victim had succumbed. The swiftness of the disease had stunned her.

Not only her parents were gone, but also Beatrice's dreams, her hopes, and the simple, peaceful life she'd known.

There were those who might say she'd put herself in this predicament by being too choosy. She might have had her own home, own family. She'd received an offer of marriage but not, however, from the person she expected.

Jeremy MacLeod was a handsome young man who'd been her friend since she was twelve, their relationship changing to a form of awkwardness, and then interest as they'd both aged. He was kind, possessing a gentle temperament, and had a bright way of looking at the world. He was ambitious, filled with plans about the mill he'd inherited from his father. If he had one flaw, it was that he deferred too much to his mother. As the last surviving child of three, he was her baby. She was fiercely protective of him, and he allowed it.

After her parents died, Beatrice had expected Jeremy to come to her cottage and explain, in that earnest tone of his, why they should marry. Instead, he'd stayed away as if she were still contagious.

The only offer of marriage had come, surprisingly, from the young minister who had taken the place of the Reverend Matthew Hanson. She'd known him for all of three days when he'd proposed.

"The people here at Kilbridden Village speak highly of you, Beatrice."

"That is very kind of them."

"They also say that you're a very sensible woman."

"Thank you."

"You're no longer a girl, however."

She'd only glanced at him, wondering if he would correctly interpret her annoyance. He didn't.

"But you're not too old to be a helpmate."

"I suppose not."

"I have two children."

"Do you?"

"I'm a widower. Did you not know?"

She shook her head.

"My children will be joining me as soon as I'm set-tled. They need a mother, and I need a wife."

Hardly a flattering proposal, but he'd looked shocked when she refused.

She'd been too foolish, perhaps, in turning her back on his offer. Now she was alone in the world and forced to find her own way in it, a circumstance the minister had predicted.

"My offer will not stand open for long, Beatrice. In fact, I doubt you'll receive another like mine."

Bride—even the word sounded odd. She'd long since given up the thought of being a bride. She'd never felt desperate or even despondent about her single state. She'd been pleased to assist her father with his work.

It wasn't that she didn't wish to marry. She had, like other girls, her own chest of linens. Over the years, she and her mother had embroidered a dozen napkins with thistles and roses. There always seemed to be enough time to consider marriage, even if there were a paucity of candidates for husband.

She'd occupied herself with one task after another, and if she were occasionally lonely and longing to be a wife or mother, she assuaged her yearnings by minding her friend Sally's children. There were times when she'd confided in Sally that she might not ever be mar-ried, given the lack of men of her age in the village.

"Then he shall have to come from somewhere else,"

Sally had said, imminently practical. "You'll fall in love with him as he's riding through the village on his white horse."

"The only white horses in Kilbridden Village are used for plowing," Beatrice had said, and the two of them had laughed together.

Beatrice pulled on the bell rope and waited at the door, wondering if she should be at the entrance to Castle Crannoch instead. She was not, after all, a guest, but little more than a servant. A toady to the irritating young duke.

There was no choice. She had to take the position. Either that or return to the frigid cottage and starve silently to death. She wouldn't last the winter.

Chapter 5

❧⟨◦⟩❧

Gaston arrived at her door less than five minutes later. He bowed slightly to her, a gesture she wished he wouldn't make. Beatrice followed him through the castle, but this journey was not in the darkness. Nor was she required to walk through a series of narrowing serpentine corridors. Castle Crannoch was not as wholly medieval as it had appeared the night before. Instead, this part of the structure was built less with protection in mind than beauty.

"Have you been with the duke long, Gaston?" she asked him in French.

"I have been with Mr. Cameron since before he was born, miss."

"I thought you were in the duke's employ."

He didn't comment.

"I understand his mother was French."

He nodded. "May I say your French is excellent?" he said.

That comment certainly put her in her place. Evidently, there were some questions she was not to ask.

"Thank you, my grandmother was French. I've spoken it since I was a child."

She halted at the top of the stairs, amazed. A pair of staircases began at the bottom, met at the second floor, then branched out again to sweep up to Castle Crannoch's third story. Both the banister and pilasters were heavily carved of a dark, well-polished wood, a stark contrast to the pale yellow silk of the adjoining walls.

In the center, suspended by a long chain from the third floor, was a massive chandelier. One of the footmen was balancing on a ladder, in the process of replacing the candles. He looked at her curiously, then evidently decided she was of no more interest than his chore.

Beatrice descended the steps slowly, glancing at the paintings on the walls. Each of the men featured in the life-size portraits resembled Cameron Gordon. Or his son.

"Are they the Dukes of Brechin?"

Gaston did not glance back at her. "No, mademoiselle, they are not all dukes. Some are men of importance to the family."

There was no time to ask any further questions, because Gaston had outdistanced her. She hurried to catch up.

The massive front doors looked to be old, banded with iron and studded with bolts. Gaston opened the left one and stepped aside, bowing lightly to her. "If you will, mademoiselle."

She stepped out onto the broad stone steps, transfixed by the view of the ocean to her left and the rolling hills before her. The sun was over the horizon, pink bands of clouds stretching like ruched ribbons across the sky.

In the night, winter had come. The grass was coated in a dull frost, and her breath clouded in front of her face. Soon, ice would hang from the trees, and snow would blanket the ground. The world would still, barely breathing, until spring.

She gripped her shawl tightly, feeling the cold seep past her skin into her bones.

A large shiny black carriage stood in the circular drive, four ebony horses being restrained by a liveried driver. The driver tipped the handle of his whip to the brim of his hat and bowed slightly. Beatrice nodded in return.

"Is that Devlen's carriage?"

"No," Devlen said from behind her. "It belongs to the Duke of Brechin, Miss Sinclair."

She turned and surveyed him. He was attired in a greatcoat that looked substantially more suited to the temperature than her shawl. She envied him the warmth of it.

"Aren't you cold?"

He studied her too intently, his gaze resting on her face, then her hands clutching the shawl around her shoulders. Finally, he looked at her shoes. Did he measure her appearance by her possessions? If so, he would judge her poorly indeed. She'd sold everything that might bring her a few coins. What was left was shabby and threadbare, hardly befitting the Duke of Brechin's servant.

"Have you nothing else to wear, Miss Sinclair?"

He unbuttoned his greatcoat and removed it, swinging it over her shoulders. Immediately, she felt warmer, and also dwarfed by the size of it. The coat puddled on the ground as he proceeded to button it.

"I can't take your coat."

He ignored her. Despite being attired only in a white shirt and black trousers, he didn't look affected by the cold.

"My father tells me you've accepted the position he offered you. Are you certain you've made the wisest decision?"

"Yes, quite sure."

"You might wish to consider the question for a moment before answering, Miss Sinclair."

"Why should I, Mr. Gordon? My decision has already been made."

She did wish he wouldn't smile at her in that annoying way.

When she stepped aside to descend the steps, he reached out and gripped her hand. She glanced down where his hand rested, then back up at his face. His smile had disappeared, replaced by a look so intent that she was startled by it.

"You need gloves as well."

"Please, let me go." She didn't tell him that her only gloves were shredded until they were nearly useless.

He released her but didn't step back.

"I don't think it's wise for you to remain at Castle Crannoch, Miss Sinclair."

"I thank you for your concern, sir, but I have made my decision and conveyed it to your father. He seems to think I would be acceptable in the role."

"You serve my father's purposes by being here, Miss Sinclair. Haven't you asked yourself why he would be willing to hire you for such a prestigious position? Candidates for the post are not normally interviewed in a bedroom."

Her face flamed. "If you will let me pass." She concentrated on his knee-high, shiny black boots. His clothing was plain but of an evident fine quality. He smelled of something pleasant, something she couldn't quite identify.

"You are a sheep in a den of wolves, Miss Sinclair."

Startled, she glanced up at him.

"Do you consider yourself one of the wolves, Mr. Gordon? The head of the pack, perhaps?"

She clapped her hand over her mouth, horrified at what she'd said.

"You're not prepared for the position you've assumed. Go home."

"And starve? This is the one position for which I have some training, and you would take it from me?"

She wanted to bite back the words the minute they were said. Who was he to know her circumstances? She wanted neither pity nor charity, simply a way to support herself.

"Is there no one to help you?"

Beatrice drew herself up, angered at having found comfort from the loan of his coat. She began to unbutton it, but he stopped her by placing his hands on top of hers.

"Keep it, Miss Sinclair. I refuse to watch you shiver for the sake of pride."

They looked at each other, the moments ticking by too swiftly.

"The cholera epidemic took everyone I loved," she said finally. "There is no one left. I'm alone."

"Not even a sweetheart?"

"No."

"Did the epidemic take him as well? Or was there more than one?"

The best course was simply to remain silent. He didn't need her participation in this conversation. He was doing quite well on his own.

"If you will forgive my impertinence, Miss Sinclair, you're an oddly striking woman. Once you've lost your thinness, you'll be beautiful, I think. Still, even now there's something about you that interests a man."

"No."

"No?" One of his eyebrows danced upward.

"No, I will not forgive your impertinence. Let me pass."

All this time, Gaston and the driver had been observing them with interest. Neither man made any pretense of ignoring their conversation. In fact, they looked as if they were taking mental notes, the better to describe it in detail for the rest of the staff.

The very last thing she needed was gossip to accompany her, especially when beginning a position that would keep her from poverty and ensure she was fed.

"Please," she said, deciding to soften her demand, "let me pass."

"Are you going home, Miss Sinclair?"

He really shouldn't say her name in that fashion. It had the effect of teasing her, as if the words traveled up from the back of her ankles to her spine. His voice was low, the syllables softly uttered, almost whispered.

"Yes, Mr. Gordon, I am going home. Now, will you let me pass?"

"Will you stay there?"

"No."

He nodded as if he weren't the least surprised by her answer.

"I hadn't intended to remain at Castle Crannoch long, Miss Sinclair, but I see I may have to delay my departure."

"Do not do so on my account, sir."

He placed his hand on hers again, but this touch was not to restrain. Instead, he trailed his fingers from her wrist to her forearm, inciting a shiver of sensation. She jerked away, a gesture that only deepened his smile.

"A few days, Miss Sinclair. Just to make certain you're settled in."

This time, he stepped back, allowing her to escape. She almost ran down the steps.

Gaston moved to open the carriage door. She gave him directions to her cottage before entering and sitting in the middle of the seat, away from the windows at either side, deliberately keeping her gaze on her feet. She didn't want to see Devlen Gordon. Not now, and certainly not when she returned.

She pulled the wool of his greatcoat up around her ears, smelling that strange and wonderful scent.

Gaston climbed up beside the driver. As they began to move, she glanced out the window. Why did she feel a surge of disappointment when she didn't see that most irritating man?

*   *   *

The last person they needed at Castle Crannoch was Beatrice Sinclair, with her soft blue eyes, restrained manner, and the hands that shook so very visibly.

Her hair was too black, and her complexion too white. Someone should tell her red lips were not in fashion. Did she color them?

She had a sharp tongue when she allowed herself to use it.

I was thinking you were Black Donald.

Someone really should do something about her wardrobe. Her clothes were too loose, but her bodice was entirely too snug. Her legs were too long as well, but he didn't suppose there was anything she could do about that.

She wasn't going to go away easily. For that matter, he couldn't blame her. His father had, no doubt, made being Robert's governess/nursemaid an enviable position while the truth was something else.

Still, it must have been better than what she'd experienced in the past year. Parts of Scotland had been decimated by the influx of cholera. In fact, he'd taken Robert to Edinburgh for the period, feeling a little more secure being away from Kilbridden Village. The stories he'd heard from Gaston had not been pleasant ones.

The last thing he wanted was to feel a surge of compassion for her. She wasn't safe at the castle. But even that revelation, subtly couched as it was, had been rejected. What would she have said if he'd told her the entire truth?

"Thank you, but I don't believe you." Or, "I'll take the position, regardless." Or, "Don't be absurd, Mr. Gordon. You've exaggerated." He could easily hear her make any of those responses.

He should be back in Edinburgh, where there were a

hundred details to see to. If nothing else, he could travel to Inverness and be about some of his business there.

Perhaps he should have accompanied Miss Sinclair to her home. There, he could have taken the measure of the woman more completely. But no one can measure where a man wants to go, or a woman for that matter, from their past. Futures were buried deep in the mind and soul, and rarely voiced.

He folded his arms, ignoring the cold as he watched the carriage begin the descent to the village.

She was going to be a problem.

Chapter 6

〜⚬⚬〜

From a distance, Castle Crannoch appeared a somber gray, but the bricks were actually nearly black, and the mortar a much lighter shade. Only part of the older section of the castle was visible from the bowl of the valley, but the villagers could not see the four turrets with their crenellated tops so perfectly constructed they appeared like teeth, or the curving drive leading to the massive arched front doors.

But the stout lone tower, behind which sat the crumbling original castle, was easily visible. A facade, perhaps like the inhabitants of Castle Crannoch?

The descent to Kilbridden Village was done with great haste, as if the driver was a seasoned traveler of the curving road. Twice, Beatrice was nearly thrown to the door, and both times had to grab hold of the strap mounted above the window.

The lower half of the road, filled with serpentine twists and turns, was even more hastily navigated, which made her wonder if this particular driver had also been responsible for the carriage accident that had killed Robert's parents and put Cameron Gordon in a wheeled chair.

At the bottom, they hit ruts in the road that jarred the carriage and once made it sway so much Beatrice thought they would surely overturn. Instead of reducing his speed, the driver only cursed the horses so loudly Beatrice could hear his shouts inside the carriage.

With frenetic speed they drove on through the countryside, as if wolves were on their heels, the driver making no effort to slow or to even take the pitted roads into consideration.

Beatrice closed her eyes, both hands clutching the strap, and prayed all through Kilbridden Village.

A scant ten minutes later, she heard a high-pitched whine and a wheel went flying by the window, followed by the carriage lurching to one side and coming to an abrupt halt.

They'd snapped an axle.

Beatrice held on to the strap until the carriage stopped moving.

"Miss Sinclair?"

Gaston's voice was close to her left ear. She raised her head to find he had poked his head into the now open door. He extended his hand to her.

"Are you all right, Miss Sinclair?"

She nodded, even though her stomach still felt a bit unsteady.

"I'll help you out, Miss Sinclair. It would be more comfortable for you to wait outside the carriage while the wheel is being mended."

Since the carriage was perched at an angle, getting

out of the vehicle meant climbing up to the door on the left side, then allowing Gaston to lift her down. The feat was done as delicately as possible, given she didn't want her petticoats to show. On the descent, her skirt ballooned, and she revealed entirely too much of her legs. She hoped Gaston didn't notice, or if he did, he'd simply forget.

She bunched up her skirts demurely and maneuvered her way around the mud puddles to reach the side of the road. Only then did she realize exactly where she was. The mill. Jeremy MacLeod's property.

Beatrice must have made a sound because Gaston glanced in her direction. She waved her hand at him to signify everything was fine.

"It might be some time, Miss Sinclair. Thomas will have to return to Castle Crannoch for the parts. Or another carriage."

She was tempted to mention that if Thomas had had some degree of caution about the state of the roads, they wouldn't have been in this situation at all. But she only nodded.

The day kept getting worse and worse. The one person she had not wanted to see was striding toward her, his sandy hair uncovered, his face a little more bronzed by the sun.

Jeremy MacLeod.

"Beatrice, do you need assistance?"

"Good day, Jeremy. No, thank you."

"As you can see," Gaston said, gesturing toward the carriage, "we have had something of an accident."

Beatrice wondered if he deliberately pointed out the ducal crest, or if Jeremy had noticed it on his own.

"What is this you're about then, Beatrice?"

Beatrice clasped her hands together. "I've accepted a position at Castle Crannoch, and I've come to get my things."

"Castle Crannoch? I've done business with the castle before." That, it seemed, was all he was going to say.

She wanted to ask him questions about the inhabitants, but to do so would indicate she had lingering doubts about her decision. Therefore, she remained silent, and so did he.

Gaston interrupted, easing the awkwardness. "If you would give me instructions to your cottage, Miss Sinclair, I could go ahead on one of the horses and fetch what you need."

"That won't be necessary," Jeremy said. "I have a wagon you can borrow. The cottage is not far from here. Easy walking distance."

He should know. He had walked it often enough as a young man.

"Very well," she said, with as much grace as she could muster. "I would be grateful of the loan of your wagon."

Beatrice sincerely hoped the day would get better.

At that thought, it began to rain.

"Tell me about the nightmares," Devlen said.

Robert sat on the floor, busy arranging his troops. The oriental carpet in the Duke's Chamber served as a military battlefield, the various patterns being hills and valleys, rivers and streams. The toy soldiers had been Devlen's gift to his cousin last Christmas, a battalion of Hessians and English soldiers adding to Robert's already considerable army.

"Have they gotten worse?" Devlen sat beside his

cousin, took a handful of toy soldiers, and began to arrange them in a line.

"Not like that," Robert said, brushing away his hand. "I'll do it. They have to win, you know."

His cousin had an unholy love of war games, an interest that had been regrettably fueled by his father. Where other boys would have been content with tales of heroism, Robert wanted to know details of the battle. How many men had been killed, how many skirmishes until the war was done, topics Devlen was certain did not interest most seven-year-olds. But then again, he could be entirely wrong. Perhaps Miss Sinclair would know better. Or perhaps she was as inexperienced with children as he.

"So, you haven't been having any nightmares?"

Robert glanced at him but didn't say a word, evidently content in arranging his soldiers. Which battle were they fighting today? Robert knew an amazing wealth of detail about the placement of regiments and such. Since he'd never been militarily inclined, even as a child, Devlen fell back to watching Robert line up the troops. From Robert's scowl, his lack of activity wasn't approved of either, so Devlen scooped up the remaining men and put them on his side of the carpet like chess pieces he'd acquired.

"It's Hannibal," Robert said, leaning over and taking back the soldiers while giving Devlen an admonishing look. "The general who marched his elephants across the Alps."

Devlen leaned back on his hand and wondered if his cousin knew there were not many occasions when he crawled around on the floor. For that effort alone, he should be applauded. His memory furnished him with one unique episode with a former mistress, but it wouldn't do to dwell on that particular escapade. His knees had been chafed for a week.

Robert was intent upon reenacting some battle far back in history. Devlen decided not to ask more about Hannibal, in case it was a subject on which Robert was voluble. A sentence or two and he would be out of his element.

Devlen was quite able to converse on a variety of subjects, having spent many years in London as well as on the Continent. He'd traveled to America for one blissful summer, but he remembered more about the woman who'd accompanied him on that trip than he did the scenery of Washington and New York. His journeys through the Orient had been the most fascinating of all his travels, and he vowed he'd return one day. He'd become somewhat familiar with the Russians, although he doubted he'd ever return to that country. Too damn cold for his taste.

Yet, none of his experiences provided him with fodder for a conversation with his cousin. Still, he'd always liked the child, and Robert must have sensed his genuine affection, because he'd gravitated to Devlen ever since his parents had died.

The responsibility of being the only adult in the child's family who could tolerate him was heavy indeed. But there was something about Robert, as irritating as he could sometimes be, that summoned forth Devlen's compassion. Perhaps it was because Robert had suddenly been made an orphan. One moment he was the cherished son of a man older than his father and the next he was told his mummy and daddy had been killed in a carriage accident.

The intervening months had not been easy ones.

First, his home had suddenly been overtaken by an entourage. His uncle, now guardian, had arrived with his wife, her maid, and countless other servants, their sole purpose on earth to look after one very lonely child.

He'd been given a series of tutors, each selected by his uncle and each more disagreeable than the last. Robert, however, had defeated them to a man with the sheer brilliant tactic of being such a monstrous child they'd quit out of desperation.

Did his young cousin realize he was the greatest pawn in this invisible war? The enemy was not the French, or the English of a century earlier, but his own uncle.

Things were not well at Castle Crannoch or with Robert. Robert, however, was not talking. For the first time, his cousin wasn't sharing his misery, and his reticence was disturbing.

Yet, it wasn't Robert's fault he was suddenly and not unexpectedly irritated. Any more than it was his fault Cameron Gordon intensely disliked him.

"How's your ankle?" he asked, glancing at the wrapping visible below Robert's trousers. "You took a nasty fall down the stairs."

A fall that might well have killed an adult.

Robert nodded.

"You must be more careful."

Once again Robert glanced over at him. Those young eyes suddenly looked too old. In that moment Devlen wondered what, exactly, the child knew. Or suspected.

"You're going to get a governess tomorrow."

"I don't need a governess."

"To that I would probably agree. Nevertheless, Miss Sinclair is to begin tomorrow. Try to treat her nicely. No itchweed in her bed."

Robert looked intrigued by the thought, so much so Devlen wished he hadn't given the boy the idea. But Robert had managed to get rid of three tutors on his own; he didn't need Devlen's suggestions.

"Perhaps you can see your way clear to being polite to her. At least talk to her from time to time. I understand Miss Sinclair is an orphan as well."

Robert's face suddenly closed; there was no other word for it. The light in his eyes went out as if there were no intelligence behind them, as if nothing lived behind the face of Robert Gordon, twelfth Duke of Brechin. Devlen had never seen anyone vanish so quickly, and the effect was so complete it stirred the hairs on the back of his neck.

They could not travel fast in the farm wagon, but it was just as well. Beatrice had time enough to savor the view of the cottage she'd always known as home.

Although most of her memories were of Kilbridden Village, she'd come from somewhere else, a place near the border of Scotland and England. Her parents laughed about it sometimes, about her father acting as a reiver and her mother being the prize he'd stolen. But those were comments not for her ears. Even as a child Beatrice had known that.

Her parents had both come from large families, she'd been told. Yet in all these years, she'd never met any relatives. No aunts or uncles had come to Scotland to visit them, nor had she ever witnessed any correspondence.

There was an air of mystery about her parents. Once, when Beatrice had asked her mother why she never talked about the past, the older woman looked as if she might cry.

"There are some memories that shouldn't be recalled," she said, and wouldn't comment further.

When her parents had died, Beatrice had carefully searched through their belongings. She'd found nothing. No links with the past, no letters or documents that might lead to missing relatives.

Her father was an educated man, always talking about books and his lessons. He was a poor farmer, inept in those necessary tasks as if such menial work was unknown to him. The crops were often scraggly, and the chickens sickened and died more often than not. He was happiest when he was deep in his study of his few books, or when he called out to her mother and the two of them discussed a topic of interest.

Even with their poverty, life was pleasant for the three of them. The only time she could remember sorrow in the small cottage was when her mother gave birth to a baby boy who lived only an hour. She'd seen her father weep then as he sat beside her mother's bed. That was the first and only time she'd ever seen him cry; but as the years passed, she realized that of the two of them, her mother was the stronger person.

When she was fourteen, the village elders came to her father and offered him the newly created position as schoolmaster. All pretense of farming was forgotten, and from that day forward the family fortunes were different. There were never times in which money was plentiful, but they were less likely to starve. Her mother kept the chickens, and maintained a small garden, and her father left for the school each morning bearing a smile that was half anticipation, and half excitement.

Now the cottage looked forlorn and empty. Should she board up the windows, close the shutters? It would be some time before she returned here, if she could bear to return at all.

The cottage was far enough from the village that she had no neighbors. She'd often felt isolated during the past year. Perhaps that had been a good thing after all. No one had known of her precarious state, that she'd completely run out of money or objects to sell a month ago.

"Is it a difficult thing, miss?"

She glanced at Gaston, realizing the wagon had stopped, and Gaston was standing in the road.

"Is what difficult?"

"Leaving your home?"

She nodded.

How strange she'd given no thought to the care of the cottage while she'd be living at Castle Crannoch. Who would check the thatch to make sure it was repaired in the spring? Who would chip away the ice from the door and oil the latch and hinges? Who would guard her father's books and her parents' possessions, those she could not bear to sell in the last month?

She should tell Gaston she could not leave. A moment later, she chastised herself. Why would she stay? There was nothing here but the past, and she needed to put it aside, both memories of the happiness and laughter and the darker recollections of loss and grief.

"Miss?"

She came back to the present and left the wagon, walking down the path and deliberately blocking out memories. But they came flooding back despite her will. Her father had laid the path, and the task had taken him a full two months—six weeks for the planning of it and only two weeks to do the work. She and her mother had helped, hauling in the stones from the back of the property, laying them down exactly where he'd planned. She remembered he'd been so pleased at the finished result while she and her mother had merely been grateful the chore was done.

Her parents were so complete, so happy to be together, that she wasn't unduly surprised Fate had taken them within days of each other. Now they lay buried together, in the churchyard facing east. "In sure and certain hope of the Resurrection," the minister had said. "With a smile in their hearts and their souls enlivened with peace."

That was all very well and good for her parents, but what about her?

An entirely selfish thought, and she recognized it as such. However, she didn't chastise herself as much as she had in the beginning when grief was such a raw wound she would sit alone in the cottage staring out at the day and wondering how she was ever to live through the pain.

She had learned, in the last year, that she could live through anything, including the loss of her parents and her friends. She could endure loneliness and heartache, grief, pain, and even despair. But her body required food, water, and warmth.

For that, she'd agreed to Cameron Gordon's offer.

She entered the cottage, gathering up her belongings: a small brush, her mother's silver-backed mirror, her father's book of *Aesop's Fables,* her remaining two dresses, a spare set of stays, and two shifts. She was wearing everything else she owned. Within five minutes, she was done.

Beatrice left the cottage and closed the door behind her, taking care the latch caught and the wind couldn't blow it open as it had a habit of doing.

She turned and smiled resolutely. "I'm ready, Gaston."

He reached out to take the valise from her. "Are you certain, mademoiselle?" She half expected him to heft the bag in his hand as if measuring its contents.

"I'm certain," she said. The belongings were hardly worth the effort of the journey.

Should she contact her parents' friends, let them know where she would be? Just in case something happened, and any of them needed to reach her.

Who should she contact? Mrs. Fernleigh? A widow of indeterminate age, Mrs. Fernleigh had been old when Beatrice was a child. In the last few years, Mrs. Fernleigh had been increasingly forgetful, referring to people who were no longer alive as if she'd just spoken with them. The cholera epidemic had been difficult on her. She was often confused. Perhaps not Mrs. Fernleigh.

Mr. Brown? He'd lost his wife and son in the epidemic and often spent his days more intent on a tankard than the world around him.

Other than Jeremy, all her friends had perished in the epidemic. There was no one to tell, in the end.

With one last, lingering glance, she left the home she'd always known, walking down the path toward the carriage to, if not a better life, then one filled with less sorrow.

Chapter 7

Rowena Gordon surveyed herself in the mirror with a critical eye, not only to her appearance but her demeanor. She must show exactly the right appearance to the world. Her family was quick to judge, and she didn't want an errant tongue commenting she looked tired, or her lace was frayed, or there was a glint of disappointment in her eyes.

There must be nothing about her comportment to give anyone a reason to comment. If someone must say something, let him say the weather in Scotland agreed with her, her complexion had never looked clearer, the years had not seemed to touch her. Above all, dear God, do not let one of them whisper a word of pity or compassion about her husband.

Dear Cameron, what a shame for such a vital man to be trapped in a chair. How do you cope, my dearest Rowena?

Please, not that.

She was wearing red today, a daring color, a shocking one. Her jacket was cropped above the waist and trimmed in fur, as was the hem of her ankle-length skirt. There were little pompoms on her boots as well as on her hat. Another new outfit. Her relatives had not hesitated to comment on her spending habits, as if they envied her wealth. As if money could ever make up for the constant sorrow of her life.

She picked up the reticule and turned to address her maid.

"Well, Mary, will I do?" she asked.

Of all the people in the world, Mary was privy to her secrets more than anyone else.

Mary had sat beside her during those terrible hours when she hadn't known if Cameron would live or die. Mary had brought her countless cups of chocolate when she couldn't sleep. Mary had surreptitiously handed her a new handkerchief when she left her husband's room every morning. And Mary was the one who hung about like a wraith, an almost invisible creature simply waiting for the opportunity to be of service.

Mary nodded and smiled in response. "You look beautiful, madam."

"Thank you, Mary. If I do, it's no small thanks to your ministrations."

Mary's cheeks turned a becoming rose as she hurried to get the door.

"Will you be ready to leave by lunchtime?" Rowena asked as she left the room.

"Oh yes, madam. My bags are packed." She looked as if she'd like to say something, but kept silent.

"Will you not be anxious to see your brother again?" Thomas was one of Cameron's drivers, a most trusted employee.

"Indeed I will, madam. It's just that London is so very exciting a place."

"It is all that and more, Mary. But we must return to Castle Crannoch."

Mary nodded. "Yes, madam."

Did Mary know how desperately Rowena had wanted to leave Scotland? The despair of her life had become too much to bear. Mary had no choice but to accompany her. But these past two months in London had not eased her life one whit. Instead, she'd missed Cameron with every passing day.

Perhaps coming to London had been a good thing after all, because it had borne home to her the truth. She couldn't escape no matter where she was. She adored her husband, without his legs or not.

These past months, he'd withdrawn from her completely. He no longer even touched her in passing or friendship. She used to sit beside his chair and press the back of his hand against her cheek, remembering so many other times when such a gesture would lead to passion between them.

Now, however, there was not even that.

He would slowly withdraw his hand and look at her impassively, almost as if he didn't quite know her. Or didn't wish to.

Sometimes, she wondered what he would do if she told him just how lonely she was. Would he look right through her? Or would he allow her back into his bed? There were things they couldn't say to each other, even though they should and needed to be said.

She left her room, descending the steps holding her head high and feeling for the treads with her feet below her full skirts. Her mouth was arranged in a fixed smile and her face in a pleasant expression. She was on a stage of sorts, and the final curtain was about to rise.

Her family had changed, or perhaps she'd just now realized how sharp and aggressive they were in their curiosity. They didn't care that each one of their questions were like darts thrown at her exposed skin. Everywhere they landed they caused a wound.

As she entered the drawing room and faced her five cousins, two aunts, and her mother, Rowena realized she'd been an absolute fool. She'd come to London for comfort and been greeted by a hungry pack of she-wolves.

Not one of these females had once embraced her, or expressed their sorrow for her life's predicament. Instead, they had been jealous of Cameron's wealth and her stepson's notoriety.

She took a deep breath and greeted them.

The journey back to Castle Crannoch was delayed due to the repairs to the coach. Beatrice sat back against the cushions and folded her hands on her lap and made a pretense of looking out the window. She had planned to be back at the castle before the afternoon was well advanced. When they finally got on their way, it was gloaming. The saddest time of day, as if nature itself wept to see the coming of night.

She hated the darkness, the total blackness of it, the absence of light. Night reminded her too closely of death. She was a person who craved mornings, who sought the dawn. The first tentative touch of sunlight against a blackened sky brought a feeling of peace, of incipient joy.

Yet here she was, approaching Castle Crannoch once more with night looming on the horizon.

Was this the hand of God demonstrating that perhaps she should not feel such relief upon leaving her village? Had she been foolish to accept the post of governess?

They began the long arduous journey up the winding mountain to Castle Crannoch. Once again the trip was done in full darkness, the moon coming out from behind a bank of clouds to witness the ascent.

Beatrice tried to concentrate on anything but the knowledge of how steep the drop was to her right. Were the horses as afraid as she? Or were they simply immune to the danger?

"Tell me about Robert," she said, directing her attention back to Gaston, who'd remained silent and watchful for the last quarter hour. Instead of sitting with the driver, he rode with her inside the carriage.

"What would you like to know about him?" For the first time, she sensed his approval and felt ashamed she'd not asked about the child earlier.

"What are his favorite subjects to study? His favorite foods? That sort of thing."

"I think it best if you learn about His Grace on your own, Miss Sinclair. I will say this about the child, however. He loved his parents dearly and suffers for their loss even now."

"That is one thing we have in common, Gaston."

"Which is why I think you will do well for each other, Miss Sinclair. You're both orphans, and you will find there are other things you share as well."

"Tell me this, then, Gaston. Has no one seen to him

since his parents died? Is there no one to give him direction and to correct his manners?"

"He is the Duke of Brechin," he said, and shrugged. "He outranks anyone who would correct him."

"I don't care about his rank, Gaston. But I do care about his manners. If I am to be his governess, that must be understood."

Gaston sat back against the cushions and surveyed her. In the moonlight she could see the edge of the smile, as if he were genuinely amused.

"Before you can discipline a child, you must have affection for him."

"That might be a French sentiment, but it's not exactly what we Scots would say."

"What would the Scots say, Miss Sinclair?"

"That if a child is to be lovable, he must be disciplined first."

"Then these next weeks will prove interesting." His smile abruptly disappeared. "But you must promise me that if you need anything, anything at all, please seek me out. I will never be far from Robert."

"Are you his protector?"

"I have never known anyone—child or adult alike—who needed me more, but no. I tend to his uncle's needs."

She didn't respond, only subsided back against the cushions.

The carriage returned to the circular drive in front of the castle. Gaston left the vehicle first, then extended a hand to help her descend. She did, holding the greatcoat up so it didn't drag on the ground. She'd gotten mud on the hem earlier today, and regretted having to give it back in such bad condition.

Two lanterns on either side of the front door were

blazing brightly, and even the steps were adorned with candles, as if for a party.

"Are they entertaining?" Beatrice asked, surprised they would be doing so less than a year after the deaths of Robert's parents.

Gaston smiled again. "No, Mr. Devlen is profligate with candles. Whenever he is in residence, he orders them lit. Sometimes I think he would like to push back the night itself."

Perhaps she should have asked about Devlen as well as Robert.

It was too late, because he was suddenly there, dressed in a black formal suit of clothes and a white cravat. She'd thought him arresting in his day clothes but had to admit that now he was sartorially elegant. Perfectly handsome. As perfect as a prince.

"Gaston," he said. "My father is asking for you."

Gaston bowed once to her, then looked toward the castle.

"I should see to Robert," Beatrice said.

"Nonsense," Devlen said. "You can begin your duties tomorrow." He and Gaston shared a look. "I will see Miss Sinclair to her chamber."

Gaston bowed again and was gone, melting into the dark as if he were a creature of night itself.

Chapter 8

"You needn't escort me," Beatrice said. "I believe I can find my way back to my chamber."

"Are you entirely certain? Castle Crannoch is a large and confusing structure."

"You saw me off, and here you are to welcome me on my return. Why?"

"Perhaps I have set myself up as the majordomo of Crannoch. Perhaps I simply missed you."

Did she take him seriously? Was he flirting with her? For some reason, she felt uncomfortable in his presence, as if he were larger than life and therefore made her feel so much smaller in comparison.

What a silly way to feel.

Devlen Gordon was simply a man. No more, no less than that. In that he was like a baker or a butcher or a silversmith or any of the men she'd met in the course of her lifetime. Some were braver than others, some more daring in their speech or dress. Some were courteous, and others used the courtesies they'd been taught in an offhanded way that made her think they truly didn't mean to be polite but only did so because it was less effort than rudeness.

None had been so handsome, though. Nor had any of them been graced with such a low voice, its tone having a strange effect on her. She wanted to hear him say mundane things, simply to hear his voice.

She was no doubt tired, and still suffering from near starvation.

"I can assure you, Mr. Gordon, I'm quite aware of how large a castle this is. At the same time, it is no great feat to find the room I slept in last night."

"How will you find the dining room from there, Miss Sinclair?"

He stopped in front of her and held out his arm, leaving her with the choice of being insufferably rude or putting her hand upon it.

She had not been reared to be impolite, and it would have caused her as much embarrassment as it would have caused him if she slighted him right at this moment. She reached out tentatively and rested her fingers as lightly as possible upon the fine material of his jacket. But her hand had a will of its own and her fingers moved over the cloth, her thumb stroking over and over as if to test the resiliency of the muscles she felt.

He glanced at her as she lifted her head. The look they exchanged made her breath tight. She felt as if someone had relaced her corset so she couldn't breathe. The bone and the leather pressed into her flesh, making her acutely conscious of her entire body. She could almost feel the outline of her hips, her waist, and the breasts that didn't feel like hers at all, but creations too full and pillowy to belong to her.

She almost said something to him then, some word to make him look toward the sea or the sky or even toward her feet. Anywhere but keep staring at her. She couldn't look away, and the lanternlight flickered over his face, alternately painting it as the face of an angel or a devil. He was too handsome and too arresting a personage to be standing here in the dark with her. The horses moved; one stamped and the others blew through their noses. No doubt a reminder to the humans that the night was growing colder, and they wanted their stalls and feed.

"I must go inside," she said, drawing his coat closer to her shoulders. She really should return it to him, but she didn't unbutton it, didn't surrender the garment.

He is dangerous. She didn't know why she thought those words, but she understood their meaning well enough. He was the type of man mothers warned their daughters about, the type of man who was mentioned in whispers and shocked expressions. Gossip would follow him all of the days of his life. Women, even virtuous women, would forever notice him. And the other kind of woman would wonder, deep in her heart, if the look in his eyes was really a promise.

"You're a guest. It would be the height of crudeness to allow you to find your chamber on your own."

"I am not a guest, or have you forgotten? I'm the governess."

"Still, the same courtesies apply."

"Then fetch the chambermaid," she dared him. "Or one of the footmen. Or even one of the stable lads with some knowledge of the castle. Any of them can assist me."

"We have a very small staff at Castle Crannoch. My father believes in being penurious to a fault. We employ only a fraction of the individuals needed to maintain my cousin's birthright. It would be a hardship to take one of them from their duties."

"Do you resent him?"

"I beg your pardon?"

The moment the question was out of her mouth, she wished it back. How could she have dared? She wanted to blame him for bringing out the worst in her, but Devlen Gordon was not at fault here. The flaw was unfortunately in her own nature.

"Do you always say exactly what you think?"

"I apologize. It was not well-done of me, and I do know better."

"I find you remarkably refreshing, Miss Sinclair. Perhaps you're what my cousin needs after all."

"Why do you object to my taking the position?"

"I have a whole host of objections, I'm afraid, Miss Sinclair. You're too young. Too attractive. You are, no doubt, naïve. You're no match for my father, and I doubt you can control my cousin."

She stared at him, nonplussed. What did she say to such a litany? She decided to address the insults alone. The compliment she would mull over later in the privacy of her chamber.

"I'm not naïve. I'm very well read."

"Reading, while virtuous in and of itself, cannot grant any true experience in life."

"Nor am I a child, sir."

"If I had seen you on an Edinburgh street, Miss Sinclair, my first thought would not have been your resemblance to a child."

She could feel her fingers and toes tingle, not to mention the tip of her nose. She was certain she was in full blush right up to her hairline. Beatrice desperately wanted to ask him what he would have thought, but restraint, absent until now, finally made itself known. She didn't dare walk into his net of words.

"Very well," she said in her most matronly tone, "I will just have to prove you wrong. I will show you I can do a very good job as Robert's governess."

For the longest moment he didn't say a word, simply looked at her as if she had issued him a challenge of some sort, and he was debating whether or not to accept.

"Did I insult you, Miss Sinclair? I can assure you I didn't mean to do so."

"I can assure you, Mr. Gordon, I am not in the least insulted."

He looked beyond her to where the driver stood patiently at the head of the restless horses. He nodded, only that, and the driver began leading them away, toward the road branching off from the entrance. Beatrice assumed the stables were in that direction, as well as the other outbuildings necessary to support the castle.

"Gaston tells me you're responsible for all the candles," she said, staring at Castle Crannoch lit up to greet the night. The building was an impressive sight indeed, tinged golden by the hundreds of flickering beeswax candles.

"I find it foolish not to use my wealth where it might bring me the most comfort. I dislike night."

She glanced at him, surprised by his admission. "Are you afraid of the dark?"

"Not at all. But darkness limits my movements, robs me of time, and I dislike wasting time intensely."

"So you change night into day."

"If I can."

"Are you very rich? Does it make you happy?"

Why on earth had she said that? To mitigate her words, she asked him another question, "Do you travel with trunks of candles?"

"As a matter of fact, I do, Miss Sinclair. I also travel with pistols in my carriage, and other objects that provide me with some protection. My dislike of the darkness is not simply limited to Castle Crannoch."

"What happens when you travel by ship? I understand fire is a very real concern. Do they allow you your candles?"

"I travel aboard my own ships, and therefore do not have the difficulty of trying to convince a captain to overlook my peculiarities. However, I restrain myself to lanterns and only in fair weather. I had a very interesting, if pitch-dark journey, around Cape Horn during a storm. It was not an experience I wish to duplicate. It was like going to hell by way of the ocean."

She had never met anyone like him, so aware of his own idiosyncrasies and yet so uncaring of them. He simply accepted that his dislike of darkness was part of his character, but he didn't offer excuses for himself.

"I am not fond of the darkness as well," she said, as he opened the door for her. She entered the castle and immediately looked up at the chandelier above their heads, now filled with hundreds of lit candles, which cast a honeyed glow over the entranceway. "Unlike you, I've never been wealthy enough to change night into day."

"So how do you manage, Miss Sinclair?"

"I simply endure, Mr. Gordon."

"Ah, there is the difference between us. I don't have the patience for endurance. I think it a specious virtue."

As they mounted the steps, he glanced down at her. "What do you do when you wake in the middle of the night? Or do you always sleep the sleep of the just?"

She smiled at his curiosity and her own pleasure in it. "I shut my eyes very tightly and pray for sleep. As a child I used to spend most of my nighttime hours below the covers. I would create a little cave for myself with my doll, my imagination, and my dreams."

"What did you dream about?" he asked, holding his arm out for her again.

She gripped the banister instead. The journey upward was done slowly and leisurely, almost as if they were taking a walk in the garden. She thought about his question.

"I dreamed of singing, even though I have no voice. Or of being a storyteller. In my imagination, people were always sitting and listening to me as if my words were important."

"So you were a teacher in your imagination."

"I've never thought about it that way, but perhaps. Or perhaps I simply wanted someone to pay me attention. I was an only child and, as such, I was lonely a great deal of the time."

"We have that in common, it seems. My mother died shortly after my birth."

"What did you dream about as a little boy? Were you a knight or Robert the Bruce?"

"If anything, I probably fought on the English side," he said, smiling. "My family has not been nationalistic for a good hundred years. I think the events at Culloden had a tendency to expunge those sentiments from most Scots' hearts."

"Another thing we have in common. My grand-mother was French, and she believed France was the greatest country on earth. She ridiculed anything Scottish or English, for that matter. I was left thinking, even as a child, it was best not to be any one thing, but to be an amalgam of all countries. So, I have a great deal of English practicality, and the fervor of the Scots."

"And the passion of the French?"

There was that warmth again, sliding up her body and down, and pooling in places where she'd never felt warm before.

"The French aren't the only people who have passion, Mr. Gordon. The Scots have their share of it as well."

At the head of the stairs he turned left. She didn't tell him that perhaps it was a good thing he'd accompanied her. She would have turned right.

Here the candles were not as abundant, but they were in evidence in the embrasures and wall sconces.

Despite the fact that the staff of Castle Crannoch was not abundant, the wooden floors were highly waxed and polished. There was not a speck of dust to be seen on the occasional tables and chests lining the hallway. Even the mirrors at both ends of the corridor were brightly polished.

They turned left again and up a short flight of stairs to another wide corridor. At the third door, he stopped.

They stood facing the door for a moment, neither speaking.

He turned and faced her, retrieving her hand and holding it between his. Her skin felt cool against his warmth. She tried to pull away, but he increased his grip so she gave up the effort, telling herself it would be a rudeness to continue.

"Why are you pulling away?"

"Because you won't let go. You shouldn't hold my hand like this."

"I like holding your hand."

"I like it, too. That's what makes it disturbing."

He smiled at her, and she had a silly notion to reach out and push that errant lock of his hair back into place so he'd look less approachable.

"You make me feel protected, Mr. Gordon, as if someone actually cares about me. But that's a foolish and naïve thought."

"Dinner will be in an hour," he said, staring down at her palm. "You have a fascinating palm, Miss Sinclair. You reveal all sorts of traits."

"Do I?"

Once more, she gently tried to extricate herself from his grasp but he wouldn't allow it. His hold on her wrist tightened lightly but firmly enough that she knew he would release her only when he was ready.

"It seems you have a passionate nature. Do you?"

The warmth had never truly receded and it was returning in full measure.

"I also believe you have a very long life ahead of you. An enjoyable one, if one believes in such things."

"In a long, enjoyable life? Or in reading palms?"

This time she did succeed in pulling her hand away.

"Thank you very much for your kindness in seeing

me to my chamber, Mr. Gordon. I appreciate your courtesies."

His smile deepened as she entered her room, and as she was trying to close the door, he sniffed her hair.

For a moment all she could do was stare at him in disbelief. She pressed her hand against her temple, and patted her hair into place, discomfited by his gesture.

"You smell of roses," he said, drawing back. "Or violets. I can't tell which. Do you perfume your hair, or do you simply use scent when you wash it?"

No man had ever asked her such an intimate question. Not even her father, who sometimes looked taken aback at living with two women.

"Did you ask me such a thing to see if it would fluster me? To see if I would fall apart in girlish giggles or tears? I can assure you I will do nothing of the sort. You're a very annoying man, Mr. Gordon."

"Ah, but just a moment ago, I was your protector."

"How would you know such things about women, being a bachelor yourself? Unless, of course, you have a score of mistresses?" A second later, she pressed her hand over her mouth as if to call back the words.

He laughed then, as if he were pleased with her response, as if her irritation had been his aim all along.

She closed the door so quickly she caught her skirt and petticoat. He was the one who opened it again, bent down, and pushed the offending garments to safety.

"I'll send a maid to show you to the dining room, Miss Sinclair. You must believe me when I say I am looking forward to dinner."

Chapter 9

Beatrice told herself she was a fool, but that didn't stop her from brushing her hair at least a hundred times as she did every night, in the vain hope it would grow faster. She studied herself in the mirror and made a face.

A maid had left a fresh pitcher of water and a few clean cloths at the washstand. She unbuttoned the dress to her waist and washed herself, taking care especially at her throat and chest where the heat still gathered.

He'd said her hair smelled of perfume. She put a tiny drop of scent, the last of the bottle she'd been given for her birthday two years ago, behind her ear and on both temples. Would he think she smelled like attar of roses?

She really should show a little more care in his presence. Oh, but he was so handsome, and there was something about him that excited her. Even when he did nothing but stand close to her, she could feel her pulse leap. She was silly to be so affected by his charm, especially since it was quite evident he was practiced at it. She was awkward at social events, and especially with men.

The only person who'd ever shown her so much attention was Jeremy and only for a few short weeks, that was all. After that, his mother had probably sat him down and explained to him Beatrice was a poor teacher's daughter and no match for him, up and coming in the world as he was.

What would Jeremy say to know she was being charmed by the cousin of a duke?

Did she look too gaunt? A little. A few weeks of eating three meals a day, and she would not look so lean and hungry. Her eyes did not look as haunted as they had a few days ago. It was remarkable what employment could do for one's hope.

She didn't fool herself that the position was permanent. She didn't know if she'd last the week, especially if Robert was as difficult as he appeared to be upon their first meeting. But she would try her very best, and perhaps when this experience, however short-lived, was over she could obtain another position. Surely it would be a good thing to have worked for a duke?

Finally, she sat on the bed and tightened her stockings, then took a cloth and wiped off her shoes until the scuffed leather was clean. She stood again and smoothed her hands down her bodice and skirt before readjusting the fabric at her waist. Should she relace her stays? No, they were tight enough. Perhaps too tight, because they thrust her bosom forward like the prow of a ship.

At least the dress had been ironed that morning by one

of the maids and was in better shape, in all honesty, than her other two garments, since it had been her mother's and rarely worn. The hem still showed where she'd let it out, but there was nothing to be done with that.

She buttoned the bodice, smoothing her hands over her skirt one last time. Her palms were damp, so she washed her hands, and dried them, facing herself in the mirror when she was finished.

The knock on the door was expected, but it wasn't a maid come to show her to the dining room. Instead, it was Cameron Gordon on the other side of the door, seated in his wheeled chair. A large package sat on his lap, and as she watched, he handed it to her.

She took it from him, and opened the door wide, uncertain whether to curtsy or to invite him into her chamber. He was such a personage, even seated as he was. He gave her the impression of a king on his throne.

He ended her awkward dilemma by putting his hands on the wheels and wheeling himself into the room. With a hand gesture, he indicated she should close the door behind him.

"It's not a gift," he said, pointing to the package she'd yet to open. "But a necessity."

He waited, and she realized he wanted her to open the package right away.

Inside was a beautiful dark blue wool cloak, the fabric so thickly woven she could feel the warmth against her stroking palm.

"It's lovely."

"It belonged to my first wife. You're of the same size, Miss Sinclair. It's more appropriate than wearing my son's greatcoat."

She felt the blush creep to her cheeks. Did he know everything that happened at Castle Crannoch?

"I regret to say I am here in the guise of your employer, Miss Sinclair."

He wheeled himself to the window and indicated she should sit beside him at the table.

Part of her awkwardness around Cameron Gordon was due to the fact she was so much taller than he. Also, she'd never before known anyone who was confined to a chair.

She wanted to express how very sorry she was that he couldn't walk. How did she do that, especially when the object of her pity so obviously didn't want it? Instead, she remained silent, sat and folded her hands on top of the table, waiting for him to continue.

"As your employer, I feel it only fair to warn you about certain things here at Castle Crannoch."

"Have I done something wrong, Mr. Cameron?"

"Nothing except be a young woman without family, Miss Sinclair." He paused for a moment. "My son is a very handsome man."

The warmth was there again, the blush no doubt in full force. Had she blushed so much while living at Kilbridden Village?

"I would hate for you to become one more of his conquests."

Now she was doubly embarrassed. Being foolish was one thing; to be called on it was quite another.

"You and my son have held several intimate conversations, have you not?"

"I have spoken to him upon occasion, yes."

"That's how it begins, Miss Sinclair. Impressionable

young ladies such as yourself are caught first by conversation, then charm. Before they know it, they are engaged in behavior that would shock their parents. Since you are alone in the world, I find it necessary to warn you."

She pressed her hands flat against the table, linking her fingers together. She focused on her nails, clasped her hands together again, then placed them on her lap.

"Simply because I am alone in the world does not make me foolish, sir."

"I'm heartened to hear it. Therefore, I'm sure you'll understand why I think it best you not join us for dinner. At least, not until my wife returns from London. We have a bachelor household until then. I think it would be advisable for you to have a tray in your room."

"Of course." She kept her gaze focused on her hands, unwilling to show her disappointment.

Cameron Gordon left her, and as she closed the door behind him, she had the oddest thought it wouldn't be wise to reveal her emotions to any of the Gordons.

A few minutes later, a maid brought her a tray, and like the morning, there was a huge selection. Once laid out, the plates and bowls covered the entire top of the table.

She was still too close to hunger not to savor a meal. After a taste of the onion soup, it simply didn't matter she was eating alone in her room.

There were potatoes and carrots and beans in a sauce tasting like vinegar and sugar at the same time. There was roast beef so succulent she didn't need a knife to cut it, and crusty rolls and pots of butter and one of honey. The maid had brought her a carafe of wine, enough for one large glass. She sipped it as she ate, taking an hour for her dinner and enjoying every single morsel.

She didn't close the drapes while she ate but sat and looked out at the view of the hills and the village below. The lights twinkling on and off looked like faraway stars, but she knew they were candles being lit in rooms where people met and sat and talked and argued, perhaps.

The rest of the world was coming together. The day was being discussed, problems being aired, questions about life and love and the sheer drudgery of living being asked and answered.

Sometimes she missed the touch of another person so much she could cry. Sometimes she simply missed the conversation, the laughter. There was no one in the world who cared whether she lived or died.

For a moment, the temptation to give in to the despair of that thought was too tempting, but she pushed it aside. If she had no one left to love her, then she would simply have to find someone who would, a friend, an acquaintance, perhaps even a child like Robert. Someone who would find some comfort in being with her.

People were not designed to live alone, to live without affection or caring. Nor was it normal to go through days and days without one person saying: How are you? Are you well? Why are you smiling? Are those tears I see?

She'd sipped the wine slowly, but she looked at the empty glass with annoyance. Perhaps the wine had brought about this maudlin mood.

She stood and opened the window, breathing the

night air. The wind was mild, but the temperature had lowered. Instead of closing the window, however, she gathered her new cloak and covered her shoulders, staring out at the flickering lights below in the village. She was both ferociously lonely and angry about it.

Her friend, Sally, would laugh at her. "Silly girl, you never know what's going to happen tomorrow. Something wonderful could happen, and here you are, moping about now." But she had never been as optimistic as Sally or as much of a dreamer. In the end Sally's dreams had not saved her from the cholera.

The knock on the door roused her from her mood. She opened it, thinking it was the maid come to gather up the dishes. Instead, it was Devlen Gordon.

While she'd felt no reluctance in allowing his father into her room, the voice of caution urged her not to be as welcoming with him. He was not confined to a wheelchair. He was young, handsome, and, according to his father, a rake.

She was not going to be his conquest.

"Miss Sinclair," he said bowing slightly, "I came to ensure myself of your health. My father said you're not feeling well."

"Did he?"

"I wanted to make sure such was not the case. You appeared in good health when I left you earlier."

"I am well, thank you."

How very polite they were. His eyes, however, were entirely too invasive. His face suddenly changed. His smile disappeared and his expression became somber.

"Have I done anything to offend you?"

The question so surprised her that she stood looking up at him, her hand on the door. "No, you have not."

"Then why didn't you come down to dinner?"

She'd been employed for less than a day and already she was being caught up in family drama. What did she tell him? That his father had warned her against him? Devlen Gordon was not a resident of Castle Crannoch. He was only a visitor, and his father was her employer.

Still, she felt guilty about lying to him, so she didn't answer him directly. "I thoroughly enjoyed my dinner here," she said, hoping he would cease questioning her.

He looked dubious, but didn't say anything else.

She felt too vulnerable at the moment, too desirous of another human being's company. But he was one man she should not wish to be near. What had his father said? First it begins with conversation, then charm. Oh, and he had charm in abundance, didn't he?

He reached up and touched her cheek.

"How fascinating you are, Miss Sinclair. Why do you look so sad?"

It was the very worst time to ask a question of that sort. She wanted to tell him she had no armor against kindness. Instead, she began to close the door. When he pressed one hand against it, she looked up at him again.

"Please." The only word she could manage.

"Miss Sinclair." He really shouldn't say her name in such a fashion, in such a low tone it sounded almost like an endearment.

"Please," she said again, and slid her hand up until it covered his. Slowly, she pulled his fingers away from the wood and then held his hand in midair. He reached out with his other hand and cupped hers.

Shouldn't she be closing the door?

Then he leaned over and did something entirely shocking. He pressed his lips against her cheek. A kiss. She'd never been kissed.

She expected more of it, and conversely less.

His lips were warm, soft and comforting; his breath against her skin surprisingly and strangely exciting.

He drew back and bowed slightly once more. In apology? Or mere politeness?

She shut the door and leaned against it, her forehead pressing against the wood. She placed her fingers against her cheek. He was gone and yet the memory of this kiss was there still, confusing and unsettling her.

"Leave the sparrow alone."

Devlen turned to see his father sitting in the shadows at the end of the hall.

"Miss Sinclair? Why do you call her sparrow? Do you see yourself as a hawk? If so, your wings have been clipped, Father."

"If you were close enough, I would backhand you because of that comment."

His father rolled himself out into the light. Not for the first time, he gave Devlen the impression of a malevolent spider, creeping around on leather-bound wheels. Cameron had had a series of ramps built at Castle Crannoch so he could navigate almost anywhere, except atop the towers.

"I think it's time for you to go back to Edinburgh, Devlen. You wear out your welcome very quickly."

"I think you're right."

He walked away, then stopped midway down the hall.

He turned and addressed his father again. "Leave her alone. Do not make her another one of your victims."

Cameron laughed. "Strange, Devlen, but I told her the very same thing about you."

Chapter 10

B eatrice readied herself for bed, pulling out the nightgown from her valise.

In the morning she would tell Devlen Gordon she wasn't to be kissed whenever he felt like it. Such expressions of affection were only between couples who were engaged, and only surreptitiously.

As the governess, she was to be considered above such dalliances. She was not the upstairs maid to be grabbed in a shadowy corner, her skirts upturned while she was groped.

How odd the vision came so quickly to her mind of Devlen Gordon doing exactly that. And how very strange that it made her angry to think of him engaged in such an immoral act. Exactly how many conquests had he made at Castle Crannoch? No doubt every single maid employed here had experienced the full extent of his charm.

How dare he kiss her?

As children she and Sally had often talked about such things, wondering exactly what loving was like between a man and woman. Each had ventured several theories as to how it must feel and what exactly a man does. What would Sally have said about Devlen Gordon?

Her friend would no doubt have teased her about that kiss. A kiss on the cheek, that was all it was.

She went to the bed, plumped up the pillows, and pulled down the coverlet.

A snake was in the middle of her bed.

In the middle of the lovely bed, on top of the ivory-colored sheets was a very dead snake with its head bashed in, and its poor twisted body stretched down the middle of the mattress. On the whole, it was an innocuous-looking creature. She'd found one in the garden often enough.

She went to the bell rope and tugged on it. When the maid appeared, looking tired and more than a little groggy, Beatrice asked for directions to Robert's room.

"You need to know where His Grace's room is?"

Surely, it couldn't be a good thing for a seven-year-old to be constantly referred to as His Grace.

"Yes, please."

"The Duke's Chamber is at the end of the hallway, miss. The big double doors."

Beatrice stuck her head out the door and looked down the hall. Just as the maid had said, at the end of the hall was a set of double doors.

"When his parents died, His Grace insisted upon moving to their suite. It's customary for the Dukes of Brechin to live there."

"Even if he's seven?"

The maid looked a little confused at this question, and Beatrice took pity on her and bid her good night.

Before the girl left, Beatrice called out to her. "What is your name?"

"Abigail, miss," she said, bobbing another curtsy.

"Thank you, Abigail. I'm sorry to have troubled you."

The girl smiled, her plump cheeks reddening as she did so. "It's quite all right, miss."

Beatrice donned her wrapper, buttoned it closed, then gathered the poor snake and left her room. At the end of the hallway, she knocked firmly on one of the doors. When her knock wasn't answered, she turned the handle and entered.

A small lamp was burning in the foyer. A set of drapes separated the area from the rest of the suite. She pushed them aside and stood marveling at the sheer size of the room. From its dimensions, she gauged it took up the whole eastern portion of Castle Crannoch.

On a dais at the other side of the room sat a massive canopied bed draped in crimson and gold. The bed itself was easily twice as wide as hers and at least that deep. As she approached it, a small figure sat up in the middle of the bed and stared at her.

"What are you doing here?" Robert asked.

"I came to deliver your snake," she said, "and to ask you one question."

She still held the poor dead creature in her hand. Carefully, she laid it on the end of the bed. "Did you kill it? Or did you simply leave it in my bed to frighten me?"

"What difference does it make?"

"If you killed it, I would think you a monster. The snake did nothing to deserve its death."

He sat back on his haunches, his fists on his thighs.

"It might have bitten me."

"If it did, it was to protect itself. You're much larger than it."

"I didn't kill it. It was already dead. I think a carriage ran over it."

"Good," she said, and turned to leave.

"Weren't you afraid?"

"I've lived through a cholera epidemic. Nothing could frighten me after that. Besides, some snakes are our friends. They eat rodents and bugs."

"How do you know that?"

"It was in a book I read, I think."

"Would you show me that book?"

"Perhaps," she said. "If you don't put any more snakes in my bed."

"I command you to show me that book."

"You can command me until hell comes to earth," she said calmly. "I'm your governess, not your servant. Nor do I ever want to hear you talking to the servants in such a fashion. If you're a duke, then behave like one."

He looked as surprised as if she'd told him he had two heads.

"Now go to sleep. Tomorrow we'll bury that poor creature."

"I command you to stay."

She studied him for a moment. "I think you're a very spoiled boy who's had a great deal of sorrow in his life. But that's no excuse for you to be rude to others, especially to me."

He looked surprised again. "Why not to you?"

"Because I've experienced the same kind of sorrow, and I know what it's like to lose my parents."

"Do you sleep?"

"What a strange question. Yes, I sleep."

"I don't. When I do, I have nightmares."

Beatrice walked back to the end of the bed and put the dead snake on the floor before sitting on the end of the mattress. She leaned against one of the massive posts supporting the bed, drew up her legs and wrapped her arms around her knees.

"Tell me about the nightmares," she said.

He stared at her for a moment as if he would like to tell her to get off his bed or go away. But evidently, the lure of companionship was too great. In him, she recognized the same weakness she herself felt. They were separated by two decades, by sex, and by role, but she couldn't help but feel akin to this young duke, spoiled though he was.

"Tell me about the nightmares," she said again.

He folded his legs in front of him, placing a hand on each knee like a pasha sitting on a throne of cushions. She smothered her smile at his unconscious arrogance. Cameron Gordon had done his nephew no favor by catering to his every whim.

"I dream someone is watching me while I sleep. They're standing in the shadows and just watching."

She felt a shiver race across her skin.

"What a horrible dream. No wonder you're in no hurry to sleep. Do you ever dream about your parents?"

He nodded. "When I dream of them, it feels just like it happened. I was waiting for them to come home. But they never did. In my dream, they never do, either, and I stand there at the window waiting and waiting."

He was too young to feel the weight of such sorrow. But she could not eliminate it from his life any more than she could wave a wand and make her own situation different. The secret was in finding a way to live until the loss became bearable.

How did she help a seven-year-old child endure such grief?

"So you keep a lamp lit."

"Devlen says it helps. You can hear noises in the darkness you can never hear during the day. As if there are things there, whispering to each other. As if they know you're asleep and defenseless and can't fight them off."

She felt another chill race down her spine. The child had wanted to frighten her with the snake and had ended up doing so with his own words.

"Shall I tell you a story? It might help you sleep."

"I'm too old for fairy tales."

"I will tell you one of Aesop's fables," she said. "They are simply stories, but each one has a lesson. Anyone, even someone of your great age, might enjoy them."

She arranged herself so she was more comfortable and began: "Once upon a time, the queen bee of a very large hive traveled all the way to Mount Olympus. Everyone knows Mount Olympus is the home of the Greek gods. Once there, she told the gatekeeper she wished to visit with Jupiter. She waited some time until he could meet with her and once in front of him, she bowed low, spreading her wings upon the golden floor.

'I give you a gift,' she said. 'A gift of my honey. My workers have labored diligently these past weeks and months to produce only the finest honey for you, Jupiter.'

"Jupiter, very pleased, thanked her, and took a bite of the honey. So impressed was he at its quality, he asked what he could give her in return for her gift.

" 'I ask only one thing, Jupiter, and that is to be able to protect my people. Mankind comes and invades my hives. They steal my honey, and they frighten and kill my workers. Give me the power that I might wound,' she added, pointing to her stinger.

"Now Jupiter was a friend of man, and he was very much troubled by the queen's request. But he granted her the ability to wound any with her stinger.

"Excited her wish had been granted, the queen returned to her hive. That very next day, a man approached the hive and she flew out of it and stung him over and over until he collapsed on the ground.

"But something strange happened to the queen. Once she stung the man, she lost her stinger, and with the loss of it, she fell to the ground and died.

"The moral of this story is evil wishes, like chickens, come home to roost."

"That's a stupid story," Robert said.

"Would you like to hear another?"

"Another fable?"

Beatrice nodded.

"No. They're stupid stories."

"Then I won't tell you another one," Beatrice said.

"Why didn't you scream when you saw the snake?" Robert asked.

"Are you disappointed? I could scream now if you wish."

Robert surprised her by smiling. "You almost screamed last night."

"You're right, I did."

"But you fainted instead. Did I scare you that much?" The little boy sounded proud of himself.

"I fainted because I was hungry."

"People don't faint because they're hungry."

"Have you ever been hungry? I doubt you have."

"Why were you hungry?"

"Because there was no food to eat, and I had no way of earning a living."

"We give food to the poor." Robert moved up in the bed.

"Some people would much rather work than take charity."

He had no comment to this, for which she was eternally grateful. Despite the fact he was only seven years old, he was an arrogant seven-year-old, and exceedingly irritating.

He slid down in bed beneath the covers. "Are you going to stay here until I fall asleep?"

"Do you want me to?"

"Is it something governesses are supposed to do?"

"I don't believe so, no. But since I have never been a governess before, I don't quite know."

"I am the duke," he said sleepily. "I should have a governess with experience."

"If you had an experienced governess, no doubt she would have left you after the experience with the snake."

"Do you truly think so?"

"I do."

"Perhaps that's why my tutors left. They were all very experienced."

"Did you put snakes in their beds?"

"No."

"Then it's to your advantage I have no more experience than I do. I shall practice on you."

"I am the duke. I should not be practiced on."

"We can learn together. Whenever I do something you dislike, I give you leave to tell me. Not to put snakes in my bed, but to tell me. Together, we'll discuss the matter."

He murmured something, an incoherent response that summoned her smile.

She sat there in the darkness at the end of the ducal bed and listened to his breathing.

When she was certain she would not disturb him, Beatrice slid off the end of the bed and stepped down from the dais, walking to the windows. Not surprisingly, Robert had not drawn the drapes against the night.

The stars blanketed the sky, twinkling back at her as if to say she was not alone. But stars were so far away and they neither conversed nor held hands nor smiled. The glass was cold against her fingers, and there was a draft as if one of the panes was not properly sealed. The gentle breeze ruffled the curtains as if someone were standing there. But she knew she was alone except for the sleeping boy.

There was a certain emptiness to the cavernous chamber, as if life needed to be inserted into it. A life that was exuberant and noisy and filled with laughter. Not one that dealt in whispers and fear.

The chamber, for all its riches, and for all it belonged to Robert, somehow did not suit him. He needed a brightly painted room, one that wasn't adorned with portraits of ancestors on the walls, and ornate and heavy furnishings.

He needed to be a boy before he became a duke.

From her vantage point at the window she could see the ocean surface brightly illuminated by the moon until it looked silvery white, and the curving road winding around to the entrance and then behind the castle to the stables. As she watched, a carriage led by four striking ebony horses slowly made its way to the front of the castle.

She had seen that carriage before, more richly crafted than the duke's, but without a crest on its door. Was Devlen Gordon leaving so soon?

How silly to feel suddenly abandoned. He was a stranger who'd dared take liberties. He'd kissed her when she'd not given him leave to do so. He'd smelled her hair, and treated her as if she were a loose woman, and oh, perhaps she was, because she couldn't forget either gesture. Foolish Beatrice. She was a governess, late of Kilbridden Village, a schoolteacher's daughter with hardly any accomplishments to her name. Yet she had a yearning for more, more excitement in her life, more sin perhaps.

At the moment, she only had the energy to be safe, well fed and secure. Perhaps one day she would venture out into the world and have some excitement. For now she was content.

Then why did she feel so suddenly bereft? Devlen Gordon was about to embark upon an adventure, she knew it. Anyone else would have departed Castle Crannoch in the brightness of day, but not Devlen Gordon. As much as he disliked the night, it suited him. Who else traveled in darkness?

She put her finger to the window again and blocked out the sight of his carriage, and the feeling of abandonment eased somewhat. If she could not see him leave, then she need not feel disappointed. Some errant idiotic notion, some girlish sensibility, some silliness that hadn't been leached out of her by the travails of the past three months no doubt was responsible for the feeling. Or curiosity. That's what it was. He was simply the most interesting, most compelling man she had ever met. The most dark and dangerous.

Movement below caught her attention. Devlen strode from the castle door to his coach and stood in conversation for some time with the driver. He wore a long coat notched at the collar, his black hair uncovered. The horses stamped their feet, their breaths white billows in the night. A moment later, Devlen glanced up toward the window where she stood. She didn't move, didn't step backward, didn't hide herself from his gaze. To do so would mark her as a coward, and she had no reason to be afraid. He was leaving.

For a long moment they exchanged a look, her with her fingers on the glass and him with a question in his eyes she couldn't decipher.

She wanted to ask him where he was going and why it was so important he leave for his destination tonight.

And what question did he wish to ask of her?

She would never know.

One by one, Beatrice drew the drapes, moving along the wall of windows until she was done. She stood at the last of the windows, looking down at the drive. From here, she could barely see the coach. She didn't want to see him leave. Everyone in her life had left her, and she had come to dislike departures of any sort, transitory or permanent.

Chapter 11

She was half-hidden by the drapes when she heard a sound. Beatrice stepped back, allowing the billowing fabric to conceal her.

Soft footsteps crossed the room, hesitated.

She pulled back the fabric of the curtains to see Devlen standing at the end of the bed, staring at Robert.

Her heart beat so fiercely in her chest she thought he must surely hear it. At that moment he turned and looked directly at her.

He walked to where she stood, and pulled back the curtains.

"Are you hiding, Miss Sinclair?"

"Of course not."

"Then may I inquire why you've made no effort to announce your presence?"

She was not dressed. She was attired in only her nightgown and wrapper, but rather than call attention to her clothing, she said, "To do so might have awakened Robert."

"Is he all right?" There was a tone of concern in his voice she'd not heard before.

"Why do you ask?"

"I should think that was obvious. You are here. Why are you in his room, Miss Sinclair?"

She didn't want Robert to be punished for what was a childish prank. "I told him a story."

"And sat with him until he fell asleep."

"Yes."

"You have a tender heart, Miss Sinclair."

"He has nightmares."

"Did he tell you?"

She nodded. "Has he always had them? Or only since the death of his parents?"

"I regret to say I don't know. I hadn't much to do with my cousin before his parents died. I had other interests I deemed more pressing."

"Like the ones that are causing you to leave now?"

"I've been told I'm unwelcome. Besides, you of all people should be glad I'm going back to Edinburgh."

"What do you mean?" Her heartbeat escalated, her breath grew short. Devlen Gordon had an odd effect on her, one that was not altogether unpleasant. She felt as if excitement was flowing through her veins, as if she'd just sipped the finest chocolate, or just finished a potent glass of wine.

"Will you watch after him?" He turned back to watch the sleeping boy.

"Of course," she said. "I'm his governess."

"He needs a friend more than he needs a governess.

If anything untoward happens, tell one of the drivers, and he'll come to Edinburgh."

"What do you mean, untoward? What do you expect to happen?"

"It's not what I expect, Miss Sinclair. I expect the sun to rise every morning and those I care about to continue living happily. However, I have learned what I expect and what happens are not necessarily the same."

"If you have such dire thoughts about the future, how can you leave?"

"I would think you'd be relieved."

"I'm afraid I don't understand."

"I think you do, Miss Sinclair. But I also think you choose to remain cloaked in ignorance or virtue, either one. One of us has to be wise in this instance. I applaud your wisdom."

"Are you normally so cryptic?"

"Are you normally so obtuse?"

She smiled, startled into amusement by his rudeness.

"I'm not obtuse at all, Mr. Gordon. I have attempted to be a lady at every one of our encounters."

"Cloaked in virtue."

In the light, he was devastatingly handsome, but in the darkness, he was even more alluring.

"Tell me, Miss Sinclair, do you ever wish to be simply a woman? Simply a female? Unencumbered by rules or expectations?"

"What you are speaking of, sir, is anarchy."

"Anarchy of the self. An apt description. Do you not ever wish to rebel, Beatrice? Before you answer no, let me warn you. I see flickers of rebellion in your eyes."

How on earth was she to answer such a challenge?

"Is there not one single part of you that wants to put aside your strict upbringing, that wants to loosen your stays and laugh at convention?"

He stepped closer, reached out one finger, and traced the edge of her bottom lip, a tingling touch reaching all the way down to her toes.

"Is that how you talk women into your bed? By daring them?"

He smiled at her. "Would it work with you?"

"No."

"Do you really want to know why I'm leaving, Beatrice?"

"You'll say it's because of me, but it isn't. You can find your share of willing partners at the next inn. No doubt you have a mistress in readiness, eagerly waiting for your return."

"Is there nothing here that would tempt me?"

"Not me. I'm cloaked in virtue. I'm not an antidote to your boredom, Mr. Gordon."

"Is that what you think it is?"

She nodded.

"I could agree except for one thing. I have an eagerness to share your mind as much as your body. What do you call that?"

"Foolish."

His fingers trailed across her cheek, behind her ear, and down to her throat. Did he know how difficult it was to swallow suddenly? Did he feel how frantically her pulse was beating?

Let me go. But the words didn't come. She opened her mouth to speak, but the only sound to emerge was a sigh.

"You are the most unlikely governess, Beatrice."

He really shouldn't call her by her first name. It wasn't

proper, but at the same time she dared herself to answer in kind.

"Why, Devlen?"

"Because, my dear Miss Sinclair, you really are tempting. If I stay, I will bed you. I'll take you to my bed or to yours or to any surface we find amenable and comfortable, be it the floor or a washstand or a table. And I will plant myself in you so deeply that when you swallow you'll be certain that it's me. I'll have you again and again and again until you are as wanton and tempestuous as I think you could be. And we would both enjoy it."

She slapped him. Her hand reached up so quickly he couldn't anticipate the blow. When she did it again, he didn't flinch, didn't move away or otherwise shield himself. He merely stood there quietly, a towering presence, a shadow, a force.

Beatrice could feel the smoothness of his cheek against her palm even through the tingling. He'd recently shaved, and he smelled of spices and something delicious. A scent she'd forever associate with darkness and Devlen.

She stepped back and crossed her arms around her waist not because she was cold. Not because she was suddenly frightened at the somber look on his face, but because she needed to restrain herself from placing her hand gently against the cheek she had just slapped. Or raising up on tiptoe and kissing his skin tenderly in apology.

"Are you done?"

She nodded.

"You are quite correct to be outraged," he said softly. "I am a rake and a lecher and a despoiler of innocents. And you, Miss Sinclair, are very much in danger from me. But I suspect you're innocent only in your experience, and not in your wishes or your deepest heart."

He took one step closer to her, and she pressed herself against the window. The glass was cold against her wrapper.

"But if it makes you feel safer to deny your nature, then so be it. As I said, the reason I'm leaving is for your benefit and not mine."

"Have you no control?" The words were out of her mouth before she could call them back.

"As I said, Miss Sinclair, I've been in your company for one day. An extremely painful day, but I don't suppose you know what I mean."

She shook her head.

"At the risk of being slapped again, let me show you."

He reached out and grabbed her hand and pressed it against his waist. No, not against his waist. Against something hard and unmistakably masculine.

She jerked back her hand, horrified.

"I haven't the slightest idea why it should be so. You are not, after all, the kind of woman who attracts me. I hunger for blondes and statuesque beauties. Although your bodice is certainly plentiful and your legs long, you lack a certain flair, a certain blowsy charm I find attractive."

She could still feel him against her hand.

"Then do not let me stop you from going out and finding the type of woman who attracts you, Mr. Gordon. I wish you well. May all your conquests be easy ones."

"Will you be thinking about me, then?"

"Your coach is waiting, and the night is cold."

"You sound so very angry, Miss Sinclair. Would you like to slap me again?"

"I would very much like to, Mr. Gordon, but it would no doubt be a waste of effort."

"Then you think I'm not capable of being educated?"

"I think you're capable of being educated. I just don't think you're capable of being trained."

His bark of laughter surprised her.

Robert made a sound in his sleep, and Devlen looked back at the bed.

"Care for him, Miss Sinclair, regardless of what you think of me."

"You have some affection for him, don't you?"

"You sound surprised."

She was, but she didn't answer him.

"Have you a kiss to send me on my way?" He bent down and breathed against her hair. Was he smelling her again? "Some token of your regard for me?"

His hand came up and smoothed against her waist. Her uncorseted waist. His hand splayed until his fingertips almost reached the underside of her breast.

She jerked away from him, and to the other side of the drape, making her escape as quickly as she could. She raced across the Duke's Chamber, her bare feet making no sound on the polished wooden floor and to her own room, where she locked the door with trembling fingers, her heart beating so fast she felt faint with it.

For a long moment she stood there, palms pressed against the door until she heard a light tap. Just that. A tap of his hand as if to acknowledge she was safe, and he was leaving.

The winding drive from Castle Crannoch was illuminated at night by a series of twenty lanterns. One man—

or boy, as he sometimes was—kept watch over all the lanterns to ensure they lasted until morning. Devlen had given the orders himself when he first began visiting.

He doubted the lanterns were used in his absence, but he liked having the freedom to arrive and to leave whenever he wished.

Now he didn't want to go back to Edinburgh as much as he wanted to remain at Castle Crannoch, but the voice of his conscience, not often loud enough to be heard, warned him he would be wiser to get away as quickly as his horses could carry him.

He wanted to touch Beatrice. He wanted to touch her so badly he hurt with it.

She smelled of roses. Warm roses and woman, as the heat of her had traveled upward to tease him with her scent. He wanted to reach out, and with not quite steady fingers, unbutton that one button keeping her modest wrapper fastened.

He'd push back the full sleeves with their lace cuffs and kiss her elbow. A teasing kiss while he parted the top of her nightgown. Another, while he slid his hand inside.

One finger would smooth in between the creamy mounds of her breasts, stroking the soft, plump skin there.

His erection swelled at the thought. A button, that's all. The thought of loosening a button, and he was hard as an iron staff.

Very well, he would imagine the button gone, and Miss Sinclair standing bare to the waist, nothing covering her. The warmth would nearly scorch his palm as it rested against a hard nipple.

She would look surprised by the reaction of her own

body to his touch and then slowly, he would use two fingers to hold a nipple so sweetly she'd gasp in awareness.

He would feel the outline of that sweet protuberant nipple and measure the length of it as it grew. His mouth would suckle it, his lips provide a gentle resting place, his tongue tasting her.

He would pull up the rest of her nightgown where it bunched around her waist until it was in folds, then toss it to the floor.

He'd pull her close so he could warm her in his embrace and she would moan at the sensation of being so heated in the chilled air.

He needed to be closer to her, so he could touch his erection to some part of her body. He needed to feel her against him, move her up and down to mimic the action of love.

Do not move, sweet Beatrice, I am imagining myself inside you.

What would she say to that?

No doubt banish him for his torment, or send him away with a teasing smile.

What would it be like to bed the surprising Miss Sinclair?

Just thinking about doing so had him close to erupting in his trousers, and he had yet to press his lips against hers or against her neck or his mouth against those bounteous breasts.

Damn it.

Sleep came with great difficulty that night. Beatrice lay awake staring at the tester above her head and when that sight dulled, she turned and stared out the window at the night sky. When she was tired, she closed her eyes and thought about what Devlen Gordon had said to her.

Any virtuous woman would have been shocked and appalled at the things he had said. Any virtuous woman would have demanded an apology. Most certainly, she would have made her displeasure known to Cameron Gordon. Or she should have marched downhill with her valise beneath her arm, intent on her lonely cottage and some measure of propriety.

A virtuous woman would not be lying here, thinking of all the things he said and wondering at the heaviness of her own limbs and the heat of her body.

Finally, she threw aside the coverlet and the sheet before drawing up the nightgown until her knees were exposed. But it was not enough; she was still too hot to sleep. She sat up on the side of the bed and dangled her feet in a back-and-forth, back-and-forth movement that did nothing to assuage the restlessness inside her body.

She was lusting after Devlen Gordon. There, she'd confessed it.

She placed both hands beneath her breasts and hefted them, feeling their weight. They were entirely too large. No matter how much weight she lost, her breasts never seemed to change. The gesture made her nipples rub against the cotton of her nightgown, gently abrading them. The feeling was so strange and yet so pleasurable she continued it for a moment.

How shocking to be touching herself while thinking of a man.

As penance, she gave herself the task of reciting the books of the Bible. She got all the way to Job before she realized she was thinking of him again.

She sighed, stared up at the elaborate plasterwork of the crown molding. The guest room she'd been given was a lovely chamber, decorated in shades of deep rose. She'd never liked the color much, but it suited the heavy mahogany furniture, offsetting the darkness and adding a touch of femininity.

Had Cameron Gordon's wife chosen the fabric? Or had Robert's mother been responsible for the décor of Castle Crannoch?

How foolish to pretend she was interested in such things when all she truly wanted to know was why she felt so decidedly odd.

She unbuttoned the top button of her nightgown and spread the placket open. Reaching in one hand, she palmed her breast. Then, experimentally and feeling wicked, she pressed two fingers around her nipple and felt an answering sensation deep inside. Without much effort, she could imagine they were his fingers on her, his whispers in her ear to continue.

"Sweet Beatrice. You want so much to feel pleasure, don't you?"

In the next moment she stood and slid her nightgown off her head, tossing it to the end of the bed. With a quick glance to the door to make sure it was locked, she went to the chest of drawers and tilted the mirror on top of it until she could see her body.

She had never before done such a thing, never looked at herself with an eye to what a man might see. Her shoulders were straight and simply shoulders. Her arms were the same. Her hands were formed like hands, her fingers long. Her waist tapered nicely from her chest before flaring gently to her hips. She placed her hand on her stomach, her thumb resting at the indentation of her navel, her little finger stretched out and touching the very beginning of the triangle of hair between her legs.

Her abdomen was flat, her bones in sharp relief, but a few more meals like the one she'd eaten that night and she would not be so thin.

She placed a palm flat on each nipple, but the friction of her touch only made them ache even more.

She turned and looked over her shoulder at her bottom. She liked the shape of it. Turning, she faced herself again, placing a hand on either thigh, splaying her hands until her thumbs met, then slowly, daring herself, she touched herself where she was most swollen and aching.

A soft moan escaped her.

She remembered the feel of him against her hand, hard and erect. The shape of him felt imprinted on her palm. Instead of delighting in the memory, she should be ashamed. Or angry at the very least. He'd done something unspeakably wrong. Shocking. Lurid.

She got back into bed and covered herself with the sheet. A moment later, she left the bed again and opened the window. This time when she returned to the bed, the chill of the room cooled her and eased the unbearable heat she was feeling.

Beatrice closed her eyes, determined not to think of him. Devlen Gordon was on the way to Edinburgh. Yet, in her mind, she could see him leaning over her. She could hear his voice whispering to her, encouraging her to find release in her dreams of him.

Shame seeped through her, shame and a loneliness so desperately painful that if he were here, she might have gone to him. That's what he'd meant. He'd gone back to Edinburgh not to protect her from him, but to keep her sheltered from her own nature.

Chapter 12

The scream was so loud it awakened her. Beatrice bolted upright in bed, staring at the opposite wall, uncertain from where the noise had originated. The scream came again, and this time she knew.

She flew from the bed, threw her nightgown on, grabbed her wrapper, and raced out the door and down the hall. She was opening the door to the Duke's Chamber when Gaston appeared in the doorway of the adjoining room.

He swore, in perfectly accented French.

The lamp in the foyer was still burning, but because she had closed the curtains the night before, the room was nearly suffocating in darkness. Gaston moved in the direction of the bed while she went to the windows, opening up the drapes and letting in the light from a dawn sky.

She turned to find Robert kneeling in the middle of the bed, Gaston's arms around the trembling boy. She didn't have to ask to know Gaston had done this often.

"What is it? Is it one of your nightmares, Robert?"

"Someone was here," he said. "Someone was in my room."

"Devlen was here earlier, but he's gone now."

"I want him. I command you to get him."

She walked toward the bed. "I'm sorry, I can't. He's gone back to Edinburgh."

He shot her a look of such dislike she almost reeled from it. How foolish she'd been to think the hour or so they'd spent together the night before might soften his manners.

She reached out and touched his shoulder, but he jerked away, burying his face against Gaston's chest.

"I don't want you here," he said. "Go away."

"Perhaps it would be best, mademoiselle. Just until he recovers."

Since she was scantily dressed, and Gaston was in his nightshirt, she decided retreat was the best option for the moment. She nodded and left the room, closing the door behind her.

Once in her own chamber, she took care of her morning ablutions before dressing in the same clothing she'd worn the day before. She brushed her hair, uncaring if it grew or not.

She stared at herself in the mirror. She was too pale, but at least she no longer felt as she had last night, confused, uncertain, and heated from her own thoughts.

She tapped her cheeks with her fingers, but she still looked pale, and her lips appeared nearly bloodless. Perhaps she needed embarrassment to bring color to her face. Or shame.

She wrapped the shawl around her shoulders. Castle Crannoch was drafty and cold, despite the fact it was a ducal residence.

In the corridor she hesitated, uncertain where to go next. Should she go back to Robert's chamber? Or to the dining room? Surely Cameron Gordon wouldn't insist upon her eating breakfast alone?

As she was debating, the doors to the ducal suite swung open, and Robert stood there.

He looked as he was, a seven-year-old boy. A title could not change the fact his hair would not quite lie down in the back. He had dressed in an outfit the miniature of his cousin's, even down to the white stock, but Robert's was tied less than perfectly around at the throat. He bowed slightly to her, his chin at an arrogant angle.

"Did you sleep well?" she asked. "Before your nightmare, I mean?"

"It wasn't a nightmare. Someone was in my room. Was it you?"

"I can assure you it was not."

He nodded as if he believed her. But she decided to change topics and start the day off in a better frame of mind. Consequently, she forced a smile to her face, and asked him, "Would you mind escorting me to breakfast?"

For a moment he looked as if he would refuse, and as she was contemplating an impasse, he came and offered his arm to her.

"I will be happy to escort you to breakfast, Miss Sinclair. And perhaps over the meal we can discuss your duties."

She bit back her retort and kept her smile with some difficulty.

"Perhaps we can at that."

Breakfast was not in the main dining room, but in something called the Family Dining Room, a dark and somber-looking place dominated by heavy mahogany furniture.

Two large cabinets filled with china sat against adjoining walls, while the fireplace was built into the third. The fourth wall was covered in heavy burgundy drapes. She would have liked to open them, to view the day outside, but no one else looked as if they were oppressed by the closed-in nature of the room.

Cameron Gordon sat to her left, while Robert was to her right. If Devlen had still been here, he no doubt would have taken the place opposite, while the setting to Cameron's right was probably reserved for his wife.

"Are you expecting Mrs. Gordon home soon?" she asked.

"My wife decides to come and go as she wishes, Miss Sinclair. I am not privy to her plans."

She nodded, feeling awkward for having asked.

A moment later she excused herself and stood at the buffet, deciding what she would eat among the huge array of breakfast foods. Surely, the staff had prepared more food than for just the four of them? The food here could have kept her for a week.

She selected a few pieces of ham, a dish of oatmeal, and a cup of something with the delightful fragrance of strong coffee mixed with dark chocolate. Her stomach rumbled, but it was not so much in hunger as delight.

For the next quarter hour, she was more intent on her meal than she was her breakfast companions. Their conversation, or the lack of it, didn't occur to her until Cameron Gordon asked his nephew a question.

"What plans have you for today, Robert?"

"I want to see the new foal. Devlen said Molly finally delivered. And then I shall play with my toy soldiers. Devlen brought me some new ones from Edinburgh."

"How kind of Devlen," Cameron murmured.

Beatrice put down her fork and folded her hands. "We shall have lessons this morning, Robert. You may see the foal later, and if you do well in your reading, perhaps you can play with your soldiers as a reward."

He ignored her.

Cameron glanced at her, a small smile on his lips, as if he were amused by the exchange.

"Is there a nursery? Or someplace set aside as a schoolroom?" she asked him.

"There are over two hundred rooms at Castle Crannoch. Surely one of them can be modified for your use."

"Did you not grow up here?"

"I did."

"Did you never take your lessons here? Or have a tutor?"

"I was sent off to school at quite a young age, Miss Sinclair. Both my brother and I were. There was never a need for a schoolroom. But I believe you can take what books you need from the library, and as for space, pick one of the rooms. I'll give the order it should be cleaned and ready for your use."

"Very well," she said to Robert. "Perhaps we can meet in my chamber this morning so I can assess your reading ability. If you have a favorite book, please bring it."

"I shan't come," he said, giving her a thoroughly disagreeable look.

She would have been sent to her room had she dared to look at any adult in such a way.

"I shall expect you at nine," she said sternly.

"I shall be with the horses."

She glanced up at Cameron, who remained silent and unsupportive.

She had the distinct feeling this was a test of sorts. Neither Cameron nor Robert Gordon knew her. She never gave up. In fact, her father had always teased her that her epitaph should read: Beatrice Sinclair—I shall prevail.

She wasn't about to let a seven-year-old child, regardless of his rank, outmaneuver her.

"I shall give orders you are not to be shown the new foal until I approve."

Robert threw down his fork and stood beside the table. "You cannot give any orders at Castle Crannoch. *I* am the only person who can give orders. Do you hear me? *I* am the Duke of Brechin."

"You're the duke of rudeness. And unless you want to grow up to be an uncivilized, ignorant creature, you'll do as I say."

He glared at his uncle, and when Cameron didn't say a word, turned and sent the same expression in her direction. She wasn't impressed.

"Nine," she repeated. Instead of commenting further, Robert left the room.

She would have gone after him, would have demanded Cameron's support but for one small, almost unnoticeable thing that kept her silent. The small hand that had been clenched beside the table, the one nearly hidden in the drape of tablecloth, had been trembling.

Beatrice watched as he stormed from the room, slamming the dining room door shut behind him.

"You have to understand, Miss Sinclair, my nephew *is* the Duke of Brechin. He is not to be treated like a normal pupil. Some allowances must be given to the fact of his rank."

She pressed her hands against her waist below the table and decided she had two choices. She could accede to Cameron Gordon's wishes, or she could choose a harder path, one that would ultimately benefit Robert.

In the end, however, it wasn't a hard decision to make.

"I am afraid, sir, I can't agree with you," she said. "He should earn what allowances he's given and not be fawned upon simply because he's inherited the title. You, yourself, have complained about his manners. He needs discipline, I believe you said. If something isn't done now, he'll grow to be a despot, and no credit to his title or his family."

Cameron looked surprised at her vehemence.

He leaned back in his chair and studied her for a moment.

"I have rarely had my words tossed so charmingly back in my face, Miss Sinclair."

"Have you changed your expectations, Mr. Gordon?"

"I have not. You're right to remind me. I was given to understand you have little experience as a governess, Miss Sinclair. Was I wrong?"

"I have a great deal of experience in learning, sir. Also, I assisted my father for many years. In addition to being the schoolteacher for the village, he was a tutor as well."

"I wasn't asking about your qualifications, Miss Sinclair, but your experience. They are two different issues."

She felt cold inside. Is this what failure felt like?

"No, sir, I have no experience as a governess. That doesn't mean, however, that my opinion is without merit."

"You surprise me, Miss Sinclair," he said calmly. "I'd no idea the heart of a tiger beat beneath your rather scrawny abandoned-kitten facade."

Before she could counter his insult, he spoke again. "I only meant you seem to be quite able in the role. Gaston tells me you were with Robert last night and rushed to his side this morning."

She nodded.

"I commend you on your duties so far. Do as you see fit. Remember, however, even if rarely, that he is the Duke of Brechin."

"Will you send word he is not to visit the stables?"

"I will send word you are to be obeyed, Miss Sinclair. That will do you more good, I think."

He snapped his fingers, and Gaston emerged from the shadows, nodded to her, and placed his hands on the hidden handles behind the tall chair and pushed Cameron Gordon from the room.

Chapter 13

~~⚬⚬~~

Robert had disappeared. There were a hundred places a boy of seven could hide.

"You might find him at the chapel, miss," one of the maids said. She glanced at her, stopped, and retraced her steps. The girl was emerging from a cunningly concealed door, a bucket and cloth in her hand.

"How did you know I was looking for Robert?"

The girl shrugged. "His Grace flew out of here like a bat from a cave. I thought it likely someone would be after him. Normally, it's Gaston."

"Where is the chapel?"

The girl gave her directions, a complicated process considering Castle Crannoch was so large.

"Does he often go there?" Robert didn't strike her as a particularly religious child.

"When His Grace is disturbed, he does." The girl turned to leave. "You know why, miss, don't you?" she asked over her shoulder.

Beatrice shook her head.

"His parents are buried there."

Before going in search of Robert, she returned to the second floor, opened the door to Robert's room, and gathered up his coat and the snake, still on the floor. She returned to her room for her cloak and followed the maid's directions to the chapel.

She didn't want to feel sorry for Robert Gordon. He was a thoroughly unlikable child. She didn't want to remember the sight of his trembling hands, or think about what it must be like for a boy of seven to endure the loss of his parents. She was two decades older, and she'd found the same loss almost intolerable.

The journey to the chapel took a good quarter hour, all the right and left turns through the old part of Castle Crannoch dizzying. An arched pair of double doors, heavily inscribed with a carved cross, marked the entrance.

For a moment she hesitated, wondering if she would find him inside. If she did, what on earth would she say to him? Perhaps now was not the time to be rigid in her requirements. But if not now, then when? Someone had to say no to the boy sooner or later, and it would be better for him if it were done earlier than not. He couldn't rear himself. Someone must be his adult.

She pushed open the door to find the chapel awash in light. Not from candles this time, but from the light pouring through the stained-glass windows in the chancellery. The altar, set across the entrance to an alcove, was covered in an ivory lace cloth and furnished with two goblets and a series of plates that looked as if they were made of solid gold. In front of the altar was a kneeling bench upholstered in a crimson fabric. At the end of the bench, his head bowed and his hands in a prayerful attitude, was Robert, the twelfth Duke of Brechin.

Beatrice did not want to disturb the child at his prayers, so she sat in a pew in the middle of the room and remained as quiet as she could.

Robert, however, began to pray aloud, his implorations to the Almighty stated rather loudly.

"Please, God, take her away. Take her back to where she come from. A big wind would do it, God. Or a lightning bolt."

"Dear God, please inject into your servant some humility," she prayed, in a voice as loud as Robert's. "Please let him see I intend to do my best by him, and that means insisting upon his diligence with his studies. His parents would not wish for him to be an uneducated boor."

There was only silence in response, and she glanced up to find Robert standing at the end of the pew.

"No one talks about my parents. It's not allowed."

"Whose rule? Yours?"

He shook his head. "My uncle's."

"Does he think it will harm you to hear of them? If so, that's silly. We need to remember those we mourn."

He sat down on the end of the pew. "I don't like you, you know."

"You don't know me. You just dislike the idea of a governess or anyone telling you what to do."

"No one else does."

"Which is why, I don't doubt, any of the boys from

Kilbridden Village could beat you in mathematics or geography."

He glanced at her out of the corner of his eye.

"Geography, Robert. It's the study of the world. If you're to be a duke, you must know as much about the world as you can."

"I am a duke."

"Then if you're to be a proper duke, you must know as much as you can."

"What do I have to know?"

"What your parents knew. What they would want you to know. How to calculate a field's production, the tally of your herds, reading the writings of the day, the authors of the past, the Bible. How to reason out a problem, protect your heritage, guard your fortune, and perhaps expand it."

"How to rid Castle Crannoch of my uncle?"

The question startled her into silence. "Yes, I suppose that, as well," she finally said.

He nodded, as if in agreement.

"Ignorant is not a good title for any man to wear, Robert. Being a duke does not equip you with knowledge. You have intelligence. You must use it to acquire knowledge, and knowledge will help you be the best Duke of Brechin."

"Did you know my parents?"

"I did not have that pleasure. Will you tell me about them?"

He shook his head.

"My parents died a year ago," she said. "Within three days of each other. I miss them every day."

"Do you ever talk about them?"

For the first time, his voice sounded like that of a

seven-year-old boy, slightly tremulous, wanting to know but too afraid to hear the answer.

"Sometimes. It took a while for me to do so. I always cried when I did."

"My parents have been dead six months."

"That's not very long, is it?"

He shook his head.

"You'll find time doesn't go by very fast when it comes to grief."

For a few moments they sat silently together. Beatrice didn't fool herself it was a harmonious interlude. Robert would either revert to being obnoxious, or he would rush off and leave her sitting there.

"My mother had a wonderful laugh," Robert said abruptly. "It made everybody smile when she was happy."

Her heart felt as if it would break. She almost wished the child was being difficult again.

"My father always said we should keep her happy because she was the queen of our castle."

Don't tell me any more. But she was as incapable of halting the child's words as she was of halting her compassion.

"She used to come and tuck me in every night."

"Did you ever have nightmares when they were alive?"

He didn't answer. Instead, he stood and walked away, and for a moment she thought he'd left her. But he called out to her. "Would you like to see them?"

She followed the sound of his voice to where he stood at the side of the chapel, in a nave she'd not seen earlier. The floor looked freshly laid, the mortar binding the stones looking too white and new.

Amee Alison Gordon lay side by side with Marcus Harold Gordon, their birth dates different, but the dates of death the same.

She carefully stepped back, but not Robert. He stood on the stones covering his parents' graves and looked down at their markers.

"Do you come here every day?"

He glanced over his shoulder at her. "Yes."

He would never heal if he kept plucking at the wound. Only time would help him understand, at least it had for her. But were seven-year-old boys different? Even in the midst of his tragedy, there must be something interesting him, that excited him.

"What is your favorite place at Castle Crannoch?"

He looked surprised at the question. "The woods. And then the towers."

"Take me there."

"Which place?"

"Your choice. But first, we have something we must do."

"What?"

She went to the pew where she'd placed their coats and handed him his before donning the cloak Cameron had given her.

Beatrice walked out of the chapel and away from Castle Crannoch, acting as if she were unconcerned if Robert followed her or not. In actuality, she was very attuned to the boy, listening intently to his footfalls behind her on the floor.

She went to a copse of trees on top of a knoll. While the child watched, she dropped to her knees, and with a stick began to dig a small hole.

"What are you doing?"

She didn't answer him. Robert demanded, and the staff of Castle Crannoch immediately gratified his every wish. She was not about to do so.

When the hole was complete, she withdrew the napkin from her cloak and uncovered it.

"The snake."

She nodded. She bent and very gently laid the dead snake inside his grave and covered it with soil. When she stood, she looked at Robert. "You must say something."

"What?"

"I don't know. A prayer."

"I don't know any prayers."

"You were praying in the chapel."

"That was a made-up prayer."

"Then make one up now."

"You first."

She decided since the departed was, in this case, a snake, she should amend the service. "Go forth, dear snake, from this world, in the name of the Almighty Father who created thee. May God receive you in His goodly habitation of light. May the angels lead thee into Abraham's bosom."

"Requiem aeternam dona eis, Domine, et lux perpetua luceat eis."

Startled, she glanced at Robert.

"Rest eternal grant to them, O Lord, and may light perpetual shine upon them," he translated, his gaze on the snake's grave.

"You learned that for your parents?"

He nodded. "For their funeral. My father liked to recite Latin."

"That's very nice, Your Grace."

She stared down at the mound of earth she'd made, a last resting place for a trampled snake.

Robert was continually surprising her.

"Shall I take you to the woods now?"

She nodded and allowed him to lead her down the path and around the castle.

Rowena Gordon folded her hands in her lap, stared out at the sky, and ignored her maid with as much determination as possible.

Mary, however, had made her presence known these last few minutes by making a series of unforgettable sounds: tiny little yelps as if she were being pinched, and deep heartfelt sighs. When those failed to garner her attention, Mary had resorted to moans and then high-pitched squeals. If ghosts truly existed, they must sound the same.

Finally, unable to take any more, Rowena slapped her reticule down on the seat beside her and stared at her maid. "We will soon be home, Mary. There is no need for such histrionics."

"But, madam, this is such a perilous journey. We could so easily fall down the mountain. Why, this road could be a way to heaven itself."

Rowena sighed. She'd heard the same thing every time their carriage approached Castle Crannoch.

"It is a very dangerous series of turns. If the horses become tired or frightened, they could easily go over the side." Mary peered out the window, then shivered before letting the shade fall back over the window.

"How many times have you made this journey?"

"In the last six months? Surely a dozen."

"The horses know the route only too well, Mary, and nothing has happened to us in all this time. Calm yourself. We'll be at Castle Crannoch in less than five minutes."

Mary subsided against the seat, a mulish expression on her face. "Very well, madam. I shall not trouble you any longer."

Rowena held back her sigh with some difficulty. Mary's feelings were often hurt. In fact, she had to be the most sensitive creature Rowena had ever known. But she'd had plenty of time to acquaint herself with Mary's idiosyncrasies since the woman had been in her employ for eleven years, ever since she'd been a young girl in London.

"Mary, there is truly nothing to worry about. If you must be concerned about anything, worry about whether or not all those items we purchased in London survived the trip."

Mary glanced over at her.

"Remember the shepherdess and the shepherd statues I purchased? And the porcelain fox for the mantel?"

"They were packed in straw, madam." But the line above Mary's nose creased in concern. "Unless they did not follow my instructions, madam; and then I'm very much afraid of what we'll find when we begin the unpacking."

Good, she'd already begun to worry about the trunks. At least she wouldn't be afraid of the sharp curves still to come.

Rowena wedged herself into the corner of the carriage and smiled determinedly. As long as Mary had something to occupy her, she was content, and bearable to be around.

The day promised to be a sunny one. Clouds had obscured the morning sky, turning it gray, but the closer they came to Castle Crannoch, the bluer the sky. An omen for her homecoming?

She hated Castle Crannoch as strongly as if it were a person and had a personality. She hated the place because it was the scene of defeat, of demoralization, of despair. She hated it because Cameron loved it and lusted after it with more affection and emotion than he'd shown her in the last six months.

The last six months had not been easy ones for Cameron or for her. There'd been times when she'd despaired of surviving from one day to the next. Not that she would ever do anything to harm herself, but there were times when her heart almost shriveled up and died.

Gradually she learned to accept that she and Cameron would never be the way they once were. Whereas previously they had never spent a night apart, now they had two separate chambers, two separate dressing rooms, two separate sets of servants, and gradually, two separate lives.

Regardless of how many times she went to London or to Paris or to Edinburgh, she always came back to Castle Crannoch again, drawn not like a moth to a flame, but like a lovesick woman for the man she adored. Because whether he walked or not, whether he acknowledged her presence or not, whether he cared if she lived or not, she loved him.

The carriage slowed, a sign they were coming close to the end of their journey. Rowena didn't bother opening the shade. She heard the driver call out to the horses and prepared herself to make an entrance. A few minutes later, the door was opened. Rowena put on her gloves and stepped down from the carriage.

Rowena fixed a smile upon her face and looked up at the edifice of Castle Crannoch with what she hoped could be interpreted as enthusiasm and not the dread she really felt.

"It seems a very long time since we've been gone," Mary said. "Two whole months. Nothing has changed one whit, has it, madam?"

"Castle Crannoch has endured for centuries. Two months will not change it."

"That's true." Mary stared up at the castle with awe on her face. Unlike her, Mary had admired the place ever since they'd moved here from Edinburgh. Romantic, Mary had said reverentially, upon first seeing Castle Crannoch.

"I imagine Mr. Cameron will be so very happy to see you, madam."

So happy he'd not yet put in an appearance. So happy no one stood at the broad front doors to greet them. Not a servant walked down the steps; the door didn't even open.

If she'd been so foolish as to confide in Mary, she'd tell her that not once in the months since she'd been gone had Cameron ever written her. She had no idea if the time without her had been a lonely one, or if he'd missed her, if his health was good. In short, her husband was a stranger.

The morning was fair, the sun greeted her brightly, but no human being of her acquaintance stood at the door and welcomed her home.

"Perhaps Mr. Gordon woke late, madam, and he's just now dressing," Mary said.

Not a good sign that her maid had noticed her discomfiture. In just a moment, Mary would be dabbing at the corners of her eyes with her ever-present handkerchief, a sign she empathized for Rowena's plight—being the unloved wife of an invalid.

"There was no way to let him know of our arrival, Mary. We shall simply let them know we are here now."

There was no need to instruct the driver, he was well aware of where to have the trunks taken. What a pity all the new clothing she'd purchased in London wouldn't mitigate this bitter disappointment.

In addition to her new wardrobe, she'd purchased presents for Cameron and Devlen, and added to Robert's collection of toy soldiers. She knew the child would be pleasantly surprised. They'd had little or nothing to do with each other, and she suspected he preferred their current arrangement as much as she.

She'd always been careful around children, cautious and reserved. She didn't go out of her way to view a child in its pram, and when a friend whispered to her she was with child, Rowena's first thought was to mentally bless the poor soul and hope she made it through the travail of childbirth.

After marrying Cameron five years ago, she'd given some thought to children, but since he was twelve years older, it hadn't been a subject concerning her overmuch. He had his heir in Devlen. After the accident, she'd had to accept the closest she would ever come to her own child would be acting as aunt to Robert, the twelfth Duke of Brechin.

She mounted the steps holding her skirts up to her ankles. Her dress was a gray merino trimmed in silk. The bodice was fitted in the waist, and the color accented her red hair. Perhaps after two months Cameron would notice she was not unattractive, at least not according to several men in London.

Would he comment upon her pale complexion? She'd been careful not to acquire any sun. Or lovers. More than once, she'd been approached by an attractive man, and more than once she'd wondered at her own virtue.

Would Cameron have been as restrained if the circumstances were reversed? That was not a question she was foolish enough to ask herself.

Mary opened the door for her, as properly as a footman. She smiled at her, a forced expression, not quite sincere. But the dear woman only smiled back at her and hurried to close the door behind her.

Dear Mary, always so accommodating.

Rowena took the stairs to the right. Her chamber was adjacent to Cameron's in the same wing, on the opposite side of the castle from the Duke's Chamber. As if Cameron did not wish to be reminded daily his nephew had ascended to the title.

How could he ever forget?

If she did nothing else, she needed to convince Cameron a few more servants would not be amiss. If for no other reason than to be able to smile at a friendly face from time to time and not make the journey from her chamber down to the drawing room without seeing a solitary soul.

At the second floor, she hesitated. A wiser woman

would have gone straight to her room to refresh herself and rest from the journey. But she had waited for this moment for the last two months, less one day.

During that first day after she'd left Castle Crannoch, she'd been happy about her decision. Then regret had crept in, and she'd been so desperately lonely she'd immediately wanted to turn around and return to the castle. During these past two months she'd imagined all sorts of homecomings, and none of them had been so dry and desolate as the real one.

How foolish she was to desperately want something that would never happen.

She stopped and turned, changing her mind and walking back to her chamber. She opened the door before Mary could do so and entered the room.

Rowena turned away from the door and went to her vanity. Mary followed, intent on helping her. For the moment, however, she only wanted to be alone.

"See to yourself, my dear," she said, with as much kindness as she could summon. "If you could come before dinner, perhaps."

Cameron insisted everyone dress for dinner, and since it was often the only time during the day when she saw her husband, Rowena took great pains with her attire.

Mary chattered at her side, and she nodded from time to time so as to appear attentive. In actuality, there were times when she simply ignored Mary. Her maid shared every thought traveling through her mind, however transiently. Given any encouragement at all, the poor dear would go on and on and on about the most trivial matter. The squeaking of the latches on the coach door, the slap of the shade against the window, all these things reminded her of when she was a child and embarked upon a journey with her father while her mother stayed behind caring for a sibling.

In addition, Mary liked to gossip, and these little snippets of conversation would shortly contain tidbits about every single individual who lived at Castle Crannoch. Rowena would be privy to the activities of every single servant, guest, or inhabitant of the castle. Except, of course, herself and Cameron. But she didn't hold out any hope Mary had any restraint whatsoever when it came to sensitive matters.

"Please, take this time for yourself."

"Very well, madam, if you're sure," Mary said. "I can stay, if you prefer. Your trunks will be delivered shortly, and we need to unpack your things. Otherwise, those lovely new gowns will be irreparably damaged."

Rowena could not see how sitting in a trunk a few more hours might ruin them when they had been sitting there for days already. But she only smiled.

"There's time enough later."

Mary finally left, closing the door softly behind her. Rowena stared at herself in the mirror, slowing removing her hat, an ethereal bit of fluff and veil that enhanced her green eyes.

She was too pale, but other than that, the last part of the journey from London had not altered her looks. She looked well, healthy, and vibrant, a woman of youth who still had the ability to turn a man's head. Her cheeks were pink, her mouth turned up in a smile, the freckles on her nose barely visible through the dusting of powder. Her eyes sparkled, but she knew it wasn't anticipation but tears making them look so deeply green.

One tear escaped and trailed from the corner of her eye down her cheek, then to her chin. She brushed it away slowly.

Cameron would know by now she'd arrived. Perhaps he was even supervising the arrival of her trunks and looking at all of the things she'd purchased with that smile of his, half-wry, half-cynical.

But he hadn't come to her room and he hadn't made the effort to greet her. Two months had evidently made no difference in Cameron's affections.

Very well, if this was how she was to live the rest of her life, she would do so with grace. He would never know how devastated she felt at this moment. Instead, let him look at her and wonder at her smile. Let him imagine what might have transpired in London. Let him think her beautiful and desirable. Let him decide she was wanton. Let him think anything at all about her other than she was a poor despicable creature yearning for the affections of the one man who wouldn't grant them. Who held his heart aloof because of what she'd done.

He had his pride. Very well, so did she, and he would learn just how very much pride she had from this moment on.

She repaired her hair, and blotted at her face so no trace of her earlier tears would show. She stood, straightened her attire, grateful for the gray wool she wore. The dress flattered both her coloring and her figure.

Once armored, she left the room, intent for the library on the first floor. Cameron had claimed the room as his, and if he wasn't in his chamber, he was holed up in the library, playing at being the Duke of Brechin. Even if he could not bear the title in actuality, he governed Castle Crannoch as if he were the true owner.

Cameron was a genius at management. He knew the exact number of cattle, sheep, goats, chickens, or horses and where they were at any one time. He knew the tally of each field and how many bushels it produced. The ships belonging to the child duke, the various possessions scattered all over Scotland, were all kept in perfect order by Cameron for the child's majority.

Once Robert no longer required a guardian, he could destroy his own birthright if he chose. When he reached twenty-one, Cameron would be forced to turn away and surrender all he'd stewarded for all these years. She'd asked him once if he would be able to simply walk away from Castle Crannoch. He'd only stared at her as if she weren't there. A ghost of who she'd been, perhaps. A wifely spirit.

She knew exactly when his love had turned to hate. Marcus and his wife had been visiting Edinburgh to celebrate his birthday. A carriage accident had killed the duke and duchess instantly, and injured Cameron to the extent she'd had to make a fateful decision.

She'd sat at the side of his bed every moment since the operation. Cameron's life force was so strong he couldn't help but survive. If anything, she would will it. For days she sat beside his bed and prayed.

When he finally awoke, it was her duty to tell him what had happened. Because his legs had been crushed beneath the carriage he would never walk again.

But he would survive, his life would go on.

"Not without my legs, Rowena." He'd turned away

from her then, and ever since, he'd treated her as if she weren't quite there, never looking at her directly and rarely addressing her personally. When he'd made the decision to move to Castle Crannoch, she acquiesced. There was nothing, after all, she could do.

How strange she could love someone so deeply and hate him at the same time.

Chapter 14

⟡

The air was chilled, but the sky was blue. The grass was lightly browned from the nightly freezing temperature. Yet there was something about the day that spoke not of winter, but of springtime. Beatrice halted on the lee of the hill and looked beyond her, to the vista of blue-shrouded hills in the distance.

There was something about the scenery, the sight of an eagle soaring high above, its wings black and gray against the blue of the sky, the feel of the air itself, holding a bite even in summer. She closed her eyes and thought she could even smell the faint odor of peat fires and smoke.

Her father was Scots, and he loved the country with the same fervency she felt. But he had no illusions as to its history, its future, or its people.

"The word no is an anthem for Scotland, my dear Beatrice. You'll never find a more recalcitrant lot than

135

the Scots. Nor will you ever find a nobler race of people or a greater friend than a Scotsman."

Her mother, half-French, always smiled in tolerance. Perhaps she'd learned it wasn't important to worry about nationalities.

At the moment, Beatrice couldn't help but feel as though she were born to this land.

She glanced behind Robert at the looming castle. From here, the older part of the castle was clearly visible, including the lone tower, now crumbling in places.

"Why is it the past seems so much more romantic than the present? Your ancestors lived here a very long time ago, and no doubt suffered a great many privations. But one doesn't think of what they suffered, only of their pride and their determination."

"Do you know nothing of the Gordons, Miss Sinclair?" Robert stopped on the path and glanced back at her. "They were a bloodthirsty lot. My father used to tell me stories of all the raids they went on, and all the cattle they stole from places along the border."

"Really?"

"My father and I used to spend every Friday afternoon discussing a Gordon. There are thirteen generations of Gordon men, Miss Sinclair, and each of them should be studied. Some were foolish, while some were heroes."

His voice proudly echoed his father's words. She looked down at him and smiled.

"I think I would've liked your father."

She thought for a moment Robert was going to say something in return, but he didn't.

Perhaps if she could get him to talk more it would be a healing step for him. She knew loss was never truly eased, but it became a part of the fabric of one's character, like a hole through a once-loved garment. Even after mending, the tear was still there, and the garment altered because of it. She didn't discard a garment because it had one flaw, and she couldn't stop living her life simply because grief had visited her. If she imparted no other lesson to Robert, she'd try to teach him this one.

The young duke was, after all, only seven years old. He had a lifetime of living ahead of him. True, his early years would always be filled with the bittersweet memories of the parents he loved, but he must begin to create other memories.

The graveled path they followed was bordered by large rocks on either side and was too narrow for two people to walk abreast. Like the road leading down the mountain, it meandered from side to side through the glen. The distance to the woods was longer, but conversely, the journey was easier, given the height they descended on the zigzag trail.

Someone, a very long time ago, had cut steps into the stone where the hill abruptly dropped, and they'd become part of the path itself. As she followed him, Beatrice noticed Robert's step became less reluctant, his arms began to swing back and forth, and his head came up as if eager to see what was ahead of him.

How long had it been since he'd ventured outside the castle? Castle Crannoch might be his birthright, but there was no sunlight there, nothing but a dark warren of lavish rooms lit by hundreds of candles. A child needed sunlight and activity, chores to perform and responsibilities, even if he was duke.

To the right, following the curve of the hill, was a

dense strip of forest. The trees were thick, and the underbrush looked as if it hadn't been cleared away for years. At first glance, the wood appeared black and unfriendly. But as they grew closer, Beatrice realized it was just the kind of place a boy would like to explore.

He thrust both fists into his pants pockets. His stock had already come untied, and there was a spot on his jacket and one on the knee of his trousers. He was not the most sartorially perfect of aristocrats.

She wanted suddenly to hug him. Though he had moments in which he was rude and unbearable, she found herself softening toward him the longer she was in his company.

"What do you do in the woods?"

"I pretend I'm duke."

She glanced at him, surprised.

"I'm not really the Duke of Brechin at Castle Crannoch, Miss Sinclair."

"Why on earth would you say that? It's your home."

He looked at her as if he couldn't believe her stupidity. It was such a boyish thing to do she found herself smiling.

"It was my home when my parents were alive. Now it's filled with people who do not like me and wish I'd never been born."

He turned and marched toward the forest again, leaving her with a choice of either to follow him or stare after him incredulously.

Finally, Beatrice lengthened her strides until she was only a few feet behind him.

"Surely you don't feel that way about Gaston?"

"Gaston is my uncle's servant." He stopped again, turned and looked at her. "Did you know, Miss Sinclair, none of the servants who were employed at Castle Crannoch when my parents were alive are here now?"

She shook her head, surprised.

"Most of the servants below stairs are rotated every three months. They come from Edinburgh or Glasgow. My uncle imports them here with a bonus and promises them they will only have to serve for a quarter of the year. Even if they wish to stay, they are not allowed to."

Was her tenure to be as short-lived? The selfishness of that thought shamed her.

"Why would he do that?"

He shrugged. "You tell me, Miss Sinclair. My uncle tells me nothing. I think he'd rather pretend I wasn't around."

"And Devlen?" she found herself asking. "How do you feel about Devlen?"

He turned away, relentless in his approach toward the woods. She had to nearly sprint to catch up with him.

"Devlen is my one true friend. I would live in Edinburgh with him if I could, but my uncle wouldn't allow it."

"Why wouldn't he?"

"Because Devlen would be a bad influence upon me." He grinned, a thoroughly masculine, albeit seven-year-old version, grin. "He stays out late, you know, and he has a great many lady companions."

"Does he?"

He stopped one more time and looked at her. "I found a deer once," he said, looking as if he were dubious about confiding in her.

"I trust you treated him with more care than the snake."

He raised his eyebrows in an imitation of his cousin's gesture. "I'm the Duke of Brechin, Miss Sinclair. I'm the only one allowed to hunt in these woods. But the deer was already dead, I'm afraid."

"You have your morbid moments, Robert. Is that why we've come to the woods? To find some other poor dead creature?"

He gave her another pitying stare, and she decided to refrain from further comment.

They were beyond the first of the trees when Beatrice heard a loud cracking noise. She looked down, thinking she had stepped on a branch, but the noise came again, this time from behind her. She glanced back toward Castle Crannoch. Something stung her face and she recoiled, pressing her hand to her cheek. When she drew it away, there was blood on her palm.

Robert ran up to her, grabbed her arm, and before she could ask him what he was about, had pulled her into the woods and to the ground.

"Someone's shooting at us, Miss Sinclair!"

Another shot rang out and this time she didn't need Robert's urging to flatten herself behind a fallen tree. The earth was a pungent combination of pine and decay, the discarded needles from the mature trees above sticking to her hands.

Her face hurt, but a delicate exploration revealed she wasn't actually hurt. Instead, she must have been struck by splinters from one of the shots.

"I'm afraid someone else believes they have the right to use your woods, Robert," she said. Another shot rang out. This one was close enough she could hear the zing of the bullet before it struck a tree. "Thank the Lord he's not a very good shot."

There wasn't much left of the tree trunk they were hiding behind. Time and the insects had hollowed out a majority of it, but the tree was enough of a shield she felt somewhat protected. She peered through the trees, in the direction she thought the bullets had originated.

In front of her was the entire hill, with Castle Crannoch to the upper left. Below was a cottage, half in ruin, evidently the gamekeeper's cottage at one time. Her eyes followed the path they'd taken. Several large boulders might shield a man with a gun.

"It wasn't a hunter, Miss Sinclair. The shots came from the castle," Robert said with a terrifying certainty. His voice was low, and if her hand hadn't been resting on his shoulder, she wouldn't have known he was trembling.

She wrapped her arm around him as they stared out at the sun-dappled day.

"It was probably a hunter with very bad aim."

"No one is allowed to hunt on Gordon land."

"Rules don't stop a man trying to feed his hungry family."

"It wasn't a hunter," he said again. "Someone was trying to kill me."

The comment was uttered so matter of factly she wanted to ask him how he had learned such *sang-froid* at such a young age. How could he view an attempt on his life so calmly?

"What a very odd thing to say, Robert."

"It isn't the first time it's happened."

Shocked, she drew back, and turned him to face her.

"What do you mean?"

"On the day my last tutor left, I'd gone to the game-keeper's cottage instead of saying good-bye." He pointed to the ruined structure down the hill.

"You mean you'd hidden there when people were trying to find you."

He looked away rather than at her.

"I was nearly caught in a trap. It wasn't there before. I almost stepped in it."

"An accident."

"We don't use traps at Castle Crannoch. Ask my uncle. He'll tell you."

He pulled away from her and stood, drawing up the leg of his trousers to reveal a bandage she hadn't noticed.

"And someone pushed me down the stairs a few days ago."

They stared at each other, Beatrice left without a word to say. What kind of hornets' nest had she stumbled into?

She stood and went to the edge of the forest, keeping Robert behind her. Several moments had passed since the last shot, and she wondered if they were being stalked. Or, had it truly been a hunter, and he'd belatedly realized they weren't game?

Her cloak was a deep blue, but Robert's jacket was a fawn color.

"You were probably mistaken for a deer," she said, even though she was beginning to be doubtful of her own claim.

He only shook his head.

A moment later, she dared herself to step out onto the

path again. Right now, all she wanted to do was reach the relative safety of the castle. But how safe was Castle Crannoch, especially if what Robert said was true?

A quarter hour later, when no further shots had come, Beatrice decided it was safe to return. They climbed the hill, taking the path back to Castle Crannoch, in full view of anyone who might wish to harm them. The only concession to Robert's safety was that he remained behind her. If what he said was correct, whoever was shooting at them would have a clear view of her, but not of him.

The journey was a harrowing one, and when they finally made it back to the castle grounds, Beatrice almost wept with relief.

"Your uncle needs to know what happened," she said when they'd reached the safety of the outer courtyard.

He stopped and looked at her in a way no seven-year-old should ever look, with wisdom and a certain amount of sadness in his eyes.

"Go ahead and tell him, Miss Sinclair. He will say it was an accident. Or that it didn't happen, and it was all my imagination. That's what he said before."

"He's your uncle. He wouldn't want anything bad to happen to you."

The child's laughter was eerie, and almost adult. He turned and looked out at the land stretching in front of Castle Crannoch.

"Miss Sinclair, my father married late in life. Up until then, my uncle believed he was the heir to the title. I was a surprise, and not a welcome one. If something happens to me, my uncle becomes duke."

Shocked, she could only stare at him. "Robert,

surely you cannot believe your uncle responsible," she finally said.

The boy began to climb the steps up to the broad double doors. At the top, he turned to face her again.

"You can talk to my uncle if you wish, Miss Sinclair. But I can tell you now it will make the situation worse rather than better."

She watched him enter the castle and wondered what, exactly, she should do. If Devlen were here, she might have confided in him. Instead, she chose Gaston, and went in search of the manservant. She found him in the kitchen.

"Do you have a moment to speak with me?" she asked.

"You've been hurt, Miss Sinclair."

She touched her cheek. Up until that moment, she'd forgotten.

"A scratch, that's all."

"We've some ointment that will aid in preventing a scar."

She had no choice but to follow him, sitting at the table when he pointed to a chair, tilting her head just this way as he cleaned the scratch and then treated it with a foul-smelling salve. He handed her a small jar of it when he was done and gave her instructions to use it twice a day.

"Now, what did you wish to talk about?"

She glanced around her at the interested servants.

"Could we go somewhere more private?"

"Certainly, Miss Sinclair." He left the tray of salves and ointments on the table and led her through a series of tunnel-like corridors. She vaguely remembered the path she took that first night.

They exited the castle to a small courtyard, and she knew her memory had been right. Devlen's coach had stopped here.

"What is it, Miss Sinclair?"

"Can you keep a confidence, Gaston? Even if it is from your employer?"

"I do not know how to answer that question, not unless I know exactly what type of confidence."

She admired loyalty, but she also needed to show some loyalty to Robert. He hadn't asked for her word, but she felt as if he deserved it, for no other reason than his courage.

"Is Robert in any danger? Has anything happened to him since his parents died that might be construed as unusual?"

She'd expected Gaston to answer her quickly and in the negative. Instead, the manservant studied her for several long moments as if to gauge the meaning behind her question.

"There have been some incidents regarding the duke. Accidents any small boy would have."

"Such as being pushed down the stairs?"

"His Grace often neglects wearing his shoes, Miss Sinclair, and takes to sliding on the floors in his stocking feet. It was an accident, nothing more."

"And the trap?"

"We were not able to find the trap he spoke of."

She almost mentioned the shots, then knew Gaston would explain them away just as she had. A zealous hunter, with an overabundance of gunpowder and a paucity of skill.

"Does Mr. Gordon know of these incidents?"

"My master does know, Miss Sinclair. He knows

everything that goes on at Castle Crannoch. Simply because he does not comment about it or make it public knowledge is no reason to think he is not aware of the situation.

"If there are more such incidents in the near future, Miss Sinclair, it might be because of you."

She stepped back. "Me?"

"His Grace might see you have a kind heart. He may use these stories to encourage you to leave Castle Crannoch."

"You believe it's his imagination?"

"Perhaps the ramblings of a child still grieving for his family."

She looked down the mountain at the torturous corkscrew of a road. If she had any sense at all, she would leave this place with its hint of mystery and tragedy. But something had changed in the last two days. She'd found herself touched to the core by a little boy who was arrogant, obnoxious, yet startlingly brave.

No, she couldn't desert Robert. She might well be the only person who believed him. Because the hunter—if he was truly a hunter—had shot at her as well as the boy.

Beatrice turned on her heel and left Gaston before she was tempted to say something she shouldn't. She didn't even ask him to keep what she'd said in confidence, knowing he wouldn't. Instead, he would no doubt visit Cameron Gordon and within the next quarter hour relate to him everything she had said.

She took the back stairs to the second floor and knocked on Robert's door. There was no answer, but this time she didn't make the effort to find the boy. No doubt he had places to hide throughout the castle. A safe place, she fervently hoped.

Instead, she entered her chamber and slammed the door, feeling both childish and frightened.

Chapter 15

"When I used to slam doors," Robert said, "My parents reprimanded me."

She glanced at the other side of the room, where Robert sat on the edge of her bed, his feet dangling over the side.

"Should I ask what you're doing in my chamber?" Nevertheless, she was oddly relieved to see him. "Are you placing another snake in my bed? Or is it to be a toad this time?"

His smile was utterly charming and he laughed like a little boy might laugh, not a serious young duke.

"Did I tell you I shot one of my tutors in the rump? It was an accident, of course, but he didn't believe that. He told my uncle I was the spawn of Satan and should be sent away to prison, not to school. I shall have to think long and hard about what to do next with you, Miss Sinclair. I suspect you are not often frightened."

"I was today. That incident," she said, using Gaston's word for it, "frightened me enough."

"Yet you were very brave," he said. "You stood out in the path and dared someone to shoot you."

"I was not daring. I was hoping with all my heart the shooter was a hunter and by seeing me clearly he might realize I wasn't a deer."

"Did you tell my uncle?"

"Ah, the real reason you're here. No, I didn't."

She sat on the bed beside him. "But I'm very surprised someone didn't hear the shot."

"They might have thought it really was a hunter. Perhaps my uncle has a yen for rabbit and sent one of the servants out."

The inference being, of course, that Cameron Gordon was responsible, either directly or indirectly, for the events of this afternoon.

"I think you're very brave, Miss Sinclair."

The compliment was said in such a calm and pleasant tone, so unlike the autocratic whine Robert normally used, that she looked at the boy in surprise. Without his cloak of arrogance, Robert was a very pleasant individual indeed. In fact, she'd enjoyed being in his company this morning, something she hadn't expected.

"What shall we do now?" he asked.

She would dearly like to lie down and put a cold compress over her eyes and ignore the throbbing headache that had grown ever since she'd been shot at, but she had to keep going for Robert's sake.

"Can you show me where the library is?"

He shook his head.

She was surprised at his sudden recalcitrance, and

wondered if she'd been too kind to think him pleasant only a moment earlier.

"My uncle uses that room during the day."

Now she understood. She didn't want to be in the company of Cameron Gordon either.

"Well, then it's impossible for us to acquire some books to begin your education. Where did you and your tutors study?"

He looked away, brushed his hands across his trousers, studied a hole that had suddenly appeared in his stockings, anything but look at her.

"Robert?"

He glanced at her and then found the view from the window to be so intriguing it commanded his attention.

"Robert."

He sighed heavily and turned to look at her finally.

"I had three tutors, Miss Sinclair."

She waited.

"Two of them thought Castle Crannoch was too far from civilization and complained from the moment they arrived, so I wasn't sorry to see them go. One of them wasn't such a bad sort, but he kept telling me how handsome my uncle was and nearly swooning whenever he saw him. I had nothing to do with his leaving, truly. The arrow didn't hurt him that badly. My uncle dismissed him."

"So they weren't here long enough for you to learn anything from them?"

He nodded.

"But where did you study?"

"There's a small sitting room next to my bedroom."

"Then we shall meet there in the morning."

Instead of answering her, he slid off the bed, his eyes

lighting up. "Would you like to see the attics, Miss Sinclair? There are lots and lots of empty rooms up there. There's one I know that is perfect for a schoolroom."

"The attics?"

He held out his hand for her. "Come with me, Miss Sinclair. I know the castle very, very well."

"Who taught you when your parents were alive?"

"My father."

She nodded, not unduly surprised. No wonder Robert resented having a governess or tutor. Their presence was a living reminder his father was not here to teach him.

As to Robert's excitement over the attic, there was an answer for that as well. No doubt Cameron Gordon couldn't navigate the stairs because of his wheelchair. She had the impression Robert's uncle oversaw everything within his domain. For the time being, Robert, twelfth Duke of Brechin, was very much within his control. She wouldn't be surprised if the child was always thinking of schemes to avoid his uncle.

Beatrice couldn't say she blamed him much.

His rebellion, however, would be short-lived. Wherever they decided to study, Cameron Gordon would no doubt make an appearance. Nor would she be surprised if he commanded them to choose an accessible room. He was, after all, Robert's guardian.

Robert led her down the hall, turned left, then right, evidently following a path he knew well. At the end of the hall, he reached out and pressed one of the decorations below the top frame of a painting. The wall instantly moved, revealing a small corridor. She'd seen one of the maids disappear into a similar one downstairs just that morning.

"A secret passage?"

"Just a way for the maids and the footmen to travel between floors. I think once they were used to hide treasure. My father said that some of our ancestors were thieves and rogues." He grinned at her. "I think they're haunted. I once saw the very first Gordon and his horse."

She raised one eyebrow at him, and he shrugged.

"My uncle doesn't like to see servants, so whenever they hear him coming, they sort of melt into the walls." He giggled, sounding like a seven-year-old boy.

"Are there places like this throughout the castle?"

"No, only the newer part. This section of Castle Crannoch is only about a hundred years old. If there are any secret passages in the old part, I haven't been able to find them."

"Do you do a lot of exploring?"

"What else is there to do?"

"Well, from this moment on, your lessons."

He made a face but didn't comment.

She followed him into the small anteroom leading to a circular iron staircase. Evidently, the space had originally been a tower. Sunlight spilled in through the archer slits, but so did the chill. In the depths of winter, it must be unbearably cold to serve the Gordon family.

He dropped his voice and whispered, "You can go down to the kitchen from here, as well as climbing up to the attics."

"Why are you whispering?"

"You have to be careful because anyone can hear you. Sound carries very well."

She held on to the railing and climbed, feeling as if

they would never make it to the top. Heights made her uncomfortable.

Finally, they were at the top, the staircase ending in a wooden landing. There was a gap of some space between the top step and the first board, and Beatrice made it across without looking down.

"It's all right, Miss Sinclair," he whispered. "We're almost there."

He pushed open the door, and she found herself in a well-lit corridor, but narrower than the second floor. There was no effort to hide the entrance to the servant's staircase.

"We're at the top of the castle," he said, and for the first time, the pride of ownership was in his voice. "There's one room on this floor that has nothing but windows for a ceiling. It's filled with trunks right now, but you can see the ocean from it."

She was intrigued by his description, enough to silence her doubts for the moment.

"When we used to have a lot of servants, they slept up here. But they use the third floor now."

"How many servants are there at Castle Crannoch?"

"Only about seven. We need at least five times as many to care for the castle."

"Why don't you employ them?"

"My uncle says he's saving my fortune. I think it's because he doesn't like to have people around him."

"You don't like your uncle, do you?"

He gave her a look that made her want to retract the question.

A moment later, he spoke again. "My father used to say people have to choose between being good or evil."

"Your father sounds like a very wise man."

"My father was the best man in the whole wide world. Nothing my uncle could ever say would ever change my mind."

She glanced down at him, wondering if Cameron Gordon was guilty of maligning the dead.

He didn't say anything further about Cameron, and Beatrice felt strangely relieved. She had held her position for only two days. Yet those two days had been very peculiar ones.

Robert walked to the end of the hall and pushed open the door. Instantly, he was bathed in sunlight. Curious, she followed him and peered into the room.

The windows started midway along the outside wall and stretched up to the ceiling and angled upward. Sunlight flooded into the room, warming the space and tinting it golden. Beatrice felt as if she were inside a bright yellow jewel.

"Isn't it nice, Miss Sinclair?"

"I think it's absolutely perfect," she said, awed.

To the right was the line of mountains, to the left the ocean sparkling in the early-afternoon sun. Ahead were the hills and valleys of the land belonging to Castle Crannoch.

"If nothing else," she said, smiling, "the vista will be an inspiration for your learning, Your Grace. You'll want to become the most learned duke of all, especially viewing your birthright each and every day."

"Do you know you only say 'Your Grace' when you're pleased with me?"

"Do I?" She glanced him and smiled. "Then you should try to make me say it often."

She studied the room. Someone had made this beautiful room a storehouse for empty crates and trunks.

"It will take some time to clear out all this mess. We'll have to remove the trunks and put them somewhere else."

Robert began to drag one out the door. "No, we can't go about this all willy-nilly. We have to have a little organization."

She began to count the trunks. "What we really need is help. It's called division of labor."

"Call one of the footmen."

She glanced at him.

"I'm the Duke of Brechin, Miss Sinclair. I can still command my own servants."

Just when she thought he was uncomplicated and childlike, Robert surprised her.

"Very well, is there a bellpull up here? Or do we need to go down to the second floor?"

He grinned at her, evidently pleased about something. He walked to the end of the corridor and waved his hands at her to get her attention.

She folded her arms over her chest and tapped her foot impatiently.

"Yes?"

Mounted on the wall above his head was a metal triangle. He jumped up to grab it, succeeding on the first try. Wrapping his arms around it, he allowed his weight to carry him nearly to the floor. When he released the triangle, the tension made it bounce back almost to the ceiling.

"What is that?" Beatrice said, coming to investigate the curious instrument.

"It's a fire alarm," Roberts said. "It only rings in the kitchen. In moments we'll have all sorts of servants here."

"Robert Gordon! Have you no sense? You will scare everyone to death."

She frowned at him, but he blithely ignored her.

Within five minutes at least four of the seven servants employed at Castle Crannoch appeared at the entrance to the servants' stair, red-faced and carrying buckets. Just as she'd feared, every single one of them looked terrified.

Beatrice dismissed them all except one footman, who looked less breathless than the others. He and Robert exchanged a glance and a conspiratorial smile, and she wanted to ask him if he'd been Robert's partner in illicit activities before.

Perhaps ignorance was the better course, at least for the moment.

The two of them set about moving the crates from the room while she investigated the trunks. Most of them were empty except for a few wedged into the corner. Two of them were badly damaged, the tops nearly crushed.

She didn't know where to put them. When she'd tried to move them, both felt as if they were full.

"They belonged to my parents," Robert said from beside her. "I wondered where they'd gone." He pointed to another trunk against the wall. "That's my mother's."

"Where should they go?"

"Could they stay here?"

Thankfully he didn't ask they be opened, only that they remain in the room, almost as if both parents would be present during their lessons. She understood, since she had done similar foolish things, such as lighting her father's pipe so the scent of his tobacco would permeate the empty cottage and putting her mother's apron on the cabinet so it looked as if she'd just stepped away.

"Of course they can," she said, smiling.

Robert made an attempt at a smile in return.

Their efforts were rewarded, two hours later, by an almost empty room. They could move a table into the center, leaving space for some bookshelves against the wall. Another discovery they'd made was the fireplace against one wall. A blaze in the hearth would warm the room on even the coldest of days.

The three of them worked together in perfect harmony, the physical labor helping to push aside the frightening events of the morning. When the room was empty, she went in search of something to clean the floor, leaving Robert behind with the footman as company. When she returned from the scullery armed with a bucket and a mop, she found the footman had disappeared, but Robert was still there. This time, however, his companion was a woman.

"You must be the amazing Miss Sinclair."

Staring at her was one of the most beautiful women she'd ever seen. A tall crown of bright red hair was piled on the top of her head and framed a face as smooth and flawless as porcelain. Her green eyes, however, were hard as chips of stone.

"Robert," she said, glancing down at the boy. "Go and ready yourself for dinner."

"I'm not hungry."

Beatrice sighed. Evidently, the child's arrogance had not dissipated completely.

"Your Grace," she said, "remember your manners."

He glared at her, but Beatrice frowned right back at him.

"Very well," he said. He made a perfect little bow from the waist. "Miss Sinclair."

She nodded, pleased with him. He turned and bowed to the redheaded woman. "Aunt Rowena."

"Forgive me," Beatrice said. "I didn't know you'd returned. I'm Robert's governess."

"So I understand. Did you know my husband prior to being employed by him, Miss Sinclair?" the other woman asked in an icy tone.

"No, I didn't."

"Extraordinary, especially since my husband likes to surround himself with attractive women."

Beatrice had never been faced with another woman's instant dislike. Nor had she ever been so certain that another person's antipathy was based on false information and misplaced jealousy.

"You won't like Castle Crannoch, Miss Sinclair. There is nothing here to keep you occupied. Nothing to interest a young woman such as you."

At the risk of sounding insolent, Beatrice remained silent.

Rowena Gordon swept by her and left the room, giving Beatrice the distinct impression life at Castle Crannoch had just gotten more difficult. Coming as it was after this morning's unsettling events, the knowledge wasn't comforting in the least.

Chapter 16

❦

Beatrice finished dressing, tilted the mirror above the bureau and surveyed herself one last time. This was to be her first family dinner, now that Rowena had returned to the castle. Frankly, she would have preferred another tray in her room.

She closed the door quietly behind her and walked down the hall to the Duke's Chamber. As Robert's governess, it was incumbent upon her to ensure that his manners were perfect for this evening. Perhaps a little conversation before they descended to the dining room wouldn't be amiss.

Her knock wasn't answered. Slowly, she turned the handle and pushed the door ajar. The room was empty. Hopefully, Robert had gone down to dinner early and was not hiding somewhere. She really didn't have the energy to find him.

Halfway down the staircase, she gestured to a maid just as the girl was sliding behind a hidden panel.

"Where is the dining room?"

"On the first floor, the third room in the east wing."

She bobbed a curtsy and disappeared from sight, much as Beatrice would like to do. The directions were sparse, but she finally found the room.

Unlike the area where they'd eaten breakfast, the formal dining room at Castle Crannoch was a monument to the family's history. There were claymores, shields, tartans, and banners hanging from the ceiling and the wall, interspersed with hunting pictures and portraits of dogs and horses. It was the most fantastic juxtaposition of really bad art she'd ever seen in her entire life.

To her relief, Robert was already seated at the table. Not at the head of it, but to his uncle's left. Rowena was on Cameron's right. Another place was set far down on the left side of the table, far enough to be considered an insult. She took her place without comment, nodding to the family. The only response she received was Robert's smile.

Dinner was a strange affair. Robert was in rare form, finding the silliest things about which to giggle. Otherwise, however, the young duke minded his manners without being prompted to do so.

Rowena Gordon ignored her for the entire meal. Whenever Cameron addressed a remark in her direction, Rowena affected to study the sconce on the far wall, no doubt measuring the length and width of the candle since the last time she had done so.

Was Rowena Gordon jealous of every female at Castle Crannoch? Was it simply because Beatrice was new or that she'd been hired without Rowena's consent?

"Were you in London long, Mrs. Gordon?" she asked.

Once again, Rowena studied the sconce. Was she going to answer her? Or simply ignore her again? Equal parts of embarrassment and irritation made Beatrice wish she hadn't asked.

"Not long, no. But long enough, perhaps."

"Two months, Miss Sinclair," Cameron said.

"Did you find London to your liking?"

"I enjoyed it as well as I was able, being separated from my husband."

"They say that sooner or later the entire world goes to London."

"Do they?" Rowena smiled absently, in that exasperating way beautiful women do, as if they could not be bothered to curve their lips. Perhaps the effort was too exhausting, and they needed to save their energy for flirtatious glances and fanning themselves.

She should not be so intent upon initiating a conversation with the other woman. Yet, politeness dictated she at least attempt to do so. Rowena, however, was making it exceedingly difficult to be polite.

Finally, the woman looked directly at her, the first time she'd done so during the whole of dinner.

"What are your qualifications to be the Duke of Brechin's governess, Miss Sinclair? Have you impeccable references?"

She had no references.

Beatrice glanced at Cameron Gordon, who was watching her with an inscrutable expression on his face, almost like a cat watching a mouse. There was going to be no assistance from him. Why? Because she'd dared to challenge him this morning?

Once again, she had the thought she'd be better off simply marching down the mountain. She'd find some

type of employment. Better yet, perhaps she'd even return to Edinburgh with Devlen when he next visited.
Surely in Edinburgh she could find a position with a
normal family.

As it was, however, she needed to answer the woman.

"While it is true my stitchery is not very competent,"
she said calmly, "I can read three languages. I speak
French as well as Italian and German, and can converse
on a variety of subjects secular or religious. I've helped
tutor young men in Latin, and I've had sufficient training in mathematics, geography, and economics."

"It seems you're talented in a variety of tasks, Miss
Sinclair. However, you need not narrow your employment to that of a governess. You could be suitable for a
diversity of employment, such as a milliner's assistant
or a barmaid, for example."

"I've no interest in hats, and while I don't object to
spirits because of any moral stance, I simply cannot
abide the smell of ale. Oddly enough, the owner of the
tavern at which I applied thought I was too old and ugly
to be employed by him." She looked directly at
Rowena. "I'm gratified you don't feel the same."

She didn't mention she'd no longer had a choice as to
what she would do. She had to become employed or sell
her body for a meal. "Virtue" was a word having meaning only for the well fed, the warm, and the secure.

Had she simply exchanged one set of problems for
another? Perhaps, but the present set of problems came
equipped with a well-stocked larder and a salary that
had been mentioned in passing but still had the power to
make her jaw drop in shock.

She forced a smile to her face, and returned to her dinner, wishing Rowena Gordon had remained in London.

Dinner was excellent, roast beef and duckling, each in a creamy sauce, vegetables, and a wonderful sweet torte that was so light it almost floated off the plate. But Beatrice couldn't help but wonder if being fed, however fulsomely, was enough to offset living a furtive life among people who suspected each other of unspeakable acts and hidden desires.

For the first time, she could understand why Robert didn't want Cameron to know about the incident in the woods. The two of them, boy and governess, exchanged a glance. She smiled, a look of collusion, and vowed to keep his secret.

"I didn't expect to see you home so soon, sir." Saunders stepped back, placed his fingers deftly around the collar of Devlen's snug jacket and helped him skin it off.

"To tell you the truth," Devlen told the other man, "I didn't expect to return home this early."

He walked into his library, satisfied when he noticed his staff had lit all the candles in the sconces and the oil lamps on the mantel and the desk.

"Was the gathering not to your taste, sir? I understand some members of the royal family were to be in attendance."

"They were, Saunders. Edinburgh society was graced tonight with a few inbred cousins and more than enough titles to throw around. They would have, I believe, gladly dispensed with the titles in exchange for another fortune or two. Why is it, Saunders, that the higher up in society one goes, the more one affects not to need money and yet the more one must have it?"

"I'm sure I don't know, sir."

"You may go," he said, dismissing the other man

with a flick of his hand. Saunders disappeared from a room with a relieved sigh.

Devlen was used to being alone, but this last week, he'd begun to crave company. He disliked mysteries, especially those of his own nature. Why was he so restless?

The knock on the door was unexpected, and he turned, waiting.

Saunders peered inside the room, his usual affable appearance marred by a disconcerted expression.

"Sir, you have a visitor."

"At this hour?" He glanced at the mantel clock. Nine o'clock. Not late enough to retire, but certainly too late for a business appointment.

"A Mr. Martin, sir. He says it's vital he speak with you."

Martin was the owner of a company he was thinking of buying. The man had developed a type of percussion powder that interested him. His company, however, was lamentably run, without organization, and in financial chaos. Martin was facing ruin, unless Devlen purchased the sagging company as well as the man's new invention.

Devlen sat behind his desk and nodded to Saunders.

When Martin was ushered into his library, he gestured to the chair opposite his desk.

Martin sat, hat held tightly between his hands.

"Have you thought about my proposal?" Devlen asked.

"I have. I don't want to sell. But I've no choice, have I?"

"You always have a choice. I don't want it said I browbeat you into a decision."

He stood, offered the man a glass of whiskey. Martin took it, drank it too quickly, and set the tumbler down on the edge of the desk. Devlen took his own glass and returned to his chair.

"I want to be partners instead of giving you everything. I'll sell you half."

He raised one eyebrow. "What good is half a company to me?"

Martin didn't answer.

Devlen leaned back in the chair, waiting.

Because I have the knowledge and you don't. Because I'll make you money. Because I'll keep my new invention unless you agree to my terms. All comments Devlen expected to hear from the man sitting opposite him.

Martin, however, simply stared down at his hat and remained mute.

Devlen had no patience with people who couldn't define exactly what they wanted and how they wanted it. A man should always be able to articulate his wishes and goals.

"Well?"

Still, the man didn't look at him.

"Why would it be to my advantage to buy half your company? I'm not used to being a partner. I prefer to own things outright."

Martin looked up. Devlen was horrified to note tears in the other man's eyes.

"It's all I have."

Devlen stood and walked to the window.

A more compassionate man might have given in at that point. But he'd never been judged as exceptionally compassionate. Shrewd, yes. Sensible, certainly. Dogmatic, intense, ambitious, all labels he accepted because society insisted upon tagging its members.

"Are you married, Mr. Martin?" He didn't turn to look at the other man.

"Yes, I am. Twenty years now."

"Do you love your wife?"

"Sir?"

Devlen turned to face the other man. "A curious question, but humor me. Do you love your wife?"

Martin nodded.

"How did you decide you loved her?"

The other man looked confused, and Devlen couldn't blame him.

"Well, it was an arranged marriage, sir. Her father knew my father."

"So, you decided you loved her after a few years?"

Martin smiled. "More like a few weeks. She was a pretty little thing, with blond hair and the prettiest eyes. Hazel-like, but if she wore a blue dress, they were blue. She has this green thing she likes to wear for special occasions, and I could stare at her eyes for hours when she does. It's like they're pools or ponds." He shook his head and stared down at his shoes.

"Do you love her for her appearance, Mr. Martin?"

He rapidly shook his head, his attention still on his shoes. "She's the kindest soul I've ever known. She'll rescue a person as soon as she will a stray dog, Mr. Gordon. You might even say she's rescued me."

"Then your company isn't the only thing you have, Mr. Martin. It's not even the most important thing in your life."

Martin looked up at him curiously. "You believe a man's marriage is more important than his business, sir? Then why have you never married?"

Devlen returned to his desk.

"You haven't given me a good enough answer, Martin. Why should I settle for half?"

Martin had run his company into the ground. He'd taken a brilliant idea and let it fester. Yet, if the man had been able to verbalize an idea, a solution, or even a proposition, he might have, for the sake of experimentation, given the man the money and written it off as a bad debt.

"What I'll pay you is more than your company's worth, Mr. Martin."

"But it's mine."

"Then keep it." He leaned back in his chair. "You came to me initially, as I recall. You asked me to buy your company. Have you changed your mind?"

"I'm ruined if you don't. I've lost everything if you do."

"Then it seems you have some decisions to make."

He stood and picked up a bell on the corner of his desk. When the door opened and Saunders peered inside, Devlen glanced at his visitor again. "See Mr. Martin to the door."

Before the man left the room, he glanced back at Devlen. "Why did you ask me all those questions about my wife?"

"Curiosity, and nothing more."

Martin didn't look convinced. As he turned to leave, Devlen spoke. "I'll give you five days, Mr. Martin. At the end of that time, I'll either buy your company or I'll walk away from my offer."

After the other man left, he returned to the chair behind his desk.

Martin wasn't the only one who needed to make a decision.

He didn't want to sit and work, didn't want to retire, read, or occupy himself in mental pursuits. He was restless, annoyed, on edge. He was never this uncertain of himself. He could always find something meaningful to do. Meaningful, in this instance, translated to expanding his empire. He liked money, liked what he could do with it, enjoyed the power of it, as well as the fact his worth—as far as society gauged it—was built on his bank balance and not his character.

Some would rate him among the most eligible bachelors in Scotland.

There was never a time when his conscience bothered him. Before he made a decision, he analyzed it thoroughly, considering every angle, every permutation of its effect. He was sometimes brutal in his assessment, but he never lied, either to his business associates or those others would classify as his enemies. Perhaps his emotions were involved, but they were so tempered by reason he didn't experience any highs or lows in success or failure. He didn't gloat.

Are you very rich? Does it make you happy?

Beatrice Sinclair. Why was she so often in his mind?

He'd never before met a woman so like him in the directness of her speech. The look of horror on her face when she'd said something particularly pointed was something he'd come to look for more than the comment itself.

Most of the time she acted as if she didn't care what he thought of her.

What *did* he think of her?

She was a woman of Kilbridden Village, a governess to his cousin, an employee, a servant of the family. A woman of mystery.

He returned to his desk and began writing his list for the next day. Every night he did the same, concentrating on the responsibilities he set for himself in the morning. He'd always had the ability to focus intently on a task until it was accomplished. Until it was done, he allowed nothing or no one to interfere.

His life was marked by goals, never further from his mind than a thought.

Ever since he had left school, he'd known exactly what he wanted: to be richer than anyone he knew, to own more property than any other Scotsman of his acquaintance, to create an empire. He'd spent every single day in the accomplishment of these goals.

That was not to say he didn't enjoy pleasure. In seeking enjoyment, he knew a respite would only make him stronger, better, and sharper for the next event, acquisition, or business meeting. He deliberately planned some time in each day for enjoyment, either through a good horse, a relaxing game of cards, or even the attention of a favorite mistress.

He hadn't ridden in days, he wasn't in the mood for games, and the fact he didn't call upon Felicia was a warning so dire it signaled the reason he was annoyed and irritated.

Beatrice Sinclair.

Why her, of all people? Why was she sticking in his mind like a particularly attentive burr?

She was a bit pale, and too slender for his taste. He wondered what a month at Castle Crannoch would do for her. Fatten her up, no doubt, and add luster to her hair. But would being Robert's governess dismiss that stricken look in her eyes?

Strange, he didn't have many protective impulses.

He was known as a demanding lover but a generous one. When he ended a relationship with a woman, he always bestowed something lovely and expensive on her, a gift by which to remember him.

Whenever he saw a recently dismissed mistress in the company of another man at one of the society soirees which nowadays bored him to extremes, she'd be flashing a bracelet, or brooch, or a particularly fine diamond necklace he'd purchased in Amsterdam. He'd nod and she'd incline her head, the two of them utterly polite to each other, conveniently forgetting the last time they saw each other she was flushed from weeping as he'd abruptly ended their affair.

He walked to the window and stared out at the night. Perhaps what he needed to do was dismiss his current mistress and install someone else in her place.

Miss Sinclair?

Hardly the type he'd pick for a mistress. She was too argumentative. Too . . . intelligent? She hadn't discussed hats once in their conversations. Nor had she asked him if he liked her dress in a thinly veiled solicitation of a compliment. He hadn't, of course—her clothing was nearly threadbare. Her hands were too red, her fingers callused. She'd done more than her share of physical work before coming to Castle Crannoch.

She was a prideful thing, with her habit of forcing a smile to her face, one that never quite made it to her eyes. He'd like to hear her laugh, long and loudly, as if genuinely amused. He'd like to buy her chocolate and watch her savor it with delight. He'd like to see her in a red dress, something to flatter her unusual coloring and bring a sparkle to those fascinating light eyes of hers.

He wanted to talk to her again, that's all. A little curiosity had never made him irritable before.

He forced himself to return to his desk and concentrate on his list. He'd just purchased part of a shipyard in Leith along with two new ships, the new clippers that would add to the China trade.

A woman didn't cause this mild irritation; it was simply inactivity.

He wasn't a man like Martin, incapable of deciding what he wanted.

Yet, it was all too clear he wanted Beatrice Sinclair.

Damn it.

Chapter 17

A ccording to Robert, Cameron Gordon had made the library his. Beatrice had no wish to be near him, and with the arrival of Rowena Gordon, it was even less wise.

For a week she and Robert had met in the attic schoolroom. His lessons were done from Beatrice's memory. He wanted to learn geography the most, and they began with the British Empire. She had a love of antiquity, and all too soon they were talking about Egypt and the recent discoveries of an entirely unknown civilization.

The time had come, however, to invade Cameron's library. Consequently, she chose dawn one morning to survey the library shelves for books she needed to continue Robert's education. From what she'd been able to ascertain, his father had grounded him well in the basics. She needed to include Latin, a study of history, and some literature to provide him a well-rounded body of knowledge.

She felt guilty for not having told anybody about the incident in the woods. She felt even worse when she realized there wasn't anyone at Castle Crannoch who genuinely cared about the child. Rowena's attitude had been cold. Cameron's had been critical. Devlen was the only one who'd shown Robert any warmth. Perhaps, if he returned soon, she'd confide in him.

The library door looked like it dated from the castle's origins, the oak studded with many tiny wormholes, and the iron banding pitted and scarred. She pushed down on the latch and opened the door cautiously, half-expecting Cameron to be seated inside. Blessedly, however, he was nowhere in sight.

Beatrice stepped across the threshold and held her breath in delight. She'd expected, perhaps, a few volumes in a room as old and worn as the door. But it was evident someone cared for the library. Of all the chambers, this was the true heart of Castle Crannoch.

The predominant color of the room was burgundy, and it was present on the upholstered chairs sitting before the desk and those in front of the fireplace. The drapes flanking the two large windows on either side of the fireplace were of a burgundy velvet as were the valances embroidered with the crest of the Duke of Brechin in gold.

There was a space behind the desk, and she realized the chair was missing. No doubt to make it easier for Cameron to wheel himself into position. Tall bookcases covered the other walls, and each of them was filled with volumes encased in leather and gilt bindings.

Sconces hung discreetly between the bookcases, and two ornate brass lanterns sat on each end of the desk, on either side of the burgundy leather blotter. She went to the desk and lit one of the lanterns from the candle in her hand. The soft glow was enough to read the spines.

A narrow ladder was propped up against one of the bookshelves. She made her way around the desk and grabbed the bottom of the ladder, pulling it out a little bit more so it would be safer to mount. She climbed the steps, daring herself as she did so. Even though she was not comfortable with heights, and could feel herself trembling, she made herself remain in place.

Her life could not be constrained by her fears.

One by one, she selected a volume, opened it, thumbed through it, and either chose it or rejected it based on a set of criteria only Robert would understand.

She wanted to combine the child's two great needs—talking about his parents and his education. Therefore, she selected volumes that might bring his father to mind, or might have once been selected by the older duke. She chose *Ivanhoe*, because Robert was a seven-year-old boy and such a tale might spark his imagination. The French poets were next, and she thought he might enjoy them because of his mother. By the time she was finished, she'd picked out six books, more than enough to continue their studies.

She took her time descending the two steps, and once her feet hit the floor, she shook her head at her own foolishness. She hadn't been but a foot or two off the floor, and yet it had felt as if it were five times that distance.

Reaching up, she grabbed the books from another step, and with her arms around them, turned in preparation to leave the library.

Devlen Gordon was standing there watching her.

Perhaps another woman would have made a sound of surprise. Or even giggled, and said something silly. "I didn't see you standing there." Or "When did you come in?"

Surprisingly, it felt as if she'd been waiting for him, as if he'd told her somehow in words she couldn't hear, in a language she didn't realize she spoke, that he'd be back, and soon. She'd kept a vigil waiting for him, clicking off the hours and the minutes and the seconds until he suddenly appeared again like a conjurer's trick.

Her arms tightened around the books and she deliberately curved her mouth into a smile. How foolish she should be expecting him and yet didn't want him to know.

He didn't answer her smile with one of his own. His face was solemn, his gaze piercing. He studied her as if he had never seen her before, or perhaps knew her too well, measuring her against some fixed notion of her in his mind.

Beatrice slowly withdrew one book and placed it on the desk beside her.

She was safer with the books in her arms, because without them she'd be tempted to go to him, place her arms around his waist, and lean her head against his chest, waiting for his hands to press against her back to hold her there, immobile and safe.

She removed one more book and placed it beside the first one.

Still, he didn't speak, only stood there with his arms folded, one leg crossed in front of the other. A nonchalant pose, if one could ignore the flex of the muscle in his cheek and the fact that his bearing, while appearing relaxed, was rigid. His shoulders were level, his hands tight on his upper arms, his face unsmiling.

She removed yet another book. Now there were three on the desk and three in her arms.

"I nearly killed my horses because of you."

She put another book on the table.

"I've spent entirely too much time on the road between Castle Crannoch and Edinburgh lately. The distance gives me considerable time for reflection. I've come to believe you're a woman to be avoided."

He moved away from the door and rounded the desk, making a show of studying the volumes in one of the bookcases. He withdrew a slim volume, replaced it, and removed a larger book and studied one of the drawings.

How did she answer him? The air was heavy was silence, and there was a beat to it as if a celestial drummer was measuring off the cadence of their discord.

He turned abruptly and stared at her, the book in his hands no more than a prop, something to justify his being in the library.

It was dawn, and the world outside was waking to yet another day. In some places it would bring delight and grandeur. In others, trauma and perhaps heartache. The circumstances varied with the locale. Some people would forever mark this day upon their internal calendars and say oh yes, this was the day when I lost my loved one. Or this was the day when my beloved was born. Outside this place, in a world regulated by the ordinary, people would go about their lives in decency and squalor, luxury and chaos.

Here, however, the world slowed, and time itself didn't matter.

She put another book on the desk. Now they were

equally matched. He held one book as did she. He walked behind the desk, coming toward her with an implacable and fierce look on his face. She turned and took a step toward him, unafraid and resolute.

"You've been gone nine days," she said.

"And you thought of me nearly every moment, didn't you?"

She extended her hand, the one still holding the book. He took it from her and tossed it on the top of the desk before doing the same with the volume he still held. Their hands met, their fingers entwined.

"Are you Satan himself, Devlen Gordon?" she asked, surprised he knew how often she'd thought of him.

"Some would no doubt say I am," he said, smiling for the first time. "But I don't think such a creature truly exists. We create Hell for ourselves here on earth. Why invent Satan?"

He pulled her to him with the most gentle touch, but she suspected he might be more forceful if she didn't acquiesce. She took two more steps toward him. Just their linked fingers joined them. Or perhaps it was their willingness to dare convention.

She wondered if her gaze was as smoldering as his, or if he could read a flicker of uncertainty there. Had she imagined it in his gaze?

Devlen Gordon had no vulnerabilities. No weaknesses. She almost smiled at that thought. There was not a man or woman alive who did not have his own share of fears. The wise person knew his and compensated for the lack. The fool pretended he was never afraid.

Which one was Devlen?

He was intelligent, charming, direct, and forceful. She doubted if he was also a fool. He would be wise to be afraid, wise to be cautious of what flowed between them. The emotion was too strong to be usual or normal.

Outside, she could hear the wind battering the castle. Overhead, the clouds raced to hide the dawn sun. It would be a stormy day, almost as tumultuous as this particular moment.

Slowly, he lowered her hand and took a step backward. One single step. A test, then. She knew it without his saying a word, just as she knew she was going to close the distance between them.

Beatrice took one step forward and raised her right hand to place it on the wall of his coat. The fabric was so thick she couldn't feel him beneath it, had no measure of his warmth or his heartbeat. She wanted to tunnel through all the layers of material until she felt him, his skin, his flesh.

She was no doubt doomed to perdition. Or the hell he said they created in their minds. If so, that was a demise she gladly accepted. What a shocking thing, to contemplate dying of pleasure.

He didn't move, didn't say a word when she took one more step, one foot sliding to rest between his. She raised her left hand and placed it on his chest, her fingers brushing back and forth over the fabric.

In the next moment, he reached out both hands and placed them on her arms and drew her gently forward.

He bent his head, and kissed her temple, his lips warm, the touch amazingly soft and amazingly wrong.

"I want you in my bed. I want you naked and impatient."

She shivered, and a feeling like ice traveled up the back of her spine to settle in the pit of her stomach.

Now was the time for her to tremble. Now was the time to feel fear. Instead, the ice heated and bubbled, and the shiver turned to a sigh of anticipation, as if a demon long living inside of her, deeper where she was ignorant and unaware, had suddenly come to life, making its presence known. She was Persephone and he was Hades. Yet there was no good reason for her surrender other than the sheer joy of it.

She hurt in places she shouldn't hurt.

He breathed against her ear. She turned her head and brushed her lips against his bristly cheek. He'd traveled all night to be with her. He traveled in the darkness like a demon, and in the dawn light, he offered her a hint of depravity.

Dear God, she wanted it so.

Her lips stretched across his cheek and rested at the lobe of his ear. Her tongue licked at the very tip of it, and she felt him jerk in surprise. He pulled back and looked at her, a small smile curving his lips.

"Are you a virgin, Miss Sinclair?"

His fingers trailed from her waist, ignoring the press of her breasts against the fabric. His finger traced a T against her bodice just below her neck, as if to demarcate where he would next touch.

As a taunt, it was deliberate. As a tease, it was goading.

What did he want her to say? Touch me? She reached out and, in another daring move, adjusted his hand so it rested over her left breast.

His smile grew wider.

"I am a virgin, Mr. Gordon."

"But an impatient one, I'm thinking. Would you care to alter your state?"

"And become like the girl in the rhyme?"

"What rhyme is that?" He slowly moved his hand so he was cupping her breast, his thumb moving back and forth over her nipple. It drew up tight until it was no bigger than a pebble, aching and sensitive.

"There once was a woman named Charlotte. She began as a virgin and died a harlot."

"Ah, virtue. Another creation of people who invent Hell, I think."

"Such as ministers and clergy? Such as the righteous among us?"

"Good God," he said in a low voice, "do you count yourself among them?"

A shuddering sigh escaped her. "I doubt anyone could think that, with your hand on my breast."

"And you enjoying it."

"I was raised to be good."

"I know."

"I was raised to be good. I was."

"I know. Poor Beatrice."

He held her nipple with his two fingers, the touch keeping her restrained, and shivering with awareness.

"Come to my bed."

"No."

"Come to my bed now, and I'll lure you to do things you've never thought of doing."

"You probably would."

"You would enjoy it, Miss Sinclair. You might even scream in pleasure."

She closed her eyes and forced herself to take one step back from him.

"I want you naked, Miss Sinclair. We'll tease each other until dinner, then feast on one another for dessert."

She took another step away, her breath shallow, her blood too hot.

Then, before he could defeat the better angels of her nature, she grabbed the books and left the room, as if he were indeed the devil.

Chapter 18

B eatrice retreated to the schoolroom, grateful to notice her hands had stopped shaking by the time she reached the third-floor landing. However, the feeling hadn't gone away. Instead, she felt as if a fire was burning inside her body, the flames licking out to touch every exposed inch of skin.

She wanted to be kissed. She wanted Devlen to whisper decadent, immoral things against her cheek. She wanted him to breathe against her ear and touch his fingertips to the nape of her neck. Perhaps trace a path with his thumbs down her throat.

Why was it so difficult to swallow suddenly?

She placed the books she'd taken from the library on the table, straightened her skirt, readjusted her bodice, and pressed her hands against her hair, hoping she looked more presentable than she felt.

Robert would be here soon, and they would have a full day of learning. Perhaps, if the weather cleared, they would go outside and take a walk after lunch. Or perhaps it would be safer simply to remain in the schoolroom, a proper governess. A woman who had a strict code of behavior ingrained in her from birth and acted in a proper fashion except in Devlen Gordon's presence.

What was he doing now? Was he going to leave again soon, and why had he come back? Was it simply to seduce her?

She walked to the window and pressed her fingers against her lips. Her lips felt swollen, as if she'd spent hours kissing him.

Beatrice smiled, recalling a memory. As a girl, she'd practiced kissing the corner of her pillow late at night, a confession she'd never made to another living soul, not even Sally.

She pressed her hands against the window, feeling the cold against her palms and feeling heated inside in contrast. The ice melted on the other side of the glass and slid slowly down to the sill.

He'd touched her breasts and fingered her nipple. She pressed her palm hard against herself, feeling a tingling between her legs. He'd have touched her there if she hadn't fled.

They'd forgotten where they were. He'd not been concerned that the library was his father's lair, or that Cameron Gordon might interrupt them any moment. Then again, neither had she.

Dear God, what kind of creature was she becoming? One of a lascivious nature, that was certain. One who craved the touch of one man. In her very thoughts, she was becoming carnal.

She returned to the table and sat, organizing her

thoughts and forcing her mind from the scene in the library. Dwelling on it would only keep the yearning alive.

Better to wish him gone than to crave her own ruin.

She arranged and rearranged the books, trying to decide where she would begin—with the French poetry or the geography, or with the essays on religion? Or would it be better to concentrate on Robert's reading?

Thumbing through the French poetry intrigued her. She began to read aloud, not having spoken French for a while before coming to Castle Crannoch. The poem she'd happened on had a special significance, as if Providence itself was demanding she aspire to better pursuits than thinking of Devlen Gordon.

> 'Twas thus those pleasures I lamented,
> Which I so oft in youth repented;
> My soul replete with soft desire,
> Vainly regretted youthful fire.

How could she regret that which she'd never experienced?

Besides, she didn't want to be good, pure, or virtuous anymore. She simply wanted an ease to her life, to wake in the morning and know the day to come wouldn't be frightening, that there was enough food to feed her and warmth to keep her from being cold. She had clothing and an occupation, and some few moments of entertainment, however she devised it. There would be, in this life she created in her mind, a purpose, even if that purpose was simply to exist without pain and without lack. She wanted nothing more than these simple pleasures, and yet it had been more than she'd had for the last three months.

If Devlen was right and we created Hell in our minds, was it done to keep mankind rigorously constrained and proper? If Hell was not real, then was Heaven? If it didn't exist, then were the virtues necessary to achieve an angelic state also false? Decency, kindness, purity, were these all spurious virtues?

Or was she, perhaps, simply seeking an excuse for her depravity?

Who was she to reorder the universe? To question all she'd been reared to believe?

She stood and walked around the table, creating a restless circle from window to door and back again. The first time she circled she clasped her hands tightly together in front of her. The second time, her hands were at her back. The third time, she folded her arms in front of her, and on the fourth occasion, she met Robert coming into the door.

"Good morning, Miss Sinclair," he said, taking his seat at the table as polite and well-mannered as any young boy of her acquaintance.

Beatrice inclined her head and looked at him and mulled over the startling thought that her pupil was becoming better mannered while the teacher was descending into madness.

She sat as well, suddenly deciding which book she'd use to begin their lessons. She handed him a small volume with an intricate sketch of Castle Crannoch on the front cover.

"Did you know your father had written a book?"

He nodded and took it from her. With his arms

rigid on the table, he held the book between both hands, studying it as if it were the most wonderful treasure he'd ever imagined. For the longest moment, he didn't speak, and when he did his voice trembled just a little.

"It's the history of Castle Crannoch," he said. "He worked on it for years and years, he told me."

"Would you like to begin reading?"

He nodded and turned to the first page.

"Aloud please."

At first, his voice was halting, and she wondered if she should spend some time with him on his reading. But then, he became more involved with the words, and his voice lost its hesitancy.

" 'Castle Crannoch,' " he read, " 'was built four hundred years ago by the third Duke of Brechin. What had once been a mound of earth was transformed in two decades to a large and sprawling castle. Although no more than the south tower currently exists of the original structure, it is enough to demonstrate the building techniques, advanced for their era.' "

He continued reading, his voice impossibly young yet filled with pride, not only for his heritage, but for the man whose words he read. She sat back and studied him, wondering what there was about Robert that was so engaging. Upon her first meeting, she could have cheerfully throttled the boy.

When he was done with the passage she congratulated him on his reading.

"My father taught me," he said. "I've been reading ever since I was little."

She wanted to point out that he was still little, then

realized doing so would be foolish. His grief alone had aged him.

But even though he appeared older, he was still only seven. There was a great gulf between the responsibilities he would one day assume and the boy he was now. He was a child, despite having inherited the title and being addressed as Your Grace.

Beatrice realized her duties might well be not those of a governess, but more Robert's protector, especially in view of the shooting incident. How remarkably ill equipped she felt for the task.

They spent the rest of the morning doing math problems. Here, the young duke was as adept as he had been at reading. They'd begun memorizing the multiplication tables when a knock at the door interrupted them.

Her initial reaction was a surge of excitement followed by a frisson of fear. She both wanted to see Devlen and didn't, needed to see him, and knew it would be foolish to do so.

When the door opened, however, it wasn't Devlen but a maid. She placed a tray carefully on the table between the two of them.

"I was sent with your noon meal, miss."

"Is it that late?"

"The rest of the family has already eaten. Mr. Cameron said you must be busy with your lessons to have forgotten and all."

The girl made a quick and perfect curtsy to Robert and backed out of the room, closing the door behind her.

Robert jumped up from his chair, leaned over the table, and peered under one of the covers.

"Soup. I don't like soup."

"Then you've never truly been hungry," Beatrice said, annoyed with him. "If you were, you'd eat anything on your plate and be glad of it."

"I'm the Duke of Brechin. I'll never go hungry."

Evidently, her charge needed some education in something other than books.

"You might go hungry if there is a drought and your lush farmland withers and dies. You might if your cattle grow sick and your sheep as well. You might, if cholera kills all your workers, if the castle itself begins to crumble. You are a fortunate young man now, and I pray your luck always holds. But it's foolishness itself to think your title will protect you from hardship. You've had a lesson in loss already, Robert. Learn from it. You need to become as smart as you can in order to grow into your inheritance, to shield it and protect it for those who come after."

He didn't say anything for a moment, and when he did, his comment surprised her. "My father said the same thing."

"Did he? Then he would be proud of your showing here today. You're a good student."

"I must be, Miss Sinclair. I am the Duke of Brechin. 'To whom much is given, much is expected.'"

"Your father's words?"

He laughed, the first time he'd done so. "No, Miss Sinclair. Thomas of Aquinas."

He peered under the second cover, allowing her time to steep in her own embarrassment for not knowing the quote. "Cook has sent us cinnamon biscuits. I *love* Cook's cinnamon biscuits."

Besides two bowls of steaming soup and the beloved biscuits, Cook had also provided a loaf of crusty bread, and a pot of tea serving both as a beverage and a restorative.

Beatrice cleared off an area at the other end of the table and moved her chair around, bidding Robert to do the same. For a few moments they were occupied with their meal. She only had to correct Robert's table manners twice. Both times he looked annoyed she'd done so, and she responded to his irritation with a bright smile.

Perhaps after lunch she might address the concept of arrogance with the young duke.

She sat back and eyed their bread. She would rather have a biscuit, she decided, and picked one up and nibbled at the edge of it. Cook had outdone herself. She closed her eyes to better savor the taste. When she opened them it was to find the remainder of the biscuits had disappeared from the plate.

Robert smiled at her innocently.

She wasn't fooled. "Are you hoarding those for this evening?" she asked. "So you might have a snack before bedtime?"

His smile didn't dim one whit.

"Or are you planning on eating them all now?"

He nodded.

"I should confiscate them, you know. Or only give one to you after you've completed your geography. But you've done so well this morning I'm going to ignore the fact five biscuits have disappeared."

His smile became a little less feigned angelic and more genuine.

"I do like you, Miss Sinclair," he said.

"Because I let you have sweets?"

"Partly. I also like you because you let me talk about

my mother and father, and because you can keep a secret."

Before she could comment on that startling announcement, he stood, grabbed the loaf of bread, and went to the window. Placing the bread on the sill, he pushed open the window.

"Robert! It's cold outside!"

He stood on tiptoe and peered outside, as if looking for something. He nodded once, as if he'd found it and then grabbed the bread, tearing it into little pieces.

"But the birds are cold, too, Miss Sinclair. My father used to feed them every day. He always said God looks after the sparrows and so must we."

Was he old enough to have learned manipulation? Or could a seven-year-old boy know, instinctively, just how to tug at her heartstrings? Every single time she became annoyed at him, Robert Gordon did something that made her wish to weep.

He stood on tiptoe and continued to toss the bread out the window, feeding the birds in memory of his father.

If she had the power of God, if she were somehow blessed with the ability to raise the dead, she would summon Robert's parents back to Castle Crannoch. Their lives had been taken too quickly and their child had nearly been destroyed because of it. But she was not the Almighty and had no such power. All she could do, in her limited way, was offer what education she'd been given, and protect the child as much as she could.

"Let's keep at your lessons," she said, reaching out and closing the window, then cleaning up the bread crumbs. "You've given the birds the entire loaf. They'll be lucky if they can fly."

"Perhaps they'll waddle," he said, tucking his hands

into his armpits and making silly little flapping motions with his elbows. When she laughed, he pushed out his stomach and walked with his toes turned in.

"An amazing demonstration, Miss Sinclair. Dare I hope other lessons will be more appropriate?"

Robert froze. Beatrice turned toward the door to find Cameron Gordon sitting there. He'd appeared silently, gliding on his leather-bound wheels.

"Mr. Gordon." There was no way to explain to Cameron Gordon they had been indulging in a simple bit of nonsense. Today was the first time she'd ever seen Robert acting like a normal boy.

Robert's uncle raised one eyebrow and stared at her.

He and his son were remarkably alike in appearance. By looking at Cameron, she could almost predict what Devlen would look like in twenty or thirty years. But would Devlen ever be as embittered? Possibly, if his life had been altered by a carriage accident. She couldn't help but think, however, that Devlen would've found a way to turn the entire situation to his advantage.

"We were just finishing our lunch, Mr. Gordon. Thank you for thinking of us."

He didn't respond.

"Robert, if you'll be seated, we'll begin our lessons again."

She glanced at Cameron. "Would you care to observe, sir?" she asked, pulling the door wider.

Instead of entering the room, however, Cameron rolled back into the hallway.

How had he ever made it to the third floor? By the look on Robert's face, he wondered as well. The sanctuary they'd found for themselves was no longer inviolate.

"I think not, Miss Sinclair. But I do expect weekly

progress reports. I would like to know what Robert is learning besides levity."

"His Grace is seven, sir. A bit of levity is not going to alter his character. Indeed, it may add to it."

"You're a very surprising woman, Miss Sinclair."

And one who was going to find herself dismissed if the fact he was clenching his hands on the arms of the chair was any indication. He was obviously annoyed by her comment.

"My only concern is Robert's well-being."

"I commend your loyalty, Miss Sinclair. And your diligence. Time alone will prove whether or not I've made a very great mistake in hiring you."

With that, he slid back into the hall and snapped his fingers. Gaston appeared, placed his hands on the handles and wheeled him away.

A sigh escaped her as she closed the door.

"Are we in trouble, Miss Sinclair?"

"I'm very much afraid we are," she said, and pushed away a feeling of doom.

Chapter 19

Devlen realized that he was a fool to return to Castle Crannoch so soon after leaving.

There were a dozen women he could have called upon in Edinburgh if he'd grown tired of Felicia. Any one of them would have been pleased to see him. Some of them would have urged him to extend his stay until morning. Instead, he'd traveled through the night to have an assignation in the library with a young miss who intrigued him every time he saw her.

How did she do it?

With a directness he found curiously erotic. He was not a satyr by any means, but neither was he inexperienced. Beatrice Sinclair made him feel as if he were a hybrid of the two.

She was a distraction he didn't need at the moment. She could complicate his life. She *had* complicated his life already.

Why, then, was he anticipating dinner like a schoolboy? Why was he taking special care in his appearance? For that matter, why had he made a special trip to his tailors to ensure his newest suit of clothing was completed? Not for his father's sake, his stepmother's, or even his own.

He wanted to dazzle Miss Beatrice Sinclair. He wanted her to be cognizant of the fact other women saw him and admired him. If nothing else, she should be aware it was a great privilege and honor for him to single her out for his attention.

He had no business seducing a governess, or even dreaming about her. She was better left alone with her books and her quill and that studious little frown between her eyes. He didn't want to recall the dawning confusion her smile awoke in him.

He looked down at his hands and thought it was a test of his will that he could still feel her. The scent she wore was either fashioned from lilies or roses or something curiously and simply Miss Beatrice Sinclair.

His tailor had told him the blue wool of his coat was flattering. He'd only glanced at the man, momentarily discomfited by the look of admiration on the tailor's face.

Instantly, he'd thought about Beatrice and wondered if she would think the same.

He didn't know the chit. His only encounters with her had been odd ones. Yet during each and every occasion in her company, he'd felt enlivened, and strangely excited. Even when she attempted to defuse his lust and spear him with her intellect.

No, she certainly wasn't a bit of fluff, but neither was she someone who should bedevil him in quite this manner. Bed her and be done with it. Go to her room and make love to her all night long. Give her what she invited with those long fluttery lashes and that wise little smile. Wear her out. Wear himself out. That should ease the enchantment, or the momentary loss of his reason.

The image of doing exactly that gave him a few uncomfortable moments as he adjusted his trousers. Dinner would prove to be an interesting affair, especially if she gave him those sidelong glances of hers. He would be hard-pressed to make it through the meal.

She was a virgin. He made it a point not to bed virgins. They were too much trouble. The first time was rarely successfully executed, and he didn't want to be the source of pain to any woman.

Virgins were for marriage, not for fun. Marriage could wait. He wasn't overly eager to form an alliance with another family and have it consummated with a show of bloodletting. No, virgins were for later, when one was unavoidable.

He should have stayed in Edinburgh. He should have devoted himself to matters of work such as the contract to purchase Martin's company if the man came to some decision.

If the need for a woman grew too strident to ignore, he'd simply call upon his mistress. Felicia was pouting lately that he hadn't visited her often enough. Perhaps she'd do better with another protector.

He'd managed to come full circle in the matter of Beatrice Sinclair. Now, he was reluctant to go down to dinner. Perhaps it would be wiser for him to turn around and go back to Edinburgh with the alacrity he had made the journey from the city.

Devlen shook his head at his reflection, patted the silk stock in place, adjusted his sleeves once more, and inspected his immaculately polished shoes. He looked the perfect picture of a wealthy man. Thank God the image he portrayed didn't reveal his confusion and his sudden annoyance.

He needed to get her out of his system—assuage his curiosity, that's all. Once he learned a little more about her, she'd just be one more woman. Just one of many.

An hour before dinner, Beatrice finished dressing and made a decision. She strode down the corridor, knocked on the duke's door, and waited until she heard Robert's voice before entering his room.

Every lantern in the room had a fresh candle now flickering against the darkness. Robert was sitting on the floor in front of the bed on a large circular carpet. Arrayed in front of him were at least a hundred toy soldiers. A sheet from the bed was bunched up on one side and formed a mountain range.

He studiously ignored her, while she overlooked the fact he was being rude.

"It's very unusual for a child of your age to be with adults every night. If you weren't the duke, you'd be having your dinner with me in the schoolroom. Would you like to do that tonight? A tray, either in the schoolroom or your sitting room?"

Without looking up, Robert said, "You just don't want to be around my uncle."

"You will not stay seven years old, will you?" She shook her head. "Whenever I think you're just a boy, you say something very old and very wise."

Robert glanced up. "I feel the same way about him. My insides always get knotted up when I go down to dinner. Sometimes, I'd rather say I was sick."

"Since you've been so honest with me, I've no choice but to reciprocate. I doubt he will allow us to avoid the dinner table completely. But you look very tired today. You've spent an entire day on your lessons. I don't want to insist that you come down to dinner when you could fall asleep in your chair."

He nodded, a slow smile coming to his face. "I am very, very tired, Miss Sinclair. But very, very hungry."

"Very well, Your Grace, if you insist," she said, sighing dramatically. "I'll ring for a tray."

"Could we, perhaps, have more of Cook's cinnamon biscuits?"

"I concur," she said. She turned and left the room, grateful she wouldn't have to suffer Rowena's glowers and Cameron's intensity for one meal. Not to mention that she was pointedly avoiding Devlen Gordon—or attempting to do so.

Less than an hour later, they were seated in the sitting room attached to the Duke's Chamber, at a large circular table that had been placed in the center of the room in front of the fire. The drapes were still open, revealing the night sky, cloudless and deep, the stars flickering like the windows in Kilbridden Village. The evening was the most pleasant time she'd ever spent at Castle Crannoch.

Their dinner done, she and Robert were attempting to fairly divide up the cinnamon biscuits Cook had sent them.

"If you eat too much," Beatrice said, "you won't be able to sleep."

"I can't sleep very much anyway," Robert said with some degree of equanimity. He reached for two of the biscuits and slid them onto his plate with no apology. "But if you eat too many, Miss Sinclair, you won't be able to fit into your dresses."

Beatrice folded her arms and rested them on the table, staring at her charge. He grinned and took a bite of the purloined pastry.

"You aren't supposed to notice a woman's attire," she said, curiously embarrassed by his comment. "At least not at seven years of age."

"You'll find Gordon men are prodigies in the realm of women, Miss Sinclair. We tend to notice females early in my family."

She removed her arms from the table and sat back in the chair, not looking in the direction of the doorway. His voice was similar to his father's, but Devlen's was lower, almost a purr.

"Devlen!"

Robert abandoned his dessert, leaving the table and throwing himself at Devlen with an exuberance only demonstrated by young boys. She turned her head to witness the reunion, smiling at his excitement. Devlen bent down and effortlessly elevated the boy until they were eye to eye.

"I've been gone less than a fortnight. Has Miss Sinclair been mistreating you that much? If I'd known, I'd have returned much sooner." He glanced at her, but his look wasn't teasing. Instead, something flickered in his eyes, a look recalling this morning and their almost kiss.

"We found a schoolroom, Devlen. We cleaned and cleaned, and it's where I take my lessons now."

"Have you? No more sitting room for you, then?"

Robert shook his head from side to side.

"I missed you at dinner," he said, not looking in her

direction. The comment was for Robert, and not for her, but she couldn't help but feel a frisson of pleasure nevertheless.

"If I'd known you were here, Devlen," Robert said, "we would have come down to dinner." He glanced over at her. "Did you know Devlen had returned, Miss Sinclair?"

"Yes," she said. "I did."

Robert frowned at her. "You should have told me."

"And I will do so in the future," she said, carefully smoothing the napkin on her lap.

She wished she had the power to read thoughts. The look Robert was giving her right at this particular moment was so inscrutable she'd no clue to what he was thinking.

"Are you annoyed with me, Robert?"

He remained silent.

"Very well, Robert, whenever your cousin returns to Castle Crannoch," she promised, "I will make sure you know immediately."

Robert nodded, evidently satisfied.

Devlen turned and addressed his remarks to Robert. "Let this be a lesson to you about women, Robert. They twist the truth from time to time. The sin of omission is as great a sin as a lie."

"Are you lecturing Robert on virtue, Mr. Gordon?"

"No, Miss Sinclair, simply on women. As a species, they're not the most forthcoming of creatures."

She stood and faced him. "Have you been wounded by a woman in your past?"

His eyebrow arched and tugged a corner of his mouth with it. "Not to my knowledge."

"No unrequited loves?"

"Indeed not."

"Were you left at the altar?"

"Since I've never proposed to a woman, that would be an impossibility."

"Has a woman ever stolen anything from you?"

"Just my time."

"And your good name? Has it ever been besmirched because of a woman?"

"Isn't that normally what happens to women, Miss Sinclair?"

"Then why your antipathy? Before you continue lecturing Robert, perhaps it would be wiser for you to remember that it was not a woman who betrayed Jesus with a kiss."

"Let that be another lesson to you, Robert," he said, his gaze never veering from her face. "Do not trade barbs with an intelligent and beautiful woman. You will lose most of the time. When your mind should be on the next rejoinder, you'll be thinking how fetching she looks in candlelight. Or in dawn light, for that matter."

"And if you would like to know anything about your own species, Robert, then please be advised there are times when men are ruled by their baser instincts and not their higher ones. The mind is to be obeyed, but too often it is the loins that rule a man."

"Spoken as a woman not unaware of her capacity to stir the loins," Devlen said, smiling an altogether wolfish smile.

Theirs was hardly an appropriate topic of conversation, especially since Robert was looking from one to the other as if he were thoroughly enjoying the sparring.

She smoothed her hands down her skirt, thinking it would be better to make a hasty retreat from this room as soon as possible. Certainly before Devlen Gordon moved closer to her.

He looked splendid. He was dressed in blue, so dark it looked almost black. His eyes were crinkled at the corners as if he had spent a great deal of time outdoors or in the act of smiling. His teeth were white and even. His neck. Her thoughts stopped. Why would she suddenly notice a man's neck? Because even his neck, the part that appeared above his stock, was splendidly made. Everything about him was glorious, from his broad shoulders tapering to a narrow waist and long legs that were so muscled she could see the hint of their shape below the fabric of his trousers. And it wasn't entirely fair a man had such an attractive backside.

That was one subject she and Sally had never discussed, the fact a man could look as attractive from the rear as he did from the front.

The longer she was in the same room with him, the worse her agitation became. All day long, she had not been able to stop thinking about him. Seeing him here so finely attired, so handsome and utterly charming, was a guarantee she wouldn't be able to sleep well either.

Perhaps she and Robert should keep themselves company tonight. She'd play games with the boy through the long hours, anything to avoid experiencing this fevered longing for Devlen Gordon.

Touch me. The need was so strong she almost said the words. The yearning was there in the clasp of her hands tightly at her waist, in the fact she couldn't look up at him but stared at the pattern of the carpet under her feet.

She would have to pass him to leave the room, but coming too close to him was as dangerous as teasing the flames in the fireplace with her petticoat.

He was tall, large, and commanding. In addition, he smelled as he had before, the scent reminding her of spices and hinting at exotic locales. Never before had she noticed how a man smelled. Not once had she ever wanted to touch someone as desperately as she did now, or have him touch her. Just a fingertip, please, on the edge of her jaw, or tracing the curve of her lips.

Or, and this could be too much to ask for, then give her a kiss. Just one kiss, and she would be satisfied until the next dream, or the next time she saw him, or the next time she felt lonely.

A dangerous man, Devlen Gordon.

"Are you leaving us?"

"Yes, I must concentrate upon my lesson plan for tomorrow. I must admit," she added, smiling down at Robert, "that I didn't expect my pupil to be so advanced in so many ways. It will mean I will have to reassess what I plan to teach him."

"Indeed. Will this lesson plan take so much of your time you must leave now?"

"Are you implying something else, Mr. Gordon?"

"Every time we meet, you seem anxious to depart. Have I offended you somehow?"

He knew it wasn't that.

"May I join you in the schoolroom tomorrow?"

"Please don't," she said, too quickly for it to be anything but rude. "I prefer you don't," she said, amending her statement. "It disrupts the learning process," she said, and smiled, genuinely relieved to have come up with some plausible explanation.

"When will I see you again?"

"Why is it necessary to do so?"

"Perhaps I'm concerned as to my cousin's education."

"No."

"No?"

"It wouldn't be wise."

"I don't like being told what's wise or not, Miss Sinclair. When you know me better, you'll realize it's a challenge. I'm not a man to back down from challenges."

"Nor am I a woman to avoid them, Mr. Gordon. But don't take it as a challenge. Rather a plea."

"I can't."

She faced him finally, tilting back her head.

"I've come all this way. What a pity if the journey is wasted."

Robert was being too quiet, his interest in this conversation too apparent. If nothing else, she must think of him. She moved past Devlen and out into the hall. Unfortunately, Devlen followed her.

"When are you returning to Edinburgh?"

"I have no plans at the moment. The length of my stay depends on nothing more than my whim."

"There are no doubt matters awaiting you in Edinburgh."

"But none here? I think you're wrong, Miss Sinclair. I think there are pressing concerns at Castle Crannoch."

"Do you have a mistress?"

He smiled as if charmed by her rudeness.

"I do. Felicia is her name. A lovely woman, quite talented in a variety of ways."

"Go back to Felicia. She no doubt yearns for your presence."

"While you don't?"

"I do not, Mr. Gordon."

"I think you're lying, Miss Sinclair. A governess ought to be a paragon of the virtues she thinks to instill in her pupils, don't you agree? How can you possibly teach Robert to be an honest man if you lie?"

"I must leave," she said, hearing the quaver in her own voice and hating it. Not because it revealed her trembling uncertainty, but because every time she was around him her fascination about him grew. He knew it, surely he must.

"I must leave," she repeated, and this time he stretched out his hand to touch her as she moved past him. His fingertips grazed her hand at her waist.

She halted for a moment, and they exchanged another look. Slowly, his fingers dropped from her hand.

"I'll not keep you, Miss Sinclair. Sleep well and deeply."

The look on his face didn't quite match the amiability of his words. In fact, he looked as if he wished her a sleepless night, and tormented dreams. She didn't tell him it was altogether possible he would get his unspoken wish.

"You look disappointed that your little governess wasn't at dinner," Rowena said, standing at the threshold of Cameron's room.

She was surprised he'd answered the door or that Gaston was nowhere in sight. Was this a sign of his softening toward her? Cameron wheeled himself to the other side of the room, and Rowena closed the door behind her.

Could it be he was lonely?

"On the contrary, my dear wife, it was my son who looked bereft. Didn't you notice? Any interest I express about Miss Sinclair is simply because I'm concerned about Robert's well-being."

"To the exclusion of anyone else."

He didn't say anything, only sat and studied her. He hadn't lost his looks in the last six months. Her longing for him would have been easier to bear, perhaps, if he had.

"I admit, she is lovely, but not your type. I've always thought you liked a certain dramatic sort of woman."

"Like you, Rowena?"

She smiled.

"Like me, dearest Cameron. Except, of course, you haven't given any indication of liking my looks of late. Strange, I thought your legs didn't work. Not your manhood."

He looked startled at her bluntness. She had never before assaulted him with words. She'd attempted to seduce him. She'd hinted at her loneliness, and when nothing else worked, she'd taken herself off to London, only to realize the only way to storm the citadel was by a direct and frontal attack.

She'd no intention of allowing someone like Beatrice Sinclair to take one iota of her husband's attention away from her.

"She's frightened of you, you know. I don't know if it's because you're in that chair or simply because she doesn't like you."

"How did you come to that conclusion?"

"She avoids you at all costs, does she not?"

"What Miss Sinclair does or does not feel for me is none of my concern, Rowena."

"I could have told her, of course, that you were kinder when you were walking. You've changed, Cameron, become more angry, more embittered, more annoyed with life."

"Is there a reason for this litany of my sins, Rowena?"

"You have always enjoyed my humor, Cameron. You once said you enjoyed my intelligence. Perhaps you'll come to admire my bluntness."

She advanced on him, then changed her mind and walked toward the door and locked it.

A small smile was playing around his lips, and it angered her. She wanted to punish him for all of his avoidance, for the nights in which she'd lain awake desperate for his touch. Now, however, was not the time.

She pulled up a chair and sat beside him, loosening her wrapper. She was naked beneath the thin garment and the cold had tightened her nipples, making them as hard and erect as if she were aroused.

He didn't need to know she was almost desperately afraid at this moment, afraid he would reject her. She reached out and grabbed his hand and pulled it to her, placing his palm over her nipple.

"How you used to love my breasts, Cameron. You used to love to touch them, to pull on my nipples. To taste me."

Despite the fact he was attempting to pull his hand away, she was stronger in her need than he was in his annoyance. She took two of his fingers and deliberately stroked herself with them.

"Do you remember being inside me, Cameron? Do you remember when we would exhaust ourselves with each other?"

Before he could respond, before he could pull away and renounce her with words that would no doubt hurt and wound, she reached out her left hand and gripped him between the legs.

"You're hard for me. What do you do every night?

Do you will it away? Or you think of your Miss Sinclair and bring yourself to satisfaction?"

"I am but an animal in several ways," he said, allowing his hand to drop. "The sight of a lovely woman, any lovely woman, is enough to get me hard."

She pulled back. "Why do you hate me?"

"You know the answer to that, madam, more clearly than I could ever articulate."

"We've only been married five years, Cameron. Five years. Am I to live like this for the rest of my life?"

"Go back to London, Rowena. Find yourself a lover."

He wheeled himself to the door, turned the lock, and swung it open.

"Or coax one of the footmen to your bed, I don't care. Just don't come here again."

She stood and pulled her wrapper around her, affecting a nonchalant pose she didn't feel.

He didn't say another word to her as she left his room.

Chapter 20

Surprisingly, Beatrice slept well, waking at dawn as she normally did. This morning, like her entire stay at Castle Crannoch, was different from the mornings of the past three months, however. She was not awakened with a raging headache, an empty stomach, and an obsession for food.

She'd have liked some of the biscuits from last night, but she doubted if Robert had left any. Never mind, she'd find something to eat.

Dressing took no more than fifteen minutes, talking to herself sternly took a half an hour.

You will not flirt with Devlen Gordon.

You will not even look in his direction.

You should not wish for excitement. Or adventure. You have had enough of those since coming to Castle Crannoch.

There was something to be said for a placid life, for a sameness of routine. Ah, but that life didn't include people like Devlen Gordon, handsome and dangerous. She sighed.

Ensuring every hair was in place, and her attire was suitable for a governess took a little longer, as did washing her face and staring at herself in the mirror until the color on her face subsided. Her eyes sparkled too much, but she doubted if there was anything she could do about that. She tried to think sober thoughts, but her mind was not cooperating either.

An hour after she rose, she walked down the hall in search of her charge.

There was time before breakfast for a brisk walk. Doing so would no doubt enliven the constitution, and make it easier to sit for hours in the schoolroom during lessons.

When she mentioned as much to Robert, he looked startled at the suggestion.

"Miss Sinclair, do you think it's safe?"

Until that moment, she'd forgotten about the shooting incident. What kind of governess was she, that she could forget such a horrid thing?

"We'll stay close to the castle," she said. "But we need some fresh air. And despite the fact it's cold, it looks to be a fair day."

In fact, it was nothing of the sort. The sky was cloudy, and it looked like snow, but her mood was such it could have been a bright summer day.

She bundled Robert up in his greatcoat while she wore her dark blue cloak. Once they were out of the castle, she turned to Robert.

"Are you going to tell your cousin about what happened?"

He looked straight ahead, and she wondered if he

was going answer her. After several silent moments, he sighed.

"Do you think I should?"

They walked for a few minutes, rounding the front part of the castle.

She hadn't expected him to ask her opinion. She turned the question on its ear and back to him. "Do you think you shouldn't?"

He stopped abruptly, and stood there thinking. After a moment, she noticed he was trembling.

"Robert? What is it?"

He raised his arm and pointed, his finger shaking.

"Look, Miss Sinclair. The birds."

She followed his glance, then walked past him, staring down at the dozen or more birds lying dead on the ground, their plump gray bodies surrounded by a few chunks of frozen bread.

"Go and get Devlen," Beatrice said, as calmly as she could.

Robert didn't ask any questions, only set off in a run to obey her.

She thrust her hands into the cloak and tried to assume an aura of nonchalance, of outward calm. Inside, however, she was panic-stricken. She clasped her hands together, and stood looking down at the dead birds. Above them was the schoolroom. She tilted her head back and viewed the window where yesterday Robert had been so excited to be feeding the birds. If she thought about what she saw, she might well scream. Or run as far from Castle Crannoch as she could.

Neither action would be helpful or productive.

Despite her resolve, however, she couldn't help but

feel the first cold icicles of fear. Someone was trying to harm Robert. First, the shots, which she had tried to pretend were an accident, and now the birds. This, however, was even more horrible. Someone had actually poisoned his food. Someone inside Castle Crannoch. Someone who wanted a child dead.

Who?

Was Cameron Gordon so bitter about being disinherited by a seven-year-old child that he'd want Robert dead?

Another icicle of fear slid down her back. She could have easily eaten the bread, too.

If it hadn't been for the child, she might have given her notice on the spot. Though poverty, the loss of her pride, possibly even starvation was all that awaited her back in her village, at least she would be alive, and it's doubtful anyone would care enough to wish her dead.

Beatrice heard the running footsteps and felt an easing of that curious, immobilizing fear. She turned her head and watched as both Devlen and Robert entered the clearing.

Devlen didn't say a word either in greeting or reassurance. He glanced down at the dead birds, looked up to the window high above, then bent to retrieve a piece of the bread.

"Did I poison them, Devlen?" Robert asked, his small voice out of keeping with his usual bravado.

He was an intelligent child. Too intelligent, perhaps. Surely she should say something to assuage his worry, to ease his mind. But she had never been a good liar. There was no hope of sheltering him or shielding him from the truth. But she reached out anyway and enfolded him in her arms, pressing his cheek against her waist.

She spoke to him the way a mother might, saying, "It's all right. It's all right." Nonsensical words, in actuality, because she wasn't at all sure things were going to be all right. But he didn't challenge her, only held on to her waist with both arms, as if she had suddenly become his anchor.

Even through the heavy wool of his coat, she could feel him tremble, and suddenly the child's fear made her angry.

Devlen stood, and she looked up at him, her eyes dry and furious.

"This is not right," she said. "For whatever reason someone is doing this, it's not right." She glanced down at the child. "Tell him, Robert," she urged.

He looked up at her, then over at Devlen.

"He'll get mad."

"I doubt he will."

"Why am I being talked about as if I'm not standing here?" Devlen said. "What will I get mad about, Robert?"

"He won't get mad, Robert. I promise," she added, glancing at Devlen.

He nodded.

Robert told him about the shooting. As the story progressed, she watched Devlen become more and more rigid until his spine could have been made of iron.

"Go and pack your things," he said.

Her grip tightened on Robert. "You do not have the power to dismiss me. Nor will I leave."

"Your loyalty is admirable," he said in an unconscious repetition of his father's words earlier. "However, I have no intention of dismissing you. Pack Robert's things as well. You're coming to Edinburgh with me."

Robert was in danger, but then again so was she. Not, this time, from someone who wanted her dead. As they exchanged a look, she knew full well if she went to Edinburgh with him she might well be putting herself in peril.

"Will you come?" he asked, his voice soft, low, and dangerous.

She had no choice, and yet she had a world of choices.

"Yes," she said, in agreement with her own ruin.

Devlen turned to his cousin.

"Would you like to come to Edinburgh, Robert?"

Robert pulled back, releasing his grip on Beatrice's waist.

He nodded. His eyes were red, traces of tears still on his cheeks. Beatrice smoothed his hair back and placed her palm on his hot cheek, feeling an incredible tenderness for the young duke.

"Then we should go and pack," she said. "Shall we make a game of it? Who'll be the first to finish?"

"You, Miss Sinclair. I have so much more than you. I must take my soldiers, you see."

"Do not pack too much, Robert," Devlen said with a smile. "Think of my horses."

She forced an answering smile to her face and took Robert's hand. There were times as an adult when she had to feign an emotion until it was real. But now she found herself in the curious position of having to hide what she felt.

"I'm half-tempted to put you in a carriage now, without giving you time to pack. How soon can you be ready?"

"A quarter hour," Beatrice said, shortening the time she needed by half. But she was nearly desperate to leave Castle Crannoch, and if doing so quickly meant her valise was packed in haste and her clothing was wrinkled, she truly didn't care.

"Then do so," he said. "I'll have my coach brought around."

She walked with Robert to the front of the castle, realizing she could easily have abandoned anything in her room. She didn't feel comfortable staying at Castle Crannoch anymore. Something was desperately wrong here, something so evil and pervasive it seeped through the very bricks.

Suddenly, she wanted her old life back. Not the way it had been a month ago, but as it was a year ago, with her parents alive and her content, if a little restless.

She had wanted something to happen, and dear God it had, but not quite in the way she'd expected. Was God a literal deity? Should she be careful about the wording of her prayers?

Then let her amend them. She wanted peace in the morning and a feeling of contentment during the day. She wanted laughter and lightness in her heart, and a dozen other pleasant emotions.

"Is it going to be all right, Miss Sinclair?"

"Of course it is," she said crisply, her voice conveying no uncertainty, no hesitation. Robert mustn't know of her own fears.

Less than half an hour later, they left Castle Crannoch. Together, she and Robert walked slowly to the coach, all the while Beatrice expecting to hear her name being called. But Cameron Gordon didn't shout for her to return with her charge. No one knew they were leaving.

She opened the coach door herself and unfolded the steps, urging Robert into the carriage. She followed him and sat next to him, taking his hand and holding it between her ungloved ones. The day was cold, the hint of snow still in the air, but someone had thought to furnish a brazier and it sat on the floor of the carriage, the glowing coals inside the pierced brass vessel radiating heat.

"I think someone's trying to kill me, Miss Sinclair."

"Don't be silly," she said, her voice pure governess. "The incident in the woods was a hunter, and the poor birds outside the schoolroom window had just frozen to death. The temperature is cold enough for it."

Robert didn't look convinced.

Finally, she relented. He was too intelligent, and she'd been too dismissive. "I don't know what's happening, Robert. But I don't like it."

He nodded, as if he approved of her honesty.

She opened up the shade.

"I think it's going to snow soon, Robert, perhaps during our journey to Edinburgh."

He nodded and stared out the window. She would much rather have him be acting like the aristocratic little snob she'd first met than this silent waif.

"Do you like the snow, Robert?"

He shrugged, but otherwise didn't answer her.

"I like the snow very much," she said, well aware she was sounding a little like a woman she knew in her village. The poor dear had a comment about anything and everything, and couldn't manage a quiet moment in the entire day. "I think it's beautiful to see, especially when it clings to the branches of the trees. At night, when it snows, it's like a full moon. The night is not quite so dark, is it? Snow seems to glow."

A thought struck her, one tinged with horror. Had someone tried to kill Robert in his sleep? Was that why the child was plagued with wakefulness?

I think someone comes into my room at night.

Dear God.

"I don't think I've ever seen the snow at night, Miss Sinclair," he said, looking interested.

"Then we'll just have to arrange it, won't we?"

"My father used to say you can't arrange nature. If we could get rain when we needed it, all farmers would be wealthy men."

"I think I would've liked your father." The eleventh Duke of Brechin sounded like a very pragmatic man with a generous spirit, a father who honestly loved his child.

The door opened, and Devlen stepped into the coach. Instantly, it felt warmer inside, and much smaller.

His fingers brushed against her skin in passing, alerting the fine golden hairs on her arms.

Gently, she pulled away, disliking the touch. No, liking the touch, but disliking the feeling of vulnerability being so close to him gave her.

He made her feel weak and feminine, as if she needed his strength and the very fact he was male. She wanted him to put his arm around her and hold her close, shelter her, protect her. She'd never before had such thoughts.

Devlen gave the signal to his driver, and the carriage began to move. Blessedly, he concentrated on the passing scenery and the faint flutter of snow.

"Do you still have your guns in here?" Robert suddenly asked.

Devlen smiled. "I do. I carry them with me at all times."

"In case of robbers," Robert said to Beatrice. "Devlen sometimes carries a lot of gold with him."

"Really?"

"I only carry the pistols to protect myself." He reached over and pushed against the wall of the carriage. Instantly, a small rectangular section popped open, revealing two gleaming guns mounted inside. "I dislike being unprepared."

"Have you ever used them?"

"Once."

"I trust you will not have to do so on this journey."

"I will protect that which I believe to be valuable."

What did he consider valuable? Or whom? His cousin, surely. Her? A woman who'd exchanged barbs with him, a village inhabitant with an expansive education taught by books but little experience in life. Would he consider her as valuable?

He said something to Robert, who smiled in return, the exchange one of longtime friends, confidants, almost brothers.

The descent down the mountain was done with some caution, she was happy to note. There was little need for haste even though she wanted to be as far from Castle Crannoch as she could be, as quickly as possible.

She glanced at Robert to find him yawning. "You didn't sleep well last night," she said.

He only nodded.

Robert shifted in the seat, leaning his head back against the cushion. She spread the blanket over his legs.

"You can put your feet up here," she offered, "if you'd like to stretch out a little more."

"It isn't polite," he said, once more the proper young duke.

Beatrice smiled, amused that Robert vacillated between an old-fashioned courtliness and an autocratic arrogance.

She patted her lap, and he was finally convinced to prop his feet up on the lap robe. He arranged one of the blankets behind him as a makeshift pillow and burrowed beneath another until only his nose showed.

Within moments, he was asleep.

In the snug carriage, with the brazier heating her feet and her legs kept warm from the blanket she and Robert shared, it was difficult to remember they might be in danger.

She pretended an interest in the increasing snowfall, but in actuality she was studying Devlen.

All in all, it was an arresting face, one drawing her gaze time and again. Was she the only woman to feel so attracted, or did Devlen Gordon simply have that effect on all females in his environment? When he walked into a crowded ballroom, did every woman there turn to regard him? Were they coy in their glances? Or did they make no secret of their fascination for him?

He glanced at her then, as if he had the power to understand her confusion and her curiosity. A corner of his lip curled upward, a mocking acceptance of her studious assessment.

"What can you be thinking, Miss Sinclair?"

"I was thinking you must charm women," she said, giving him the truth with no reluctance whatsoever.

He looked momentarily disconcerted, and she vowed from that moment always to be direct with him. Doing so equalized them. He was evidently unfamiliar with those who spoke the truth, and she was equally so with those who spoke falsehoods.

"I have no lack of companions, if that's what you're asking."

"I wasn't, actually. You've already spoken of Felicia. Are you bragging? Or simply letting me know how many women you have?"

"You're very constrained, Miss Sinclair."

"Am I?"

"I've never seen a woman as constrained as you."

"Is that as great a sin in your eyes as the ability to stretch the truth?"

"It's a characteristic that concerns me, oddly enough."

She fisted her hands in her lap and glanced at him. "Why is that?"

"You're too calm. I've never seen you angry, although I've given you ample reason to be. You might be afraid, but you don't appear to be."

"Why should I indulge in drama?"

"Who hurt you, Miss Sinclair?"

For a moment she could only stare at him, flummoxed.

"Was it life itself? Too much unexpected grief? Too many disappointments?"

"Are you this rude to every woman of your acquaintance?"

"Most women don't incite my curiosity. They bore me, instead. But you, Miss Sinclair, are a different situation entirely."

"Should I pray to be boring, Mr. Gordon?"

"It's too late for that. I'm already intrigued."

She looked out the window at the falling snow. The winter scene was starkly beautiful. There was no reason to be touched to tears, but she suddenly wanted to cry. Or worse, confide in him about the previous year, living in the cottage after burying her parents. Systematically burying her friends, too, while she waited for cholera to sicken her.

Over the years, she'd developed her mind, and whenever emotions persisted, she allowed them some freedom before restraining them and tucking them back into their proper place. Even her grief had been similarly controlled. She needed to concentrate on living in the present.

After all, she was pragmatic and practical, a survivor.

She turned to face him again. "Shouldn't you be more concerned about what's been happening to Robert?"

The incident in the woods and the dead birds were enough to be concerned about.

"I'll protect Robert. You needn't worry. For that matter, Miss Sinclair, I'll protect you."

"Physically, Mr. Gordon? Or morally?"

There, the challenge was out in the open.

He only smiled.

An image of his black-on-black coach thundering through the countryside, faintly illuminated by the lanterns on the outside, came to her. He'd terrified her the first time she'd seen it.

She'd be a fool not to be afraid. How odd she wasn't. The emotion coursing through her wasn't remotely like fear.

"For someone who dislikes the dark, you certainly use it to your advantage."

"I don't sleep very much. Three hours at the most. Why waste the time?"

She had no answer for that.

The snow fell in a cloud of flakes, as if they were feathers wafting on the chilled breeze. They clung to every surface, trees, bushes, and grass, transforming the world into a white fairyland, a place so delicate and ethereal it stopped her breath.

Her eyes tickled with unshed tears. An odd moment to cry. Or perhaps the best moment, after all. There was so much loveliness in the world, the same world in which there dwelt so much horror. A paradox, one in which they were forced to live.

She wanted something at this moment, something she couldn't quite define or explain. Something that would answer the restlessness deep inside her. She was either hungry or lonely or distraught and more than a little curious as to why she couldn't identify the feelings completely. Perhaps it was because all this time, she'd cocooned herself, protecting herself from the grief and fear that were too painful to experience on a daily basis. Perhaps she was separated from her own discomfort, like stubbing her toe and not feeling the pain until hours later.

Was she just now recognizing the full extent of her own loneliness?

Devlen Gordon made it difficult not to feel. Every time she was in his presence, she was different . . . alive, somehow. As if he had the capacity to stir her— or awaken her—in some way.

He was too strong a personality, too forceful to ignore. Nor could she avoid the fact that he was so quintessentially male. There were times, like now, when she wanted to reach out and touch him, to see if the muscles hinted at below his shirtsleeves were truly real.

Her gaze was entirely too intent on his trousers. She was even curious about his feet, encased in knee-high boots. His chest looked too broad to be completely real, and she had the absurd and horrified thought that perhaps he wore padding beneath his clothes.

Not Devlen Gordon. He wasn't the type to engage in artifice. He was more the kind of man who would dare society to judge him for what he truly was—handsome or ugly, short or tall, rich or poor.

But of course he was handsome, tall and rich, and the relative of a duke. No doubt he was extremely popular in Edinburgh.

"Why haven't you ever married?"

"Is it any of your concern, Miss Sinclair?"

"None at all."

"You're very curious. In that, we're alike. If I answer your question, will you forfeit one to me?"

She didn't answer for a moment.

"Afraid?"

"Not afraid," she said. "Wise, perhaps."

"Perhaps I'll ask you something improper."

"I expect you to."

"Then why the hesitation?" Devlen asked.

"I'm trying to decide if I'll answer."

He smiled at her again.

"Shall I start then? The answer to your question, Miss Sinclair, is that I've never made the time for marriage."

"The time?"

"Courtship takes a measure of time I've never been willing to spare."

"Not to mention emotion," Beatrice said.

"There is that."

"Have you ever been in love?"

"Ah, but it was only one question. I think it's my turn now. Have you ever been in love, Miss Sinclair? Not an improper question after all."

"No. Never."

"A pity. The emotion is said to be very heady."

"Really?"

"Love makes fools of us all, I've heard."

"Have you?" Beatrice asked.

"Can't you envision me playing the fool, Miss Sinclair?"

"Not unless it was to your advantage, Mr. Gordon."

His smile broadened. "You think me a cynic?"

"Aren't you?"

"Cynicism is just another word for wisdom."

"So, you're too wise to fall in love?" she asked.

"I don't think love has anything to do with wisdom. I think it simply occurs when it will."

"Like a bolt of lightning?"

"Do you believe in love at first sight, Miss Sinclair?"

"No."

He laughed softly. "Now who's the cynic?"

"Why fall in love with someone's appearance? People get sick, or grow old. The character matters more than looks, Mr. Gordon. Wit, intelligence, kindness, all matter more than appearance."

"So, you would have love come after a conversation?"

"Perhaps."

"How long would it take?"

"The conversation?"

His smile chided her. "Falling in love."

"How should I know if it's never happened to me?"

"Perhaps we should talk longer, Miss Sinclair, have a few more conversations."

He looked away, and it was just as well, because she didn't know how to answer him.

Chapter 21

The weather was growing worse. The snow formed a curtain between them and the rest of the world. She couldn't see the trees or the bushes lining the road anymore, and it was evident the driver was having difficulty with the horses as well because their speed had slowed considerably. Twice, the driver had rapped on the small window separating him from the passengers, and twice Devlen had reassured him there was no need for haste.

"Take your time, Peter," he'd said on the last occasion. "We'll make an inn soon enough."

"So, we are going to stay the night?" Beatrice asked.

He sat back against the seat and surveyed her indolently. "The weather has made further travel an impossibility."

"Is it entirely proper?"

"You and I staying at an inn together, chaperoned only by my seven-year-old cousin? You alone can decide the answer, Miss Sinclair."

"I'm not entirely certain I like the way you say my name. It always has a touch of sarcasm about it."

"My apologies, Miss Sinclair. I meant no affront."

She frowned at him.

"Unless we sleep in the same chamber, I'm certain your reputation will remain as pure tomorrow as it is today. Or perhaps I am assuming too much. Is your reputation unsullied?"

She looked over at him, more than a little offended. "Of course."

"Then I should worry about other things, Miss Sinclair. Reputation does not seem to be an important one."

"Possibly because you have none to lose," she said.

But he only looked amused at her comment. "If that is your opinion of me, then you have joined a great many other people. I wonder what it is about me that makes people immediately label me a sinner?"

He glanced at her. "Do you have a great deal of experience in recognizing sinners, Miss Sinclair?"

"My father was schoolteacher, not a minister. But it seems to me with your penchant for dark coaches and traveling at night, you encourage people to think the worst of you."

"Simply because I hate to waste time, I'm now to be punished as an evildoer. How very quaint."

"Perhaps people are afraid of you. They often label as evil what they don't understand."

"Therefore, in order to counter their bad opinion, I should endeavor to make myself understandable?"

"Perhaps."

"The fact is, Miss Sinclair, that I don't care what a great many people think of me. Does my attitude surprise you?"

"Not in the least."

"There are, however, several people whose opinion I do value. Would it further surprise you to know you are among that small and select cadre?"

"Very much," she said, finding it difficult to hold his gaze.

"I find I do care what you think about me. I am not the lecher my father would make me out to be."

"I have not often discussed you with your father."

"But you have discussed me. How novel, an honest woman."

"That's not the first time you've alluded to dishonesty being a female trait. I would venture as many men are dishonest as women."

"On the contrary, it's been my experience that women as a whole do not tell the truth unless it suits their purpose."

"I think perhaps, as a representative of my species, I should be insulted."

"But you aren't, and I wonder why that is? In fact, you're rarely upset, Miss Sinclair. Do you ever cry?"

"A rather personal question, isn't it? I demand a forfeit."

"Very well. But answer first."

"No, I don't cry often."

"Why not? And before you protest, Miss Sinclair, it's only part of the original question. A clarification, if you will."

"Because I've never found tears were worth shedding. Why cry? It will not make the situation easier to bear."

"Do you ever feel any strong emotion? Anger, joy?"

"It's my turn to ask a question."

He sat back and folded his arms, waiting.

"Why do you have such a bad opinion of women? Who hurt you?"

He smiled. "I'm sorry to disappoint you, Miss Sinclair, but no one. If I have a somewhat jaundiced view of women, it's because I only view them as companions for the evening. I have no women friends, and I've rarely spent time with them unless it was in amatory pursuits."

"You should. You'd discover that women do not, as you think, use honesty or the lack of it to manipulate others."

"Then you are very sheltered, Miss Sinclair, because I could show you five or six women in Edinburgh alone who have a singular ability to do exactly that."

Despite his words, she still had the feeling he'd been hurt in the past. But Devlen Gordon was not a person for whom she should have any compassion or pity. First of all, he would be amused at it. Secondly, she doubted those poor women were ever able to harm him. More like he'd broken their hearts.

The carriage slowed even further. She flicked a finger beneath the shade and surveyed the white world outside the carriage.

"It's gotten so much colder," she said, looking up at the gray-white sky.

"I'm afraid we're in for a blizzard, sir," the driver said, peering down into the window again.

"A blizzard?" She glanced at Devlen. "Does that mean we won't be able to travel through to Edinburgh?"

"What that means, Miss Sinclair, is we need to take shelter and wait out the storm." He glanced up at Peter. "The horses will be freezing. Make for the nearest inn."

"Yes, sir."

She glanced at Devlen, surprised he should feel such compassion for four-legged creatures and none at all for women.

He smiled at her then, as if gauging the tenor of her thoughts. If so, she should mind her features with greater skill.

Less than a quarter hour later, a tall gray building appeared out of the white blur of snow. The windows were lit like welcoming beacons.

Beatrice sat back among the cushions, grateful they'd finally found shelter.

She glanced down at the sleeping boy and reached out one hand to gently cup his cheek.

"Robert," she said softly. "You need to wake."

"Leave him," Devlen said. "I'll carry him inside." There was an expression on his face she had never before seen, a tenderness oddly suiting him.

She didn't say anything in return, merely pulled the lap robe up around Robert's shoulders and tented it so his face was shielded.

The carriage stopped, and the door opened, the driver standing there coated in snow, his cheeks red as he moved from one foot to the other to warm himself.

"After you've done with the team, Peter," Devlen told the driver, "get yourself inside. You needn't stay with the horses tonight."

The man looked surprised, and Beatrice wondered if it was his habit to sleep in the stables. That impression was strengthened when Devlen held out his hand and gave Peter a small drawstring bag to his obvious surprise.

"Buy yourself something warm to drink," he said. "You've earned it, getting us here safely."

"Thank you, sir." The driver's seat face split into a smile. "Thank you, Mr. Gordon. I'll do just that."

Devlen left the coach first and helped her out. Once she was standing on the frozen ground, he reached into the carriage and emerged with Robert in his arms, the blanket half over the boy's face to protect him from the falling snow.

"Will we be able to travel in the morning?"

Devlen's smile was remarkably warm considering she could barely see him through the snow flurries.

"Shall we let the snow take care of itself? We won't know until the morning."

Until then, she had to get through the whole long night.

Despite the fact the inn was large, it wasn't especially prosperous. The greeting they received from the effusive innkeeper was so fawning Beatrice wondered if he thought them royalty. The weather had evidently driven most of his regular clientele away, and the taproom was empty except for one man sitting huddled before the fire.

"Your best rooms," Devlen said, shifting Robert's weight in his arms. He acted as if he was familiar with being obeyed and quickly.

The innkeeper bowed, still smiling. "Of course, sir. How many would that be?" He glanced at Beatrice and back at Devlen.

"Two," Devlen said. "If you do not object to staying with Robert," he said in an aside to her. "I'd prefer someone be with him, especially in view of what happened with the birds."

"Surely you don't think . . ." The rest of her question was silenced when he shook his head slightly. Now was not the time to question him as to Robert's safety, not with the innkeeper listening. "No, I don't mind," she said. The child would serve as her chaperone.

The innkeeper gestured to the stairs, and she followed, ascending the steps and hearing the two men's conversation behind her.

She hesitated at the landing and the innkeeper pushed by her, leading her to a room at the end of the hall. The second room was next door. Entirely too close.

The innkeeper opened the door and bowed to Devlen, but he made a gesture that she should precede him. The room was cold, but the fire was hurriedly lit by the innkeeper himself as he kept up a running commentary on the weather.

"This room is larger," Devlen said. "You and Robert can stay in here."

Beatrice stepped close to the window for a view of the snow-encrusted countryside. Icicles hung like frozen tears from the branches of the trees. Bushes were laden with layers of snow until they appeared like dozens of hulking shapes huddled against the wind. The road was a mirrored path, the lanternlight reflected in its icy surface.

The snow had stopped falling, and the sky had cleared, revealing a full moon hanging like a snowball in the sky. The snow sparkled, and the ice glistened. Her breath fogged up the window, and she stepped back from the draft.

On this cold night there would be no comfort to be

found outside the inn, but inside there was the warmth from the fire, a thick mattress, and plenty of blankets.

Devlen laid Robert in the high bed and removed the boy's shoes before tucking him beneath the covers.

The room she and Robert had been given was undoubtedly the inn's very best. A massive four-poster took up much of the space. What was left was occupied by a washstand, a small folding screen, and a chair sagging so much in the seat that it looked to be a castoff from the taproom downstairs.

The innkeeper melted away after showing Devlen his room, spurred on his departure by Devlen's coin. A moment later, the tavern maid left as well, and Beatrice was oddly reminded of the time when she'd been so disappointed not to get the job at the Sword and Dragon. What would her life have been like in the last two weeks?

She would not be standing here beside the window, wouldn't be surreptitiously glancing at Devlen occasionally, would not be worrying about what he was doing when he came around the end of the bed and headed in her direction. There were so many things that would not have happened, let alone the sheer excitement of his taking her hand.

"You look frightened. Are you?"

"Should I be?"

He smiled. "You never seem to answer any of my questions directly."

"Then, yes, you frighten me sometimes. Sometimes, my own reaction to you frightens me."

There, an honest answer, one without prevarication.

"Why are you afraid of me?"

She turned and looked out the window. "Because you lure me to do what I should not. Because you entice, Devlen Gordon, and your enticements are not for maidens like me."

"I normally eschew maidens, Miss Sinclair. I avoid them with all haste and vow never to bother with them. They're too much trouble, you see, and I'm a man who knows my own worth and the value of my time."

"So maidens are a waste of time?"

"I've found so, yes."

"Then I should feel safer, shouldn't I?"

"Do you?"

"Not appreciably, no."

"I've promised to protect you, don't you remember? I never break a promise."

"What if I don't wish to be protected?"

He smiled in response. "I'll go and see if the innkeeper can find us something to eat," he said, closing the door behind him. The room was suddenly much smaller.

"You like my cousin, don't you, Miss Sinclair?"

She smiled in Robert's direction, not completely surprised he'd feigned sleep.

"Yes, I do. Is that acceptable to you, Your Grace?"

He smiled sleepily. "He's a very nice man when he wants to be. But he can be ruthless."

Not a word a seven-year-old should be using to describe an adult.

"Where did you hear that?"

He sat up and rubbed his eyes. "My uncle. But I don't think he likes Devlen very much. Devlen's very rich."

"One man's ruthless is another man's determined."

He sat up, looking around. "It's not a very big place, is it?"

"But we're lucky to be out of the storm."

"Devlen would never let anything happen to his horses. He spent a lot of money for them."

"Then we should consider ourselves fortunate he has such great concern for his horses. We are therefore protected by default."

"Oh, I'm certain he would never let anything happen to me, either, Miss Sinclair."

"Yes, you're the Duke of Brechin."

He nodded. "But he loves me, too."

She found herself silenced by the wisdom of a child.

"Remember our conversation about snow at night-time?"

He nodded.

"Come and look."

He slid off the bed and came to the window. After a moment, he smiled up at her. "It looks like you could eat it, Miss Sinclair. As if Cook had spread her frosting all over the world."

Beatrice smiled. "You're right, it does."

A few minutes later, Devlen arrived at the door followed by a chambermaid. The girl bobbed an awkward curtsy, a rather remarkable feat considering she was balancing a tray filled with food.

She laid it on the table doubling as a washstand and curtsied once again. Not to Beatrice, who was rather unused to the sight, but to Devlen, who further confounded the young girl by smiling at her.

"You really shouldn't do that," she said after the maid left the room.

"Do what?"

"Smile at young things. It confuses them entirely. I noticed at Castle Crannoch you made the maids lose the ability to talk. As if their wits had flown out of their heads."

"You exaggerate."

"I speak only the truth," she said, amused at the flush coloring his cheekbones.

Could it be that Devlen Gordon was embarrassed? Or only flummoxed because she'd called him on his ability to charm the female sex?

"My cousin has always had that effect on women."

"Do you ever sound like a seven-year-old?" Beatrice asked him. "Sometimes I think you're really twenty, and you're only masquerading as a child."

"That's because I'm very intelligent."

She and Devlen exchanged looks, and she couldn't help but wonder if he felt as bemused around Robert as she often did.

But she was grateful to notice in the next few minutes he reverted to being his age as he bounced in the middle of the bed and insisted upon having a picnic there, with the cloth spread out in the middle.

"You sit there," he said to Beatrice, pointing at the opposite corner of the bed. "You, there," he said to Devlen, indicating the pillows at the head of the bed. "We'll pretend we're sitting beneath a tree at Castle Crannoch."

She'd prefer a safer place.

"I think we should envision a different scene," Beatrice said. "Somewhere we've never seen before."

"The moors outside of Edinburgh," Devlen contributed. "Beneath a large oak tree."

"Pine," Beatrice countered. "Pines smell so much better."

"I wasn't aware oaks smelled."

"Which proves my point."

She reached for one of the crusty rolls as Devlen did. Their fingers met, touched, and she reluctantly withdrew her hand.

Robert reached down into the basket and grabbed a roll and handed it to her. "Here, Miss Sinclair."

"My troubadour. Thank you, Robert." She spent some time slicing it in half and piling some of the ham on top of it, anything but look in Devlen's direction. She was as foolish as one of the maids. His very presence had an effect on her. He needn't smile. Even one of his frowns was captivating.

"Don't you think so, Miss Sinclair?" Robert was saying.

She glanced over at the boy. "I'm sorry, but I was engrossed in my own thoughts. What was it you asked me?"

"I was saying we might be trapped here for days and days."

"Well, at least we have food to eat," she said, gesturing toward the lavish dinner Devlen had procured for them. "And we're warm." Only just, however. There was still a chill in the air since the fire was just lit.

"And Devlen's horses are in the barn," Robert added. "But I want to see Edinburgh again. I want to see Devlen's house. It's the most wondrous place, Miss Sinclair. You have never seen anything like it. It's three stories, and it's filled with furniture and marvelous rooms, and it has a hidden staircase just like Castle Crannoch and a secret passage from the library to the stables."

She glanced at Devlen to find him smiling fondly at the boy.

"Some of what I've told you is a secret just between you and me," he said, smiling.

Robert looked shamefaced, then brightened. "But she doesn't know exactly where the secret passages are, Devlen."

"Why would you build a secret passage in your house?"

"I didn't build it," he said. "I bought the house that way. Edinburgh has long been known for its intrigues, and evidently the previous owner had some connection with the court. He no doubt thought it wise to provide some type of escape for himself and his family."

"Did he ever use it?"

"I'm not entirely certain. I decided not to delve too deeply into the family history when I bought the property."

The rest of their meal was pleasant, their conversation innocuous bordering on bland, as if both of them were conscious of the innocent boy sitting between them.

They also carefully avoided discussing the attempts on Robert's life.

Their meal done, Devlen took the tray and stacked the dishes on it.

"You surprise me," she said.

He glanced at her and resumed his chore.

"Why, because I don't need a servant to do my every bidding or because I'm not afraid to do for myself?"

"Perhaps both."

He put the tray down, opened the door, and picked up the tray again.

"Things are not always as they seem, Miss Sinclair. Nor are people."

He glanced at Robert. "We'll make our travel decisions in the morning."

She nodded, and a moment later he was gone.

"You need to wash, Robert," she said, handing him a small ceramic jar she'd taken from her valise.

He didn't fuss but did as she instructed, lathering his face and hands with the soap, then making a point of shivering as he rinsed. She handed him a small towel embroidered with the Brechin crest. He dried himself off and changed into his nightshirt, making a point of stepping behind the folding screen and making her promise not to look.

Beatrice smiled and promised, and lit one of the lanterns, but because of the size of the room, didn't bother to light the other.

"It's very cold in here, Miss Sinclair," Robert said, emerging from behind the screen.

"Bundle up in bed, and you'll soon be warm enough."

"Tell me a story," he said with all the arrogance of a fully grown duke.

"Not if you command me."

"You're my employee."

"You're my charge."

"I'm Brechin."

"You're seven is what you are."

She sat down on the edge of the bed. "Do you think your father would be proud of you to hear you talk like this? From what you've said of him, he was very conscious of the feelings of others."

Robert's eyes widened, but he didn't answer her.

"Would he be glad you announce your title so often?

He strikes me as a most modest man, someone who wanted to do good in his life more than he wanted to impose fear."

To her absolute horror, the child began to cry, the huge tears rolling down his cheeks all the more powerful for the fact they were soundless. Stricken, she reached out and enfolded him in a hug.

She'd never thought herself maternal. In fact, when a baby was born in the village, she was not inclined to gather around the child and ooh and aah about its face, toes, or its likeness to either parent. But at the moment, when she began rocking back and forth in an effort to comfort the child, she felt absurdly protective.

Who would dare to hurt a child?

The thought was so sudden and invasive she was taken aback. This was not a holiday. This was not an adventure. There was only reason they were going to Edinburgh and that was to keep Robert safe.

Someone wanted him dead.

"I will tell you a story, my young duke," she said, kissing the top of his warm head. He smelled of the soap he'd used before getting into bed.

"Once upon a time, a peacock with a glorious tail noticed a tall and ugly crane passing by. The peacock made fun of the crane's gray plumage. 'I am robed like a king,' he said, 'in gold and purple, and all the colors of the rainbow, while you have not a bit of color on your wings.'

"He proceeded to parade around the crane, making a great presentation of his tail feathers, spreading them wide beneath the bright sun. Indeed, they were magnificent feathers in shades of red, blue, and green.

"The crane said not a word. When he walked, he did so awkwardly, and it's true there wasn't a bit of color on his feathers. He was nearly ugly, just like the peacock said.

"But while the peacock was laughing at the crane with the other peacocks, the crane suddenly picked up his feet, flapped his wings, and began to run. A moment later, while the peacocks watched in amazement and awe, he soared into the heavens.

"Up and up and around the clouds he flew, into the face of the sun itself.

"The peacocks could barely hear the crane's voice as he climbed higher into the sky, but hear it they did. 'It is true you are beautiful, much more beautiful than I. But I wing my way to the heights of heaven and lift up my voice to the stars. You can only walk below among the birds of the dunghill.'

"The moral of this story? Fine feathers don't make fine birds."

"Do all Aesop's fables have a moral, Miss Sinclair?"

"Every single one of them."

"Are any of them interesting?"

She only shook her head and tucked him in, taking care to ensure he was warm.

Once Robert was tucked in, he fell asleep without much difficulty. She sat and watched him, convinced he would rest tonight without nightmares. The room might be small, but there was a pleasantness to the inn somehow lacking at Castle Crannoch.

A half hour later, she stood and undressed, replacing her clothing with her nightgown and wrapper.

She was about to do something very foolish, something even Sally would caution her against. But if nothing else, the last year had taught her something. Life was fleeting and could be stripped from her without warning, without a hint.

She didn't want to waste one second of the time she had. She didn't want to pretend that there would be years and years to be wise and sensible, to find love.

Love. The word described all the incredible acts of passion mankind was capable of, all the acts of sacrifice, all the illogical and nonsensical acts. Love. She wasn't under any illusions that what she was about to do was based on love. She was intrigued by Devlen Gordon, and fascinated by him. His smile caused desire to curl up at the base of her spine, then extend its silky tail through her body, but she didn't love him.

Nor was time a certainty. All she knew was that she had this moment.

Still, she hesitated at the door, her hand on the handle. She felt greedy for life in the same way she'd been hungry for food, as if she'd been starving for experiences all these years. The hunger she felt easily overcame the soft whisper from her conscience.

She left the room, closing the door softly behind her.

Chapter 22

Beatrice stood before Devlen's room a full minute before summoning the courage to knock.

The sound was too loud in the silence, the echo of it carrying down the hall and back. She heard his footsteps nearing the door, then he hesitated, as if questioning whether or not he should open it.

She didn't knock again, but neither did she turn and go back to her room. Instead, she stood there with hands clasped in front of her, waiting.

Finally, the door opened, and he stood there, half-undressed. His stock was askew, his shift unbuttoned. But he didn't apologize for the state of his appearance.

Nor did he question her presence.

"Who do you think might have tried to harm Robert?"

It was a valid question, and one that needed to be asked and answered. But that wasn't why she was here, and they both knew it.

He reached out and pulled her into the room, then closed the door behind her.

"You wouldn't enjoy it, Miss Sinclair. In the morning, you'll wonder why you gave up your virtue so easily."

"Will I?"

"You'll wonder why you gave up so much for so little."

"You sound as if you have some experience in the regrets of virgins."

"No, I don't. Nor do I wish to. Go back to your room."

His voice was so well modulated, his smile so firmly fixed in place she would have thought him unaffected by her presence. Except, he kept his hands thrust in his pockets and there was a little pulsebeat at his neck where his skin moved up and down furiously, a cadence that was remarkably similar to her own frantically beating heart.

"Devlen?" She reached out with her hand, placed her fingers against his cheek. He jerked away at her touch.

"You tempt fate, Miss Sinclair."

"Beatrice," she said softly. "Have we not progressed to that, at least? I shall call you Devlen, since I do so in my mind already, and you may call me Beatrice."

"I would be better to call you ill-advised or foolish, Beatrice Sinclair. Without a smidgen of sense."

"You have teased me for days, if not weeks. And tempted me to your bed. Now you warn me away from it."

"Someone should warn you."

"I didn't expect you to warn me. I expected you to be my lover."

His smile abruptly disappeared.

"Have you no sense of self-preservation, Beatrice Sinclair? Nothing that warns you it isn't wise to tease the wolf?"

"Is that what I'm doing?" How utterly strange. Her pulse beat so hard she could feel it in her lips, her eyelids trembled, the whole of her body was vibrating.

She forced her hands to open. Her palms were wet.

"Is it such a terrible thing being here, Devlen?"

"You're leaving Robert alone."

"Yes, I am."

She turned to go, angry at him. He'd seized upon the one thing that could force her away. When she would have left the room, his hand on her arm held her back.

"He'll be fine."

"No, you were right to remind me of my duty. After all, I'm an employee. A governess."

"A woman."

His voice was low, his hand on her wrist warm. She didn't turn to look at him, but she wanted to. When he moved to stand close to her, her breath hitched and held, then slowly, slowly, released.

"I have never met anyone like you, Beatrice Sinclair. What kind of woman are you?"

"One derelict in my duty, Mr. Gordon, as you reminded me. Please release me."

"Tomorrow, perhaps, at dawn."

He turned her slowly.

A fingertip rested on her bottom lip, tapped it lightly. "You frighten me a little, you know."

"Do I?"

"My conscience wants to send you in all haste from this room. After all, I promised to protect you. My curiosity and my need begs you to remain."

"Then protect me tonight. Protect me from loneliness and despair. From questioning myself, from being cold."

"Beatrice."

"I can't explain what I feel, because I've never felt it before. I have no descriptions for the sensations rushing through my body, no way to convey the emotions I'm feeling. Maybe I need a poem to do so. Or a symphony. Music, as a way to express words I can't find."

"Damn it, Beatrice."

"Tell me what to do to rid myself of these feelings, and I'll do it. I won't trouble you any longer. Is there something I can drink? Something I can eat? Would sleep do it?"

"Touch yourself."

"What?" Shocked, she stared at him.

"Touch yourself and think of me. Hold your breast and tell yourself Devlen would touch me just this way. Stroke your nipple, and pretend it's my tongue. Let your hands wander over your body until you manage to convince yourself they're my hands."

"If I still crave your touch after that?"

He reached behind her, opened the door, and abruptly left the room, leaving Beatrice to stare after him.

Did she wait? Or return to her chamber?

After deciding to come to him, she wasn't going to leave. She walked to the bed, removing her wrapper, then mounted the steps and slid beneath the covers, feeling the shivery chill of the sheets.

Devlen would warm her.

Why was she here? Because she was lonely? Because he offered her something that had sparked her curiosity? Possibly both reasons, or neither of them.

Her body was capable of so many wondrous feelings, from first waking in the morning and stretching to feeling the warmth of the sun on her arms to walking bare-

foot through the spring grass. She could close her eyes
at that moment and recollect the summer breeze across
her cheek or the feel of the linen as she donned her
shift.

What would she recall tomorrow morning?

The room was cold and silent, the only sounds the
tearing wind outside and the hiss and pop of the fire.
Her feet warmed, and she burrowed deeper beneath the
covers, staring up at the ceiling and wondering if she
should have some sort of trepidation for what was soon
to follow.

The door opened then, and she was done with intro-
spection. He closed the door softly and stood with his
back to it, surveying her with a somber look.

"You have time to get out of my bed, Beatrice Sinclair," he said. "But I warn you, if you're not gone by
the time I get there, you won't be able to escape."

"Do I look as if I'm attempting to escape?" She rose
on her elbow.

"You should. You should be frightened for your life.
I'm offering you nothing, you know."

"I know."

Silence stretched between them.

"Where did you go?"

"I hired the maid to sit outside Robert's room for the
night. She'll fetch me if he awakes."

"You're a better protector than I, Devlen Gordon."

He didn't answer her. Instead, he came to the bed,
pulled the covers down, and held out his hand. Curious,
she sat up, then rose to her knees.

Her nightgown was gone in a few swift movements.

"Perhaps you have some experience in this, after

all," she said, amazed at the speed with which he'd divested her of her clothing.

"Now's not the time to discuss my experience."

"Then pray, remember that, when you would mention my lack of experience."

"Ah, but you are a virgin. Virgins are special creatures."

"You make me sound like a unicorn. Surely I'm not all that rarefied a creature?"

"In my bed you are."

She shouldn't have felt a shiver of pleasure at those words. He hadn't complimented her, after all.

"So, I'm your first virgin."

"You needn't look so pleased," he said, sitting on the bed.

"Why ever not? A woman likes to think she is special to a man in some degree or another. If for no other reason, you'll remember me because I was a virgin."

He shook his head, and she couldn't help but smile. It amused her to confound Devlen Gordon.

"Have you given no thought to your future?"

"You mean a child?"

The atmosphere in the room suddenly changed. It was no longer a secluded bower, a warm oasis from the cold. The chill of the winter night seeped in through the windows. Beatrice wouldn't have been surprised to look outside the bed to find snow piled high around it.

Devlen moved from the bed, walking to where the innkeeper had placed his trunk.

"I hadn't thought that far ahead," he said. "But luckily I do not travel unprepared."

He returned to the bed holding something in his hand. Instead of showing it to her, he slid it beneath the pillow.

"They're *les redingotes anglaises*."

"English riding coats?"

"Precisely. They're to prevent you from becoming with child."

"I've chosen well," she said. "If I had to be deflowered by anyone, it was wise to choose a rake, someone versed in the skill. Do you make a point of keeping them next to your candles and your pistols?"

"You sound annoyed."

"I am not. Truly, I'm not. Very well, I am. I want both to be protected and to be protected from the knowledge of being protected."

"You want to be loved by a rake who's a virgin."

"It does sound nonsensical, doesn't it?"

"It would be better if you went back to your room. Then we wouldn't have to discuss English riding coats or preventing children."

"Yes," she said, "it would be better if I went back to my room." It was suddenly cold, and she was chilled. She hadn't felt so acutely naked before, but she did now, with her nipples drawing up tight against the chill.

He looked at her intently, and she wished he wouldn't. She felt vulnerable now while she hadn't been earlier. Instead, she'd been caught up in the daring of her deed. Now she just felt foolish.

She raised an arm to cover herself and just as she did, he reached out and prevented her from doing so.

"If you deny me your company for this evening, then at least let me look my fill. The sight of you will fuel my dreams."

How could he do that? With just a few words, he'd made her warm again.

She reached out her hand, and he took it. She rose to her knees, put her hands on his shoulders, and placed a soft kiss on his cheek.

"Being here is foolish, I know," she murmured next to his ear. "But I'm rarely foolish, Devlen."

"You want a taste of sin."

She nodded.

"And if you're ruined for marriage?"

"I'm not titled. Nor am I wealthy, and I doubt such considerations will matter if I ever marry. My husband will have to take me as I am or not take me at all."

"You'd bend the rules, Beatrice? Challenge society itself?"

"I suspect you've done your share of bending and challenging, Devlen Gordon."

"It's different for men, I think."

"Because we are vessels. What an odd way to think about women, don't you agree?"

"I don't believe I've ever considered a woman a vessel before, Beatrice."

"You must have," she said, drawing back. "If you hadn't, you wouldn't be carrying English riding coats in your trunk."

"Why are you so content to get nothing in return?"

"In return?"

"For the gift of your virginity?"

"Is it a gift? Or a burden?"

"You won't enjoy it, you know."

She looked at him for a long moment. "Are you a bad lover, Devlen? How odd I'd never considered it."

His smile was barely there, anchored by a wisp of

emotion. A wish, perhaps, that she would cease questioning him. Or meekly acquiesce to what she'd already chosen as her fate.

She sat back on her haunches and regarded him.

He didn't look away or appear the least uncomfortable. Instead, he pulled his stock away from his throat slowly, so she could almost feel the slow slide of fabric against skin. Then his waistcoat, unbuttoned by large, long fingers, was falling to the floor with casual disregard.

"Your valet isn't here, Devlen," she said, amused.

"Perhaps I can convince you to straighten up after me."

"I have one charge. I am in no hurry to gain another."

How silly she should want to smile at this moment. The time was not ripe for humor, or the buoyant feeling in her chest. But she was absurdly happy as she watched him slowly undress, his gaze still fixed on her face and her dawning smile.

"You are enjoying this, aren't you?"

"The sight of you undressing? Very much. I must admit, however, I've never actually seen a naked man." An instant later, she corrected herself. "Not alive at any rate."

He halted in the act of unfastening his trousers. "Not alive?"

"During the epidemic, anyone was pressed into service to help bury the dead, Devlen. I was very good at sewing shrouds."

"You have a disconcerting habit of flummoxing me with your conversation, Beatrice Sinclair."

"You don't have to call me by my first and last name, you know. You could call me Beatrice. Or my middle name."

"Angelica?"

"No, nothing so ironic. Angel and devil." She smiled. "Anne. Much more prosaic."

"At first glance, however, Beatrice, it would not seem you're the angel in this mix. I suggest you're the devilish one."

"Really?" She was absurdly delighted by his comment.

He sat at the end of the bed, removed his boots and stockings, then slipped his trousers off his long, long legs.

"My," she said, and then fell into a long silence, interrupted only by the wind pushing against the windowpane. "Have you always been so large?"

A bark of laughter had her lifting her gaze to his face.

"Not a question I've ever been asked before," he admitted. "I don't think I was this large as a boy, no."

"Is it practice that makes it large? Does it get larger the more you use it?"

"Where do you get these questions?"

"Curiosity. I've always been curious."

"I find it oddly disconcerting to be questioned about my sexual exploits."

"Have you had none?"

He startled her by jumping onto the end of the bed. "Enough, Beatrice Sinclair. You have the devil's own tongue."

"Thank you," she said, and was further surprised by his dawning smile.

"Whatever for?"

"For not regaling me with stories of your conquests."

"That wouldn't be well-done of me, would it, Beatrice?" He leaned over and kissed her on the nose, a thoroughly confusing kiss.

He knelt before her, allowing her to look her fill.

She should have turned away, perhaps. But then, she shouldn't have been here at all. Instead, she looked, starting at his shoulders, rounded with muscle, to his chest, crafted like a Roman soldier's hammered breastplate, to his lean hips, to other places far more interesting.

"You look, dare I say it, enthralled."

"I've not had the opportunity to witness a naked man so close."

"One who's alive."

She nodded.

"I trust you approve of the sight."

"You're very beautiful. Do many women tell you that?"

"Considering the circumstances, perhaps it would be better if we didn't discuss other women."

"That means they have, of course," she said, stretching out her hand. Before she could touch him, she halted, her fingers resting on his thigh. As she watched, his manhood grew, stretching like a sleeping snake.

Oh my.

He picked up her hand and placed it on him.

"You're very warm," she said, when she'd regained the use of her voice. The comment came out as a croak. "Almost hot," she added.

His skin could burn her. She brushed the back of her hand against his thigh, and watched as his eyes half closed. He was like a cat she could pet. A warm cat who'd been sunning in the window. The fine black hair on his skin was not unlike a pelt. But there all resemblance to a domesticated animal fled from her mind. He was not a tame kitty, even though he was sitting patiently beneath her touch. His muscles were taut, his expression one of barely restrained civility.

His hand clenched, then moved to rest against her breast, to cup it as if to measure it against his palm. Her breast looked small and white and defenseless against his hand and she wanted to urge him to take some care with her. With all of her, naked and trembling yet too wild for maidenhood.

His thumb strummed against the tip of her breast, and she closed her eyes at the feeling. A sound trapped inside of her escaped through her tightened lips. A soft moan, or a sigh, no more than that.

Suddenly, she was on her back, and he was above her.

"Last time, Beatrice Sinclair, unicorn, if you will."

"I wish you'd urge me to stay with as much eagerness as you urge me to flee."

"I only wish to give you fair warning."

"It cannot be such a dour thing, Devlen, or the world would not hold it in such esteem. Nor would preachers sermonize about the doom and gloom of hell. Do only men enjoy it?"

"The first time, I'm afraid so."

"Then shall we dispense with the first time as quickly as possible? I shall hold you blameless if I feel the least bit ill from it."

"It's not a purgative, Beatrice."

"At least that, Devlen, or you wouldn't be warning me so."

He bent and kissed her and there were no more warnings. Or if he ventured any, she was not in the mood to hear them. His kisses were hot and drugging, leading her into a state of nothingness she'd never before known, a place where only sensation ruled. The touch of the tip of his tongue against her mouth, the soft sigh he made when deepening the kiss, the taste of him were all things she noted with the small part of her mind not adrift in wonder. The rest of her was aflame, curling beneath his fingers, his palms, her skin ablaze with feeling. Not even her toes were exempt from sensation, because they brushed against the long, wiry hair on his legs, and teased the soles of his feet.

She undulated like a wild thing, arching and retreating, enjoying each touch. He palmed her breasts, and she marveled they'd never been so sensitive. His thumb reached out and with his forefinger, teased her nipples, and she knew she'd never again be unaware of herself and her capacity for sheer enjoyment.

When his fingers explored her intimately, spreading swollen folds and entering her, it was as if he was demonstrating to her the body she'd inhabited all these years. His thumb bore down on one spot, his fingers curled into her, and she arched her back in an effort to get closer to him. Her arms wrapped around his shoulders and her lips pressed against his ear and it still wasn't close enough. Not nearly enough.

His fingers flicked against her. She felt caught up in a whirlwind, a vortex that was sucking her higher and higher. He whispered something to her, some words that had no meaning because she'd lost the ability to filter sound, so entranced was she in the magic he'd created with his touch.

She reached out with one hand and pressed against his fingers, urgent in a way she couldn't articulate. He said something else, and the only thing she noted was the amusement in his tone.

There was nothing remotely funny about what she was feeling.

He inserted another finger into her, his murmur less amused than coaxing. His thumb was insistent, probing, magic. Suddenly, her mind numbed, the sensation silvery, an explosion that crested, halting her breath. She hung, suspended, in midair, then exhaled a sigh, floating back to earth slowly on a current of bliss.

Devlen slid his hand beneath the pillow. He pulled away from her, and when he returned, he entered her with a smooth and practiced movement.

Just as swiftly, the bliss she'd felt turned to discomfort.

"No."

He halted, staring down at her, gripping the pillow on either side of her head.

"No?"

She nodded.

"For the love of God, Beatrice, you can't say no now!"

"You won't fit, Devlen. I know you think you can, but it's all too obvious you won't."

He sighed, and lowered himself until he rested his forehead against hers. "Let me show you, Beatrice. Remember how I said it wouldn't be very comfortable?"

She nodded again.

"This is the not-comfortable part. But I promise, I shall be very kind."

"Am I still a virgin?"

"Only half."

"Then, please, finish."

"If you're sure?"

She nodded for the third time and was rewarded by his very determined expression.

He withdrew, and surged forward, and she immediately wanted to scream at him that he hadn't been kind at all. She felt stretched and invaded, and where he rested it burned. But then he withdrew once more, and this time she did scream, but only a little as he buried himself to the hilt in her.

She closed her eyes and tried to distance herself from what she was feeling.

"Beatrice?"

"Yes?"

"Are you crying?"

"A little."

"I'm very sorry, but I did tell you."

"Do you feel better being right, Devlen?"

"Not appreciably."

"Is it very enjoyable for you?"

"Not at the moment, no."

"I don't think I'm a virgin anymore, am I?"

"Definitely not."

"Well, that's done."

A moment passed, and she realized he was still hard inside her, a state of affairs that surely wasn't right. Short of asking him to hurry up and finish, however, what did a virgin do?

"Devlen?"

"Yes, Beatrice."

"Are you waiting for something?"

"For you to grow accustomed to me."

"I doubt that will ever happen, Devlen. You mustn't wait any longer."

"I've never been asked to depart with such grace, Beatrice."

She didn't have anything to say to that, so she remained silent.

"You're quite large."

"That's a compliment, you know. Thank you."

"I feel very small in return."

"You're supposed to be. You're a virgin."

She flexed her internal muscles, trying to ease the ache. He glanced down at her and smiled.

"That feels interesting, Beatrice."

"Can you feel that?"

"Too much more, and so will you."

She did it again, and he closed his eyes.

"Beatrice."

Once more and he moved, raising himself on his forearms and looking down at her as he did so. The discomfort wasn't quite as bad this time.

Once, twice, three times he surged into her, and when he did, she flexed her muscles. Several more minutes went by, with him moving above and in her. Her discomfort had almost completely eased now, but his, evidently, had not.

Devlen's expression was almost pained, his eyes closed, his movements more and more forceful and less restrained. She was being moved with each forward thrust, until she placed her hands on the headboard, palms upside down, bracing herself as he surged into her.

Suddenly, he made a sound and collapsed against her, his breathing ragged, his heart beating so frantically she feared for him.

A moment later he raised his head, his face flushed, his eyes sparkling wildly.

"You're wondering what the hell you've done."

"You were right. It wasn't very enjoyable. Oh, there was a moment there, but . . ."

"On the whole, you'd rather not have done it."

She nodded.

"I very much regret that fact, Beatrice. I shall have to change your mind."

She shook her head. She didn't want to do this again. Ever.

He lay beside her and held her close, but the comfort of his embrace didn't make up for her soreness or the lingering discomfort.

However, she couldn't berate herself until dawn came. She gave up, sighed deeply, and surrendered to sleep.

Chapter 23

The first thing Beatrice was aware of the next morning was Devlen leaving the bed. He went to the window and opened the sash, scooping the snow off the sill and forming it into a ball. He closed the window with his elbow and returned to the bed and did something utterly shocking: he placed the ball of snow between her legs and pressed it against her.

She nearly flew off the bed.

"Devlen! What are you doing?"

"Be still," he said. "Try to bear it as long as you can. The snow will help the swelling."

She subsided against the pillows.

"You'll be sore, but there's nothing I can do about that."

"I think I'm numb," she said. "Hasn't it been long enough?"

He removed the snow for a moment, but then when

she thought he might cease his ministrations, pressed the snow to her again.

"For someone who has never had a virgin in his bed, you seem to know a great deal about the care and feeding of them."

"Unicorns," he said, smiling.

There was nothing else for her to do but lie back and enjoy being cared for, albeit in such an intimate manner. His attitude, his entire demeanor, made it so casual that she couldn't help but be grateful.

When he was done, and most of the snow melted, he dumped the rest of it in the basin and pressed the towel against her. True to his word, she felt better already.

"I should be leaving," she said, glancing out the window. Dawn was already lightening the sky.

He nodded and stood, returning to the window.

"It hasn't snowed for quite a few hours. We'll be able to travel today."

She sat up in the bed, folding the towel he'd placed beneath her. The silence stretching between them wasn't so much awkward as it was filled with unspoken thoughts.

She wanted to thank him for his care of her, and his honesty. She wanted to explain why she'd come to his room, what she'd wanted from him. He'd eased her loneliness and satisfied her curiosity, but in doing so had only incited so many other questions.

If she asked him, would he give her the truth?

Why were men the only ones allowed pleasure? Was it because women were given the greater blessing of carrying a child? Was she odd in wanting to experience the same type of bliss Devlen had felt?

She slid off the edge of the bed and donned first her

nightgown, then her wrapper. Still, he didn't turn from the window, obviously impervious to the cold or to the fact he was naked in full view of anyone who might look up.

What a sight they would see.

"I'm going now," she said, and only then did he turn. His gaze, when he looked at her, was somber. There was not a remnant of the sparkle in his eyes. His mouth looked like he had never smiled, and his face might have been etched in marble, so stern and unapproachable was he at that moment. If she'd never before known him, he would have given her pause. She might have been afraid of him, or at the very least wary. But they'd shared their bodies the night before, and he'd cared for her only minutes earlier.

"Let me go and dismiss the maid. If you have no care for your reputation, at least I do."

When he returned, he didn't glance at her. "Go and wake Robert. Tell him I want to get an early start." She nodded.

"We'll break our fast on the road. I'll have the innkeeper pack us a basket."

Once again, she nodded, his perfect servant.

She opened the door, glanced at him once more, but he'd turned back to stare out the window again. In the reflection, however, he was looking at her. She drew the wrapper closer at her throat as if to hide all the places on her body where his hands had made a mark, where his whiskers had abraded her, where his lips had sucked and his tongue touched.

But she didn't say a word as she closed the door behind her, regret thick in the air.

* * *

The sun was so bright against the drifts of snow that Beatrice had to shield her eyes from the glare.

Robert grumbled as they left the inn and entered the carriage. She ignored his complaints about the early hour, that he was hungry, cold, and tired.

"It doesn't do any good to complain endlessly. It doesn't make a situation easier to endure."

To her surprise, he subsided against the seat, folded his arms across his chest, and remained silent until Devlen joined them.

"How long until we get to Edinburgh, Devlen?"

Devlen closed the door behind him, choosing to sit beside Beatrice. He had never done that before and she rearranged her skirts twice before realizing what she was doing.

"In fair weather, it would be a matter of hours, Robert. But with the snowdrifts, I've no idea. If the roads are impassable, we'll simply have to turn around and come back."

"But I want to get to Edinburgh."

Beatrice leveled a look at him, almost daring him to have a tantrum at this particular moment. She was in no mood for petulant dukes, or ill-mannered children.

To his credit, Robert was very good at reading her expression, because once again he sank back against the seat without another word.

Devlen tapped on the top of the roof twice, a signal to the driver. The carriage began to move, the horses evidently restive and willing to show their mettle.

Twice they were forced to stop because of the ice. The driver and Devlen laid down a bed of straw, a large bundle of which had been purchased from the innkeeper and now sat atop the carriage for just such a use. Other than those two occasions, the journey was uneventful. As the day lengthened and grew warmer, the snow began to melt, and the danger was getting trapped by the muddy roads.

Beatrice had heard about Edinburgh all her life. Her father was enamored of the city and once they'd actually had the funds to take a coach there. He'd conferred with an academic friend, and they'd stayed in the man's narrow little house in a tiny airless room. The discomfort of their visit had never mattered to her father, who'd regaled Beatrice with every single sight of historical interest and the history of each.

As they drove into the city, she experienced an incredible sense of sadness. Her father would have been so happy to have been able to return here. As she looked around, she could almost hear him exclaim at all the changes that had taken place since she was fifteen and a wide-eyed girl.

She knew the city was divided into two sections, called Old Town and New Town, and she wasn't appreciably surprised when the carriage continued toward the newer section of the city. They stopped in front of a set of iron gates and waited as two men appeared and swung them inward.

Beneath the folds of her skirts, Devlen's hand found hers. He gave her a reassuring squeeze, as if she were a child frightened of the dark.

She turned and looked at him, but he was staring out the window. She did the same, pretending an interest in the scenery rather than the feel of his warm fingers intertwined with hers.

Here, in the city, the snow had not been so plentiful,

but what still lay on the road and on the trees was a sparkling mantle. The carriage turned, traveling down a wide road of crushed shells. A few moments later, she glimpsed his house for the first time, an enormous mansion easily the equal in size to Castle Crannoch, set in the middle of a parkland.

She'd heard Devlen described as wealthy, had known he had some business affairs, but until this moment, she'd not considered exactly who Devlen Gordon might be. As she stared at the house, she realized she'd misjudged him again.

"What kind of businesses do you have?"

He turned and looked at her. "Do you want the types of industries, or a listing of the companies I own?"

"What's shorter?"

He smiled. "The industries. The companies take up two pages in my ledger. There's shipping, textiles, import and export. I build things, and I make soap."

"Soap?"

"The soap making is a new venture, I confess. But we've been experimenting with putting all different types of scents into soap."

"Is that why you always smell so wonderful?"

His smile dimmed, and he glanced at Robert. What would he have done if Robert hadn't been in the carriage? She didn't have a chance to wonder, because he continued with his litany.

"I make a great many things as well. Nails, for example. And cotton. There's a new loom I'm trying out. Do not, I pray you, forget about my ships or my glassworks. Plus, I'm negotiating for a company that makes gunpowder."

"I had no idea."

"Did you think me a hedonist?"

She shook her head. She hadn't thought of him as an industrialist, a man interested in glassworks and ammunition. When she thought of him, it was as he'd first appeared to her, sitting in his carriage, or teasing her in Robert's sitting room.

Devlen's house was built of red brick, three stories tall with two wings outstretched like arms around the curved drive. A dozen white-framed windows stretched along each floor. The entrance was a double white door level with the drive, a sedate brass knocker the only ornamentation.

The house was as far from Castle Crannoch as she could imagine.

As she exited the coach, and stood smoothing down her skirts, Beatrice had the oddest notion her cottage could have fit inside his home at least thirty times over. Devlen extended his arm to her and she took it as if she were accustomed to always visiting such a magnificent place on the arm of its owner.

Robert, not content to walk sedately, gamboled in front of them. She didn't bother to correct him. The last several hours in the coach had only bottled up his energies. Better he should expend them now than when he needed to be on his best manners.

She and Devlen were silent as the door opened. They still had not spoken of the night before. It might not have ever happened except in her memory or except for the small aches and pains reminding her it was all too real. At the moment, Devlen felt like a stranger, proper and hospitable. They might never have talked or shared a meal or been intimate.

She had no inkling of his life, and how could he possibly understand what she'd gone through in the last year? Every single conversation came back to her and replayed itself as she made her way across the gravel drive, still holding on to the arm of the man who'd taken her virginity. The stranger who'd been almost a friend until this moment, until her awareness of the vast gulf separating them.

A man stepped out in front of the door and nodded to two footmen. Like marionettes, they bowed to Devlen before opening the door. Robert preceded them, silent for once.

Once inside the foyer, she stopped and looked around her, her breath leaving her in a gasp. She couldn't swallow, and she was certain she couldn't speak. Neither Robert nor Devlen acted as if anything was amiss.

The foyer was three stories tall with sunlight pouring down onto the tile floor. In the ceiling was a rotunda fitted with at least a dozen panes of glittering glass. Surrounding the carved dome were a dozen birds in all shapes and sizes, carved from plaster and incredibly lifelike.

The tile floor beneath her feet was black and white in alternating squares. In a smaller space the pattern would have been overwhelming, but the entranceway of Devlen's home stretched on forever.

Ahead of them was a massive round mahogany table resting on a single pedestal. In the middle of it was a silver epergne filled with flowers.

"You have flowers," she said, grateful to note she'd been able to form a coherent sentence. "There's snow on the ground, but you have flowers."

"There are greenhouses behind the house. We have flowers year 'round."

"Of course you do," she said, sounding a great deal more cosmopolitan than she felt. "You have a great many parties here, don't you? Balls, and the like."

"I've entertained some, yes." He looked amused.

She felt like a country girl who'd never been far from Kilbridden Village. But she'd come to Edinburgh before, had seen the sights. But she'd never thought to stay in one of the wonders of the city, to reside in one of its stately mansions. Devlen's house was far more grand than anything she could have imagined.

"You could fit an orchestra into one corner of the foyer and it would barely be noticed."

"Actually, they play on the second floor. There's a ballroom there."

She didn't have a chance to ask any more questions. A woman was walking down the hall, her look smoothing from surprise to one of welcome.

"Sir, I didn't expect to see you back so soon."

"Castle Crannoch proved to be inhospitable, Mrs. Anderson. I trust you will not be discommoded by our unexpected guests?"

"Of course not, sir. You know our guest chambers are always ready for any of your friends."

Exactly how many friends did Devlen have? And how often did they stay at his home? That she would even entertain such thoughts was an indication of how disoriented she was. His life was none of her concern.

Mrs. Anderson glanced in her direction, then immediately dismissed her to smile at Robert.

"Your Grace," she said, performing a very credible curtsy considering the woman was not young. "What a pleasure to have you with us again."

"Thank you, Mrs. Anderson," Robert said without being prompted. But his next words were not so polite. "Do you have any of those chocolate biscuits?"

"I believe we can find some for you, Your Grace. Shall I send them up to your room?"

To his credit, Robert glanced in Beatrice's direction. "Is it all right, Miss Sinclair?"

"Since breakfast was a long time ago, it's very all right."

"Perhaps you would like some biscuits as well," Devlen said with a smile. "Mrs. Anderson?"

Once again the woman glanced at her, then away.

"I can have lunch in the family dining room in a matter of moments, sir."

"I think we're more tired than hungry, Mrs. Anderson. It's been an eventful journey. We can subsist on biscuits for now, but let's plan on an early dinner."

"Of course, sir."

"Miss Sinclair is Robert's governess and will be staying with us as well."

"Miss Sinclair." Mrs. Anderson executed a stiff inclination of the head while her lips curved in an infinitesimal smile barely warmer than the frosty weather outside. What concessions she made to politeness were for Devlen's benefit entirely, and they both knew it.

"I'll show you to your room."

"That is not necessary, Mrs. Anderson," Devlen said, all cordial hospitality. "I'll show Miss Sinclair her chamber. The blue room, I think."

"It's quite some distance from the Duke's apartments, sir."

For a moment, the two of them, servant and employer, just stared at each other.

"Quite right, Mrs. Anderson," Devlen said finally. "Miss Sinclair is His Grace's governess, not his nurse. I think the blue room will do fine."

This time the smile he received was at least as wintry as the one bestowed upon Beatrice. Mrs. Anderson obviously didn't approve.

Beatrice's cheeks felt warm, but she didn't say a word as she followed Devlen and Robert up the sweeping staircase. She'd thought the architecture at Castle Crannoch impressive, but it was no match for this magnificent home in the middle of Edinburgh.

"How many people do you employ?" she asked, not merely to make conversation. She was genuinely interested.

"Seventeen. A damn sight more than at Castle Crannoch."

"Don't forget the stables, Devlen. He has four groomsmen and a stable master, too, Miss Sinclair."

"Truly?"

"My horses are at least as important as any dust that might appear in my home," he said, but blunted the edge of his comment with a smile. "I will have to show you my horses, Miss Sinclair."

"I'm lamentably ignorant when it comes to horses," she confessed. "We've never kept any, and they always seemed so very large."

"We shall have to see if we can add to your education. And Robert's. We'll consider it a lesson, perhaps."

They were on the second floor now, looking down at the foyer and up to the sunlit dome at the top of the house. She could see the birds more clearly, each so ornately carved and true to life they looked as if they could all fly away in a flutter of wings.

"What kind of bird is that?" she asked, extending her arm and pointing to one particularly odd looking specimen.

"A white pelican. Indigenous to North America."

He was looking at her oddly, and she supposed she was acting irrational. But she couldn't get over the impression she'd totally misjudged Devlen Gordon. It wasn't because of his wealth, but because of his industry. He was genuinely excited when he was talking about making soap, of all things.

She'd always admired people who had a fire inside, who knew exactly what they wanted to do or to be in life and who pursued it with single-minded ambition.

Because she was female, she was supposed to want, first, to be a wife, then a mother. Any other interests she pursued would be supplanted by those roles. Except, of course, she was lacking sufficient suitors, and she had only one true talent: she was very, very good at survival. In the last year she'd managed to stay alive, and that was still her primary goal and focus.

Devlen led the way down the corridor, and she followed, wondering how close her room would be to his. Had he shocked his housekeeper? Should she protest?

She wished he wouldn't look at her in quite that way, out of the corner of his eye, as if measuring the distance between them. Then he would always follow up that glance with another one toward Robert.

There were too many emotions, too many feelings to sort out, too much had happened in the last day, and she'd yet to reason it all through. First, the birds dying, then this hasty retreat to Edinburgh, and finally, most importantly, last night.

What a fool she'd been. What a silly, idiotic fool.

And yet, if the circumstances were the same again, she would no doubt do exactly what she'd done last night. Lovemaking was overrated and painful, but at least she had experienced it.

She was no longer simply Beatrice Sinclair, of Kilbridden Village. She was Beatrice Sinclair, the governess of the Duke of Brechin. A woman whose virginity had been taken by Devlen Gordon, industrialist extraordinaire.

When the time came for her to return to her village, she would never again be the same gray, nondescript person she had been. People would notice her, if for no other reason than the look of nostalgia in her eyes.

When the time came. She couldn't predict how many weeks or months or days it might be until he sent her from Edinburgh, until Robert went off to school, until Cameron Gordon was so incensed by the fact they'd left Castle Crannoch that he dismissed her.

Time was not one of those commodities she could predict with any certainty. Nor could she gauge another human being's behavior or actions. Therefore, she'd have to be content with simply living each day to its full measure, to savoring all she could when it was placed before her. If she were at a banquet, she'd be foolish to deny her hunger.

At least for the next few days, she'd be living in a beautiful home in the middle of an exciting city, with a man as handsome and distracting as Devlen Gordon.

Devlen halted before a chamber door. Robert had lost no time opening the door and inspecting the premises.

"You haven't changed it," he said.

"Why should I?" Devlen asked. "It's your room. I promised you that, the last time you were here."

Robert nodded, but still went from wardrobe to chest, opening doors and drawers as if to acquaint himself with the contents and ensure himself nothing was missing.

"Your room is in the next wing," Devlen said. "Come and see, Robert. In case you need your governess."

"We shan't be having lessons, shall we, Miss Sinclair?" he asked, as they walked down the hall. "This is a holiday, isn't it? Because of the birds?"

She glanced at Devlen, then away, startled to find he'd been watching her. "We should find a schoolroom here. Your lessons shouldn't be neglected."

His mouth was set in a mulish pout, but after looking at Devlen, he evidently thought better of protesting right at that moment.

Devlen halted before another door, turned the handle, and threw the door open wide for her.

The chamber she'd been given was unlike anything she'd ever seen. The predominant color was blue, from the draperies in front of the long windows to those that hung at the corners of the four-poster atop the dais. The mattress was easily double the size of the one she'd slept on at Castle Crannoch and covered with a thickly embroidered coverlet, again in blue, with a medallion of gold in the center. In the middle of the ceiling was a second medallion, this one in ivory, directly over a blue-and-gold-flowered carpet.

The furnishings were perfectly proportioned for the room's dimensions. A vanity with delicately turned legs sat against one wall, swags of blue damask matching the bed hangings draped from the mirror perched halfway up the wall down to the floor, where they puddled in large folds. A washstand in the corner was partially concealed by a folding screen, and a small secretary sat next to the window. The writing surface sat open, a quill, inkstand, and a supply of paper lay in readiness as if to welcome a correspondent.

"If you need anything, Miss Sinclair, all you need do is summon a maid." Devlen walked to the bell rope near the fireplace and fingered the tassel.

"Thank you," she said. "This is all rather grand."

"So are you."

For a moment she only stared at him, startled by his words. What could she possibly say to that?

There was something about him that would have attracted her even if they'd met on a street in a crowded city. She would have looked back at him if their carriages had passed, if she'd walked near him, if she'd been introduced to him by a mutual friend.

She might have caused a scandal anywhere, at any time.

"Devlen," she said in warning.

He only smiled, turned, and glanced at Robert, who was investigating the balcony beyond the French doors.

"My chamber is across the hall."

An arrangement similar to that at the inn. Did he think she was going to come and visit him?

"No wonder Mrs. Anderson was scandalized."

"Mrs. Anderson is an employee."

"So am I."

"Ah, but I don't pay your salary. My father does. So technically, you aren't."

"You look at the finer point of things, Devlen."

"I'm trained to do so."

She was as well, and yet she didn't think like him. Her education had been in using her mind to analyze a point, to converse in one of three languages, to consider the past. She had no experience in shading the truth or cutting the corners from it.

The moment the door closed behind him, Robert in tow, she let out a breath she hadn't been aware she'd been holding.

What on earth had she done?

It was one thing, her father had always said, to make a mistake. Quite another to refuse to admit it.

We are, Beatrice, my dear, a strange and wondrous species. We go willy-nilly through life making mistake after mistake, only at the end of it to look back and see where our course should have been corrected, made less difficult by a simple turn.

She needed to make a turn now, that was evident, needed a room in the servants' quarters, and not be treated as if she were a beloved guest. Nor should she be across the hall from Devlen's own suite of rooms.

Her cheeks warmed even further at the thought of Mrs. Anderson's pursed lips and disapproving glance. No doubt the woman knew, almost as if she had been standing outside the room last night, exactly what had transpired between them.

Anyone who happened to interpret the glances between them would know. Even Robert had looked from one to the other, curiously, as if he'd sensed an undercurrent.

Very well, she'd been foolish, but if they still took precautions, there was nothing to be concerned about other than her slightly dented reputation. That was something that needn't carry further than Devlen and her. No one in her tiny village would know. No one at Castle Crannoch would have any inkling. Therefore, if she wished, she could return there almost as if she were unsullied and pure and as maidenly as she had been two nights ago.

In actuality, she couldn't see what all the fuss was about. Lovemaking might prove to be very pleasurable to men, but women must simply grit their teeth and pray during the entire experience.

Besides, she had more to be concerned about than her reputation. There was Robert's safety and the mystery of who wanted him harmed, or dead. There was the uncertainty of his future—and hers. At this point, she couldn't even imagine returning to Castle Crannoch.

Although it was only early afternoon, she was tired. The night before had been filled with a fitful sleep. She was unused to sleeping beside another person and found herself awake more often than not, looking at Devlen as he slept.

Would it be acceptable to take a nap? Or would it be considered unpardonably rude?

The question was answered a few minutes later when she responded to a knock at the door. For one moment, she hoped it wasn't Devlen, coming to speak with her. He would kiss her, she knew, and the meaning of his longing glances were clear enough. He wanted to replicate what had transpired between them the night before.

How did she tell him no?

But it wasn't Devlen after all, for which she was grateful, but a footman bringing her valise. Behind him was Mrs. Anderson, bearing a tray.

"Mr. Gordon asked me to bring you something to eat,

miss. He thought you might be tired and would like to rest."

She nodded, feeling tongue-tied and shy in the presence of the older woman.

"Thank you," she said, after the woman had placed the tray down on the table. "It looks delicious."

"It's just some greens and some soup. Along with one of Cook's tarts. Mr. Gordon is very partial to Cook's apple tarts."

"I appreciate your efforts on my behalf."

"It's what I would do for any of Mr. Gordon's guests."

"Does he have many?"

"It's not for me to say."

After the woman left, she sat at the table and ate the meal, finding it tastier than anything she'd eaten at Castle Crannoch.

Once done, she removed her dress and her stays, and placed the garments in the armoire before retrieving her wrapper from the valise. She crawled into the big, wide bed and slid beneath the covers, thinking heaven itself could not feel more sumptuous.

Wealth could not bring a man happiness, she'd always been told, a saying she questioned as she burrowed into the feather pillow. Perhaps it couldn't buy happiness, but it certainly could provide comfort.

Devlen had a hundred things he could do, a dozen things that must be done. There were, no doubt, people waiting for him in his office to make decisions. He needed to go by the shipyards, and the new machinery was due to be delivered to the warehouse he was converting to a textile factory.

Instead, he sat in Beatrice's room, watching her while she slept.

If nothing else, he could be interviewing Robert, coaxing details from the boy about the poisoning of the birds, and the shot in the forest.

His mind shied away from doing that, and it didn't require any great thought to understand why. His father had always wanted to be duke. Enough to kill a child?

He would have to protect Robert, at least until he determined who was at the bottom of the incidents surrounding him. Who had shot at him, and who had poisoned his food? Why would anyone want to kill the boy? His thoughts came full circle, back to his father.

Tomorrow, he would visit with his solicitor, have him send something to his father. Anything to keep Cameron away from Robert, at least until Devlen could assure Robert's safety. Castle Crannoch wasn't the place for the boy. For the time being, Robert would remain with him. At least in Edinburgh he was safe.

His bachelor life could be expanded somewhat to include a child. He was growing tired of the endless round of parties and entertainments. The idea of staying in was growing in appeal.

How much did Beatrice Sinclair have to do with that idea? Probably too much to warrant investigation. He hadn't lied to her—he thought virgins too much trouble. She, especially, with her air of directness and her way of puncturing his conscience.

He'd eschewed the substances in life proving to be addictive. He didn't indulge in opium, or too much drink. While he engaged in selective breeding of his horses, and treated them well, he didn't think that hobby a vice. He'd been attracted to gambling, only to find himself feeling certain that he'd been singled out to be different. When he won, he felt as if his luck was special, his destiny unique. He'd felt blessed, as if a light from heaven shone down on him to illuminate to the rest of the world that he, alone, was anointed.

He had to almost lose his fortune before he realized what a fool he'd been.

Was Beatrice as dangerous as gambling?

She was proving to be a distraction of major proportions. He anticipated her smile, and he wanted to hear her laugh. Deflowering her had been one of the single most unforgettable experiences of his life. He hadn't wanted to cause her pain, and had felt acute regret when he'd done so, enough that his own pleasure had been muted. When she'd carefully avoided him this morning, he'd wanted to enfold her in his arms, kiss her tenderly, and tell her the experience would be a better one the next time. But it was all too obvious she wanted nothing to do with any further forays into passion.

Was that why he was here?

Perhaps he was more concerned about his reputation as a lover. He couldn't let her continue with the thought that lovemaking was a painful event, especially with him. That's what it was—he was simply concerned she not have a bad opinion of his skills.

He smiled in the darkness, amused by his attempts at delusion.

There was none so blind as he who will not see. Who said that? And did he ever sit in a darkened bedroom and gaze at the object who was causing him so much mental discomfort, feeling helpless and wanting?

She had the power to charm him, keep him awake.

From the moment he'd met her, only weeks ago, he'd been fascinated.

He had a hundred acquaintances, but few friends. He wasn't given to confidences, and he was so single-minded and focused in his work that he was impatient with the necessities of friendship. He didn't want to spend any time cultivating an acquaintance into a friend, didn't want to spend the time to listen to their travails, their thoughts, or the experiences of their days. There were only so many hours in each day, and he spent most of them productively.

For the first time he felt the lack of friendship, acutely lonely in a way that surprised him at his core. Was that another aspect to his life brought about by Beatrice Sinclair?

She was proving to be quite an irritant.

It occurred to him then, as he sat in the darkness, that she occupied the role of friend more closely than any-one ever had. He actually wanted to hear her thoughts, and had solicited her opinions quite often. The way her mind worked was vastly fascinating to him to a degree that startled him.

That was it. She was simply a friend, and he was act-ing in a capacity of friendship. That was all.

This time, he didn't smile at his delusion.

Chapter 24

When Beatrice awoke, the drapes had been closed against the night. She lay there in the dark, disoriented at first before she pieced everything together. She was in Edinburgh, the city she'd always wanted to revisit. Her parents and her friends were dead, her life had changed drastically. The man she'd taken as her lover was, for all intents and purposes, her employer, and he'd given her this lovely room.

In exchange for her virginity?

How foolish a thought if it were true. Devlen owed her nothing. Although the experiment itself had a disappointing outcome, she would not have traded the experience.

Knowledge was never to be shunned.

She sat up and wished whoever had closed the drapes had thought to light a candle or a lamp. But just as she was wondering where there might be a box of matches, she heard a sound. A rustle of fabric, a movement of a shoe against the flowered carpet, no more than that, but it had the power to freeze her.

She gripped the sheet and pulled it up to her chin.

"Who's there?"

"Forgive me," Devlen said. He struck a match and instantly, an oil lamp flared to life. His shadow grew to encompass the corner where he sat, looming to a point on the ceiling.

He stood, and his shadow danced down to a normal size even as the man himself grew taller.

"How long have you been there? Have you been watching me sleep?"

"Not long. I had plans to take you on a carriage ride at sundown, but time got away from us."

"I'm sorry, I didn't mean to sleep so late."

"You were tired. Neither of us got much sleep last night."

"No." She was proud of the fact she could sound so calm when speaking of last night. How utterly civilized both of them were being. Usually, such circumstance might lead to high drama, but she couldn't imagine Devlen Gordon being histrionic about anything, let alone the seduction of a woman of some naïveté.

"Could we go tomorrow night?"

"We can do anything you wish." He'd reached the side of the bed now and leaned over to smooth her hair back from her cheek. She'd not thought to braid it, and it would take some time to rid it of its tangles.

She wished he'd not seen her in such disarray.

The oil lamp barely illuminated the room; they were two shadows approaching each other.

"I really should see about Robert."

"He's fine. He's pestering the cook for more biscuits and grateful you're nowhere in sight."

"I've been an errant governess."

"Every boy needs a chance to escape from authority, even as delightful an authority as you."

"Stop doing that."

"Doing what?"

"You're very effusive in your compliments, Devlen."

"And you don't know quite how to handle them. Or me."

"Is that your intent?"

"To keep you off-balance? Perhaps. I like you discomfited, Miss Sinclair. You're charming when you're confused."

"You're just too charming."

"Ah, you're learning too quickly, I think. I must warn you, however, I'm not nearly as overcome by compliments as you seem to be. I've grown accustomed to praise."

There was silence while she wondered what next to say. She was often fighting for her verbal survival around him.

"Which brings up the subject we need to discuss."

She had a good idea what subject he wanted to discuss and she preferred to avoid it.

"I told you it wouldn't be an enjoyable experience."

"Yes, you did. I'm grateful you aren't a liar, Devlen."

His bark of laughter startled her. "Only a despoiler of innocents."

"Absolutely not. You did nothing I didn't want done."

"Tell me this, since we're so intent on the truth, you and I. Would you have done it if you'd known what it was to be like?"

She considered the question for a few moments. "Probably not," she said finally. When he remained silent, she continued, "I'd much rather not do it again, please."

"So much for honesty. I'm beginning to believe it isn't as much of a virtue as I've always thought."

She slid from the other side of the bed. "You sound annoyed."

"Not annoyed, Beatrice." He came around the end to meet her. "Very well, annoyed. I'd expected you to say differently. I wanted you to have some pleasure in our closeness, perhaps. Enough to want to replicate the experience. Only then could I show you it was a great deal more pleasurable than the first occasion."

"For you, perhaps, Devlen. I'll grant you that."

"I've never been considered a selfish lover, Beatrice. Pardon me if I'm slightly irritated by that comment."

"Shouldn't we be arguing over something that makes a bit more sense?"

He didn't say anything for a moment.

"I didn't mean to insult you, Devlen." She touched him on the arm, and the muscle jerked at her touch. "Forgive me."

When he still didn't say anything, she moved closer. "You said yourself virgins are too much trouble."

"I've come to show you something," he said. "A little renovation of mine."

"I really should see about Robert."

Suddenly he reached out his hand and touched her cheek with his fingers, trailing a path across her face to the corner of her lips, then back to her ear.

She half turned her face away, uncomfortable with his gentleness. That feeling was beginning again, where her breath was tight and her heart beat too loudly. Her mind knew what was to come, but her body had not yet learned that lesson, evidently.

"He's fine, Beatrice. When he finishes badgering Cook, he'll see the new soldiers I bought for him."

She pressed her hand against his chest, feeling the fine linen weave of his shirt. A wealthy man's garment, the stitches so fine as to be invisible, the fabric so closely woven as to feel like silk.

Leave me alone. I beg you.

But how strange she didn't speak the words. One hand splayed on his chest, and she placed the second one there, thumb to thumb. And still she didn't measure the full breadth of his chest.

"Beatrice."

Just her name, softly said. She let her eyes flutter shut and bowed her head until her forehead rested against his chest, unsurprised to feel his arms extending around her. Her traitorous body was so foolish, she took two tiny steps closer.

She wanted to be kissed, and when she tilted her head back, he obliged her. The consummate host, giving what a guest desired.

She opened her mouth below his, inviting the invasion of his tongue, feeling a spear of excitement deep inside when he touched his tongue to hers and deepened the kiss. Her hands spread wide, reached up to grip his shoulders. She stood on tiptoe and wound her arms around his neck, pressing her nearly unclad body so close a sigh could not have separated them.

His hands reached down and cupped her buttocks and pulled her closer and higher so his erection rested at the V of her thighs. He lifted her slightly, then let her slide down again, to mimic the act of love in a standing position.

The excitement she felt deepened as her body heated, and their kiss became more carnal.

Too quickly done. Within a moment, she was aflame. Her thoughts, wishes, decisions might have been thrown out the window. If he'd suggested they go back to her bed, she would have thrown herself atop the mattress. Thankfully, he did no such thing.

He slowly pulled back, gave her one last kiss, then bent his head again and pressed his lips against her cheek. His breathing was ragged, the words barely audible.

"Not yet, Beatrice. I've a surprise to show you."

She didn't want a surprise. Or dinner. Or to be proper. She wanted her breath to come back in full measure and her heart to quit its erratic beat. Most of all, she wanted that feeling inside her to ease. Her body waited for something, anticipated something, and yet her mind knew full well exactly what she wanted. His hands on her. His fingers on her pressing against her, bringing her release. But if that happened, there would be pain, and she wasn't eager for that part of the experience to be repeated.

"Come with me." His hand trailed down her arm until their fingers linked. He headed toward the door with her following.

"I'm not dressed," she protested.

"You don't have to be. In fact," he added enigmatically, "you shouldn't be."

He opened the door and looked both ways, and she fervently hoped none of the maids or footmen were in the hall.

He led her out of the room, closed the door behind

her, and walked across the hall to his own chamber. She tugged at his hand, but she was no match for Devlen's insistence.

Seduction was evidently not on his mind. Inside his suite he turned away from the bed mounted on a dais, and led the way across the room to a door set in the wall. He turned the latch and pushed in the door and let her into another chamber.

She'd never seen anything like it.

There was no carpet on the floor, nothing adorning the stone walls. The chamber would have been as cold as a mausoleum had it not been for the floor-to-ceiling fireplace in one wall. A large copper pot sat bubbling over a well-tended fire. The only furnishing in the entire room was a large copper vessel sitting in the middle of the room, a series of pipes leading from it to the fireplace, then down into a drain in the floor.

"It's a bath," Devlen said with obvious pride. "If you want hot water, all you do is turn that spigot," he said, pointing to a handle mounted at the edge of the tub. "The other leads to the cistern on the roof and provides cold water."

"Good heavens."

But the wonders weren't over.

"When you're done, merely unplug the tub and the water disappears into a drainage area in the garden."

She had never seen anything quite like it, and when she said as much, his smile was that of a young boy.

He reached into his pocket and handed something to her. She looked down at the key on her palm.

"To the room," he said. "I thought you might enjoy the experience. Alone. With no interruptions."

She'd revel in it.

They'd had a tub at the cottage, but the effort of heating all that water was a chore. It was easier to simply bathe in bits from a basin.

She nodded, grateful for his consideration, and absurdly glad he was wealthy.

Before she could thank him, he'd slipped from the room.

She turned the key in the lock, removed her wrapper, and hung it on a hook near the door. Before removing her shift, however, she went to the tub and peered inside. Devlen could have fit inside. In fact, it was commodious enough for two people.

The stopper was easy to fit into the hole at the bottom. She was leery about the hot water lever but after turning it just halfway, a steady stream of steaming water filled the tub. After adding cold water, she removed her shift and climbed the small wooden step next to the tub. She put one foot and then the other inside, sinking down into the hot water with a blissful sigh. A few minutes later, she leaned back in the water, submerged up to her neck, happier and more relaxed than she could remember being in months.

"I thought you'd like it."

Her eyes opened and she jerked to a sitting position, using her arms to hide her breasts.

"I neglected to mention I have a second key," he said, entering the room and closing the door behind him.

"Yes," she said, "you did."

"Are you angry?"

"I should be. You're very presumptuous."

"But you aren't. Good. I came to bring you this." *This*

turned out to be a tray on which a dozen or so ceramic jars were arranged, each bearing a label in a distinctive script.

"My newest venture," he said, setting the tray down beside the tub.

She read a few of the labels: SANDALWOOD, BERGAMOT, LAVENDER. "Soap?"

He nodded. "Would you like to try one?"

Before she could say yes, she would, but only in private, or ask him to leave, or a few other rejoinders that would no doubt be more proper and less suggestive, he moved the stool to the back of the tub and sat down, grabbing one of the containers from the tray.

"Sandalwood," he said, and reached out with one hand to grip her shoulder. He gently pulled her until she was resting her head against the back of the tub again, staring up at the ceiling.

A word from her would send him away, she was certain. She didn't speak.

Using both hands, he massaged the creamy soap into her shoulders and neck. The scent mixed with the steaming water and strengthened.

"It's very exotic," she said, surprised her voice sounded so level. His hands were very gentle, never dipping below the level of her shoulders, never going above her neck. Every once in a while, however, he would brush his thumbs up her throat to rest behind her ears, a gesture that had the power to incite shivers.

"I think of Far Eastern bazaars and women in veils."

"You use it, don't you?"

"Occasionally."

"I've smelled it on you."

He reached for another jar, and she let out a sigh. It was to be seduction, then. He would use his hands and bring her delight. In return, she would endure the discomfort and the pain for a few moments.

She would concentrate on the delight, and the other would take care of itself.

He lathered his hands with a scent reminiscent of flowers. He began at her shoulders, but this time trailed his hands down her arms, leaning forward until his cheek rested against hers. His breathing was steady and even, the antithesis of hers.

He had that power over her. At another time she'd feel irritated. Now, she was too occupied anticipating his touch.

His fingers entwined with hers, and she dropped her head back and closed her eyes, pretending not to know her breasts rested half-in, half-out of the water, her nipples pointed and hard and wanting to be touched.

He withdrew his hands to reach for another container. This scent was definitely lavender, and his hands, thick with soap, went immediately to her breasts.

A soft gasp escaped her at the sensuous slide of the soap, coupled with the hardness of his palms against her sensitive nipples.

He placed a gentle kiss against her ear. A tender, almost soothing kiss as if to calm her while his palms were making circles around her breasts.

She shifted restlessly, causing the water to lap near the edge of the tub.

Still, he cleaned her breasts with minute detail, careful to ensure the nipples were given their share of attention. Another scoop of soap and his fingers devoted another minute, two, to the task.

Beatrice licked her lips and turned her head. His beard was beginning to show, and she found that impossibly arousing. She licked at his skin and kissed the spot her tongue touched.

He made a sound low in his throat and gently squeezed both breasts.

The sensation flew like an arrow through her.

He removed his hands, but she didn't complain. She knew he'd pick another container and return soon enough. This scent was something herbal and green, smelling of a garden after the rain. He leaned against her back, his arms almost completely surrounding her, his cheek once more next to hers.

"Kiss me," she said, her eyes still closed.

"Turn your head."

She did so cautiously, opening her eyes slowly. His lips were so close. She wanted them on her, wanted to feel them.

He drew back, and she raised one hand, placed it on his cheek.

"Now," she said, demanding. He'd teased her into becoming this creature, and she felt no shame.

He kissed her, and she clung to his lips, parting them with her tongue, teasing him just as he'd done her.

In a few moments, he'd want to be inside her, but there was a price he had to pay first. He must pleasure her, softly and with great skill.

She pulled back and looked at him.

His hands dipped into the water, found her, and he slid one finger across her swollen folds. It wasn't nearly enough, but just when she would have begged for more, he stood, dragging her upward so forcefully she had no choice but to cling to him.

"Damn it to hell, Beatrice."

He was angry, his cheeks flushed, his eyes dancing with something that wasn't quite rage.

She didn't have a towel, but she didn't need one as long as he was holding her so close. His shirt and trousers were sodden.

He marched across the bathing chamber with her in his arms, opened the door, and stalked through his bedroom. Suddenly, she was airborne, then landing on his mattress with a bounce.

This wasn't supposed to happen at all.

"Damn it," he said, stripping off his clothes.

He was naked and atop her, but before she could say a word, he was inside, surging so deeply into her she expected the pain to be unbearable.

Her eyes widened, but the only sound she made was a gasp of surprise.

"I told you, damn it. I told you it wouldn't hurt."

"Why are you so angry?"

"Because this time was supposed to be slow and deliberate. But you've made me lose all control."

He hadn't been slow, but this felt very, very deliberate.

"Are you all right?"

She nodded.

"Are you certain?"

He moved then, and abruptly she wasn't certain at all. The sensations she was experiencing weren't at all what she'd felt the night before, and although he was still large, she was accommodating him quite easily.

She placed her hands flat on the bed and pushed upward a little. The resultant feeling was interesting. More than interesting—she felt positively exultant with it.

"I think you're enjoying this." Devlen smiled.

"Wasn't that what you wanted?"

"We should be gentle. Restrained. You're too close to a virgin."

"Unicorn," she said, smiling.

"Damn it, Beatrice."

Her smile broadened, and she felt, absurdly, like laughing.

"Does it always feel this way? Once you're not a unicorn, that is."

"How does it feel?"

"A heaviness," she said, considering. "No, nicer. Like something soothing and not at the same time. Does that make any sense?"

"Shall I tell you what it feels like for me?"

She nodded, curious.

"It's a damnable itch, and it makes me want to slide in and out of you until it's satisfied. I'm so hard it's painful, and yet every time you move, or sigh, I get harder. I want to bury myself in you so deeply you'll never be able to forget how I felt."

"Oh."

"Indeed. Oh."

He moved, sliding just a fraction of an inch out of her, and she gasped. Instinctively, her hips arched up to entice him back, and he returned, bending his head to kiss her.

She reached up and kissed him, sighing with relief when he returned to her. He pulled back a few moments later, his breathing labored, and braced himself on his elbows.

"You have beautiful breasts."

She wasn't particularly in the mood for conversation right at the moment. Again, she pulled his head down for a kiss, but he hesitated just before reaching her lips.

"Impatient?"

"Kiss me."

"Dearest Beatrice, so autocratic."

She didn't care what he called her as long as he kissed her. She flexed her internal muscles and heard him groan. He bent to kiss her then, and her lips curved against his smile.

His fingers measured her swollen folds, danced where they joined, and she almost came off the bed when his thumb circled her and coaxed her to pleasure.

Loving would cease to be simply a word. The very mention of the word *love* would summon images to her mind: his smile, the way he looked down at her with each surging thrust, the flex of the muscles in his arms, the tightening of his neck. Their bodies pushed against each other for that last bit of feeling. Again and again he arched his hips, his buttocks flexing beneath her spread fingers.

He bent his head, his lips near her ear, praising her response. "You're so tight, Beatrice. So very hot inside."

Each word, each soft stroke of his fingers on her body, was an incitement. When she lifted her hips, urging his invasion once more, he whispered to her, "Soar for me, Beatrice. Fly."

She did, feeling as if she touched the sun.

When he followed her a moment later, she held him

tight, her arms wrapped around his shoulders, and wept against his neck.

"What do you mean, he's gone?"

"I heard," Mary said, "they left yesterday. Both of them. Mr. Devlen and the governess. And the boy, of course."

"That odious child. He causes more problems than he's worth."

"Mr. Gordon is having a fit, madam. He's throwing things around in the library and threatening to go after them."

"Is he?"

Mary handed her the cup of tea, bustling around her to adjust the pillows on the settee, straighten the blanket on her lap.

Sometimes, the woman could be busy as a bee and about as annoying.

"Settle yourself, Mary," Rowena said.

The older woman did so, choosing a footstool near a chair.

"Cameron is going after them?" She hadn't spoken to Cameron since that disastrous night she'd gone to his room. Nor did she want to. Her pride was all she had left.

"He hasn't told me, madam."

"Gaston might know."

"Gaston would never tell, madam."

"That's true. It amazes me the loyalty Cameron is able to inspire."

Mary looked away.

"Not that you're not loyal, Mary. But you are not fanatical about it."

"I don't know what you mean, madam."

Rowena sighed. "Never mind." She held her hands out. "There's a draft near the window."

Mary hurried to close the drapes, throwing the room into a clouded sort of darkness. She lit a candle, and the blaze from the fire provided some illumination as well.

"The entire castle is cold, madam."

Rowena didn't bother to answer.

She wanted to go back to London. At least there she could pretend her life was ordinary. If Cameron didn't wish to speak to her, she could attend a play or an entertainment. If he barred her from his bedroom, perhaps she could engage in a flirtation with someone else.

How foolish she was being. As if anyone else could ever measure up to Cameron.

"I hate that child."

Mary looked stricken.

"Madam, you're crying."

Rowena wiped at her face with one hand. "Am I? How very odd."

She stood, returned to the dressing table, and allowed Mary to flutter around her as she usually did.

"I would like to wear the green today, I think, Mary," she said. The dress was a new one, purchased in London with the thought it might interest Cameron. The garment required a special set of stays because it was so closely fitted. At least she looked the part of Chatelaine of Castle Crannoch, at least until Robert grew and took a wife.

Damnable child.

She didn't want to hear about Robert, didn't want to worry about Robert, didn't want to even think about Robert until it was absolutely necessary. Every time she saw the child she was reminded of that horrible day of the accident.

She dropped her head in her hands and said a prayer, hoping God would forgive her because she knew Cameron wouldn't.

Chapter 25

"**D**evlen!" Two knocks on the door, followed by another of Robert's shouts. "Devlen!"

They looked at each other.

"Good heavens!" She sat up, forgetting her nakedness. Devlen's eyes traveled down her torso, and she slapped him on the chest before pulling up the sheet.

"Go into the bathing chamber, and I'll get rid of him."

"I know Robert, he won't be rid of easily."

"I'll take him down to the dining room. You can go to your room. When you're dressed, summon one of the maids to show you where it is."

She couldn't just sit across the table from him. Not now.

"Shouldn't I just have a tray in my room?"

"No."

She raised her eyebrows at him. "No?"

"I want you at the table with us."

He stood, and walked to the washstand, supremely unconcerned about his nakedness.

"I enjoy your company, Beatrice." He glanced at her, then halted. "Stop looking at me like that."

"You're very attractive. I like looking at you."

"Devlen! Answer the door!"

Beatrice pulled the sheet off the bed and wrapped it around her, entering the bathing chamber and closing the door behind her.

Devlen said something in response to Robert's summons. The child was evidently mollified because she didn't hear him shouting again.

She flattened herself against the door and looked at the disarray all around her. The towels had tumbled to the floor, the box of soaps was askew. Water puddled near the drain and in a path to the door, and the tub was still filled.

What a strange time to want to laugh.

A half hour later Beatrice was dressed, descending the staircase with her thoughts still full of Devlen. A maid greeted her at the base of the stairs, her face, if not sullen, then strangely without expression. Did Mrs. Anderson force such a conformity of expression on her staff?

She was led to the drawing room, a room of such beauty that at any other time she would have stopped in the doorway and admired the pale yellow walls and the art mounted on them.

The sight of Cameron Gordon, however, sent every thought flying from her mind.

He'd lost no time in following them.

"You're looking well, Miss Sinclair," he said.

Robert sat on a couch not far away, looking small, pale, and cowed.

How dare he frighten a child.

Devlen stood behind him, but at her entrance, he moved beside her.

"You didn't tell me you had plans for a holiday in the city, Devlen. I might have allowed it had I known."

"There was no reason to inform you since you were the reason we left."

Cameron raised one eyebrow and studied his son. "Are you going to explain that statement, or shall I use my powers of divination?"

Devlen put his arm around her back, his hand on her waist, a physical gesture of support she'd not expected.

"There were too many attempts on Robert's life for me to be comfortable with him remaining at Castle Crannoch."

"Indeed."

"And you, Father, seemed disinterested in his welfare."

"I'm his guardian. Of course I'm interested in his welfare."

"Did you know someone shot at him? And poisoned his food?" A movement caught her eye, and she glanced to where Gaston stood, silent and until now unobtrusive.

"Robert is a very excitable, very imaginative little boy. He sees goblins where there are none, Miss Sinclair."

Robert simply looked at his shoes, a miserable expression on his face.

"He didn't imagine those incidents," she said. "I was with him when they occurred."

"Then perhaps if you are no longer with him, they will not occur. I think I will dispense with your services, Miss Sinclair. Your propensity for attracting danger cannot be a good thing for Robert."

"You're dismissing me? Is that your answer to protecting Robert?"

"No, Miss Sinclair. My answer to protecting Robert is to remove him from your care. He belongs at Castle Crannoch. Robert," he said, turning to the boy, "we'll be leaving in the morning. Edinburgh is not the place for you."

"I'm not going." He stood and faced his uncle, his fists balled up at his sides. Beatrice wondered if he was trembling as he was the last time he confronted Cameron.

"Indeed you are, child."

"I wouldn't be so certain, Father." Devlen stepped closer to Robert, standing behind the boy and placing his hands on Robert's shoulders. "Robert isn't going anywhere. I've already contacted my solicitor. I'm contesting your guardianship."

Cameron's face changed. In that moment he was no longer the charming, almost courtly invalid. Instead, he was obviously angry, his hands gripping the arms of his chair so tightly his knuckles were white.

"Robert is going to stay here with me, Father, until the courts decide," Devlen said. "I suggest, however, that you return to Castle Crannoch."

"You can pretend to be duke without me there," Robert said.

The look in Cameron's eyes did not bode well for the child. He signaled to Gaston, who stepped to the rear of Cameron's chair and deftly wheeled him to the door. When he was gone, Beatrice turned and looked at Devlen.

Robert stared at the empty doorway. "He wants me dead."

She had no answer to such a statement. The horror was that Robert uttered it in such a calm voice, as if accusing his uncle of murderous impulses was an every-day occurrence.

"I don't have to go, do I, Devlen?"

"No, you don't, Robert," he said somberly. "I promise."

She almost wept at the look in the child's eyes, and was certain she'd worn the very same expression after her own parents' deaths: grief, loss, and pain so deep it was almost tangible.

"Go and ask Cook if she has some treats," Devlen said.

Robert nodded, leaving the room without a backward glance.

"My father has always been dissatisfied with his life," Devlen said. "My earliest memories are of his anger toward his brother for being duke. He always told me that his brother would much rather prefer to be a scholar than head of the family."

"While he would much rather be the head of the family."

He nodded. "He was destined to be duke, at least in his mind."

"Could he harm Robert?"

He didn't answer her. Instead, he walked to the fire, stirred the coals with the poker. Several minutes elapsed before he turned back to her. "I've been asking myself the same question for weeks, ever since I learned of Robert's penchant for accidents."

"If not your father, then who else could be behind it?"

"Gaston?"

She must have looked surprised, because he smiled. "Gaston is my father's loyal servant. He would be the most likely candidate, being my father's legs, so to speak."

"I went to him," she said. "When Robert was shot at in the woods, I went to Gaston." He had been in the kitchen, she remembered. Not far from the courtyard. He could have seen them descending the hill.

Devlen came to her side. "It's too easy to blame yourself in hindsight. I do the same. Why didn't I take Robert from Castle Crannoch in the beginning?"

"If you had, we never would have met."

"A circumstance that would have occurred in some fashion, I'm sure."

"Fate?"

"You sound as if you don't believe in it," he said, with a smile.

She shook her head. "You can't say you do."

"Actually, I don't."

"But for Fate you might be a duke yourself one day."

"I am content to be a mister, nothing more."

She tilted his head and surveyed him. A corner of his mouth turned up as she continued to study him. The moments ticked by as their gaze held.

"Are you disappointed that I'm not a duke?"

She laughed, genuinely amused. "Heavens, why should I be? You've created your own wealth, and you look the part of a prince. The title would just be redundant."

"I created my own wealth because I didn't want to depend on anyone for my livelihood, and my looks are beyond my control."

"You've just proven my point. You have the arrogance of a duke."

He smiled at her. "Why, I wonder, does your opinion matter so much to me?"

"It shouldn't. I'm just a governess. And not even that, now."

"You're my angel of goodness."

Amused, she reached out and let her fingers stray over his coat, palm flattening over his heart. "You're my devil of delight."

"You frighten me," he said.

A confession that disturbed him, she could tell. His eyes were suddenly somber, and the expression on his face was that of a man forced to speak the truth.

She placed her palm against his cheek. He frightened her as well—or more correctly—what she felt for him frightened her.

"Devlen."

He bent and kissed her, a soft and charming kiss, but not a passionate one.

"I have duties to perform," he said. "Work I could do."

"Yes."

"We haven't eaten dinner yet."

"No." She shook her head.

"Every time I kiss you, it always leads to more."

"I'm sorry." She smiled.

"I believe you plan it that way," he said.

"Not truly."

"I thought, once, you would change my life."

"Have I?"

"More than you know."

"Perhaps it would be better if I left," she said.

"Perhaps it would. But I haven't always done the wisest thing in regard to you, Beatrice."

"Nor I you."

"We are a pair, aren't we?" he asked.

She stepped away, allowing her hand to drop. "For the meantime."

His face darkened, as if he didn't like the truth she'd offered him. They didn't belong to the same life, and they'd only borrowed this time.

"I'll go and see about dinner. Robert is probably coaxing Cook into giving him all sorts of forbidden treats."

"He'd be happier that way."

"Yes, but life isn't all cake, Devlen."

"Beatrice."

She glanced at him, but he only shook his head, as if his thoughts must forever remain unspoken.

Beatrice left before she, too, could say more.

Chapter 26

Two weeks later, Devlen stood in a ballroom staring out at the newest crop of virgins, all too aware that he was being watched by the matrons of society to ensure he didn't violate any unwritten rule, therefore proving himself good enough for their daughters. The daughters, on the other hand, were less judgmental.

One brave young miss reminded him of Beatrice, not because of her appearance—she was short, blond, petite, and graced with a bodice that must be half handkerchiefs for all the overflowing lace—but because of her daring. She was batting her eyelashes and her fan at him.

"That one has her eye on you, Gordon."

He turned to see a business acquaintance staring at the same young lady. She looked pleased rather than daunted by the increased attention.

"I think I'll pass. Be my guest."

"Haven't the money. Rumor is her mother is trolling

for a title. Barring that, a fortune. Too bad, the girl really is a looker."

Devlen didn't comment, an omission that had the other man glancing at him curiously.

"Surprised to see you tonight. These types of things aren't usually your style."

"I felt the need to show myself."

"In the marriage mart are you?"

"God, no."

"Wouldn't think so with that gorgeous creature of yours."

"How the devil do you know about her?"

"Hell, Gordon, everybody knows about Felicia."

"Oh, her."

"Whom did you think I meant?"

He shook his head, but the other man wasn't satisfied. What the devil was the man's name? Richards? Something like that.

Devlen wished his hostess approved of something more potent than a sugary sweet pink punch as a refreshment. Whiskey, for example.

"Is the fair Felicia about to get the boot, then?" He leaned closer. "Want to share who your newest mistress is?"

"No."

"But you do have a new one?"

"I don't know why the hell I'm here," Devlen said. He turned to the man beside him. "Why are you here?"

"I'm being harassed at all sides to marry," his acquaintance said. "I just need to find an heiress, myself. Someone with a penchant for poor men who will worship at their feet forever."

"Is that what women want?"

"Damned if I know," the other man said, smiling ruefully. "I have five sisters, and they all seem different. Sometimes different from themselves, depending on the mood."

Beatrice had been herself, consistently. She had a variety of moods, however, each of them more fascinating than the last. He even enjoyed her annoyance, and found himself going out of his way to argue a point of view he didn't even agree with simply to see her impassioned anger.

How idiotic was that?

They discussed literature, languages, history. He'd even found himself expounding on his plans for a new racing stable. They argued politics, religion, women's rights, and various other subjects he'd never once discussed with a male acquaintance.

"Never seen you look so down, Gordon. Deal fall through? Heard Martin is being stubborn."

"He can keep his munitions works if he wants. I've offered him a fair price."

"Then you don't really want it. The word is out, you know."

"I didn't know I was that easily deciphered."

"If you don't want something, it's not worth buying. Surely you've seen that most of the market follows your lead like carp? They're bottom feeders, Gordon."

At another time he might be amused by the analogy.

The orchestra was beginning again, and the girl with the fan was fluttering a little madly.

"You really should give her a go."

"I don't dance."

His companion glanced at him. "There's nothing to

it, Gordon. You simply go out there and resign yourself to playing the fool. It's done all the time."

"Not by me."

"Then it's a good thing you're not in search of a wife. It's a requirement, you know."

He fingered the box in his pocket. It was time to leave. He'd come to this idiotic evening to prove, at least to himself, that his life hadn't changed in the past few weeks. He could go and come as he liked, unfettered by conscience or guilt. He'd enjoy himself, and when it was time, he'd return home.

The problem with his plan was that it didn't work. He wasn't enjoying himself, and he wanted to be home more than he wanted to be in company. Every woman of his acquaintance was either insipid or too obvious, and none of them was graced with wit or intelligence or the ability to tell him what she really thought.

None of them was Beatrice.

He bid farewell to the man at his side and spent the next quarter hour locating and saying good night to his host and hostess. That done, he made his way to the entrance and spent an enjoyable few minutes chatting with another man of his acquaintance while waiting for his carriage to be brought around.

When it arrived, he gave Peter a destination the driver knew well.

The interior lantern was lit and illuminated the necklace as he drew it out of its box. A magnificent collection of yellow diamonds. "A necklace fit for a queen," the jeweler had said.

He hoped Felicia thought so as well.

* * *

Beatrice sat in the middle of Robert's bed in the room Devlen had set aside as his. Unlike the Duke's Chamber at Castle Crannoch, this room obviously belonged to a child. The walls were painted a soft blue, and there were blue silk draperies on the windows. There were three armoires aligned against one wall, and two of them held an abundance of toys, anything a duke—or any child—might want.

Beatrice was an observer as Robert arranged his toy soldiers around the pillows and featherbed coverlet. He had already described several battles to her, and since her knowledge of anything military was somewhat lacking, she could only nod sagely and pretend an interest she didn't have.

From time to time she glanced at the mantel clock, then away, pretending the lateness of the hour didn't matter. In actuality, she was conscious of the passing of every minute. Robert, however, having readied for bed, was professing to not being able to sleep.

"I feel like I might have a nightmare tonight, Miss Sinclair."

Of course she hadn't believed him. Was it even possible to predict when one might have bad dreams? Nor had Robert had any nightmares since leaving Castle Crannoch.

It wasn't concern for him that held her there or allowed him to remain awake and playing. She was lonely and angry and sad, and all three emotions were keeping her unsettled. Perhaps a little guilt kept her here as well. She hadn't been the best or most attentive governess since leaving the castle.

The last weeks had been part of an idyll, weeks of hedonistic pleasure, and if she made up for it by playing toy soldiers until midnight, then it was a small price to pay.

Still, he was yawning every few minutes.

Earlier, she and Robert had had their dinner on a tray. Devlen had a social engagement he'd had to attend, and the house was oddly empty without him.

As the minutes advanced, she was all too certain that, for the first time since coming to Edinburgh, she was going to spend the night alone.

Where was he? What was he doing?

The clock struck midnight, and despite Robert's protests, she began to gather up his toy soldiers.

"If you don't sleep now, or at least try, you will be worthless for your lessons tomorrow."

He gave her a rude look, and she returned it with a strict expression.

"You'll be too sleepy to go on an adventure."

"An adventure? Are you bribing me, Miss Sinclair?"

"I believe I am, Robert. But we should explore Edinburgh a little, don't you think? Perhaps we can go and find a sweet shop."

"Really?"

She nodded.

He allowed her to tuck him in and light one lantern. It was hardly necessary. Devlen's home was lit up as bright as a harvest moon.

He was the most unusual man she'd ever known, and the most fascinating.

"You haven't had nightmares since we left Castle Crannoch, have you?"

He shook his head. "Castle Crannoch doesn't feel like home," he said, scooting up in the bed and gathering the sheet around him. "Not since my parents died."

Since she felt the same way about her own little cottage, she only smiled.

There were some things a child, even one of seven, was certain to understand. Death was regrettably one of them. Loss of parents changed everything, made the world a dark and unfriendly place.

Beatrice stretched out her hand and smoothed back his hair. He yawned in response.

"Tell me a story. But not a fable."

"They're the only stories I know."

"Tell me about when you were a little girl."

"When I was little? How little?"

"My age."

"You don't seem very little at all. One moment you're seven and the next you're twenty-seven."

"You're avoiding the subject, Miss Sinclair."

She smiled. "I am, actually. I haven't had a very exciting life. My grandmother lived with us until her death, and it was from her that I learned French. When she died we came to live at Kilbridden Village. I was almost twelve. I remember because two days after we arrived was my birthday."

"Did you have a celebration? Get a present?"

She shook her head. "There was so much chaos no one remembered. It wasn't until nearly a month later my mother realized it."

"I should have had a fit, Miss Sinclair. No one should forget my birthday. It's June 26," he added for good measure.

"I shall make a note of it."

"But where did you live before?"

"In a small house on the border of Scotland and England. A very small farm but a lovely place. I don't re-

member very much about it, but I know I was happy."
She tucked the sheet around his shoulders. "That is the
extent of my adventures. See, I told you I didn't have a
very exciting life."

"Didn't you have any friends?"

"My very best friend lived at Kilbridden Village. I
met her on my birthday, as a matter of fact. Her name
was Sally."

"Is she still your friend?"

Sally had been among those who'd died in the cholera
epidemic. On the day Sally had died, a storm had suddenly appeared, turbulent and wild, stripping the
branches bare until it appeared to be raining leaves. The
birds had ceased their song, and even the raindrops, drip-
ping ponderously from the heavens, were more like tears.

But for Robert's benefit, she only nodded.

"But what's all these questions about friends?"

"I haven't any. I'm the Duke of Brechin. Shouldn't I
have friends?"

She bent and before he could draw away, kissed him
on the forehead. "Indeed you will. When you go away
to school, perhaps."

"Why not here in Edinburgh?"

"I shall have to send out notices to all my business
acquaintances, I see. Announce to all of them the Duke
of Brechin is accepting visitors, but only those around
the age of seven." Devlen strode into the room.

Robert grinned. "Could you do that?"

Beatrice turned and smiled at Devlen. He was so utterly handsome, her heart stilled at the sight of him.

She stood and walked around the end of the bed.

Devlen joined her there and grabbed her hand, bringing it up to his lips to kiss her knuckles.

"How have you been?"

"In the four hours since you've been gone? Fine."

He bent his head, but just before his lips met hers, he glanced to the side.

"Turn your head, Robert. I'm about to kiss your governess senseless."

"I'm a duke," Robert said. "I should learn about such things."

"Not at this particular moment. And not from me."

He turned her so his back was to Robert's bed, and proceeded to kiss her until her lips were numb.

"May I escort you to your room?" he asked when he released her.

"I would like that."

She stood at the doorway and watched Robert for a moment. "Sleep well."

He feigned sleep for a moment before opening his eyes. "I'm hungry."

"Tomorrow."

"I'm thirsty."

"Tomorrow."

He sighed dramatically. "Good night, Miss Sinclair."

"Good night, Robert."

"Good night, Devlen."

"Go to sleep," Devlen said. He still held her hand, and she felt as if they were children themselves, walking swiftly down the corridor to the next wing. For the first time, she was grateful for his advance planning in having installed her in a room far from Robert's.

Instead of saying farewell to her at her door, he opened it and stepped aside. When she entered the room, he followed her and closed the door behind him.

They were immersed in shadows. The darkness gave

her a freedom she'd never before felt. She linked her hands to the back of his neck and stood on tiptoe to press a kiss against his lips.

"Thank you," she softly said.

"Why am I being thanked?"

"For your kindness to Robert."

"Anyone would be kind to the child," he said.

"Someone isn't."

"Must we talk about that at this moment?"

"Must we talk?"

"Beatrice, I'm shocked."

"Are you?" She reached up to kiss his smiling mouth.

"The dress looks very complicated."

"On the contrary, it is supremely easy."

He placed both hands at her waist, his thumbs meeting in the front. Slowly, he drew them upward until he cupped both of her breasts.

"Have you many dresses? I would just as soon tear this one from you."

"I only have three, and before you suggest it, no, I shall not accept any clothing from you."

"How did you know I was going to offer?"

"It sounds like something you'd do. You're very generous."

He bent and placed his cheek against hers. "I'm not especially generous with other people, Beatrice, but I find myself wanting to give you things."

"Then restrain yourself with the knowledge I will not accept them."

"Do you dance?"

"Dance?" She pulled back to look at him, but the room was too dark to see his expression. "I do. Country dances mostly. Why?"

"I'd dance with you. I just realized that tonight."

"You would? How very sweet of you to say that."

"I'm not sweet. I despise the word."

"Very well. You're kind and well-mannered."

"If I am, it's because you summon forth my better nature."

Slowly and with great dexterity, he unfastened her bodice, and spread it wide, unlacing her stays with such skill it was as if his fingers could see in the darkness.

In a matter of moments she was down to her shift, her dress thrown on the nearest chair, along with her stays.

Her fingers found his coat, eased it off his shoulders, uncaring it fell to the floor. His waistcoat was next, and she unbuttoned it with the same skill he'd shown earlier. Over the past weeks, they'd learned each other's clothing. His shirt came next. She unbuttoned one button and bent forward to kiss his bare chest. Another button, another kiss.

While she was intent upon removing his clothing, he was equally intent upon learning her curves beneath her shift. His hands roamed from her shoulders to her elbows to her hips to her buttocks and up her back, soothing strokes that made her shiver.

They were matched in sensuality, the only part of their lives where they were equals. His wealth was enormous, his position enviable, his possessions covetable. Her status was not so high-flown, and she had nothing to her name but a cottage and the contents of a well-worn valise. No one would ever clamor for her presence at dinner, and there would not be hordes of invitations awaiting her perusal as there were for him daily.

Suddenly, she was in his arms, and he was taking her to bed. This loving would be slower, less fevered, and perhaps more devastating. There was a component of tenderness now that made her want to simply hold him to her. She framed his face with her hands and kissed him sweetly.

Don't ever forget me.

They didn't speak, didn't tease each other with words.

When he entered her, a lifetime later, she arched off the bed, a small gasp of wonder escaping her.

"Please," she said, knowing he was the only one who could end this eternal wanting.

When it ended, and she was sated, she turned in his arms, exhausted. She heard him whisper her name, just before she slid into sleep, feeling safe and protected for the first time in a very long time.

Devlen left the bed and donned enough clothes so that he wouldn't shock a footman if he were seen. He left her room, soundlessly closing the door behind him.

The lovemaking was one thing, but it had a remarkable ability to put him in a reflective mood, and he was damn tired of feeling guilty about Beatrice Sinclair.

She was driving him mad.

He wanted her constantly, and it was obvious she felt the same. But her conscience was evidently not bothering her as much as his; witness the fact she'd rolled over and gone to sleep, and he was prowling through his home like some nocturnal creature.

He should leave her alone. Why couldn't he?

He should send her back to her village with enough money to live for the rest of her life. A dowry, if you will. She'd marry a farmer, maybe a brewer or a shop-keeper, and bring to that union assets of her own.

Why should he banish her?

Because hiding in the shadows was no life for a woman like her. Because he was not used to skulking around like a passion-crazed weakling who couldn't get enough of a woman.

Because he didn't want to keep her as his mistress.

She was probably better educated than he was, and no doubt had a more traditional upbringing. Her manners were impeccable, her speech upper-class, and she had an annoying tendency to be right during most of their arguments.

Then why treat her like a doxy on the London wharves?

Damn it.

Chapter 27

When Beatrice awoke Devlen was gone. Her first thought was that she missed him, and her second was that she was being foolish. He hadn't been in her life long enough for her to miss him. He wasn't firmly fixed in place, wasn't someone to whom she could point with pride and announce he belonged to her.

Devlen Gordon was so much himself that the idea of him belonging to anyone was amusing.

The snow was full on the ground, and they were months away from spring. The squirrels were hiding away in their burrows, and there was a wild and fierce wind blowing against the building, but nevertheless the day looked to be one of promise. She felt like the happiest person alive. Was that tempting Providence?

The garment she chose was a dark blue dress with red piping along the cuffs and collar. It was cinched at the waist and fastened up the front. Very proper attire by any standards. Perhaps not grand enough for a guest at Devlen's Edinburgh home, nevertheless, it was the best of her three dresses and must do.

In the last three weeks, Devlen had tried to convince her to accept the services of a dressmaker, and she'd repeatedly declined. It was one thing to engage in an idyll, sharing weeks of hedonism for the sake of it. Quite another to be kept openly like a mistress.

Devlen's mistress. The label should have shocked her, and the fact it didn't was an indication of how utterly depraved she'd become.

She left her chamber and went to Robert's room, not unduly surprised to find it empty. The child was no doubt down in the kitchen again. He was often to be found there, chatting away with the cook and her helpers, and stuffing himself full of purloined treats.

The staff had still not warmed to her, and she wasn't surprised. During the day, she and Devlen practiced a careful avoidance of each other in front of the servants. Were they fooling any of them? Or was the staff at this enormous home busy speculating behind closed doors about the master and the governess?

She found her way to the kitchens, and there was Robert, perched on a chair, one hand braced on the top of the table, the other in a large ceramic bowl.

At the sight of her, he grinned.

Evidently, the Duke of Brechin was in the process of picking another biscuit. One or a dozen, she couldn't be certain. A selection was already arrayed on the table in front of him.

She reached him and brushed off the crumbs from the front of his shirt.

"Biscuits for breakfast?"

"Annie's biscuits," he corrected. "The best."

"Do not talk with your mouth full."

He nodded and smiled.

"Good morning, miss," Cook said, turning from the stove. She performed an awkward curtsy, especially as she had a spoon in one hand and a pot in the other. The odor of chocolate filled the room, and she suddenly understood why Robert couldn't stop grinning.

When his biscuit was finished, he said, "We're going to have chocolate to drink, Miss Sinclair. In honor of the day."

"In honor of the day?"

"It's Wednesday. Don't you think every day should be special?"

She smiled at him and reached to take a biscuit herself. Tomorrow, she'd fuss at him about eating a proper meal.

"I'm sure Annie wouldn't mind if you had some chocolate, too."

"Thank you, Your Grace, you're more than kind."

He grinned at her and took another bite of his newest biscuit acquisition. She was tempted to ask if he intended to hoard the others, but didn't.

Beatrice smiled her good-bye and made her way into the family dining room, where the table was set for breakfast. In a sense, the chamber was indicative of her life. From the kitchen, she could hear the sound of laughter and conversation. Somewhere, Devlen was no doubt occupied in a myriad of duties. Here, in this room, she was alone, strangely segregated from others. Proper, alone, and suddenly lonely.

In the year since her parents had died, she'd learned to accept the silence of her life, learned to live with the aloneness of loss and grief. It had been a habit she'd suddenly lost the ability to endure. She suddenly knew she'd never be able to go back to that life.

She moved to the line of serving dishes and inspected the contents one by one before replacing the lids.

At the cottage, she had been occupied with a daily tedium. Washing, weeding her tiny garden, carrying water to the struggling plants, cleaning, mending her garments and those she could still use that had once belonged to her mother. Her life hadn't been interesting, but it had been busy. Her new life was fascinating and yet was steeped in tedium.

She sat at the table and folded her hands, intent upon studying her nails. They'd lost their bluish tinge since she'd been eating well. Her hands no longer looked so frail or skeletal. Her body had filled out, her clothing was almost too snug. There were no lasting ill effects of her near starvation during that last hideous month before coming to Castle Crannoch.

After a few moments, she stood again and walked around the table and took another chair. The view was different, and she could look out the lone window at least. The day was a gray one and looked to be cold. Too cold for a walk, perhaps? She needed to stretch her legs, to do something other than simply wait until breakfast was done to begin her teaching chores.

Even that was not onerous. Robert was a good student when he wished to be, and when he didn't, one look from Devlen changed his mind about misbehaving.

The morning that had begun with such promise was now proving to be interminable.

She stood once again and left the dining room.

The fact they were lovers did not give her the authority to invade Devlen's privacy. Otherwise, she'd have used some of her free time to explore, to investigate some of this grand house Devlen had created for himself. She should retreat to the library and pick out a book. But she would be there soon enough to begin Robert's lessons. She needed something to do other than think of Devlen, some occupation that would take her mind from her enthrallment.

What was she but a slave to Devlen Gordon? A slave to pleasure, one who had begged him to bind her with chains.

Finally, with nowhere else to go, she retreated to her room, but before she entered, she turned and stared at the double doors leading to Devlen's chamber.

She strode across the hall and knocked gently on his door. There was no answer. Had he already left for the day? With such an empire to run, he must be occupied every moment of the day. If so, she was envious. She wanted something to do other than to think of him.

She heard a sound, and pushed on the latch, surprised to find the door unlocked.

He'd opened the drapes, and the weak sunlight spilled into the room, illuminating the midnight blue of the carpet and the draperies surrounding the bed.

The sound came again and she suddenly knew where he was.

Slowly, she pushed open the door of the bathing chamber and leaned against the jamb, watching him.

He was reclining in the copper tub, his arms on the sides, his head back with his eyes closed. Steam rose around him as he hummed a tune, some little ditty that had bawdy lyrics, no doubt.

After a moment, she stepped into the room, closing

the door behind her, but taking the precaution of locking it before turning to face him.

He glanced behind him and now sat looking at her, his features impassive, but a twinkle sparkling in his eyes.

"Are you going to tell me what's sauce for the goose is sauce for the gander?"

"I should, shouldn't I? But I must confess any thought I had has simply flown from my mind."

"At the sight of me?"

"Of course."

Beatrice retrieved the three-legged stool and set it beside the tub. She sat and dipped her hand into the hot water, playfully flicking water onto his chest.

"Dare I hope you're going to bathe me?"

"Do you want me to?"

"I'd be a fool to say no, wouldn't I?"

"We're both fools, of one kind or another."

He was dangerous, addictive, fascinating, and bad for her. She was virtuous, educated, and—to the world outside this house—imbued with sense and decorum. There was some type of future ahead of her now that she'd been the Duke of Brechin's governess.

She resented him at the same time she was fascinated by him. Nothing good could come of her relationship with Devlen Gordon.

He smiled at her, as if he understood her sudden irritation.

"You didn't use the English riding coats last night."

"I know. I remembered later."

"Does that mean I'm going to have a child?"

"Not necessarily. But it does mean I can't be trusted around you. I've never forgotten before."

What a silly time to feel a surge of pure, feminine pleasure.

His erection broke the surface of the water like a creature emerging from the deep.

"Does it always grow like that? Is it the hot water?"

His laughter echoed against the stone walls. "Not the hot water, Beatrice. It's you, I'm afraid. Frankly, even the idea of your hand being so close."

"Oh."

"Indeed. Oh. You see, I have been sitting here thinking of you touching me, and in you come, locking the door behind you."

"Really."

"You have the most fascinating look on your face. Why?"

"If you must know, I'm trying to envision what it must look like right at the moment."

He abruptly stood, water cascading from his body in sheets. "There, does that help?"

He was most gloriously made, a man in his prime, muscled and splendid. His buttocks were round and formed like two perfect buns. She trailed her fingers over one and watched as it flexed beneath her hand. But it was his impressive array of male attributes that caught her attention and held it.

His erection was long and thick, growing as she watched. It pointed to his stomach, and he pushed it down with a hand as if preparing to use it as a lance. If she'd still been a virgin, she would have been terrified.

She knew, however, what absolute wonder he could perform with such a weapon, and was only fascinated at its girth and length. Slowly, she extended one finger and trailed a path from its bulbous head to the nest of surprisingly soft hair at its base.

"It's very hard," she said. "And hot. Does it hurt?"

"Yes."

She glanced up at him to see him watching her intently. Her finger strolled from base to tip, and then softly circled the head.

"Indeed?"

"I'm in great pain at the moment."

"You should take advantage of a long, soaking bath I think. Something that would take the swelling down."

"Is that what you would recommend?"

"A snow pack, perhaps, would be better."

"It would certainly cool any ardor."

She stroked his erection again, and it trembled beneath her ministrations.

"You must certainly seek some treatment for it."

"Kiss it."

She glanced up at him, shocked. His eyes were glittering, his face ruddy with color. "Kiss it, Beatrice."

Slowly, she rose and, with one hand on the edge of the tub for balance, reached over and pressed her lips against him. His erection bobbed in response, hot and eager, and so soft she was tempted to kiss him again. She held him with one hand, her fingers gently resting against his length as if to coax him still. Her other hand curved around one buttock as her lips found him, and opened just a little.

The bulbous head was soft against her lips. She opened her mouth just a little wider, enough for her tongue to dart out. A teasing touch, one eliciting a groan from Devlen.

She smiled, her lips curving against the shaft.

The steam from the water dampened her face, plastered the fabric of her bodice against her chest. She wished she was naked with him. She ran her palms up his thighs, combing the hair on his legs with playful fingers. His buttocks were smooth, so beautifully shaped she couldn't help but caress them with her hand.

All the while, he stood motionless, his hand on the back of her head, fingers spread through her hair. She didn't move her lips, but from time to time she would blow a warm breath on the head of his erection to see it jerk and throb in response.

She loved having him under her power.

He smelled of the soap he'd used, something scented with sandalwood. Reaching out with her right hand, she scooped some up from the tin and placed it on his knee, rubbing it into his skin in a circular pattern.

"Beatrice."

She sat back and looked up at him. "I want to wash you, Devlen."

He grabbed her hair, and tugged gently. "There. Wash me there."

She only smiled.

One leg was washed slowly, from the knee down to his foot, submerged in the steaming water. Then the other, using the same slow, rhythmic touch.

His erection grew as if to attract her attention. She was not likely to forget about it.

When she was done with his legs, she lathered the base of hair between his legs, taking care to soap the testicles with a gentle circular motion. Finally, it was time to wash his erection. She covered both palms with the sandalwood soap before placing them on the shaft.

He made a noise halfway between a groan and a laugh.

Beatrice smiled.

Using both hands, she stroked him from the base to the tip, her grip firm and unrelenting. He said something to her, some caution she blithely ignored. She wanted him to explode in her hands, wanted him to lose control as she did every time he touched her.

She grew breathless and heated—she wanted the same from him. Her heart pounded so loudly her chest quivered with it. Her mind opened and her soul poured out to him. She wanted him as desperate and longing as she felt.

Both hands were on him, holding him still, and she bent forward and opened her mouth, encircling the head with her lips. He arched his hips forward, and she felt an answering response deep inside, where her body readied for him.

A few drops of water splashed from the faucet into the tub, a log dropped in the fire, but they only accompanied the kissing sounds she made when teasing the head in and out of her mouth. Devlen whispered something, a warning perhaps, and she only moved slightly so she could grip one of his buttocks with each hand.

She moved, releasing his erection, compelled to do something shocking. She bit him tenderly on that beautiful backside, kissed the spot, and then rubbed her cheek against his buttock. He made a sound in his throat, a cross between a laugh and an oath.

The moment was so decadent, completely sensual, and probably wrong, but her breasts tightened, and her body heated.

She trailed a path of kisses back to his erection.

He was arching his hips back and forth as if to urge her to mouth more of him. But despite pressing her head forward with his hand, she wouldn't do what he wished. This moment was for his satisfaction, but she would be the architect of it.

She pulled back and gripped the shaft again, looking up at him.

He'd always used words to such advantage with her. Could she do the same?

"I want you to explode in my hands, Devlen." She gripped him tightly, using the remainder of the soap as a lubricant to slide her hands tightly down his shaft to ring the head with her fingers.

"A waste, Beatrice."

He looked fierce and proud and almost angry with passion. At that moment, she wanted him in her, rising over her and into her. But her satisfaction would have to wait.

One more stroke and he closed his eyes.

"Open your eyes, Devlen. Look at me."

She licked the head of his erection, never breaking eye contact.

His gaze grew even more fierce as the color on his cheekbones deepened.

"You taste sweet. Is that your soap? Or you?"

One more lick.

"Did you make the formula of your soap for just this purpose? How inventive of you."

She licked him again, tightening her grip around his shaft and sliding her hands up and down once more. He felt hotter and harder than before.

"What a marvelous instrument this is," she said,

speaking to his erection. She licked the head again. "You taste of salt."

He tightened the grip on her hair.

Another stroke, and a rhythm began between them, not unlike when he was inside her. He arched, she stroked, her gestures accompanied by words of encouragement.

"It will be soon, won't it, Devlen?"

"Is that what you want?"

"Oh yes."

"If you don't stop teasing me, I'll be more than happy to deliver."

"Please do. I want to taste you."

"Damn it, Beatrice."

That's when she knew he was hers. She had him between her hands, at the end of her licking, teasing tongue. She smiled and bent to taste him again and he swore once more, his hips jerking forward before his erection shivered and arched and throbbed. His testicles drew up and she held him as he exploded between her hands.

He dragged her up against his body. His eyes were glittering, the flush on his face had darkened. His kiss was punishing and exhilarating. She held on to his shoulders for balance as he pulled her closer, her dress sodden.

For once he was powerless, and her mood was exhilarated and wild.

A strange and wonderful time to realize she was in love.

Chapter 28

B̲eatrice sat on the leather sofa in Devlen's library, Robert on the floor in front of the circular table. The room was palatial in comparison to the library at Castle Crannoch, both in terms of numbers of volumes on the shelves as well as the furnishings. Two leather couches, tufted and designed for comfort, sat sideways in front of a roaring fire. Between them was a low round table adorned with a crystal bowl filled with flowers.

When they studied, Beatrice took the precaution of moving the crystal bowl to the floor.

The mahogany shelves surrounding the room were crafted with intricate dentil molding and filled with leather-bound books with gilt titles. She'd examined most of them, fascinated with the depth and breadth of Devlen's curiosity.

The room was shaped like an L; at the other end was Devlen's desk where he sat working on a stack of papers. He glanced over at her from time to time, and smiled, then returned to his task.

"We're going to discuss Pliny the Younger this morning," she said, forcing herself to pay attention to Robert's lessons. She would have liked to sit and study Devlen, instead, since he was such a commanding personage, especially dressed casually as he was this morning. But that wouldn't be proper, not to mention a colossal waste of time.

She wouldn't be any closer to understanding him than she was now. Nor would she have an inkling of what plans she should make.

Time. Time had never before raced by as quickly as it had these last weeks. Some permanent provisions would have to be made for Robert, and she was very much afraid the plans wouldn't include her.

Beatrice didn't want the child returning to Castle Crannoch, however. If she could do nothing else, she'd convince Devlen not to allow him to return to that dark and brooding place.

As for her, she needed to find another position. Cameron Gordon had dismissed her, and she was without prospects. She wasn't going to starve again.

She could always remain as Devlen's mistress. If he wished her in that role, that is. What kind of life would she have if she remained? One of pleasure and luxury, no doubt. But little regard from others, and she doubted she'd have friends. And security? As much money as Devlen would promise her, perhaps. She'd be a rich man's mistress.

She'd be Devlen's mistress.
She'd be Devlen's lover.
Life was quickly done and easily over. She'd

learned that lesson in the past year. Even Robert in his youth had learned how temporary life could be. Should she return to her cottage to spend the rest of her life as a virtuous woman, repentant of her time of lust? Or should she live her life as best she could, as fully as she could?

She bent to her lessons, blocking out the sight of Devlen with some difficulty.

Instead of looking for another room in the house to do their lessons, Devlen had urged her to use his library, which was all well and good, but he had occupied it as well.

At first, she'd been a little self-conscious to instruct Robert in front of his cousin, but Devlen rarely appeared to be listening. A few times she caught him smiling, however, like now.

"Do you think my methods amusing?"

"You're so very earnest, Miss Sinclair. You seem to care very much whether or not Robert learns from you."

"Of course I care. What sort of governess would I be if I did not?"

"My tutors didn't seem to care," Robert offered.

"That's because you put frogs in their beds."

"I put a snake in yours."

"Did you?" Devlen asked.

"He did."

"What did Miss Sinclair do?"

"She gave the snake a funeral," Robert said.

"Miss Sinclair has a very soft heart."

She glanced at him and then away.

"You're a very good teacher," Devlen said.

She really shouldn't have been so pleased, but she was, of course.

"I have an errand to do this afternoon," Devlen said. "Would you like to accompany me?"

Her initial response was the same excitement Robert immediately showed. Instead, caution reared its head, and she shook her head. During the day she was Robert's governess. At night she was Devlen's lover. The two roles never overlapped. In the library she was Miss Sinclair. In the bedroom she was dear Beatrice.

"I think it would be better if Robert and I take a walk. The snow has kept us inside for days. I need to stretch my legs."

"There are several shops you might enjoy not too far away." He glanced at Robert. "You must make a point of stopping by Mr. McElwee's Confectionary Shop. They make excellent sweets."

Robert looked hopeful again. Beatrice smiled at him and nodded. "You've been working very hard lately. I think that deserves a treat."

They finished their morning lessons. Devlen left the room before they did, calling her attention to a pouch he left on his desk.

"A little money for your outing."

She didn't bother arguing with him, only thanked him and watched as he left the room. Instantly, she missed him.

The day was cold, but the sun was shining. Beatrice bundled up in her cloak and ensured that Robert was similarly attired. He needed new gloves but for this outing was using a pair of Devlen's. They were much too large, of course, but he insisted upon wearing them, waving the fingers comically at her.

She wrapped a scarf around his throat and wished the

snow was not so deep, but they would look for a well-traveled route so they could avoid the worse of it.

"Shall we take the carriage, Miss Sinclair?"

"I am heartily tired of riding in a carriage, Robert. Aren't you?"

He nodded a moment later, but she could tell his heart wasn't in it.

"You'll see. The walking will do us good. We'll be hungry for lunch when we return."

"I'm hungry now."

"You," she said, ruffling his hair, "are hungry anytime."

He didn't fuss any more about the walk, and twenty minutes later she was grateful she'd decided to go on foot.

Edinburgh's streets were narrow in places, and mostly cobbled. London had the reputation of being the city the world came to visit, but it felt as if Edinburgh also shared that distinction this morning. She heard French being spoken as well as three other languages, one of which was German. The other two she couldn't identify, but she stood there unabashedly listening to the speakers in an attempt to do so.

The city was perched on several hills, so walking was a vigorous exercise. Devlen's home was in the newer section of Edinburgh, its neatly arranged streets and parks a marked contrast to Old Town.

"The residents of Edinburgh are certainly well-read," she said, when they passed yet another bookstore.

"Yes, but do they eat any sweeties?" Robert frowned up at her, a not-too-gentle reminder they were on a quest for a confectioner's shop.

She consulted her directions and led him to the shop

Devlen recommended. There, she spent some of the money Devlen had given her on fudge in various flavors, including chocolate with raisins, hazelnut, and something delicious called Highland Cream. At Robert's insistence, she tried a sweet that made her feel as if the top of her head was coming off.

"It's hot, isn't it, Miss Sinclair?"

She waved her hand in front of her mouth. She'd tasted cloves and cinnamon, but there was something else in the chewy toffee as well—pepper and ginger?

"You put another snake in my bed, didn't you?"

The boy laughed, the first time he'd done so in so long that her discomfort was worth it.

She saw the carriage as they left the confectioners, but other than to remark upon its similarity to Devlen's vehicle, didn't pay it much attention. But when it was still there, lingering on the crowded street when they emerged from a bookshop, she studied it with more care.

The horses looked the same. She wasn't an expert on the animals, but their coloring was similar, and they were perfectly matched.

Had Devlen sent a carriage to wait for them?

She walked a few feet before realizing that Robert wasn't with her. She turned to see him standing at the edge of the street, his attention caught by a dead rodent.

"Come away, Robert."

"It's dead."

"Robert."

He glanced at her and for a moment she thought he might disobey, but he kicked at the animal, then stepped back when a score of flies swarmed upward.

The coach was looming directly in front of them.

There was something oddly reminiscent of the first time she'd seen Devlen's carriage on the winding road to Castle Crannoch.

Before Robert reached her, however, the carriage swerved, heading directly for the boy. For a horrified second, Beatrice froze. In the next breath, she ran for Robert, grabbing him by both arms and pulling him with her. They both slammed into a retaining wall beside the road.

Beatrice reached down and grabbed the boy under the arms, pushing Robert up to the top of the wall. His shoes scraped her forehead as he scrambled to reach the top.

Please, please, please. There was no way she could escape the carriage. She buried her head below her arms, and pressed herself as close to the wall as she could.

She couldn't think, could only feel time measured in tiny blips of seconds. She wanted to run, as quickly as she could, but was trapped against the wall. Her arms stretched wide to minimize her breadth. The horses were so close she could feel their heated breath on her face.

Screams of equine terror echoed in her ear.

Help me.

"That's all," Devlen said to his secretary.

"Sir?"

"I can't work."

"Are you feeling all right, sir?"

"Fine, damn it."

"Could I bring you something to drink, sir? Or ring for Mrs. Anderson? She could bring you some tea. Or chocolate."

"I'm not hungry, Lawrence. I simply can't work."

"You must make a decision, sir, on the new cotton mill."

"Later."

"What about the new hull design?"

Devlen leaned back in his chair. "Tomorrow."

"But the negotiations for the mine, sir, in Wales. That can't wait. Sir?"

"Have you ever been in love, Lawrence?"

"Sir?"

The young man's face flamed. Deven had employed Lawrence because he'd been impressed with the young man's business acumen. His youth, however, was always an issue.

"Never mind." He thumbed through the stack of papers on his desk. "Do you think my empire is going to be in shambles if I don't work today?"

"With all due respect, sir, you haven't worked very much for the last three weeks. Not since . . ." His face deepened in color.

Devlen didn't bother to answer his accusation. Lawrence was right.

Even if his own business affairs were done, there was the matter of the solicitor's report. He wanted to amend Robert's guardianship, and there was a slight chance the courts would grant him custody of the child, only because of his father's infirmity. He didn't want to fight Cameron, especially in the courts, and he didn't want to bring to light—and to the public—what had happened to him. But Robert's welfare was greater than Cameron's reputation, and if the latter needed to be sullied in order to protect the child, then Devlen would do so.

If, however, he could get his mind off Beatrice. He'd
come to the wharf office to do some work, approve the
off-loaded inventory, and meet with two of his cap-
tains. Not sit here like some weak-minded lad, remembering Beatrice as if he hadn't just left her.

One particular memory was his favorite. They were
studying Plutarch's Lives, and when he'd inquired as to
whether doing so was a little advanced for Robert,
she'd smiled.

"He dislikes *Aesop's Fables*, and Plutarch offers stories about mortal men who really lived. But the study of
their lives also offers a moral."

"Did you always learn that way? Every lesson having
a moral?"

She considered the question for a moment. "My father once said animals can teach their young without
seeming to do so. A kitten will obey its mother, or perhaps its nature, while a baby has no inkling of the lessons the parent has learned. Education must fill the gap.
We must learn from the mistakes and triumphs of others. It's not enough simply to know the sum of a column
of figures, or to be familiar with a poet's work. Learning must be about a man's life. How to make it better."

"Has learning made your life better?"

She glanced at him and then smiled. "Some would say
learning is wasted on women. I've heard that thought es-
poused on more than one occasion. Plutarch taught me
to be resigned rather than angry about my life."

"I think a little anger wouldn't have been amiss. Less
logic and more feeling, perhaps."

"Do you think I don't have any feelings?"

"I think you push them down so deep inside so
they'll not trouble you. Even Plutarch acknowledged

the weaknesses of men. He believed men could be pro-
moted to angels but for their passions."

"He also believed men are subjected to death and re-
birth. Do you believe that?"

"A clever way of deflecting the subject, Miss Sinclair."

He'd stood, then, and left the room. Otherwise, he
would have kissed her, in front of Robert and the
young maid who'd entered with a tray of biscuits and
chocolate.

She had the most alluring voice. Low, but imbued
with a rounded tone to it, as if laughter hid just behind
the words. She looked as if she hid a smile as well, her
lips curving as if teasing him to leave his desk and
come across the room to kiss her.

Beatrice. The name truly didn't suit her, and yet at
the same time it did. It was much too modest a name for
such a wanton creature. Only he knew how wanton. He
leaned back in the chair and contemplated a series of
memories, plucking one at random. Until the day he
died, he'd remember how she looked this morning as
he'd opened the curtains and watched her sleep. The
sun had filtered into the room, stealing across the carpet
to rest at her feet, and then, catlike, creeping to bathe a
hand, and then a cheek. She'd blinked open her eyes,
shielding them with that same sun-warmed hand, and
smiled at him, a look of such beauty and delight he'd
been charmed to his toes. And something else. He'd
been struck by a fear so pervasive and sudden he'd lost
his breath because of it.

What would he do if she left him?

She couldn't.

Where were they now? Had they already visited the
confectioner's shop? Was she tired of walking Edin-

burgh's endless hills? Should he send a carriage to bring her home?

How could he keep her with him?

Too many questions, and regrettably, he didn't have the answers.

The carriage missed her by an inch, no more. Beatrice could feel the heat of the horses, then the slap of their leads against her back. The axle of the wheel grazed the back of her legs, tearing her skirt.

The wheels ground against the cobbles, combined with the whinny of the frightened horses, and Robert's shouts.

When it was gone, she sagged against the wall, feeling herself slip to the ground, her palms abraded against the brick.

"Miss! Are you all right?" She was suddenly surrounded by strangers, people she didn't know, whose faces were as white as hers must be.

"Criminal, the way some people drive!"

"You're bleeding, miss." A woman pressed her lavender-scented handkerchief into her palm, and Beatrice dabbed at the cut on her lip.

"Miss Sinclair! Miss Sinclair!" She folded herself against the wall, her cheek pressing against it. The carriage was careening down the crowded street, pedestrians turning to witness its departure, more than a few people surrounding her, inquiring as to her well-being. She had to get up. She was causing a scene, sitting there.

She stood with some difficulty, her legs shaking beneath her.

"Miss Sinclair?"

She turned to see Robert standing there. How had he descended from the wall?

"Miss Sinclair, are you all right?"

She wasn't, but she forced a smile to her face. "How are you, Robert?"

"It happened again, didn't it?"

There was no point in mistaking his meaning. Someone had tried to run him over, in a carriage looking too much like Devlen's for comfort.

"It was Thomas, Miss Sinclair."

"Thomas?"

"The driver. He works for my uncle."

She pressed her hands against her waist, and prayed for composure.

Beatrice grabbed Robert's hand and started retracing their steps to Devlen's house. The return trip was mostly uphill and too long. She was trying not to think as she walked, but she couldn't do anything about the fear. It was there like a third person.

Robert was silent at her side and she wanted to reassure the child they were safe, but she couldn't lie to him. Edinburgh was proving to be as dangerous as Castle Crannoch.

As they walked past the wrought-iron gate and entered Devlen's property, Beatrice felt some of the tension leave her. Devlen would know what to do. The thought brought her up short. When had she begun to place all her trust in Devlen?

"Miss Sinclair."

She glanced down at Robert. The boy had stopped in the drive and was staring at the carriage parked in front of the house.

"It isn't your uncle's."

She tugged at his hand, walked behind the carriage, and opened the front door. There, in animated conversation with Mrs. Anderson, was one of the most beautiful women Beatrice had ever seen.

The black cloak she wore was made of a soft wool, Beatrice could tell that much by the way the garment draped. Pearl buttons held it closed at the neck, while a white fur collar emphasized the blue of the wearer's eyes, the delicate pale complexion, and the shine of her auburn hair, arranged in a style designed to be taken down with the artful removal of only a few pins.

She was shorter than Beatrice by some measure, enough that she felt like a giant in comparison. Everything about her was petite, from the pointed shoe peeping out from beneath her cloak, to the hand holding the white fur muff.

"Who are you?"

Even her voice was small. Small, and breathy, as if she was too delicate to take a full breath. No doubt doing so would test the stamina of her chest, and it looked like she was doing all she could to stand upright with such a massive bosom.

"Mrs. Anderson, who is this woman?" she asked, her voice accented with the barest hint of a Scottish burr. No doubt the men of her acquaintance thought it charming.

Mrs. Anderson didn't even look in Beatrice's direction. "His Grace, the Duke of Brechin and his governess, Miss Sinclair."

"Devlen's cousin," she said, dismissing Robert as unimportant. Why not? He was only seven and therefore too young a male to attract.

"I'll wait for Devlen in his library."

Beatrice glanced at Mrs. Anderson. "Is that wise?

Devlen doesn't like people in his library when he isn't there."

The other woman turned and surveyed Beatrice again. "You're a bit forward to be the governess, aren't you?" She hesitated for a moment, then began to smile. "You think to coax him to your bed, don't you?" An instant later, her eyes narrowed. "Or have you already? How very convenient for Devlen to have installed you as the governess." She smiled. "You're available both day and night, and he gets two positions in paying for only one. Devlen does have a head for business."

She calmly unbuttoned her cloak, revealing a green silk dress clinging to her overripe curves before falling to her ankles in a long, shimmering cascade of fabric.

"Does he give you presents as well?" She fingered a diamond necklace at her throat. "It's his latest gift."

Devlen's mistress.

"It's too showy for my taste," Beatrice said calmly. "I prefer pearls. So much more understated."

Felicia smiled, but the look in her eyes could have melted ice.

"You might want to thank him in the bathing chamber. He has a partiality for that room."

Before Felicia could say another word, or the estimable Mrs. Anderson could comment, Beatrice took Robert by the hand, turned, and walked out the door.

"Where are we going, Miss Sinclair?"

"Somewhere safe," she said.

"Will anyone be able to find us?"

"No."

"Miss Sinclair? You're shaking."

"I'm cold, that's all."

She was shaking, but it wasn't cold or even fear.

Anger raced through her, as spicy as the chocolate she'd eaten earlier. How dare he! How dare he keep her in his house and keep his mistress as well.

Was Devlen to blame? Or was she the more culpable? She'd wanted adventure and excitement to the exclusion of good sense. She'd pushed down every condemning thought, every weak whisper of her conscience because of pleasure.

She should have been wiser, smarter, less innocent, unwary. Instead, she'd given him everything: her affection, her body, her trust. Her love.

"Miss Sinclair?"

"It's all right, Robert. It will be all right."

She reached into her reticule and pulled out the money Devlen had insisted she take for their outing. He'd been incredibly generous, and they'd purchased enough sweets to give Robert a stomachache for a week. The remainder of the money would be enough to leave Edinburgh.

Beatrice halted at the corner and wondered where she could go to hire a carriage. A simple enough question as it turned out. She inquired of a passerby, who pointed her in the direction of an inn. The innkeeper in turn directed her to a stable. The owner was not happy to rent his carriage for a one-way journey, so she ended up paying twice as much as it was worth.

"I need to go to Kilbridden Village," she said, giving him directions.

"I know the place, but it's an out-of-the-way hamlet, miss. Inverness might be more to your liking."

Robert had been silent beside her, his eyes wide. But it was an indication of how desperate their straits that he didn't question her actions.

"Return in an hour, and we'll leave then."

"Now."

He stared at her and then spit on the ground. "I've not had my dinner."

"Your horses are rested, are they not? Have they been fed and watered? What else must you do?"

"Are you fleeing for some purpose, miss? I'm not carrying a felon, am I?"

"I've done nothing. But my son and I need to travel this afternoon."

"The roads might be bad, we might need to spend the night."

"I've the money to pay for lodging."

"Son is it? He doesn't look like you."

"Mommy," Robert said just at that moment, "I want a candy."

"Not now. Later." She brushed his hair back and wondered at the speed at which they had both become accomplished liars.

"Very well, get inside, and we'll be off." He added a few more moments of grumbling before he began to lead the horses to the front of the coach.

She and Robert climbed inside, and in the silence he asked her the one question she dreaded.

"Does Devlen want me dead?"

"I don't know."

She didn't want Devlen to be involved. He couldn't be. She couldn't be that wrong about someone. He loved Robert; that was plain to see by anyone who viewed them together.

And her? What did he feel about her?

"I'd give it up if I could," Robert said. She glanced down to find Robert crying. Large tears all the more touching for the fact they were silent. "I don't want to be duke."

She wrapped him in the folds of her cloak. At the moment, she wanted to cry, too. She was so frightened, and she didn't know what to do.

Robert slid his hand into hers, and she was grateful for the comfort of it. Together, they sat as the driver made the carriage ready. She was grateful for the silence. There was nothing she could say to the child.

She'd almost failed him.

Chapter 29

⌒◇⌒

The journey home took them five hours, far longer than it would have taken if the driver had made an earnest attempt to hurry. Perhaps the roads were as bad as he complained. They were certainly icy, but neither snow-filled nor rutted. If he'd been paid by the distance instead of the hour, Beatrice was certain they could have reached Kilbridden Village in half the time.

The cottage looked more than empty; it looked deserted and oddly sad, its thatched roof drooping beneath the night sky. The stone of the walls was from a quarry outside of the village and was the color of mud when it rained. In the spring they were saved from dullness by climbing ivy. But now it looked forlorn and humble, hardly a fit place to bring the Duke of Brechin.

She left the carriage and paid the driver the rest of his money, before taking Robert's hand and following the path to the front door.

At the door she turned the latch and entered, feeling

as if she'd been gone for years instead of just a few weeks. She halted on the threshold, feeling the memories flooding back.

"Father, why did they build such funny-looking buildings?"

"They're called pyramids, Beatrice, and they're for worshiping their gods."

"Beatrice Anne Sinclair. What are you doing? Come down from there this instant!" But in the next moment, her mother had dissolved into laughter to see both her husband and her daughter sitting in the high branches of a tree.

"It's a nest, Mother. Father thinks it's an eagle."

"I shall not ever want to leave you. I promise and cross my heart, Father."

"Ah, but you will, Beatrice, and it will be a good thing. One's children are only on loan, you see. They are gifts to be surrendered when the time comes."

Robert entered the cottage after her, and she wondered what he saw. A plain structure, with three windows and a door, a wooden floor sagging in spots. There was one place near the hearth where the floor squeaked.

The kitchen table was square and old, two of the chairs matched, but the third did not. Her mother had made the curtains over the windows a few years ago, sitting by the fire and hemming the embroidered linen with careful stitches. A rug in front of the fireplace had been her resting place many evenings as she'd sat and listened to her parents talk or her father read aloud. Two overstuffed chairs sat in front of the fire with a small table between them. On it sat a lantern, and a store of candles. A door led to her parents' room, and a staircase to her loft bed.

All in all, a snug place to live. Nothing as grand as Castle Crannoch. But there was love here, the remnants of it clinging to the very air. At Castle Crannoch there were only dark shadows and suspicion.

And in Edinburgh? She could not think of Edinburgh right now.

After lighting the candles on the mantel, she knelt and prepared the fire. The room was chilled, and it would take several hours for the cottage to warm.

She opened the door beside the fireplace, revealing her parents' small but comfortable room, one she'd never occupied.

"You'll sleep here," she told Robert, who was still looking around him with wide-eyed wonder. Ever since they'd left Edinburgh he'd been strangely quiet.

There was nothing to eat in the larder or pantry, so she and Robert sat at the end of her parents' bed and ate the rest of the sweets for dinner. When she tucked him into bed, his voice was subdued and more childlike than she'd ever heard.

"Miss Sinclair? Could I have a candle lit, please?"

"Of course," she said, and bent down to brush his hair off his forehead. Before he could object, she kissed his cheek, feeling a curious and maternal protectiveness for the Duke of Brechin.

"Sleep well, Robert."

"You'll be close?"

"Just in the loft," she said, pointing to the ceiling. "A call will bring me running."

He nodded, evidently satisfied.

She sat in the main room of the cottage, staring at the fire. She was cold, but it wasn't the type of chill that could be warmed.

Had she made a mistake in leaving Edinburgh without meeting with Devlen? Robert's safety came first, and her wishes and wants far behind. Did she suspect him? That was the question, wasn't it?

She stood and walked around the room, touching the table where she and her parents had taken their meals, the mantel where her mother's most prized possessions, a pair of statues of a shepherd and shepherdess, had once rested. She'd sold them after the epidemic, in order to afford the gravestones for her parents.

She gripped the mantel and leaned forward, resting her head on her hands. The heat from the fire warmed her face.

What would her father have thought of Devlen? He would have warned her to be wary of men with such a charming smile and way with women. A despoiler of innocents. A hunter of unicorns. Her mother would have adored him.

She stood, and walked back to the chair her father had often occupied. The upholstery still bore the scent of his pipe.

Dear God, how was she to endure this, too?

The pain felt like a bandage being removed from a wound. Until now, until this exact moment, she'd thought everything was bearable. The discovery there was agony beneath the surface was shocking, stripping her breath from her.

She wrapped her arms around herself and bent over,

stifling the sharp, keening cry. She wanted to scream, but the sound traveled inward, careening through her mind and heart and forcing her to her knees. Beatrice slid to the floor, holding on to the arms of the chair to keep herself upright. She could barely breathe for the pain.

Devlen.

Her tears came grudgingly. She wept for her parents, for Robert's loss, for the girl she'd been and was no more. She cried for the lost innocence not of her body but of her heart. She cried because she was betrayed, and in love, and the enormity of those twin emotions was too great a burden after all.

Devlen couldn't remember ever being as angry as he was right at this particular moment.

He'd come home, only to find that Beatrice and Robert hadn't returned from their outing. He'd paced in the library for a few hours, calming himself with the thought that they were no doubt enjoying the day. But by dusk he was summoning the servants, intent on retracing their path through the shops.

He told himself it was annoyance that incited his search, but he couldn't maintain that pretense for long, especially after visiting a shopkeeper along the route.

"Aye, sir, it was a close call. I seen them both, the little boy and the woman. Why, the woman nearly got herself trampled trying to save the lad. Magnificent horses, though. Matched pairs, both of them. Rarely seen the like."

"But you haven't seen them again?"

"The horses? Oh, you mean the woman and the boy. After a close call like that? I'd go to the nearest tavern and down a whiskey." The shopkeeper shrugged. "No, I never saw them after that."

The carriage was too slow, and he pounded on the top of the roof as a signal to the driver to pick up speed.

The idea she'd almost been hurt had caused him no end of grief. His stomach still rolled thinking about it.

Where in blazes was she?

He'd sent Saunders to Castle Crannoch to ensure she wasn't there. He didn't believe she'd go back to the castle but he couldn't afford to overlook any possibility. At dawn he'd visited Felicia, which proved to be both interesting and profoundly disturbing. Up until Mrs. Anderson told him he'd no idea the two women had ever met, let alone that Beatrice had returned to the house earlier. At least one question had been answered: Why hadn't she come to him? She had, and found Felicia.

"What did you say to her?" he asked.

"Nothing of consequence. Has she gone away, Devlen?"

Felicia began to smile, reaching up to place her hands on his chest. He had the strangest thought she was not unlike a cat. He didn't particularly like cats.

"Why, Devlen darling. Are you lonely?"

"What did you say?"

She pulled back, and then stepped away.

"Are you this proprietary with your women, Devlen? If so, I should have been flattered during our time together."

She began to laugh, her wrapper falling open to reveal a plenteous bosom. He should know. She'd been his mistress for two years.

"You're in love with her. Oh, Devlen, that truly is a jest."

There was nothing he could say. To argue the point would be futile, especially since it occurred to him just at that moment, standing in his former mistress's parlor, that she might be right.

Beatrice couldn't have simply left. She wouldn't have, not after last night. Or this morning. She'd glanced at him before he'd left the room and he could swear there was something warm in her look, an affection, some type of fondness.

But there was nothing to tie her to him. No reason for her to stay. Perhaps he should settle an obscene amount of money on her and bribe her to remain with him. Or hire her in some capacity. Perhaps he could lock her up in his house for a year or two. Keep her sated and well loved in his bed, so exhausted she couldn't leave it. The idea of her needing to sleep to recuperate from their loving and then being seduced again was enough to deflect his anger for a few moments.

She'd come from Kilbridden Village. Is it possible she might have returned there? Where else would she go? Beatrice was alone in the world, with few options. She had no money, nothing but the care of an occasionally obnoxious seven-year-old duke.

The thought they were in danger was sudden, overwhelming, and nearly paralyzing.

Beatrice ended up sleeping in her father's chair, fully dressed. Her feet were swollen when she awoke and her shoes pinched, so she slipped them off and wished the fire hadn't burned down to cinders. She eased up from the chair, feeling stiff. A price to pay for sleeping sitting up, her head braced against the chair's side. She'd caught her father doing that only too often in the past.

Last night they'd survived on sweets, but today she must arrange to buy some food. She'd become accustomed to eating three times a day in Edinburgh, and her stomach rumbled as if to remind her a meal was due.

Later, she'd go to see Jeremy. He'd know the name of the magistrate, or some other official to whom she could tell her story. There must be someone impartial who could offer protection to Robert. If nothing else, his title should be able to garner some interest in his plight.

There was enough money to tide them over for a week or two, especially if she were careful. And after that?

That decision could wait until later.

She pulled at the wrinkles of her skirt, slipped on her shoes, and went to the well in the back garden. The rusted pulley wheel squeaked as she hauled the bucket up from the bottom. Once the bucket was full she returned to the cottage, intent on her morning's chores.

Mary stood in the middle of the cottage's main room. Rowena's maid was dressed for the weather in a full cloak trimmed in fur. Both hands held a basket.

"Miss Sinclair," she said, inclining her head. "How tired you look."

"What are you doing here? For that matter, how did you know I was here?"

"Devlen sent his man to Castle Crannoch looking for you. My brother and I wondered if you'd be here, instead. You do remember my brother, don't you? Thomas? The driver? Or perhaps you don't. People often ignore servants, as if they're not there. We're invisible."

She strode forward and put the basket down on the table. "I've brought you some pastries. I'm quite a skillful cook, you know."

"That was very kind of you."

"You look wary. I wonder why."

"I don't know you. Why should you bring me pastries?"

"Miss Sinclair?"

Robert came out of her parents' room, rubbing his eyes. He had clearly just awakened. Before she could go to his side, before she could urge him back into the room, Mary grabbed her.

The knife in her hand bit deep into her throat.

She gasped, half in shock, half in pain.

"Take a muffin from the basket, Robert." Mary moved the knife closer. Beatrice could feel the blade cut into her skin and the warmth of her blood trickle down her neck.

Beatrice didn't understand. Not until Mary moved closer and unfolded the napkin from the basket. There was an assortment of plump muffins resting there, each of them sprinkled with what looked like sugar.

The birds. The bread.

"Don't," she said, the only word she was able to get out before Mary tightened her grip.

"If you don't want your governess to die, Your Grace, you'll do as I say. It won't be bad. You'll just get sleepy, that's all. Then you'll go and meet your father and mother. You miss them, don't you, lad?"

Robert reached out and picked up a muffin, his eyes wide and frightened. He was only seven, young enough to trust the words of an adult, even a madwoman. But Beatrice knew the moment he ate the biscuit, Mary would kill her.

She made a noise in her throat, and the knife sliced deeper.

Her neighbors were too far away to be of any assistance. No one else knew she'd returned to Kilbridden Village.

"I'm the Duke of Brechin," Robert suddenly said, putting the muffin down. "No one commands me to do anything."

Mary made a sound in her throat. "Do you want Miss Sinclair to die, you foolish child?"

He picked up the muffin again and looked away, his attention momentarily distracted. Beatrice wanted to shout at him to move, to run away, anything but allow himself to be poisoned.

What a hideous time to discover Robert felt some affection for her.

A sound at the door made Mary turn, still holding the knife. Beatrice was bleeding freely now, and she didn't know if the sudden dizziness she felt was from loss of blood or terror.

A thousand cannons suddenly exploded. The small cottage absorbed the boom of thunder and a high tinny ringing Beatrice realized was only in her ears.

Mary dropped to the floor, her mouth forming a perfect O as she fell. Instantly, a crimson flower formed on the floor around her. No, not a flower. Blood.

Beatrice looked toward the door, eyes wide. Devlen stood there, holding one of his carriage pistols, a look of such ferocity on his face she almost flinched from it. As Robert ran to him, she sank down into her father's chair, holding a hand to her throat.

Chapter 30

"**W**hy?"

Devlen glanced at her, and Beatrice tightened her arms around Robert. "Why would Mary do such a thing?"

"Unfortunately, the person who really knows the answer to that question can no longer tell us."

The wheels of the carriage were loud on the gravel-covered road. The wind, sharp and fast, sounded a high-pitched keening as if to mourn Mary.

"But you suspect," Beatrice said.

"For the sake of love. It makes fools of all of us."

"But did it make her a murderer?"

"I suspect she wanted my father to be duke," Devlen said.

"Did she love him so much she was willing to kill a child?"

"Not for him. For Rowena."

She closed her eyes, placed her cheek against Robert's

357

head, and exhaled a breath. "To make her the Duchess of Brechin."

"There was that, but I don't think she thought of it like that. Rowena and my father have not seen eye to eye since the accident. My father wanted the dukedom. If he was happy, perhaps Rowena would be."

"But when Robert was shot at, they weren't even at Castle Crannoch."

"No, but I think if you look closer to Mary's family, you'll find her accomplice."

"Thomas."

She looked out the window. The day had been spent with the magistrate, a very somber gentleman who owned land to the north of Kilbridden Village. He hadn't been overly impressed with either the Duke of Brechin's title or Devlen's wealth.

"How did you come to find Miss Sinclair, sir?"

"I asked in the village. I woke up more than one person, I admit, until I got an answer."

Evidently, Thomas had driven his sister to her house, and waited outside while Mary carried out her plot. Devlen had easily overpowered him and given the other gun to his driver, with instructions to shoot if Thomas moved.

Now, the magistrate was taking Thomas somewhere to be held for trial.

"You'll be here to testify, sir?" he asked Devlen.

"I will."

The magistrate also arranged to have Mary's body taken back to Castle Crannoch.

The man had had some training as a physician, and insisted upon inspecting the temporary bandage Beatrice had placed on her own throat.

"If she'd cut you any deeper, miss, you wouldn't

have survived the wound." He'd wrapped her throat tightly and given her some precautions. She'd listened and nodded from time to time, trying to ignore the fact Devlen was glowering at her.

Robert was being so quiet every few moments she bent forward to look at his face. He was awake, but only barely. He looked tired, his face too pale. A few minutes later, he grew heavier in her arms, and she glanced at him to find him asleep. She couldn't blame him. The day had been a long one with the interviews with the magistrate, and the inquiry about the shooting.

"Was Thomas responsible for pushing Robert down the stairs as well?" she whispered, not wishing to wake the child.

Devlen looked down at his cousin. "I'm afraid the incident on the stairs was a genuine accident. Too much haste, combined with a young boy in his stocking feet. The floors are well waxed."

"Will there be any ramifications for you because of what you did? Will you be arrested?"

"For killing a woman who was going to kill you? No. Don't forget, she'd planned to kill Robert as well."

She nodded.

"I wouldn't want you to be punished."

"I shall not be."

"Thank you for what you did."

"I would have protected anyone in my care."

Her eyes flew to his, but then she looked away, anything but try to interpret that stony stare.

"What about Felicia?" she asked.

"What about Felicia?"

"She came to see you."

"And met you instead. Is that why you left Edinburgh?"

She glanced over at him. He didn't look the least ashamed.

"I thought you weren't seeing her anymore."

He didn't answer. "Is that why you left Edinburgh?"

She blew out a breath. "Perhaps." She'd been angry and afraid, emotions that didn't necessarily lead to logic. "I wanted to get away, to be safe."

"And you didn't think it would be safe with me."

"I couldn't stay there."

"Because you thought I was still with Felicia."

She looked away, and only then nodded. "Yes," she said in the silence.

"I haven't been with her since I met you. I've only seen her once, to give her a ruinously expensive diamond necklace."

"She mentioned it."

"You should have stayed in Edinburgh."

She turned her head and stared at him. "I'm no longer your employee, Devlen. Don't presume to tell me what I should or should not have done. I did what I thought was right at the time."

"Forgive my impertinence, Lady Beatrice."

"Is that your attempt at humor?"

"Believe me, I'm not feeling at all amused at the moment."

The moments stretched between them, silent and uncomfortable.

"You could have asked me," he said finally. "About Felicia. I thought we had that much trust between us."

She didn't speak.

Finally, several moments later, she spoke again. "Does it ever ice up so you're trapped at the castle?" There, a casual question, one not containing emotion of any sort.

"No. There's always a way down, even if it must be done on foot."

The weather was growing colder, and a fine mist was falling. The fog was rising as they mounted the hill, their journey slower than usual.

Devlen didn't speak again. She was forced to silence only because she didn't know what to say. It was only too clear he was angry. No, not angry. Not even furious. He appeared encaged by rage. The wrong word might set him free. She wasn't entirely certain she wanted to face an infuriated Devlen.

At the entrance to the castle, he exited the carriage first and reached in to take Robert from her, all without a word spoken. She was left to follow him, up the winding staircase and to the Duke's Chamber. Robert still slept, but she wasn't surprised.

Devlen left the room after placing Robert on the bed, leaving her to remove the boy's shoes and tuck the counterpane around him. Later she would worry about undressing him properly. For now, she wanted to let him sleep.

The room was the same. The maid had straightened the bed and replaced the toweling, but otherwise the room looked as if they'd just left it and not been gone a month.

The pillows smelled of fresh herbs, and it was evident someone had beaten the dust from the four-poster's drapes. The circular table near the window had been treated with lemon oil and the scent permeated the room. Everything was in readiness for the Duke of Brechin.

Home and safety. For the first time, Robert might feel a little of both.

"You wanted to see me?"

Rowena tried, and failed, to push hope away. But it was the first time since the accident Cameron had sent for her, and she stood on the threshold of his library dressed in one of her new purchases from London, a blue silk that flattered her complexion. She'd taken the precaution of coloring her lips a soft pink and adding drops to her eyes so they gleamed in the candlelight.

In the mirror she'd looked like a woman going to her lover.

"Mary is dead."

"Yes, I heard."

"You don't seem overly affected by the news."

She shrugged. "She was a good maid."

"Is that all you have to say? She's been with you for what, a decade?"

"Do you wish me to weep for her, Cameron? Doing so would hardly put me in a good light, would it?"

"I can't remember you being this calculating when we first met, Rowena. But perhaps I was blind to your true character, being as besotted as I was."

"Were you besotted, Cameron?"

She took a few steps toward his desk, wishing he wasn't sitting on the other side. He used the sheer size of it like a barrier, a bulwark behind which to position himself. That was very well when he was addressing the staff, but hardly necessary when he was talking with his wife.

"I've decided it's best if you return to London."

She stared at him, disappointment rapidly overcoming any other emotion. "Why?" she finally said.

"Because I cannot bear the sight of you, my dear Rowena. Even the scent of your perfume renders me nauseous."

She took another step toward him. "I don't understand."

"I'm much happier when you're nowhere to be seen. London is far enough away, I think."

"You can't be serious, Cameron."

"On the contrary, Rowena. I don't believe it's possible to measure the exact degree of my hatred for you."

She took a step backward, almost physically affected by his words. The contemptuous look in his eyes made her suddenly wary.

"I spoke to the doctor, you see. At length, as a matter of fact. While you were in London. We had an interesting conversation, he and I."

Her stomach lurched, and she placed a hand against her waist. She was going to be sick, she was certain of it.

"What I cannot comprehend was the reason for it. Did you hate me so much?"

"I love you."

Her skin was so cold she could feel the heat of her own blood racing beneath it.

"You will never get me to believe that, Rowena. Not now, not ever."

He emerged from behind the desk, wheeling himself toward her. She remained where she was, determined not to flee in the face of his hatred.

"What about Robert? Did you know about Mary, about what she and Thomas were doing? Let's have a little honesty between us."

"No, I didn't know. I don't like the child, but I wouldn't harm him. And you, Cameron? Don't tell me you're unhappy she almost succeeded."

"Unlike you, Rowena, there are certain things I won't do in order to get my way. Killing a child is one of them."

He studied her, such a disinterested glance she felt the coldness of it. It was over. Finally, it was over. She turned, intent upon leaving the room, the castle, and him.

Before she could leave, he spoke again. "Don't ever come back, Rowena."

She hesitated at the door, squared her shoulders, and forced a smile to her face. She glanced back at him once. "I won't, you can be assured of that. But you will miss me, Cameron. Perhaps you'll even long for me."

"No, madam, on that score, you're wrong. I would sooner wish for the devil himself."

Devlen was determined not to be an idiot about Beatrice. However, he was very certain he was going to do just that, which is why he was intent on his errand.

Gaston was driving him, but before he got into the carriage, he ventured a question to the other man.

"Have you ever been in love, Gaston?"

The other man looked surprised at such a question. Just when he thought it wouldn't be answered, Gaston nodded.

"I have, Mr. Devlen. It's not a gentle emotion, for all that the books would have you believe."

"On that I agree. It's a damnable feeling, isn't it? It gets a hook right into the middle of you and won't let go."

"Even when it does, sir, you remember the feeling."

Devlen nodded. "Like being a salmon, Gaston. A salmon with a smile on his face."

He entered the carriage and closed the door, staring back at the castle.

She needed to follow the magistrate's instructions about that cut on her throat. Would she? She'd always have a scar. He was damned if all she thought of when she looked in the mirror every day was the memory of nearly dying for Robert.

He'd been a fool—he wouldn't deny that. From the very first moment he'd ever seen her he'd been an idiot. A lustful idiot.

There was her window. If he threw a stone at the glass, would she look down?

He'd never been so confused, uncertain, and definite about a woman in all his life. She made him want to pull his hair out, wander around naked in his own home, and vow monastic celibacy all at the same time.

She couldn't stay here. While the danger to Robert had been eliminated, the atmosphere still wasn't suitable for Beatrice. She needed laughter and a touch of silliness. She needed to attend the opera and listen to music. He'd take her to his soap factory, and she'd sample the new scents. Or to the glassworks and let her see the new patterns.

Anywhere.

Instead, he nodded to his driver and got in the carriage.

Maybe he'd be better off simply riding down the mountain on a surefooted horse. The faster he was about his errand, the better.

"Devlen told me what happened. Please accept my apologies as well as my thanks, Miss Sinclair. I truly didn't know."

Beatrice turned, surprised she hadn't heard Cameron's

arrival. She glanced at the bed, grateful Robert was still asleep. For his benefit, she left the room and stepped out into the hallway.

She waited until Cameron followed her to answer him.

"I don't care about your apology or your thanks, Mr. Gordon. All I care about is that Robert is safe. Can you promise me that?"

"I can see why you fascinate my son so much, Miss Sinclair."

"I don't know how to respond to that comment. Do you expect me to be flattered?"

"You don't hesitate to speak your mind while at the same time insisting upon being very female. And yes, I promise to protect Robert to the best of my ability, Miss Sinclair. Not for your sake or mine, but for his."

She walked down the corridor, wondering if he would follow her. He did, his manipulation of the wheelchair done gracefully.

"My son may be enamored of you, Miss Sinclair, but he's ruthless, all the same."

When she didn't comment, he continued, "How do you think he created his own empire? With a please and a thank-you? He's accustomed to getting his own way, to doing exactly what he wants."

"Is there a reason you're telling me this?"

"I feel a curious responsibility for you, Miss Sinclair, especially in view of all you've suffered on our behalf."

"I would think you'd be proud of him."

"I am, but I'm not blind to his faults. My son is stubborn, opinionated, aggravating, talented, generous, loyal, and the most irritating human being I've ever loved."

"He's determined, Mr. Gordon," she said, turning and facing him. "As determined in his way as you are in yours."

One eyebrow rose, an expression so similar to Devlen's that she smiled.

"Just how am I determined?"

"You could have easily died in the carriage accident, I understand. Yet you survived."

"On the contrary, Miss Sinclair. I was barely injured."

He smiled, an expression so odd she felt a trickle of ice slide down her spine.

"Do you know what it's like to love, Miss Sinclair? To love so desperately you would surrender your very soul?" He glanced at her. "Ah, I see you do. People can twist the force of that love into something else, something distorted and possibly evil."

Slowly, he drew the lap robe off his legs. All this time she'd thought he was paralyzed, but there were only neatly hemmed trousers beneath his knees. Nothing else.

"My wife did that." He stared at himself, his smile mocking. "She instructed the surgeon to amputate both my legs, even though there was no need. I might have lost a few toes, or had to use a cane perhaps, but that was the extent of my injuries."

She stared at him, horrified. "Why?"

"Why does one cage a bird, Miss Sinclair, but to hear it sing? We don't think about the bird's freedom, only our own gratification."

She held on to the doorjamb.

"My wife believed I was interested in other women. Are you up to hearing a confession? I was not a faithful husband. But I hardly think I deserved this punishment for my sins."

She shook her head.

"All this time, I thought she was somehow behind the incidents involving Robert. She was capable of it." He rolled to the end of the hall, stared out the small window at the vista of mountains in the distance. "I thought she wanted Robert to die to absolve herself of her great crimes. She would present me with the dukedom as if it could make up for the loss of my legs."

Speech was beyond her. She'd never heard of anything more horrible. She'd been right all this time to think the atmosphere at Castle Crannoch malevolent.

Beatrice opened her door, suddenly wanting to be away from Cameron Gordon.

"He's left, you know." He glanced at her. "Devlen's left the castle."

"Has he?" She folded her hands together, determined not to betray any of her emotions.

"You can still catch him, if you try."

"I doubt he wants to see me again."

"Love should always be given a chance, Miss Sinclair. Real love." With that, he wheeled himself down the hall. In her mind, he'd always been an object of pity. Now she saw him as he was, a man altered by circumstances but not yet felled by them.

She walked to the window, staring down at the entrance to the castle. Devlen's carriage rounded the corner of Castle Crannoch and disappeared from sight. From here, she couldn't see the serpentine curves leading down to the valley.

How strange that anyone would begin a journey at the edge of nightfall. The sun was setting, the dying rays touching remnants of snow, and casting the world in a golden glow.

She might catch him. If she were brave enough.

The road curved back on itself in at least three places. The area closest to the castle was too high and too perilous to climb, but halfway down, embankments jutted out beside the road. By cutting across the retaining walls, she could shorten the distance. If she could make it past the first long curve not long after Devlen's coach, she had a chance of reaching him before he made it to the bottom.

She left the cloak behind since it would only weigh her down, and raced for the stairs. Sunset colored the steps of the castle orange and red, and she blessed the fact night had not yet fallen. Even so, she would have taken the chance.

Beatrice took a deep breath, and began to run. She fell once, when slipping on a patch of ice, but picked herself up and raced for the curve. In the distance, she could see Devlen's coach.

Dear God, please don't let him leave. Don't let him leave me.

She made it past the first curve, nearly falling again, but managing to find her balance as she skidded to the edge. Finally, she made it to the second curve, and without stopping to think, to reason, or to be afraid, she put one leg over the edge and said a quick prayer that the ground was stable and not covered with ice. A few scrub bushes aided her descent, and she held on to them as she made her way past the last curve. She was now almost even with the carriage. Either Devlen was traveling uncharacteristically slowly down the road, or she was blessed by Providence.

And faster than she thought she could be.

At the base of the mountain, she only had a few moments to spare. She stood in the middle of the road, stretched out her arms, and closed her eyes, wondering if she was destined to die by coach after all.

The driver shouted, standing and pulling on the reins in an effort to halt the horses. The road was slick beneath the carriage's oversized wheels, and it began to slide around the last curve.

In that second Beatrice wondered if all she'd succeeded in doing was sending the coach catapulting off the mountain. Instead, the horses lost their footing, and the carriage slid sideways into a snowdrift like a ship nestling into its berth.

The driver was still shouting at her in French, the comments not polite in the least. She recognized Gaston finally, but she didn't move, only lowered her arms.

The door opened, and Devlen emerged, looking like an emissary of the devil himself. In the faint light of a waning sun, she flinched from the look in his eyes. She tilted back her chin and took a deep breath as he reached her.

"You stupid fool! You could have been killed!"

"I couldn't let you go. I couldn't let you leave without knowing."

She was hiccupping softly while she cried, the tears falling freely.

"Knowing what?"

"I never thought you were responsible." Honesty compelled her to add, "Perhaps for a little while. After Edinburgh. But I knew that a man who'd taken a child to safety wouldn't have then tried to kill him."

"How very reasonable of you."

"You couldn't have done it." Her tears continued. She didn't know how she would be able to stop them. Right now she felt as if she could cry forever.

"I knew you would prove to be a problem."

"You hate me, don't you?" She looked up at him, uncaring that tears sheened her face.

"I don't hate you, Beatrice."

"Then why are you so angry?"

"Anger is one of those essentially worthless emotions."

"One of those? What would be the other ones?"

His smile grew more genuine.

"You're expecting me to say love, aren't you? Or a host of other gentle feelings. Dear Beatrice, you lay such sweet traps for me."

The snow began.

His look was intent, somber. She was reminded of the first time she'd seen him, on this same road, at almost this same spot. She'd been transfixed by the sight of him as she was now.

Finally, he spoke again. "It's better to be angry than afraid. It's foolish to feel fear when a little knowledge will normally overcome it. Fear is caused by uncertainty, by ignorance."

"I'm not afraid of you." Well, perhaps she had been, but only in the first five minutes of their meeting. Fascination had easily taken the place of fear.

"My dearest Beatrice, I wasn't referring to you. But of myself. I've been afraid ever since I met you."

"You have?"

"All this time, I was afraid you'd leave me."

"I never wanted to."

"But you would. One day you would."

Perhaps he was right.

"Stay with me."

"Are you asking me to be your mistress? I thought Felicia held that post. The beautiful, tiny Felicia."

"Thank God I didn't witness that meeting," he said, smiling. "As to being my current mistress, I think it would be amusing to have a wife who acted the part."

For a moment she couldn't speak.

"Where did you think I was going?" he asked.

"To Edinburgh."

He shook his head. "I was in search of a minister, my dearest Miss Sinclair. I have no intention of losing you again. The bonds of matrimony must surely be strong enough to keep you with me."

The snow was piling up on his shoulders, and she reached up to brush it away.

"You love me?"

He smiled, and the expression was a faint effort at best, not quite reaching the somber expression in his eyes.

"With all my heart, dear Beatrice. Or do you think I kidnap governesses without a care to their reputation or mine? It's not my way of doing things."

"You love me?" The thought was so alien she found repeating it the only possible solace.

"Even though you thought I was a murderer. We shall have to work on trust, I think."

"I never thought you were a murderer. I thought your father was. I didn't want to put you in a position where you'd have to choose."

"Between you and anyone else? I choose you. Between you and the world, Beatrice? Surely you know that answer."

"Your father says you're ruthless."

"Indeed."

"I suspect he's right, Devlen."

"You're correct, Beatrice. In certain matters, I am. With you? Of a certainty. I feel it only fair to warn you I'm about to kidnap you again."

"Are you?"

"And Robert as well. I think the boy would do better in Edinburgh for a while. Although, while we're on our honeymoon, he should attend school."

"You want to marry me, even though I'm a governess?"

His laughter echoed up the mountain and back. "You're the most unlikely governess I've ever known."

She took a deep breath. "You asked me once if life had affected me. Maybe it has, I don't know. I do know I don't want to dread every day. I want a roof over my head, and food to eat. I want to be warm and have pretty clothes. I want to be healthy, and I want to be happy. But most of all, I want you. I deserve you."

She wiped her tears away with her fingertips, but they kept coming.

He placed his hands on her waist and pulled her to him. "I think you deserve a great deal more than me, but I'm afraid I won't let you go. You'll have to say yes."

She looked up at his face, thinking a year ago she wouldn't have thought there was any reason to feel joy or wonder or such delight it spread through her body like a warm flood.

"Do you have such great experience with being in love, Devlen?" She'd asked him the question once, and he'd never answered her.

"None. It feels like an ache, Beatrice, a damnable irritation right here." He reached for her hand and placed it over his heart. "You're the only one who can heal me."

"It's a contagious disease, Devlen."

"I should hope so."

"I do love you."

"I know, dearest Beatrice."

"You love me, too."

"With all my heart and what's left of my mind." He smiled and enfolded her in his arms.

There, in the darkness, just below Castle Crannoch, they kissed. When they broke apart, it was with a smile toward the sky, at the large snowflakes wafting down on them like a celestial blessing.

"Yes, Beatrice?"

"Oh yes, Devlen."

With a laugh, they turned and walked hand in hand toward the carriage.

We know you expect the very best love stories written by utterly extraordinary writers, so we are presenting four amazing love stories—coming just in time for Valentine's Day!

Scandal of the Black Rose by Debra Mullins

An Avon Romantic Treasure

What is the secret behind the Black Rose Society? Anna Rosewood is determined to find out. Dashing Roman Devereaux has his own reasons for helping Anna—even though he *thinks* she's disreputable. Soon, their passion causes scandal, and what they discover could be even worse . . .

Guys & Dogs by Elaine Fox

An Avon Contemporary Romance

Small town vet Megan Rose only sleeps with a certain kind of male—the four legged, furry kind! But when she finds herself on the doorstep of millionaire Sutter Foley she starts changing her mind about that—and more! But how can she like a man who doesn't love dogs?

Pride and Petticoats by Shana Galen

An Avon Romance

Charlotte is desperate—driven to London to save her family's reputation, which is being assaulted by Lord Dewhurst. He's insufferable, but sinfully handsome, and soon she finds she must play the role of his bride, or face the consequences.

Kiss From a Rogue by Shirley Karr

An Avon Romance

Lady Sylvia Montgomery has no choice but to involve herself with a band of smugglers, but she needs help, which arrives in the irresistible form of Anthony Sinclair. A self-proclaimed rake, he knows he should seduce Sylvia and have done with it. But he can't resist her . . .

Visit www.AuthorTracker.com for exclusive information on your favorite HarperCollins authors.

REL 0106

Available wherever books are sold or please call 1-800-331-3761 to order.

Avon Romantic Treasures

Unforgettable, enthralling love stories, sparkling with passion and adventure from Romance's bestselling authors

SIN AND SENSIBILITY
by Suzanne Enoch
0-06-054325-6/$5.99 US/$7.99 Can

SOMETHING ABOUT EMMALINE
by Elizabeth Boyle
0-06-054931-9/$5.99 US/$7.99 Can

JUST ONE TOUCH
by Debra Mullins
0-06-056167-X/$5.99 US/$7.99 Can

AS AN EARL DESIRES
by Lorraine Heath
0-06-052947-4/$5.99 US/$7.99 Can

TILL NEXT WE MEET
by Karen Ranney
0-06-075737-X/$5.99 US/$7.99 Can

MARRY THE MAN TODAY
by Linda Needham
0-06-051414-0/$5.99 US/$7.99 Can

THE MARRIAGE BED
by Laura Lee Guhrke
0-06-077473-8/$5.99 US/$7.99 Can

LOVE ACCORDING TO LILY
by Julianne MacLean
0-06-059729-1/$5.99 US/$7.99 Can

TAMING THE BARBARIAN
by Lois Greiman
0-06-078394-X/$5.99 US/$7.99 Can

A MATTER OF TEMPTATION
by Lorraine Heath
0-06-074976-8/$5.99 US/$7.99 Can

AuthorTracker
Don't miss the next book by your favorite author.
Sign up now for AuthorTracker by visiting
www.AuthorTracker.com

Available wherever books are sold
or please call 1-800-331-3761 to order.

RT 0705

Avon Romances
the best in
exceptional authors and unforgettable novels!

SOMETHING LIKE LOVE
by Beverly Jenkins
0-06-057532-8/ $5.99 US/ $7.99 Can

**WHEN DASHING
MET DANGER**
by Shana Galen
0-06-077315-4/ $5.99 US/ $7.99 Can

BEYOND TEMPTATION
by Mary Reed McCall
0-06-059368-7/ $5.99 US/ $7.99 Can

THE RUNAWAY HEIRESS
by Brenda Hiatt
0-06-072379-3/ $5.99 US/ $7.99 Can

MORE THAN A SCANDAL
by Sari Robins
0-06-057535-2/ $5.99 US/ $7.99 Can

THE DARING TWIN
by Donna Fletcher
0-06-075782-5/ $5.99 US/ $7.99 Can

DARING THE DUKE
by Anne Mallory
0-06-076223-3/ $5.99 US/ $7.99 Can

COURTING CLAUDIA
by Robyn DeHart
0-06-078215-3/ $5.99 US/ $7.99 Can

STILL IN MY HEART
by Kathryn Smith
0-06-074074-4/ $5.99 US/ $7.99 Can

**A MATCH MADE
IN SCANDAL**
by Melody Thomas
0-06-074231-3/ $5.99 US/ $7.99 Can

SCANDALOUS
by Jenna Petersen
0-06-079859-9/ $5.99 US/ $7.99 Can

RULES OF PASSION
by Sara Bennett
0-06-079648-0/ $5.99 US/ $7.99 Can

Visit www.AuthorTracker.com for exclusive
information on your favorite HarperCollins authors.

Available wherever books are sold or please call 1-800-331-3761 to order.

ROM 0805

DISCOVER CONTEMPORARY ROMANCES *at their*
SIZZLING HOT BEST FROM AVON BOOKS

Hidden Secrets   by Cait London
0-06-055589-0/$5.99 US/$7.99 Can

Special of the Day   by Elaine Fox
0-06-074059-0/$5.99 US/$7.99 Can

She Woke Up Married   by Suzanne Macpherson
0-06-051769-7/$5.99 US/$7.99 Can

**Midnight in the Garden
of Good and Evie**   by Marianne Stillings
0-06-073476-0/$5.99 US/$7.99 Can

Running on Empty   by Lynn Montana
0-06-074255-0/$5.99 US/$7.99 Can

The Hunter   by Gennita Low
0-06-059123-4/$5.99 US/$7.99 Can

How To Marry A   by Kerrelyn Sparks
Millionaire Vampire
0-06-075196-7/$5.99 US/$7.99 Can

Wanted: One Sexy Night   by Judi McCoy
0-06-077420-7/$5.99 US/$7.99 Can

Flashback   by Cait London
0-06-079087-3/$5.99 US/$7.99 Can

The Boy Next Door   by Meg Cabot
0-06-084554-6/$5.99 US/$7.99 Can

CRO 0805

Visit www.AuthorTracker.com for exclusive
information on your favorite HarperCollins authors.

Available wherever books are sold
or please call 1-800-331-3761 to order.

New York Times Bestselling Author

ELOISA JAMES

KISS ME, ANNABEL
0-06-073210-3/$6.99/$9.99 Can

According to Annabel Essex, a husband must be rich, English and amiable. So what cruel twist of fate put her in a carriage with the impoverished Scottish Earl of Ardmore?

MUCH ADO ABOUT YOU
0-06-073206-7/$6.99/$9.99 Can

Tess Essex is forced to contemplate marriage to the sort of man she wishes to avoid—one of London's most infamous rakes.

YOUR WICKED WAYS
0-06-056078-9/$6.99/$9.99 Can

Helene has suffered ten long years while her scoundrel of a husband lives with strumpets and causes scandal after scandal. Now Rees makes her a brazen offer, and Helene decides to become his wife again...but not in name only.

A WILD PURSUIT
0-06-050812-4/$6.99/$9.99 Can

Three years after she caused a sensation by being found in a distinctly compromising position, Lady Beatrix Lennox sees no reason not to go after who she wishes—Stephen Fairfax-Lacy, the handsome Earl of Spade.

FOOL FOR LOVE
0-06-050811-6/$6.99/$9.99 Can

Simon Darby has vowed he will never turn himself into a fool over a woman. So while debutantes swoon, he ignores them all . . . until a steamy love letter from Lady Henrietta Maclellan becomes public.

DUCHESS IN LOVE
0-06-050810-8/$6.99/$9.99 Can

Directly after the ceremony Gina's handsome spouse Camden, the Duke of Girton, fled to the continent. Finally Cam has returned home to discover his naïve bride has blossomed into the toast of the town.

Visit www.AuthorTracker.com for exclusive information on your favorite HarperCollins authors.

EJ 0905

Available wherever books are sold or please call 1-800-331-3761 to order.

AVON TRADE... because every great bag deserves a great book!

Paperback $12.95
ISBN 0-06-078478-4

Paperback $12.95
($16.95 Can.)
ISBN 0-06-081587-6

Paperback $12.95
($16.95 Can.)
ISBN 0-06-078636-1

Paperback $12.95
($16.95 Can.)
ISBN 0-06-077875-X

Paperback $12.95
($16.95 Can.)
ISBN 0-06-075474-5

Paperback $12.95
($16.95 Can.)
ISBN 0-06-073444-2

Visit www.AuthorTracker.com for exclusive
information on your favorite HarperCollins authors.

Available wherever books are sold, or call 1-800-331-3761 to order.

ATP 0106